CONSEQUENCES
SOUTHERN SECRETS SAGA, BOOK 2

JEANNE HARDT

Gina —
All Deceptions
lead to Consequences —

Jeanne
Hardt

Chapter 1

Sunday, the second of June. Claire's *supposed* due date.

Of course Michael had been born on April twenty-fifth, more than a month before he should've arrived.

Thank goodness Gerald was none-the-wiser.

He still believed Michael had been premature. Simply a healthy, *full-grown,* premature baby. Gerald had enjoyed teasing her. He'd said if Michael had been carried a full nine months, he'd have been the size of a watermelon and nearly impossible to deliver. She'd responded with a gratuitous smile and laugh.

Deep down, she hated herself for deceiving him.

Keeping up with the new baby, as well as her chores, had her spent. Being a devoted husband and daddy, Gerald had driven to Beth's and brought her back to help Claire until she'd completely recovered from the delivery.

Beth's amazement at Michael's dark hair and eyes could've caused issues, but Claire managed to convince her that he'd gotten them from her own daddy, John Martin. Since Beth had never seen the man, she'd accepted her explanation and raved about her new nephew.

Sadly, after three short weeks, she had to return home and go about her own business. Time with her passed much too quickly. At least it had given Claire the chance to become well-rested, and she'd found a comfortable routine with the baby. They parted with promises to see each other again soon.

Her sister-in-law's departure reminded Claire of another promise she'd made at Christmas. She and Gerald were supposed to visit Aunt Martha so *she* could see the new baby. Their visit was way overdue.

"What's wrong with you, Claire?" Gerald kept his hands on the reins, but looked sideways at her.

"Wrong?" She gave him what she hoped was a convincing smile. "Nothin's wrong." She held Michael a little closer.

"Then why are your eyebrows dancin' like a caterpillar?"

Opening her eyes wide, she grinned. "Didn't know they were." After letting out a sigh, she decided to be partially truthful. "Reckon I'm nervous 'bout havin' Martha see Michael. You know how she is."

He reached over and patted the baby. "Ain't nothin' bad she can say 'bout our baby. He's perfect."

Since he looked just like his daddy, of course he was perfect. Andrew was the finest-looking man she'd ever met. But would he be smart? It would be months—maybe even *years*—before they'd know.

"Claire?"

Lost in her thoughts, she barely heard him. "Yes?"

"Why are you so scared for folks to see Michael? You told me *no* when I wanted to take him to the Baptist church, and now you act like you don't even want your aunt to see him. It don't make sense."

"He's tiny, Gerald. I don't want him to get sick."

Gerald let out a laugh. "He's the healthiest baby I ever seen. You're just a nervous mama. I'm proud a our baby. You should be, too."

"I am. It's like you said. I'm a nervous mama." She looked away and scrunched her eyes tight.

I hafta do better or he's gonna know sumthin's not right.

She couldn't keep Michael hidden forever. Worrying about someone guessing the truth would have to be set aside.

Approaching Martha's, memories of the last time she'd been there rushed in. She'd made that ten-mile walk with her heart broken in two.

Looking down at Michael sleeping soundly in her arms, she saw Andrew.

He looks just like you.

She spotted Martha sitting in the front porch swing.

The woman jumped to her feet and let out a whoop. Lifting her skirt, she ran to the wagon. "It's high time you came for a visit! Why'd you wait so long?"

Gerald hopped down. "It's good to see you, too, Aunt Martha."

Claire handed him the baby, then Martha took her by the hand and helped her down, all-the-while ignoring Gerald.

Martha eyed Claire from head to toe. "Yep! You lost weight since I last saw ya."

"Oh, Martha!" Claire gave her a big hug.

"Let's go inside so I can get a good look at that baby." Martha led her into the house, with Gerald and Michael following after.

Once they'd gotten comfortably seated in the living room, Gerald pulled back the lightweight blanket and revealed Michael's face. "Martha, this is Michael Andrew Alexander." He beamed, presenting his son.

"Look at that head a black hair!" Martha's eyes popped wide. "Lawdy! Where'd he get hair like that?"

Gerald grinned. "Claire said her daddy had dark hair an' dark eyes. That's where he gets it."

"John Martin?" Martha's lip curled. "He never—"

"Martha doesn't like to talk 'bout my daddy." Claire stopped her before she said too much. She peered over Gerald's shoulder and gave Martha one of her *please don't say another word* looks. "Do you, Aunt Martha?"

Martha leered at her. "Nope. Never liked talkin' 'bout him a-tall."

"Go ahead and spit now, Martha," Claire said, then turned to Gerald. "Aunt Martha always spits when she says his name. She's never cared much for my daddy."

"That's right," Martha said flatly, then spit.

Gerald wrinkled his brow and looked to Claire for help. *The poor man doesn't have a clue.*

Martha fidgeted in her seat, mumbling.

Gerald returned his attention to Michael, talking to him and rocking him gently. Claire simply watched and waited, wondering what else would be said.

Martha cleared her throat and Claire jumped. "Your husband sure loves that little baby, don't he?"

"Yes, Martha, he does."

They were silent again.

Martha sighed. "Gerald? S'pose you could go out to my barn an' take a look at my wagon? One a the wheels ain't right. Needs some fixin'. George ain't here today, an' I'm afraid the wheel might come plum off if it ain't tended to. You mind?"

"Course not. I'd be glad to." He smiled, placed Michael in Claire's arms, kissed her on the forehead, and headed to the barn.

Michael craned his head toward Claire's breast, ready to nurse. The timing couldn't have been better. Claire draped his blanket over her shoulder and positioned him for feeding.

Martha stood and paced the floor. Aside from the squeaking floorboards, silence hung in the air.

After going to the window and peering outside, Martha moved to Claire and hovered over her. "What the devil was that all 'bout?"

"What's wrong, Martha?" The question was unnecessary. She already knew the answer.

"You know well as I do John Martin never had dark hair an' eyes. His hair was 'bout your color and his eyes was blue!" Martha breathed heavily. "He was a good-lookin' snake in the grass!"

"Shh!" Claire scolded. "You'll scare the baby."

"That's not why you're shushin' me. You don't want Gerald to know the truth, do ya? An' don't you start playin' games with me." Martha pointed her finger in Claire's face. "I know sumthin' ain't right here."

Claire hung her head, tired of all the lies.

"Your baby's beautiful, Claire. Don't get me wrong. But as sure as the sun rises . . ." Martha took a deep breath. "Gerald Alexander ain't that boy's daddy. The looks of him makes me think you was with some Injun."

Claire's eyes filled with tears.

Martha shook her head. "Don't you start blubberin' now. Your husband will be back here 'fore we know it, and I aim to get to the bottom of this. Am I right? Did some savage have his way with ya?"

"Please don't say that. Andrew's nothin' like that." His name slipped from her lips so easily, but once it fell, she wished she'd never said it.

"Andrew, huh? Ain't that the child's middle name? Was that your idea? Some sorta bad humor aimed at your poor husband?"

"No. It was Gerald's idea. It's a long complicated story." Claire wasn't ready to go into detail.

"Don't know what to think a you, Claire. When you came here all broken-hearted, you convinced me it was over Gerald. An' to think I was tryin' to give you advice 'bout the birds an' the bees. I had no idea you'd already been buzzin' all over the hive!"

Martha finally sat down. "Claire . . ." Her voice had softened. "I love you more than anythin', but what you've done to poor Gerald—deceivin' him so—ain't right. Now, I ain't gonna say nothin' to him. He loves you an' that baby more than he loves life itself. He'd do anythin' for ya. But I also know this. Lies got a way a comin' out an' bitin' you in the butt. When that happens, everyone gets hurt. I hope I ain't around to see it."

"Martha, please believe me. I thought I was doin' the right thing. I can't explain it all, but I promise you, I won't hurt Gerald. I love him. I really, truly, love him." She peered deeply into the woman's eyes, hoping to convince her.

Martha stood and crossed to her, then laid her hand on Michael's head. "He's the innocent one in all this."

Claire nodded, gazing at her precious son. "I know I've disappointed you. I disappointed myself, too."

"No matter what you done . . ." Martha lifted Claire's chin with a single finger. "Or what you figgered was right, you've involved other folks that might be hurt from the choices you made. From here on out you should always listen to your heart. It won't lead you astray."

Gerald came back in through the front door and caught Claire's eye. He inched his way up behind Martha.

Claire touched her finger to her lips. Michael had fallen asleep.

"Ain't he beautiful, Martha?" he whispered.

She put her arm around Gerald. "Yes, Gerald. Your son's the finest baby ever was." She kissed Gerald on the cheek, then walked toward the kitchen. "I reckon it's time for some sweet tea punch."

Gerald raised his hand to his cheek, then turned and watched her walk away. "I'll never understand your aunt. Reckon she finally likes me?"

"She has a new respect for you," Claire whispered. "She's realized what a good man you are."

He bent down and kissed her on the lips, then kissed Michael on his tiny head. As he stood upright, his face beamed.

* * *

Keeping a baby cool in the heat of an Alabama summer wasn't easy. Claire spent most of the afternoons with Michael on a blanket in the shade beneath a large oak tree not far from their house.

Gerald had told her he'd suspend a swing for Michael from one of the large branches, but Claire reminded him it would be some time before he'd be big enough to use it.

The man would do anything and everything he could to help with the baby. He'd even offered to feed him, until she reminded him he wasn't equipped to do so. Of course, he'd laughed about it. His temperament was a blessing she tried to deserve.

Henry had become more distant than ever, but it was for the best. He stayed busy in the shop in the daylight hours, coming inside only to eat. In the evenings he'd retire to bed early.

Gerald commented on the man's strange behavior, suggesting perhaps he was ill, but Claire assured him his uncle merely needed his own space.

Fortunately, Gerald accepted her explanation, but his complete trust of her intensified her guilt.

Guilt.

Another July had almost come to a close. Only a year ago her life had been completely different.

Andrew.

Could he be thinking of her as well?

She'd just fed Michael and passed him over to Gerald, who sat beside her on the sofa. Luckily, Henry had already gone to bed. She tilted her head and watched her husband gently rock the baby. He'd become quite good at putting him to sleep.

How had she come to this point in her life? He'd always been there for her. Even now, he helped her through her troubles and wasn't even aware of it.

She stood and took Michael from him. "I'll put him in his crib," she whispered. "I'll be right back."

After ascending the stairs, she carried him into his room and laid him down on his belly. He'd already outgrown his cradle and Gerald had crafted a lovely replacement. She covered him with a light blanket and gave him a sweet kiss on his cheek. Returning to her husband, she sat down beside him, then laid her head on his shoulder.

"I reckon he stayed asleep?" Gerald asked, then turned his head toward her and kissed her lightly on her forehead.

"Yep." Her heart thumped.

She wanted him.

For the first time, *she* wanted to make love to *him*. They hadn't coupled since Michael was born.

It's time.

She sat upright, then took his face in her hands and kissed him longingly.

He pulled back and looked at her with wide eyes, then eagerly returned the kiss.

"It's been a long time, Claire," he rasped.

Without saying a word, she took his hand and led him to their room. Keeping her eyes affixed to his, she undressed before him, then climbed into bed.

He stared at her. "You sure? I don't wanna hurt you."

"I'm fine. I've never been surer of anythin'."

She watched with anticipation as he removed his clothing and crawled into bed next to her. Never wanting him to doubt her love, she kissed him with all the tenderness she held. She belonged to him and knew he'd always be there for her.

"You feel so good, Claire." He breathed the words against her skin.

"So do you, Gerald." With surprising hunger, her hands moved over his body.

Their lovemaking lasted into the late hours of the night. She put aside all thoughts of Andrew and finally made love to Gerald—her husband. Just as she should.

CHAPTER 2

Claire.

Andrew lay wide awake staring into the darkness, wondering if she might be thinking of him. It had been an entire year since he'd held her in his arms.

A sound outside the window brought him to his feet. As he peered through the glass, light from the full moon illuminated the figure of a man looking at him from the other side.

With a racing heart, he ran to the door and flung it open. "Who's there?"

No one answered.

Ignoring the lump in his throat, he stepped outside. Step-by-cautious-step, he walked the perimeter of the house. His body jerked around. Someone had stirred the branches of the trees.

"I know you're there! Show yourself!"

This was the third time he'd seen someone watching him. He'd been leaving a chair propped against the door any time he was at home, even after installing a lock.

Who would want to harm me?

A man stepped from the trees. Andrew's breath hitched.

A Negro. Tall and extremely large. Not the size of Elijah, but a big man nonetheless. Then it struck him. "Tobias? Is that you?"

The man sprinted away, not saying a word.

Andrew could've sworn it was Tobias Lewis—the husband of the woman who'd died, along with her child, in Andrew's care. Of course, their deaths weren't his fault, but he'd always known Tobias saw it differently.

Has it been Tobias watching me all this time?

A horrible chill run down his spine.

Though he wished it didn't, somehow it made sense.

* * *

Alicia invited Andrew to her home for dinner and a one-year birthday celebration for Betsy. He gladly accepted the invitation, but before going, decided to pay a visit to the Lewis's home. He needed to confront Tobias.

He'd admired the people in the shanties who'd come together to help Tobias with the children ever since Emma's death. They did what they could to make certain the children were properly fed and clothed, but he feared what might be going on behind closed doors. If vindictive, Tobias might be taking it out on the children.

Andrew knocked on his door. Feet shuffled from the other side. "Get away from there!" A gruff voice yelled.

Tobias opened the door a crack and grimaced at Andrew. "Wha' do *you* want?"

"Tobias . . ." Andrew did his best to remain calm. "I'd like a word with you, please?"

"What for?" He stood in the doorway, not opening it further.

"Who is it, Daddy?" A tiny voice asked.

The man's head whipped around. "Shut your mouth!"

"Please, Tobias?" Andrew wouldn't give up. "Can you step out for just a moment?"

The man came outside, then closed the door behind him. "Well?" He glared with so much hatred, Andrew's skin crawled.

"I believe I saw you a few nights ago at my home. I called out to you, but you didn't answer." Andrew folded his hands in front of himself—feigning composure— though his heart raced.

"Wadn't me."

"I disagree. I think you've been at my home on several occasions and I'd like to know why?"

Something struck the wall inside the shanty.

Tobias huffed, then opened the door. "I'm gonna whoop whoever done that! Now, keep it down!"

Andrew looked away, having a difficult time holding his tongue. "Tobias, do you need help with your children? I'm certain I could find someone to assist you."

"Wha' do you know 'bout children? I don't want no hep from you with nuttin'. I seen what kinda hep you give." The man's upper lip curled and twitched.

"You know I did all I could for your wife. Please let me help you."

"Don't never mention her again! You killed her! You was s'pose to be a good doctor, but you din't do nuttin' for her. Look at me now. I got nuttin' because a you."

Andrew doubted he could reason with him. "I'm sorry you feel that way. As for the other matter, I believe you *have* been at my home. You're not welcome there. If I have to, I'll involve the law, but I'd much rather we settle this here and now."

"Ain't got nuttin' to settle." He jabbed at Andrew's chest with two forceful fingers, then spat at his feet. "You ain't welcome here neither. You best keep to the white folk. We don't want you here no more."

Tobias went back inside and slammed the door.

A pair of tiny eyes peered at Andrew from behind a tattered blanket draped over the front window of the shanty.

"Stay away from that winda!" Tobias yelled.

The eyes disappeared.

"No, Daddy! Please?" The tiny pleading voice grew faint after being followed by a loud smack and a child's cry.

Andrew grasped the door knob, sickened by the sound.

I have to do something to help.

Slowly, he pulled his hand away. Now was *not* the time. Tobias could be capable of anything and might have a weapon. And his interference might make matters worse for the children. He'd have to find another way.

He stood momentarily staring at the rundown shanty, then mounted his horse and headed for the Tarver's.

They greeted him with a warm welcome that lifted his spirits; however, he couldn't erase the sounds and images etched in his mind from the home of Tobias Lewis.

"You ain't eatin' much. What's wrong, Doc?" Alicia asked. "Don't tell me you're pinin' over a woman again?"

"No, it's nothing like that." He pushed some of the food around with his fork, but very little made its way into his mouth.

The children stared at him, having already eaten every bite on their plates.

"Jenny," Alicia said. "Take the children outside to play. Go on now . . ."

"All right, Mama." Jenny took Betsy by the hand.

Andrew grinned, watching little Betsy toddle out the door. She'd recently learned to walk and hadn't quite gotten used to her legs.

"Keep an eye on the baby," Alicia said.

Jenny rolled her eyes. "I always do, Mama."

Joshua and Samuel were already out the door, but Clay hesitated.

"You're fourteen now, Clay," Elijah said. "You can stay."

Clay beamed and returned to the table.

Alicia poured a round of coffee for all of them, including Clay. He grinned when she handed him the cup. After loading it down with sugar, he drank it, confirming his rank as a full-fledged adult.

"Now then," Alicia said, taking a seat at the table. "What's troublin' you, Doc?"

Andrew sighed. "Tobias Lewis." Simply saying his name made him wince.

"Tobias?" Elijah asked. "What's Tobias got to do with ya?"

"He's been watching me—coming to my home. I've seen him a number of times staring at me through my window. I came home one night and heard someone running off into the woods. When I went inside I could tell someone had been there. I'm certain now it was him."

"What do you s'pose he wants?" Clay asked.

"I think he's trying to scare me. And it's working." Andrew folded his hands on the table. "I went to his home to confront him before I came here. He denied everything, but I'm sure he was lying."

Alicia's brow drew in. "Makes no sense, Doc."

"Actually, it makes perfect sense. He still blames me for his wife's death. I think he knew the baby didn't have a chance, but he's never forgiven me for not saving her." Andrew hung his head. If only he could've saved them.

"You an' me both knows you did all you could for Emma." Alicia reached her hand out to him. "She was my friend, but I *never* blamed you for her dyin'. I know you, Doc. You're a good man."

"Thank you." Andrew gave her hand a squeeze. "And, yes, I did all I could. There was nothing else I could've done to save her. She'd lost too much blood. But Tobias will never accept it. He's seeking vengeance."

Elijah shook his head. "'Twas more than a year ago. Reckon he's been followin' you 'round all this time?"

"Maybe so. I've started looking over my shoulder now more than ever. I hate feeling this way." Andrew sipped his coffee, then held the cup in his hand, staring at it.

"*I* needs to go have a talk with him," Elijah said.

"I'll go with ya, Daddy!" Clay exclaimed, wide-eyed.

"No, Clay," Alicia said. "You may be drinkin' coffee, but you ain't ready for that sorta confrontation. I agree it might be a good idea for Lijah to talk to him. We was all friends at one time."

"I appreciate it," Andrew said. "But I hate to think of anyone having to deal with that man. He's unreasonable. *Hateful.* And the way he treats those children . . . God help them." He set his cup on the table and stood to leave.

"Them poor children." Alicia frowned. "Emma loved 'em so much. All the folks 'round here have been tryin' to hep with 'em. But there's only so much we can do. Tobias is their daddy. He has the final say."

"Seems to me he's been speaking loudly with the back of his hand," Andrew said. "I heard it myself as I was leaving."

"Elijah . . ." Alicia's tone hardened. "You go see him t'morra. You make shore them children are all right."

"I will, Leesha." Elijah smiled at his wife, then patted Andrew on the shoulder. "Doc, you be careful goin' home now."

"I will. I've never been afraid living here. But I have this awful feeling something terrible is going to happen, and I've learned to listen to my feelings." Andrew walked to the door. "Or perhaps I'm a bit paranoid."

As he turned to leave, he thanked Alicia for the meal.

"What little you ate," she chided and waved him on.

He mounted Sam and urged her homeward, faster than normal. Frequently, he looked over his shoulder, and for the entire ride tried to calm his rapid heartbeat. Once home, he secured Sam in the barn, then locked himself inside the house.

Will Elijah be able to reason with Tobias?

He doubted he would.

CHAPTER 3

Victoria O'Malley was on a mission. Since Dr. Fletcher had accused her of being a girl; she intended to prove him wrong and show him how much of a woman she truly was.

Izzy had told her she needed to learn *how* to be a woman. So she set out to discover what Izzy meant.

After watching how her mama interacted with her daddy, she determined their relationship to be boring.

If that's what it's like bein' a married woman, I want no part of it!

Granted, her parents showed one another little affection and slept in separate bedrooms. But they had good reason. After Victoria, her mama had been unable to carry another pregnancy to term. So, she *had* to keep her distance from the man. Pregnancy endangered the poor woman's life.

Victoria wanted a man who would dote on her, buy her lavish gifts, and show her off to all his friends. If she married a doctor—namely Andrew Fletcher—all of her dreams of the *perfect* married life would come true. They would likely attend all sorts of parties and events, and as a doctor's wife, she would naturally be well-respected.

She'd settle for nothing less.

She invited Penelope to go with her into town to spy on the women of Mobile. They visited the tearoom. Victoria found it even more boring than her own home.

"What fun is it sittin' around sippin' tea with your nose in the air?" she asked Penelope.

"I don't even like tea," Penelope grumbled.

They strolled down Main Street watching other women as they passed by them. Being a hot summer day, most of the fine ladies carried parasols to keep the blistering sun off their delicate skin. Victoria and Penelope were no exception. They weren't allowed out of their homes without one.

Victoria had the most fashionable parasol that matched her dress to perfection—lace and all—in a lovely white fabric with dainty pink roses. Of course she wouldn't go anywhere without a corset and bustle, and her neckline plunged in its usual fashion.

She batted her eyes at every man who crossed her path, and they returned her gaze. However, they weren't looking her in the eye. That was her sole reason for showing her bosom. She *wanted* them to look. The only man who'd ever been disinterested was Dr. Fletcher.

Why must he act so differently than every other man in Mobile?

She hoped the rumors about him weren't true.

The last man she passed licked his lips as he went by, prompting her to giggle and pull her shoulders back even farther.

"Don't worry, Penny," she said. "Though they're lookin' at me, if you're fortunate they *might* notice you."

"I certainly hope so," Penelope said with a sigh. "All I need is one man. However, doesn't it bother you that they don't look you in the eye?"

"Why would I want them to look *there?*" Victoria laughed. "Eyes are eyes. I have much more to offer a man."

"Aren't you concerned they might get the wrong idea?"

"I *want* them to get that idea. I only wish Dr. Fletcher would behave like all these other men." She lifted her chin into the air. "I believe Izzy's wrong 'bout me. By the behavior of the men we've seen today, I'd say I'm plenty a woman."

She and Penelope giggled, then held hands and walked home. Victoria needed to come up with another plan to catch her doctor. Her afternoon with Penelope affirmed she had all the right equipment; she just had to prove to Dr. Fletcher that she knew how to use it.

Izzy stood in the entryway waiting for Victoria when she arrived home. She jerked the parasol from her hand. As soon as Penelope exited, Victoria prepared for a scolding. Izzy's demeanor indicated it would be a good one.

The woman's fists rested on her hips and her face scrunched tight. "You been up to no good again. Ain't ya, Miss Victoria?" Her hands left their place at her side and she shook the parasol to accentuate her final words.

"Why, no, Izzy. Why would you say such a thing?" Victoria tilted her head and strolled into the living room.

"I knows ya. An' I knows you're upta sumthin'! You keep showin' yourself the way you does an' you may not like the kinda attention you're gonna get!"

"Don't be silly, Izzy. Men like to look at me, an' I like it. They'd *never* try to do anythin' else. Besides, there's only one man I want, an' I can't seem to get *him* to notice me at all." She sat down hard on the sofa and pouted.

"There you goes again actin' like a baby. Now you listen, an' listen good." Izzy bent down, mere inches from Victoria's face. "You keep advertisin' your wares an' someone's gonna expect you to sell. You understan' me?"

"I can take care of myself, Izzy. I know what I'm doin'." Victoria stood, and with her nose in the air, went up the stairs to her room.

Izzy doesn't know what she's talkin' 'bout.

She took a seat at her vanity and gazed into the mirror. Taking a bottle of perfume, she dabbed some across her rounded breasts, then inhaled deeply and sighed. One day soon she'd have a man who'd bury himself there and appreciate every ounce of her femininity.

Blood boiled inside her veins. She had needs only a man could satisfy, and she had no doubt a doctor would know exactly how to do it.

CHAPTER 4

September.

Time had ticked by quickly for Andrew.

Once Elijah told him Tobias had left town with his children, Andrew felt exceedingly better. He'd heard that the man had taken the children to live with their aunt in Birmingham. Shortly thereafter, Tobias couldn't be found anywhere.

Andrew shuddered remembering how Elijah had described the condition of the vacant shanty. Soiled blankets on the floor crawling with cockroaches, clothes strewn about, and dirty dishes piled high in the sink. Andrew assumed it hadn't been much different when they'd lived there.

At least with Tobias gone, he could sleep again. Still, he frequently woke from nightmares with a wrench in his gut. Though the man had left, from what Elijah had said, he hadn't forgiven him. He despised Andrew and blamed him for his wife's death. When Elijah had tried to convince him that Andrew was a good man, Tobias spat at his feet, just as he'd done to Andrew.

He hated that his friend had to endure the man's disgusting treatment. Especially since they'd been friends at one time. Elijah had defended him and placed *their* friendship even higher. Something Andrew would never forget.

While at work, Andrew did his best to leave personal matters at home. After an exhausting, full day, he was ready to leave the hospital.

As he started to exit, Sally stopped him. "Dr. Fletcher! Mr. Schultz would like to see you in his office right away!" Her eyes were wide with urgency.

"Thank you, Sally." Since Mr. Schultz currently had no grievances with him, he headed down the hallway to the man's office and knocked on the door without trepidation.

"Come in!" The man sounded even more urgent than Sally.

Andrew opened the door to find Mr. Schultz in the company of another man.

The stranger held himself upright and proud, with an air of sophistication. He wore a fine business suit that had a waistcoat decorated with a watch chain.

The moment he saw Andrew, he stood even taller, although he was much shorter and rounder than him. He clutched a hat in his hands, exposing a partially bald head. What little hair he had was reddish-brown in color. The majority of it formed into bushy, but stylishly trimmed sideburns.

"Dr. Fletcher," Mr. Schultz said. "I'd like you to meet Mr. Patrick O'Malley."

Andrew extended his hand. "It's a pleasure, sir." Mr. O'Malley shook it.

Andrew's mind raced. *O'Malley? I know that name.*

"I appreciate the formalities," Mr. O'Malley said in a heavy Irish brogue. "But me daughter's ill, and I need a doctor at me home right away. Mr. Schultz tells me you're the finest."

"Thank you, sir." Andrew sensed his earnestness. "I'll get my bag."

Mr. O'Malley rushed out the door with Andrew right behind him. But Mr. Schultz stopped him.

"Yes, sir?" Andrew was anxious to leave.

"Take all the time you need. He's an important man. Funds many things for the hospital. Don't worry about your duties here. I'll make certain you're covered. " Mr. Schultz waved his hand, motioning him to leave.

Andrew thanked him, then hastily followed Mr. O'Malley down the hall, stopping only briefly to retrieve his bag.

"Me buggy's right outside," the man said. "Hurry now!"

They flew down the steps and hopped into the buggy.

"It's me daughter, Victoria!" O'Malley snapped the reins. "I believe she has the fever. I've never seen her so ill in all me days."

Victoria?

Andrew gave no indication he'd ever met her. Frankly, the meetings they had weren't worth remembering. She annoyed him. She acted like a spoiled child, and he had no appreciation for such behavior. However, being a doctor, any patient—spoiled or not—deserved his finest care.

Arriving at the O'Malley's home, Andrew wasn't surprised by its magnificence. The house suited Victoria. *Immaculate*, like the lady herself.

A large Negro woman, whom he assumed to be a housemaid, opened the door. She gave him a warm smile and he liked her immediately.

"Up the stairs to the left!" Mr. O'Malley bellowed.

Andrew raced up the stairs to Victoria's room.

A woman, presumably the girl's mother, sat beside her on the bed, wiping her brow with a cloth. She was an attractive middle-aged woman with red hair like Victoria's, but accented naturally with gray streaks. She wore it up on her head in a large twist. Though no *small* woman, she was far from obese. He had no doubt where Victoria inherited her striking looks.

She locked eyes with him. "*You're* the doctor?" She had a brogue as thick as her husband's.

Strange that Victoria has no trace of it.

"Yes. *Mrs.* O'Malley, I presume?"

"*Shannon* O'Malley," she replied, with a slight nod.

"I'm Dr. Fletcher." He set down his bag and removed the stethoscope.

"You don't seem old enough to be a doctor," she huffed. "Do you know what you're doing?"

"Yes, ma'am, I do. Now please, let me take a look at your daughter." In no mood to argue regarding his age or ability, he tried to be as patient as possible.

Mrs. O'Malley arose from the bed and moved back, allowing him to get close to Victoria.

"She's burnin' up," the woman cried. "Please help her!"

Andrew sat on the edge of the large bed. A satin canopy encased it. The room had European-style elegance, but he quickly determined Victoria to be the most beautiful part of it.

He took her pulse and listened to her heart. Her body was fighting the fever, causing a rapid heartbeat.

Hmm . . . dried blood in her nostrils. Not good.

There hadn't been a case of yellow fever in some time. He'd been told the worst epidemic in the city had been before the war, and the hospital had been filled to capacity with patients suffering from it. No one knew what had caused it, but it was common knowledge that yellow fever could be fatal.

He attempted to raise her eyelids. Her eyes appeared vacant, unaware of his presence. Delirious, she moaned and mumbled unrecognizable words.

"How long has she been like this?" he asked.

Mr. O'Malley had entered the room during the examination and stood beside his wife with his arm around her. "She was vomiting this morning and we thought she'd merely eaten something that didn't agree with her. Then this afternoon, the fever set in. That's when I went to the hospital."

Mrs. O'Malley sniffled. "Can you help her, Doctor?"

"We have to get her fever down. Do you have any means of getting ice? A lot of it?" If he couldn't get her temperature down soon it could damage her brain.

"I'll go to the icehouse. Whatever you need!" Mr. O'Malley flew out the door.

Without her husband's support, Mrs. O'Malley trembled. She stood staring at her daughter. Grief covered her face as if the girl lay at death's door.

"Mrs. O'Malley," Andrew said. "Your daughter will be fine. I promise you." It had been wrong to make such a promise, but he wanted to ease her. "Can you bring her a glass of water?"

With a nod, she gave him a timid smile and left the room.

Andrew studied Victoria. She looked different lying here in bed with her hair loose and flowing over the pillows. Without thinking, he moved his fingers through it.

The color suits her.

He much preferred it loose this way than in the tight ringlets she wore each time he'd seen her. Her gown was a plain nightgown, not a fancy dress with her body pushed and pulled in every direction. The simplicity of her appearance made her more attractive.

Her lips were slightly swollen from the fever.

What would it be like to kiss those lips?

He scolded himself for such thoughts. He'd been called to care for her, *not* make advances. Fortunately, it didn't take long before her mother returned with the water.

Reaching under Victoria's shoulders, he lifted her to a more upright position. "Victoria," he whispered. "You need to drink."

She opened her eyes and her mother gasped.

"What?" Victoria's voice sounded weak and shallow.

"You need to drink. You've lost a lot of fluid." He held the glass to her lips.

She took a small sip, then her eyes opened fully, taking him in. A frail smile lifted the corners of her lips. "Dr. Fletcher?"

"Yes, Victoria?"

Thank God she knows me.

Mrs. O'Malley cast a wary glance. She'd obviously realized their familiarity, but now was *not* the time for him to give an explanation.

"Try to drink a bit more," he said. He tipped the glass and she dutifully obeyed.

"I don't feel well," she rasped.

"I know. I'm going to make you better." He rested her head against the pillow. "Sleep now. I'll be close by."

Her eyes closed and soon she fell asleep. Even in sleep, her body shook from fever.

Mr. O'Malley had better hurry.

When the man arrived with the ice, only thirty minutes had passed, but they had no time to waste. Andrew helped him wrap the large blocks in burlap, then they carried them into the kitchen.

Mr. O'Malley formally introduced Andrew to Izzy, the housemaid, who immediately set to chopping at the ice blocks with a pick, breaking them into smaller pieces.

While Izzy chopped ice, Andrew and Mr. O'Malley hauled a large bathing tub from the lower floor to Victoria's bedroom. Making every effort to keep her comfortable, they didn't want to move her down the stairs.

Izzy placed the ice into large bowls that were then dumped into the tub. Once the bottom became full, they lifted Victoria into it, then put more ice over the top of her.

She shivered, but it was necessary to bring the fever down.

Andrew left her there until her temperature had lowered enough to risk putting her back into bed.

"We can take her out now," he said, nodding to her father.

Her mother stepped up beside him. "Her gown is soaked. You can see . . ." Her face glowed red as she tried to shield Victoria's most private parts from his gaze.

"I'm her doctor, Mrs. O'Malley. Not a common bystander." He'd already noticed how the melted ice had dampened her gown and revealed every part of her body.

Still, he intended to do everything in his power to make her well, seeing her with the eyes of a physician, not those of a common man.

"But . . ." The woman's mouth pinched tightly together as she pointed to Victoria.

"Mr. O'Malley," Andrew said. "Why don't you have Izzy come to the room to help your wife dress Victoria in a clean, dry gown?"

"Of course," the man said, and left the room.

When he returned with Izzy, Andrew walked out with him so the women could tend Victoria.

Several hours had passed since Andrew's arrival. The evening waned.

"I'll have Izzy prepare a room for you, Dr. Fletcher," Mr. O'Malley said in a tone indicating a demand rather than a request.

"Thank you, sir." He had no intentions of leaving.

"Will me daughter live?"

"Yes, sir. She'll be fine." Since her fever had come down, Andrew had become more confident. However, he hoped the illness hadn't advanced so far as to cause jaundice. If her liver became damaged, he doubted he could save her. It was different from little Betsy's jaundice, which was common in premature babies and easily treated. It wouldn't be so simple for Victoria.

Andrew returned to her room. Izzy and Mrs. O'Malley had finished dressing her and she rested comfortably in bed. She'd already drifted off to sleep.

He sat next to her once again, took her pulse, and listened to her heart. Her heartbeat sounded closer to normal, and her skin felt cool to the touch. He caught himself running his hand down her arm, caressing her without even thinking.

Fortunately, the girl's parents were busy talking to one another, but when he shifted his eyes to Izzy, she smiled at him.

Did she see the way I touched her?

He'd be more careful in the future.

* * *

The next day, Victoria's fever spiked again. They repeated the ice treatment and brought it down, but Victoria's exhausted body had become extremely weak.

She couldn't keep food in her stomach and Andrew was worried. He left her side only to sleep and occasionally stretch his legs; otherwise he remained beside her in a chair her father had brought up from the living room.

Through the course of his time there, Andrew found a new friend in Izzy. Not only did he appreciate her cooking, but she was a fine conversationalist.

She brought his meals to Victoria's room and would sit with him while he ate, talking all the while. Victoria seemed unaware of their presence for the most part, drifting in and out of sleep and speaking only a few words.

"Yessa," Izzy said. "I been workin' here since the war. When I heard a white man wanted a good cook, I came to their door." She leaned in close. "Ms. O'Malley don't cook too good," she whispered. "Knows how to cook Irish Stew, but nuttin' else." She chuckled. "I works every day but Sunday. On Sunday, Mista O'Malley gets Irish Stew." She shook her head. "Don't never come here on Sunday."

"I appreciate the advice," Andrew laughed.

They discovered they both knew Alicia and Elijah Tarver, as well as Tobias Lewis. Izzy knew most everybody in Shanty Town, because she lived there. She walked two miles each way six days a week to work for the O'Malley's from sunrise until sunset.

"I's glad Tobias done left," she said with a sigh.

He nodded his agreement.

"Odd he left behind some a his things. Din't have much. Figgered he'd take it with him. Some folks say someone be squattin' in his home. Don't know why anyone would wanna live there. Place was a mess."

"As long as the children are cared for. That was my biggest concern."

Izzy's face lit up with a grin. "You gots a big heart, Doc. I seen it with my own eyes. The way you care for Miss Victoria."

"Thank you, Izzy. I've noticed *you* care for her, too."

"That I do. Been fixin' her hair, washin' her clothes, dryin' her clothes, pressin' her clothes . . ." She chuckled. "She gots lots a clothes. Most important . . . I cinch up her corset tight as I can. I's shore you appreciate that!"

Andrew shook his head, laughing under his breath. He believed Izzy knew more about Victoria than her parents did. Even through Izzy's light humor, she obviously loved the girl. Maybe he'd misjudged her. Perhaps Victoria was more than a beautiful spoiled child.

"I's tellin' ya, Doc. That child can be demandin', but least I gets paid for my frustrations." She raised her voice a bit too loudly, causing Victoria to moan. "Don't get me wrong. I loves her with all my heart."

"I know you do, Izzy. And I'm sure she loves you, too."

* * *

Victoria handed the empty cup to Izzy. The clear broth had tasted good. She'd been told that she'd been sick for three days already. At least she could finally sit up in bed, but it bothered her not remembering what had happened.

Dr. Fletcher had assured her parents the worst had passed, and with more rest, she'd be herself again in no time.

Because of his assurance, her daddy had returned to work at the bank and her mama had left the house to meet with some of the ladies from St. Mary's Parish.

Izzy stood holding the cup, looking between her and the doctor. "You say she be just like her old self?"

"In time, yes," Dr. Fletcher replied.

"Not shore that's a good thing," Izzy mumbled and left the room.

Never before had Victoria been at a loss for words, but then again, she'd never had a man alone with her in her bedroom. She stared at her hands, then pulled the blankets up toward her chin.

"Are you cold?" he asked.

"A bit," she whispered.

He lifted a quilt from the foot of her bed and laid it over her. "Better?"

"Yes, thank you." Truth be told, she'd become rather warm. "Dr. Fletcher? Have you been here the whole time —while I've been sick?" She gazed deeply into his dark eyes, never having been so close before. It would've been easy to reach out and touch him.

"Yes, I have. You're my patient. My responsibility."

"So you only stayed because my daddy's payin' you to be here?" She turned away, unable to look at him any longer.

He took her hand. "I *wanted* to stay."

Her heart doubled its pace. "You're holdin' my hand, Dr. Fletcher. Is that common practice?"

"No. Nothing about you is common, Miss O'Malley."

"I prefer you call me Victoria. I heard you say my name the first day you were here. It's all I really remember 'bout that first day—aside from the ice."

"I'm sorry about the ice . . . but it was the only way. I didn't want to lose you. That is . . . I never give up . . . on a patient." He stumbled over his words.

She laughed. It was the first time he'd fumbled since she'd met him. He'd always had an air of confidence that intimidated her. She liked this side of him. It made him attainable.

"Dr. Fletcher . . ." She sat upright, more confident than ever. "Isn't your given name, Andrew?"

"Yes, it is."

"May I use it?"

"Yes, you may." He smiled.

"Thank you . . . *Drew.*"

"*Andrew.*"

"No. To me you'll simply be *Drew.*"

"No one has ever called me *Drew* before." He frowned.

"And I'm certain you've never met anyone quite like *me* before." She bit her bottom lip, then reached out and touched his leg.

He took a deep breath. "I think it's time you rest. Perhaps when you wake you'll feel like eating a bit more. I can ask Izzy to fix you whatever you like. How's your stomach?" He'd started to behave too much like a doctor again. She intended to change that.

She took his hand and pulled him toward her, placing it on her abdomen. "You tell me," she said, batting her eyes.

"I'd say you're feeling much better." He pulled away and started to leave.

"Where are you goin', Drew?"

"I need some air."

And just like that, he was gone.

Even though he'd left the room, she was satisfied. Not only was she on a first name basis with the handsome doctor, she'd given him her own pet name. No one had ever called him Drew.

She giggled.

She'd staked her claim. Soon, she *would* have her doctor.

CHAPTER 5

September 2nd, 1872.

Gerald had wanted to buy Claire a new wedding ring for their first anniversary, but she'd insisted the one he gave her was the only one she ever wanted. Having lost all the weight she'd gained with Michael, she had to wrap it again with yarn to keep it on her finger.

For their celebration, Henry offered to cook them a meal. She gladly accepted his offer, though Gerald teased him about not being up to her standards.

"Don't mind him, Uncle Henry," Claire said, pleased to have a free evening. "We appreciate your generous offer."

"You work hard. Both a ya," Henry said. "Now go on an' enjoy what's left a the day."

Gerald grinned. "Let's go for a walk."

Since Michael was taking a nap and Henry had busied himself cooking, Claire liked the idea. They seldom got away alone. They didn't mind having the baby with them, but it was nice to have some quiet time for just the two of them.

"Where do you wanna go?"

He wiggled his brows, took her by the hand, and led her to the stable.

"What are you doin'?" She already knew.

He took her to the stall where they'd first made love. "Remember this?"

Had he planned this all along? The stall had been filled with fresh straw.

"How could I forget?" She couldn't look at him and stared at the ground. "I'm ashamed for puttin' you through that."

"Why'd you do it, Claire? Why'd you hafta give yourself to me before we was married?" He took her hand, pulling her closer.

What should I tell him?

She hesitated, gathering her thoughts. "I was scared. Scared I couldn't do it. I didn't wanna deny you that part of our relationship. So I had to . . . well . . . you know. *Do* it."

Please believe me.

"I was scared, too. But I'm glad you done it. Reckon you gave us both some confidence. We made Michael here that day." He placed his hand on her belly.

"Yes." She still couldn't look at him. "I know."

"I'd like to try again. Maybe there's sumthin' magic 'bout this place. You *do* want more babies, don't you?"

Yes, she did. But it wouldn't be possible for him to father a child. He didn't know it and she wasn't about to tell him.

"Course I do." She kissed him, but he deserved much more from her.

He knelt in the straw, then pulled her down beside him.

"Gerald, it's the middle a the day. What if someone comes in?"

"They won't come back here. I want you, Claire." He laid her back against the straw.

He'd learned how to kiss her gently, how to caress her body, and how to make love to her in a way that satisfied both of them. And she'd learned how to love him back wholeheartedly.

It was different than the love she'd made with Andrew. There'd never been fireworks with Gerald. Instead, each time felt like coming home to a warm fireplace and snuggling up with her best friend. Her husband had become the sparkling fire that warmed her to the core.

They were in love and they were happy.

After finishing, they lay in the straw, holding one another. She placed her head on his chest and his heart beat strong against her cheek. She sighed with contentment. If only it would last.

Rain pattered against the rooftop. It would've been easy to fall asleep listening to the soft rainfall, their bodies exhausted from their exertion.

She glided her fingers over his skin, exposed from his open shirt. "We best be gettin' back." Rising up, she kissed him one more time. "Henry's gonna be callin' us for supper, an' we need to check on Michael." Reluctantly, she stood and extended her hand.

He gave her a warm smile, then took it. After brushing the straw from their clothing, they walked hand-in-hand back to the house. The soft rain cooled them.

When they entered, Henry studied them as if he knew what they'd been doing. Heat filled her cheeks, though it shouldn't have mattered. They were married after all and had the right.

At times, the man behaved like a jealous lover, making her more uncomfortable than ever. Eventually, she and Gerald would need to move into their own home. And one day she'd have to tell him why. For now she'd go on trying to ignore Henry and be the most loving wife and mama she could be.

Supper wasn't quite ready, so they went upstairs to check on Michael and found him stirring in his crib. They watched him until he became aware of their presence. He looked back and forth between them, his little eyes full of life.

"Did you have a nice nap?" Gerald asked, as he reached in the crib to pick him up.

Michael made some tiny baby sounds and nestled against his daddy's shoulder.

They were a perfect picture.

He can never know the truth. It would break his heart.

Tears formed in her eyes and she had to turn away. She'd just made love to the man. Even after losing herself in his arms, guilt always had a way of creeping back in.

"You all right, Claire?" He rested his hand on her back.

Wiping away a tear, she faced him. "Course I am. I'm the luckiest woman alive."

Obviously believing her tears to be the *happy* kind, he kissed her on the tip of her nose and grinned. "We're both lucky. We got the finest baby ever born."

She nodded and cupped her hand over Michael's head. "I love you both."

"Hey up there!" Henry's loud voice interrupted the solemn moment. "Supper's ready!"

They headed to the kitchen and Gerald passed Michael into her arms. Instantly he craned his neck ready for his own supper.

"Go on an' eat," she said. "I'm gonna feed Michael, then I'll join you." She carried him into the living room and sat on the sofa.

While he nursed, she couldn't help but think about his daddy—wondering what he might be doing now. But she had to dismiss all thoughts of him if she ever hoped to find lasting contentment.

That evening as she crawled into bed beside Gerald, she thanked him for a wonderful anniversary, then laid her head against her pillow and laughed.

"What you laughin' 'bout, Claire?" He sat up and stared at her.

"I was thinkin' 'bout our weddin' night. Remember how the bed squeaked?"

He grinned. "Yep. But I hate it's a *funny* memory."

"I can't help it. I was so embarrassed that night, I thought I'd die. What with Uncle Henry downstairs beatin' his cane. How'd we make it a whole year?"

"With a lot a love." He brushed her hair back from her face. "It's been the best year a my life."

"You mean that?"

"Course I do." He circled his fingers over her belly.

"Again, Gerald?"

"Well, it *is* our anniversary. Seems like a good idea." He continued to caress her, then rolled over onto her.

"Happy anniversary, Gerald." She gave him a memorable kiss.

"Happy anniversary, Claire."

They made no more conversation.

CHAPTER 6

Victoria had fully recovered from her illness. Though still weak, she'd been getting stronger every day.

Fortunately, she had no lasting side effects and the time had come to go shopping. It had been far too long since she'd been to Parker's. After spending some of her daddy's money, she planned to *drop in* on her dear Drew.

She chose to wear a warm royal blue dress with long sleeves. The late September air was cool, but not cold enough for a coat or shawl. She never liked to wear coats, believing they covered up too much of her clothing. Priding herself in the way she dressed, she made certain to always be the pinnacle of fashion.

"Izzy! Come to my room and help me with my corset!" She'd positioned the thing and was ready to be *enhanced.*

Izzy walked in, shaking her head. "Don't know why you hafta wear this. You're thin nuff 'thout it." She jerked on the strings.

"Tighter Izzy," Victoria huffed. "I wear it to make me shapelier."

"Oh, you's shapely a'right. Don't know why your daddy lets you go out lookin' like this. You need to be locked in your room." The woman pulled and yanked until Victoria was satisfied.

"Daddy thinks I'm pretty." She tossed her head. "He wants me to attract a husband."

"There's other ways. You keep drippin' all this honey, an' the flies is gonna come. Don't want no flies." Izzy lowered the dress over her head. "Why are all your dresses cut down to your navel?"

Victoria laughed. "It's the style. That is . . . it's *my* style." She gazed at herself in the full-length mirror in the corner of the room. After adjusting her bosom, she flashed a satisfied grin.

"Where you goin' today?" Izzy asked.

"To catch me a doctor."

"Ah . . . I likes that Dr. Fletcher. If I was younger, I might try for him myself."

"Oh, Izzy." Victoria giggled and waved her hand. "The man's white."

"He ain't *that* white. Mmm, mmm he's fine."

"Well, no matter. He's *mine*." She finished dressing, had Izzy help with her hair, then headed out the door.

As she walked, her stomach began to flutter. She felt quite certain someone was following her. But every time she turned around, the footsteps stopped.

She brushed her worry aside and continued her stroll to Parker's. The mercantile was only ten blocks from her home and she made the walk even shorter by taking a shortcut through an alleyway that ran alongside it.

Mr. Parker had catalogs full of merchandise. She simply made herself comfortable at the counter, pointed, and he wrote up an order.

She'd already begun planning her Christmas attire. After purchasing a lovely dress that had large green and red ribbon stripes on a white background, she found the perfect hat to match. A new style held on by long hatpins, rather than tying at the neck with a bow. She wanted to be the first woman in Mobile to wear such a hat. So of course she had Mr. Parker order it.

"That all for today, Miss O'Malley?" Mr. Parker asked, smacking his lips.

His eyes were glued to her bosom, giving her the attention she desired. She purposefully bent low over the counter while perusing the catalog. Something about making a man's mouth water stimulated her.

"Thank you for your help, Mr. Parker." She gave him her sweetest smile. "I'll be back soon." She wiggled her fingers at him, then turned to leave.

"My pleasure. I'll look forward to it."

I know you will.

Whether it was her daddy's money or her voluptuous figure that the man liked more, she didn't care. She happily obliged him on both accounts and gave him a little taste of something he'd never fully have.

When she reached the door, she glanced over her shoulder and delighted in watching him wipe the sweat from his brow.

Continuing her stroll down Main Street, she headed for City Hospital. Entering through the main door, she approached the front desk.

"I'd like to see Dr. Fletcher." She didn't ask, she demanded.

"I believe he's with patients now, ma'am," the desk clerk said. "If you'd like to have a seat I'm sure he can see you eventually."

"I don't care if he's with other patients. I happen to *be* one of his patients. I'd like to see him *now*. I don't want to wait!" Victoria crossed her arms and glared at the girl.

"Yes, ma'am. I'll see if I can find him." She scurried off down the hall.

You'd better run fast, little girl.

It wasn't hard to get what she wanted, especially when dealing with incompetent little girls. It didn't take long before she returned with an uptight man at her heels.

He pinched his lips together and looked her over from head to toe. "I'm Mr. Schultz, the hospital administrator. Is everything all right?"

Victoria lifted her chin. "No, it is not. In case you don't know who I am, I'm Victoria *O'Malley,* and I'd like to see Dr. Fletcher *now*. Is that a problem?"

"Oh . . . my. Miss *O'Malley.*" Mr. Schultz fumbled for his words, jerking his body as if he'd sat on a nest of ants. "We . . . that is . . . uh . . . I'm so happy to see you feeling well. I'm certain Dr. Fletcher will be happy to see you."

"Thank you." She pursed her lips. "I'm not surprised a fine man like you could help a lady in distress." She batted her eyes and touched her hand to her breast.

"Think nothing of it. That's what I'm here for." He puffed out his chest. "I'll go now and help Sally find Dr. Fletcher."

Sally? I simple name for a simple girl. Why on earth did the hospital employ someone so young and inefficient?

As Mr. Schultz hastened down the hallway pulling Sally along be the arm, Victoria giggled.

Yes, little girl. I always get my way.

* * *

Andrew looked up, attuned to rapid footsteps approaching. Mr. Schultz and Sally seemed to be upset.

Perhaps an emergency?

"Dr. Fletcher, thank God!" Mr. Schultz exclaimed. "Hurry to the front desk."

"What's the matter?" By the tone of the man's voice, it *had* to be an emergency.

"Please hurry!" He grabbed Andrew's arm and yanked him down the hallway. "You have an important woman waiting to see you."

Andrew peered over his shoulder to find Sally following behind them. The poor girl seemed terrified.

As they neared the main entrance, Mr. Schultz waved his arms in the air and pointed at Andrew. "We found him, Miss O'Malley!"

Victoria?

Instantly, Andrew's chest tightened. If the matter was urgent, perhaps she'd had a relapse. But she certainly didn't look ill.

"I'll leave you alone," Mr. Schultz said, then walked away pulling Sally along with him.

"Victoria?" Andrew placed his hand on her arm. "Are you all right?"

"Of course. I'm fine, Drew." She smiled, and placed her hand into the crook of his arm. "I just wanted to see you."

"I happen to be working. You can't just come by and expect to see me." Once again her behavior annoyed him.

The only time she *hadn't* annoyed him was when she'd been partially unconscious. He attributed her poor behavior to youth.

She has a lot of growing up to do.

Her lower lip protruded. "But Drew, I haven't had the chance to properly thank you for savin' my life. The least you could do is let me buy your dinner."

"You're asking me to have dinner with you?"

She's so bold.

"It *is* almost your dinner time, isn't it? We could go to Sylvia's. I know you like the food there." Coyly, she bit her bottom lip.

He didn't want to be rude. "Yes, it's almost time for my break." *How could it hurt?* "I'll have dinner with you. Especially since you're buying."

An unusually loud whimper turned his head. Not from Victoria. It came from Sally who'd returned to her desk.

He crossed to her. "Sally, Miss O'Malley and I are going to eat. I'm certain Mr. Schultz won't object to my leaving. If he asks, please tell him where we've gone."

"Yes, Dr. Fletcher." The frown on her face proved he'd sorely disappointed her.

As they walked the short distance to Sylvia's, he took note of Victoria's demeanor. She strutted with her chin in the air, and her arm linked through his. The exact thing he hated—being paraded like a prize.

They sat at the table at the far end of the café. The same one where she'd first introduced herself.

"Drew? Were you surprised to see me?"

"Yes *and* no. Nothing you do surprises me. But then again, I don't understand why you're being so persistent. I haven't exactly been *nice* to you."

"I don't know what you mean." She tilted her head and touched her hand to her breast. "You saved my life. Stayed by my side. How much nicer could you be?"

"I could be considerably nicer, and I'm sorry I haven't been." Since she kept trying so hard, maybe he should at least give her a chance.

They ate their dinner and attempted conversation. Victoria picked at her food and ate little. She seemed to be more interested in keeping an eye on who happened to be coming and going.

"Drew," she cooed. "You and I should start spendin' more time together. I believe you'll find we have a great deal in common. You aren't seein' someone *else* are you?"

Claire.

Why he thought of Claire at that moment wasn't really clear to him. It had been over a year. "No, I'm not seeing anyone. And I *would* enjoy spending more time with you. What do you have in mind?"

She bit her lip, then took a deep breath. "Lots of things."

Her blatant meaning shouldn't have surprised him. "Slow down, Victoria."

"But I don't like goin' slow."

He held up his hand. "Perhaps we should start with supper on Friday night?"

"I suppose, but I hate to wait so long. That's three whole days." Out popped the lower lip.

"You'll survive." He grinned. Even though she acted childish, he found something grown up and exhilarating about her. "I'll let you choose the place. I imagine you're more familiar with the restaurants here than I am. I don't get out much."

She reached across the table and ran her fingers over his. "I intend to change that." Her sultry voice warmed him.

His eyes were glued to her hand as she moved it slowly along her neck, then down toward her cleavage. Breathing became almost impossible.

She's a temptress.

"Are you certain you're eighteen?" he asked, licking his lips.

"Why? Do you still believe I'm a child?" Her thick, rich voice told him otherwise.

"No. Far from it." He swallowed, attempting to moisten his dry throat.

She's trying to seduce me in a public café.

"Is sumthin' wrong, Drew?" She met his gaze, then breathed deep and slow, causing her breasts to noticeably rise and fall.

"Y—Yes. It's a bit warm in here. I should return to work." He stood, wanting to flee. "Thank you for dinner." He extended his hand to assist her to her feet.

She stood with slow deliberation. Rather than taking his hand, she let it glide along her body as she arose.

He didn't move it.

"It's been my pleasure," she said. "Until Friday. I'll expect you at six. Don't be late."

"Right!" He quickly exited the café.

She'd affected him. Made him feel things he hadn't in some time.

But, why? She's nothing like Claire.

They couldn't be more opposite.

Maybe that's what I need.

Then again, the woman could be poison.

CHAPTER 7

Andrew's mind spun.

Maybe suggesting they have supper together hadn't been wise.

Though young, Victoria's actions were far from youthful. Aside from pouting, her behavior indicated she was ready for a good bedding. But *he* certainly wasn't ready for it. He'd made up his mind not to bed a woman again unless he married her first. Fearing he'd rushed Claire when she hadn't been ready and therefore left him, he swore he wouldn't let it happen again.

Thursday afternoon, Sally stopped him as he was leaving the hospital. "Dr. Fletcher, I have a message for you." As she handed him an envelope, a waft of Victoria's perfume floated into the air around him.

"Thank you, Sally."

"You're welcome, Doctor." The smile she gave him was by no means *happy*.

He opened the note while walking out of the building.

Drew,

Dress casually tomorrow. The place I've chosen is simple and does not require a coat and tie. I assure you the food and company will be quite tasty.

Or, if you would prefer, don't wear anything at all. That would suit me as well.

Until then . . .

Victoria

His assumptions regarding her were correct, but he'd have to disappoint her.

* * *

"Izzy!" Victoria yelled and stomped her foot.

Where is that woman?

Tonight had to be memorable and she needed Izzy's help.

I must look exquisite for Andrew.

"Izzy, where are you?" She couldn't scream much louder.

I shouldn't have to leave my room to find her.

She put on her lacy undergarments, then started to position the corset. "Izzy!"

"What you fussin' 'bout?" The woman finally came in, but with an enormous frown. "What you wearin' them fancy underpants for?"

Victoria giggled. "Oh, Izzy. Sometimes you ask too many questions."

"You're upta sumthin' an' it ain't good."

"Truthfully, it could be *very* good." Anticipating what might happen made her shiver with delight. "Now, I want the corset good and tight."

"Chastity belt might be better," Izzy mumbled, jerking on the strings.

"I'm not a little girl, Izzy. I'm a grown woman. So stop talkin' and keep pullin'."

"Fine. I just hopes that doctor knows what he's gettin' into." She wrenched the corset so tight Victoria nearly fell over.

"Thank you, Izzy. That'll do. I'll finish up from here." Victoria shooed her away.

Even though she'd told Andrew to dress casually, she would never lower herself to such a standard. She wore a scarlet-colored dress trimmed in black lace. Her hair was in ringlets, but fell loosely over her shoulders.

After dabbing perfume in all the appropriate places, she admired herself in the mirror. "Drew, you *are* a lucky man."

* * *

It was six o'clock on the dot when Andrew knocked on the O'Malley's door.

Hopefully she'll approve of my attire.

He'd chosen a pair of black pants, white shirt, and frock coat. But no hat. He'd never cared for them.

Izzy swung the door open.

"Good evening, Miss Izzy," he said, bowing his head. "Is Victoria ready?"

"Mmm hmm," Izzy muttered. "She is." She stepped to the side. "Just hope *you* are."

"Excuse me?" Had he heard her correctly?

"Never mind. I'll get Miss Victoria." She bustled away.

Patrick O'Malley came around the corner accompanied by his wife. He extended his hand. "It's good to see you again, Doctor. I'm thankful it's for a pleasant reason."

Andrew shook his hand. "Thank you, sir." Would he be so gracious if he knew Victoria's intentions?

Doubtful.

Mrs. O'Malley took Andrew's hand and gave it a pat. "You be sweet to our little girl. She's a fine lass. We don't want her hurt."

Her husband narrowed his eyes. "How can you say such a thing, Shannon? He saved her life."

"Don't worry about your daughter, Mrs. O'Malley," Andrew said. "I promise I'll be a perfect gentleman." He took her hand and kissed it.

"Oh, my." She blushed, then looked away toward the stairs. "Victoria! Don't keep the good doctor waitin'!"

Andrew followed her gaze and beheld Victoria slowly descending toward them.

"Me lovely daughter," Mr. O'Malley beamed.

Her mother clasped her hands together and shook her head from side to side. "Isn't she a vision?"

Once she reached the bottom, Andrew took her hand. "You're beautiful, Victoria."

"Thank you, Drew." She smiled and coyly tilted her head.

Andrew observed her father's raised brows, and her mother's eyes pop open at their daughter's chosen name for him. The smiles that followed indicated they might already be planning a wedding.

Not so fast.

Andrew escorted Victoria to the buggy and helped her up. Since they'd be going someplace new, he'd chosen Sam for the evening. Charger didn't do well in new surroundings.

"She's a beautiful mare," Victoria said.

"Yes, she is." He wasn't referring to the horse. The woman sitting beside him was stunning.

She directed him to an out-of-the-way restaurant at the pier. "I hope you like oysters, Drew," she said, twisting her mouth. "It's their specialty."

"I do." It wasn't completely true, but the concern in her eyes made him want to ease her.

As they were led through the restaurant, Victoria kept her head held high. The eyes of every man they passed turned to admire her. She'd overdressed, but he expected no less from her. The woman loved being the center of attention.

They were seated at a table in the corner. Once they ordered their meal, they conversed in small talk. As usual, she paid more attention to who'd noticed her, rather than engaging in intelligent conversation.

"I chose this place because of the oysters," she said, taking a bite of soup.

"You must like them a great deal."

"Not especially. Though I've heard they're an aphrodisiac." She looked him in the eye, then licked her lips. "Are they workin'?"

He nearly choked. "Victoria, you happen to be a *walking* aphrodisiac. You could've chosen another restaurant."

Why is she in such a hurry?

She tittered. "So, you admit you find me stimulatin'?"

He glanced around the restaurant, embarrassed by their conversation.

"This isn't the place for such a discussion," he whispered, leaning in.

"We can leave soon. I thought it might be fun to go somewhere and make love." She made the statement as if she were talking about taking a casual stroll or playing a game of checkers.

"Fun? Making love is more than having *fun.*" He kept his voice low, hoping no one heard them.

"I feel it *should* be fun. That's the problem with most married couples. My parents for example. They've had separate bedrooms for years. What fun is that?" She continued eating.

He leaned even closer. "I assumed you were saving yourself for marriage."

"Don't be silly. I've already done it." Her words were flippant. "Only once though. I was fifteen, he was sixteen. It just . . . *happened.*" She grinned. "I liked it. It was fun. I've wanted to try it again for some time."

"Aren't you Catholic?" His hands had started to sweat.

"Yes."

"I thought the Catholic Church frowned on that sort of behavior outside of marriage."

"They do. But I go to confession every week. God forgives me." She spoke so nonchalantly he wondered if she had any morals at all. "So," she held her spoon in the air. "Are *you* Catholic?"

"No. I'm not really anything. I believe in God, but don't practice any particular faith." He'd never make light of this subject and took it to heart.

"Hmm. You should go to church. It's good for the soul." Her voice took on a more serious tone than it had all evening.

Why is she so earnest about my religious practice when she seems so unconcerned about following hers?

"My father is Methodist," he said. "And my mother was Cherokee. They have their own unique beliefs."

"What do you mean, *was*? Is she dead?" Her voice held no compassion.

"Yes, she died when I was ten." Just saying the words wrenched his heart.

"That's a shame. She never got to see what a handsome man you grew into. Oh, well. At least *I* get to appreciate you." She left it at that. No other questions. No real concern.

God, I miss Claire.

They finished their supper, he paid the bill, and he escorted Victoria to the buggy.

"Drew, let's drive down the shore a bit. I know of a pretty beach." She rested her hand on his leg.

"It's already dark. Sam's unfamiliar with this part of Mobile." He'd had enough of her and wanted to take her home.

"Dark is a good thing. Please, Drew?" She stuck out her lip and pouted.

"All right. As long as it's not far." Why did he agree? He'd likely regret it.

The beach *wasn't* far, and didn't have a trace of another soul around—something that made Victoria overly happy.

"Drew, it appears we're all alone," she cooed.

Yes, I'm going to regret this.

He helped her from the buggy and they walked toward the water.

"Don't you just love Mobile Bay?" she asked, gesturing to the waves that lapped against the shore.

"Yes, I do." He found himself thinking of Claire and *their* walk on the beach.

Shaking his head, he attempted to focus on the woman beside him.

A cloth satchel dangled from her wrist. She opened it and removed a small package.

"It's chocolate," she said. Her tongue glided along her lower lip. "All the way from Europe." She broke off a piece and held it in her fingers. "Mr. Parker ordered it special—just for me. Have you ever had barred chocolate?" Moving within inches of him, she teased him with the candy, waving it in front of his nose. But she didn't stop there. She ran it along his lips.

Her teasing caused his heart to thump hard. "No, I haven't."

"Then why don't you have a bite?" After pursing her lips, she lowered the piece into her cleavage.

How can such a young woman be so sexually bold?

He shook his head and didn't comply.

With a grin, she removed the chocolate, then placed it in his mouth and licked her fingers. "I was teasin', Drew. I'm just tryin' to keep you on your toes."

He swallowed the candy. "What did you say?"

"I'm tryin' to keep you on your toes." She gave him a large inviting smile.

Claire?

He took her face in his hands and kissed her.

No, she's not Claire.

Aside from her lips, he felt nothing. She didn't even move them. She just stood there letting him kiss her. He'd have had more response from a dead fish.

As he backed away, she smiled.

"It's 'bout time you did that," she said, twisting a strand of hair around her finger.

"You've never kissed a man before, have you?"

"Not exactly. Only my daddy. But that's different." She tipped her head, staring at him.

"What about the boy? The one you were with? Didn't *he* kiss you?" He couldn't comprehend coupling without kissing.

She giggled. "He was too busy doin' *other* things. Now, will you make love to me or not?"

"I *won't*, Victoria. It's time I take you home." She appalled him.

"Don't you want me?" She pouted.

"Not like this. You may find it hard to believe, but I plan to wait until marriage for lovemaking. I hardly know anything about you, and you're throwing yourself at me. It cheapens what you want to do." He turned from her and headed for the buggy.

She ran after him. "I'm sorry. I thought all men wanted it."

"Maybe so, but there's a time and place for it. You can't just give yourself to every man who takes you to supper. You're better than that." He scolded her like a child.

"So, you *do* like me?" Tears pooled in her eyes.

His heart softened seeing them. "Yes, I do. But you've got to stop trying so hard. Let things happen naturally. If it's meant to be, it will be." He placed a soft kiss on her forehead.

He helped her into the buggy and took her home.

After walking her to the door, he raised her hand to his lips and kissed it. "Goodnight, Victoria."

"Goodnight, Drew," she whispered. She touched his face with her hand, then turned and walked into the house.

Andrew went home, glad to be somewhere comfortable.

As he settled into bed, he gasped. A shadowed figure appeared outside his window.

Not again.

His heart pounded.

Though he'd locked his door, he doubted it would matter.

CHAPTER 8

Victoria cried so hard following her outing with Andrew that it made her head ache. But it also made her more determined than ever to discover what she'd done wrong.

"You did what?" Izzy gaped at her. "Girl—you don't just come out an' tell a man it might be *fun* to make love! You gots no sense."

Victoria folded her arms and pouted. "At least he liked me enough to kiss me."

"And what did *you* do when he did it?" Izzy faced her with her hands on her hips.

"I stood there and let him kiss me."

"Stood there? A good-lookin' man had his lips on ya, an' you just stood there? You ain't got a clue, do ya?"

Victoria plopped down on the edge of her bed, then rubbed her temples trying to ease the dull throb.

Izzy sat beside her. "Don't worry yourself. I can hep." She patted her on the leg.

Thank goodness for Izzy. She certainly couldn't talk to

her mama about such things. How could a woman who'd been married to the same man her entire life know anything about relationships?

"First," Izzy held up a single finger. "When a man kisses ya, you gotta kiss him back. Move your lips. Grab onto him. Don't just stand there waitin' on him to do it all."

"Wouldn't that be too forward?"

"Do what?" Izzy erupted into laughter. "You already throwed yourself at him!" She shook her head, calming. "If the man's serious 'bout waitin' till marriage, you'll hafta convince him he *needs* to marry you." She sighed. "Best be marryin' soon. I won't have you endin' up in someone else's bed cuz you're too impatient to wait for the doctor. May need to give you more ice baths to cool you off!"

"Is it wrong to want him so bad, Izzy?"

"He's an easy man to want. God broke the mold when He made that one. Mmm . . . mmm." Izzy stood, fanning her face.

"He is *fine*, isn't he?"

"Finest man in Mobile, an' you's the finest woman. The perfect pair."

Victoria hopped off the bed and hugged her.

"What's that for?" Izzy asked.

"For bein' my dearest friend." She kissed the woman's cheek. "I hope you know I appreciate you. I may not always show it, but you're the only one I can talk to 'bout things of this nature."

"Well . . ." Izzy rubbed her back. "I loves ya. I don't wanna see you hurt. You just hafta behave yourself for a while. Go slow like the doctor said. Just not *too* slow. I'll have your daddy buy more ice just in case."

"Oh, Izzy!" Victoria laughed. Certainly she couldn't be serious about the ice.

Could she?

* * *

Andrew couldn't stop thinking about Victoria. Part of him wanted to be with her—no doubt *which* part—but his mind indicated she couldn't be more wrong for him.

And yet, his father would approve of her. She was beautiful, wealthy, refined . . .

Though she pouts too much.

Without a doubt, she was eager to let him bed her. In his father's eyes, Victoria represented the perfect woman by every standard. The type every man wants, and she could be his. So, why hesitate?

He needed to know more about her. Find out what lay below her beauty. She'd made all the advances up until now. *His* turn had come.

He asked Clay to tend his home for a few days, warning him of his fear someone might be lurking around again. Not wanting to endanger the boy, he also told Elijah. He'd added that if Tobias had returned, he doubted he'd harm anyone other than *him.* Especially Clay.

To ease his guilt, he offered him extra pay. Clay jumped at the opportunity, stating that with Christmas coming soon, he wanted to buy something special for his mother. The additional income would help.

Andrew rented a room at the Mobile Hotel, conveniently located beside the hospital. He intended to call on Victoria, and this would make it easier on him. He wouldn't have to travel so far. Because he lived close to

Shanty Town, he didn't want to take her to his home. In more ways than one, her father would disapprove.

It'd been a week since their supper together. Following work, he went to his room and changed clothes, then dabbed on some cologne.

Why am I doing this? Why encourage her when I have no intentions of taking things further?

Something about her kept drawing him back and he wanted to find out what it was. He'd give her another chance. Besides, he was lonely. Tired of spending his nights alone, pining over a woman he could never have again. In a strange way, he'd started following his father's advice. That alone should've told him it was a bad idea.

After purchasing flowers, he waited long enough to be certain she'd finished supper, then went to her home.

His hand shook as he knocked on the door.

"Doc Fletcher!" Izzy's eyes lit up. "Them for me?"

Instantly, he relaxed. "Miss Izzy, I'm ashamed of myself. I purchased these for Victoria. I should've gotten some for you as well."

She grinned and waved her hand, chuckling. "Come on in. I'll get Miss Victoria." She exited and left him standing in the entryway.

* * *

Victoria sat at her vanity brushing out her long hair.

"Miss Victoria!" Izzy rushed in, frantically waving her hands. "You gots company."

Andrew was the only *company* that would cause the woman to act so crazed. "Truly?"

"He brung flowers, too. Maybe you done sumthin' right." Izzy tried to force her from her seated position.

"But look at my hair," Victoria whined. "It'll take me forever to roll it again. I'm not prepared."

"Get your tail down them stairs. You looks fine." Izzy jerked her to her feet.

"At least help me put on my corset. I don't want him to see me all droopy."

"Fine. Hurry up now." Izzy pulled her dress up and over her head, then positioned the corset. The woman yanked with more force than ever before.

Once properly *placed*, Izzy put the dress on her again. "There!" she huffed. "You ain't droopy no more. Now get your tail down there." She swatted Victoria's behind.

Victoria paused at the top of the stairs to compose herself. Her parents had joined Andrew in the entryway.

"Andrew Fletcher?" She began her descent. "Did you bring me flowers?"

He looked up with his gorgeous smile. "Yes, Victoria, these are for you. However, if you don't care for them I'm certain Izzy will take them off your hands." He winked at the older woman who'd come down the stairs behind her.

"Let me put those in water," Izzy said, taking the flowers.

"Just don't forget," Victoria said. "They're *mine*."

"I won't forget. I'll put 'em in your room." She scuttled off to the kitchen.

Andrew moved directly beside her. "Your parents were telling me they're planning a getaway this year at Christmas to see some of your family in Birmingham."

"Yes, Uncle Sean is in steel. He has a large mill there. Daddy keeps up with him. Advises him on his investments. They have a lovely home and I enjoy spendin' time with my cousins. But it breaks my heart not to be *here* for Christmas." She lowered her eyes.

"Don't be so sad," her mama said. "We'll only be there two weeks. Besides, there's lots of shopping to do in Birmingham." That *did* raise her spirits a bit.

"Yes, Dr. Fletcher," her daddy chuckled. "Me daughter's good at spending me money. I've spoiled her, but how could I not? Just look at that face." He gave her cheek a gentle squeeze.

She wrinkled her nose in a manner he adored.

I know how to manipulate you, Daddy.

"Sir, if it's all right with you, I'd like to take Victoria for a ride." Andrew looked at her for approval. "My buggy's outside. That is—if Victoria's interested in going."

"Of course I am!" she exclaimed. "And I'm certain Daddy doesn't mind at all. Do you Daddy?"

"Anything my baby girl wants."

"Thank you." She rewarded him with a kiss on the cheek.

"Don't keep her out too late, Doctor," her mama said, shaking her finger.

"I'll have her home by nine," Andrew promised.

"Nine?" Victoria protested. *Not if I have my way.* "I'm not a child, Drew. I can stay out past nine o'clock."

"But it's not appropriate to have you out so late." He gave her a look similar to those she received from Izzy. "I'll have her home at nine, Mrs. O'Malley." He nodded to her mama, then extended his arm.

Victoria happily took it and they exited out the door.

* * *

Andrew helped Victoria into the buggy.

"So, tell me, Drew . . ." She spoke softly, unlike her usual tone. "Why did you come back? After our last outin' I assumed I'd never see you again."

"Honestly, I don't know. I simply needed to see you."

"I'm glad. Where are we goin'?" Her soft-spoken tone sounded refreshing.

He chuckled. "I thought we'd go back to the beach. If that's all right with you."

"Yes. Whatever you like."

The change in her charmed him. Passive and not so arrogant.

She's so much more attractive this way.

The sky shone bright with shimmering stars. The air felt crisp and clear. Being late in October, he'd worn a coat, but she'd not put one on.

She shivered.

After stopping the buggy, he pulled out a blanket from behind the seat and wrapped it around her shoulders. "Is that better?"

"Yes, thank you." She lowered her head.

"What's wrong? I can tell something's bothering you."

"I look terrible."

"What? You can't be serious. I think you look beautiful. More so than ever."

"My hair's a mess and I'm not even wearin' a proper hat."

He tenderly pushed her hair away from her face. "I like it like this. It's softer. You don't look so uptight." He smiled, hoping to lighten her mood.

"Truly?" She sat up straight. "Do my ringlets make me appear bad-tempered?"

"Somewhat. Seems like a waste of time when it's naturally lovely."

She placed her hands against her cheeks.

Did I make her blush?

That would be quite an accomplished feat with Victoria O'Malley.

"I'm curious, Victoria. Why don't you have an Irish accent like your parents? I find it odd you display no trace of it."

"Years of private schoolin' at St. Mary's Parish. They sent me there to learn how to be a proper southern woman. Do you like how I talk?"

"Oh, yes. You speak beautifully." He found her soft southern lilt enchanting. Their outing had started off just as he'd hoped. Her behavior remained calm. *Compelling.*

They arrived at the beach. After helping her out of the buggy, he took her hand and led her toward the water. "You aren't hiding any chocolate anywhere tonight are you?"

"No." She tipped her head and smiled, but then instantly frowned. "Drew, I don't know what you want from me. Why'd you come to see me?"

"What do you mean? I *wanted* to see you."

"But . . . *why?* You've made it clear you don't want to make love to me. What else is there between a man and a woman?"

He shook his head, finding it hard to believe she really didn't know. Her demeanor proved the question's sincerity.

He lifted her up onto a large smooth rock. The perfect place for her to sit.

"A man and a woman can share everything," he said, standing below her. "It's not just about *making* love. It's *loving*. It's simple things like sharing Christmas morning, eating a meal together, taking walks on the beach, listening to music, sharing a good book, and when needed—drying each other's tears." He paused, peering deeply into her eyes. "Sometimes, it's simply holding each other."

"I won't be here for Christmas mornin'." Unshed tears glistened in her eyes.

Andrew sighed, realizing it hadn't been a good example. "There are other mornings and many more Christmases in our lifetime. I just want to know who you are. Is that so hard?"

"No, it's simple. I'm what you see." She looked away from him. "I'm not very smart and I can't cook. But if you give me the chance, I could prove I know how to love."

Lifting her down, he gazed at her face. Her eyes appeared softer and warmer than before, or perhaps he just saw her in a different light. He decided to try again.

He bent down and kissed her, slower than before. This time she responded and wrapped her arms around him, returning the kiss. He didn't want to stop.

Dropping to his knees, he pulled her down beside him onto the sand, then gently lowered her onto her back. With no one in sight, it would've been easy to make love to her. He wanted to desperately.

No, I can't.

Hovering above her, she looked at him with infinite questions in her eyes.

He kissed her again. Longer and harder.

God, let me stop.

A vision of Claire came to mind, pressing her hand to his lips and telling him not to stop. Why couldn't he shake her memory?

Victoria wanted him. His *body* wanted *her*, but his heart wasn't ready.

He pushed away from her and stood. "I'm sorry, Victoria. I can't do this." He extended his hand and lifted her to her feet.

"It's all right. We can wait."

No anger? She's not even pouting. Has she truly changed?

He held her close, then ran his hands down the length of her hair and over her perfect body.

I'm insane to walk away.

"I'd better get you home." He needed to before his body won the internal battle.

"But it's nowhere close to nine," she whined.

"It is for me. I can't trust myself alone with you much longer."

"You worry too much. We can stay here if you want to. I'll do whatever you want." She placed her hand on his chest, then slowly ran it down to his groin.

He grabbed it, stopping her. "That's what I'm afraid of. I've made a promise to myself that I plan to keep. You're making it difficult."

"Some promises are made to be broken," she said like an experienced woman, then proceeded to kiss and nibble on his neck. The old Victoria had returned.

"Not this one." She'd set his body on fire. He had to stop her. "Let's go now."

Though she frowned, he took her hand and headed toward the buggy.

Immediately, his heart began to race, sensing an unwelcome stranger. "Hurry, Victoria! We're not alone!"

She tightened her grip and ran with him. "Who do you think it is, Drew?" Obviously sensing his fear, her voice trembled. Her body shook as he helped her into the buggy.

"I'm not certain, but I have my suspicions." He popped the reins hard and Sam took off. The sooner he had Victoria safely home, the better.

"Why are you so early?" Mr. O'Malley asked, the moment they stepped inside.

"It was cooler than I thought it would be," Andrew replied. "I didn't want Victoria to catch a chill."

"You're such a thoughtful lad," Mrs. O'Malley said and pinched his cheek.

Andrew smiled, then turned to her husband. "Mr. O'Malley, may I have a word with you privately?"

"Of course. Come to me study." He led the way down the hall. After lighting a lantern, he motioned for Andrew to sit in one of two leather chairs, then took the other himself.

The room was filled with shelves of books and had a large desk at its center.

"You seem a might serious, Doctor," the man said, lighting a pipe.

"I am. There are two things I wish to discuss. First and foremost I'd like your permission to court your daughter." Andrew swallowed hard.

Is that what I truly want?

"I thought you already were." Mr. O'Malley chuckled. "You have my blessing and that of me wife." He leaned in and his laughter subsided. "So tell me now. What's troubling you?"

"You *do* have locks on your doors, don't you, sir?"

"Aye. We seldom use them. Never saw the need. People respect our property." His eyes narrowed. "Why do you ask?"

"It's complicated, but there's a man who blames me for his wife's death. A patient I attended who died in childbirth. I swear it wasn't my fault. I did everything I could for her, but he hasn't forgiven me. Says I killed her. I believe he's been following me. Even here."

"You think he may try to harm you or someone you care about?"

"Yes. I doubt he'd harm anyone else. He wants *me*. But just in case, lock your doors."

"I will." Mr. O'Malley stood. "I appreciate your candor. Takes a good man to look after those he cherishes. You must truly care for me daughter. I'll be happy having you court her."

"Thank you, sir." Andrew shook his hand.

"As for the other matter." The man sucked on his pipe, then blew a ring of smoke into the air. "The man you say wants to harm you? Is he a Negra?" His upper lip curled.

"Yes, he is. Why?"

Why should the color of his skin make a difference?

Mr. O'Malley rubbed his chin. "I know people who can take care of the likes of him. Do you understand my meaning?"

The way he said it made Andrew shiver. "Yes, sir. I hope it doesn't come to that."

"You mark me word." Mr. O'Malley pointed a sharp finger. "Sometimes it's the only way." He took another drag from his pipe. "Now then, time we get back to the lassies."

He draped an arm around Andrew's shoulder. "Do you happen to be Catholic?"

"No, sir, I'm not."

"We'll have to see about changing that. Everything in time."

He smiled at the man, but his stomach twisted.

Am I doing the right thing?

They returned to the ladies who'd seated themselves in the living room.

"Victoria," her father said, puffing out his chest. "I've agreed to let this fine doctor court you."

Her eyes opened wide. "Truly?"

"Yes, me dear. Are you agreeable?"

"Oh, yes! Thank you, Daddy!" She wrapped her arms around him.

"Saints be praised!" her mother exclaimed.

Victoria shook her head. "It's just courtin', Mama. He hasn't proposed. *Yet.*"

Andrew folded his hands in front of himself and smiled. Victoria could be quite charming. But there was something more to her than her obvious beauty. Courting hadn't been his intention when he'd arrived, but he'd followed his feelings and landed somewhere unexpected.

Right in the middle of an Irish stew.

CHAPTER 9

Andrew went back to his room, looking over his shoulder at every turn.

The hotel had two stories. Each had long enclosed corridors with rooms on both sides. They didn't have exits directly outdoors. The only way to leave was through a common hallway. This alone made him feel more at ease. He felt comforted having guests in the rooms abutting his. If he cried out someone would surely help. At home he was completely alone.

He hated being afraid and refused to let Tobias disrupt his life this way. But he wasn't about to take Patrick O'Malley up on his offer. The thought alone made him ill.

O'Malley must have ties to the Klan.

He didn't approve. O'Malley's connections could harm any chance of a relationship with Victoria. Hopefully it wouldn't come to that.

Tomorrow he'd see Elijah and ask his help seeking out Tobias.

He fell asleep with thoughts of Victoria.

* * *

As always, Andrew received a warm welcome when he arrived at the Tarver's.

Alicia left the men to discuss business and took the children with her to visit a friend.

Elijah motioned Andrew to sit at the table. "Can't believe Tobias is back," he said, shaking his head. "You shore 'bout that, Doc?"

"I haven't seen him plainly, but I've been followed. More than once. Who else could it be?"

If only I'd gotten a good look at him.

"I reckon you's just nervous. Tobias knows better than to mess with ya. Knows he'd hafta deal with me if he do."

"You're a good man, Elijah. I appreciate you more than you know. It's just that—well—it's not just *me* anymore. I'm seeing someone." He looked at the ground.

Do I really want him to know?

"You seein' a woman, Doc?"

"Yes. Her name's Victoria."

Why is it so hard telling him about her?

"Sounds nice. *Dignified.* She pretty?"

"She's beautiful. Red hair. Green eyes. She's young, though." Andrew couldn't look at him.

"How young?"

"Eighteen."

"Eighteen be woman enough. You serious 'bout her?"

"I don't know. I *care* about her. It's just . . . *different.*"

"Different from the woman what left ya?"

"Yes. I don't understand *what* I'm feeling. Why can't I let go of her and love Victoria?" He finally looked the man in the eye.

"Cuz you still loves her. You needs more time, Doc."

"I don't *want* more time. I want to feel whole again. I get lonely." He put his head in his hands. "If you saw Victoria, you'd think I'm insane for not taking her for myself and forgetting there'd ever been anyone else. But something's missing. I'm confused."

"Doc." Elijah patted Andrew's arm, drawing his attention. "When I met Leesha, I knew she was the one for me. My heart told me. I admit other parts a my body told me, too, but I listened mostly to my heart." He grinned. "Lotsa men don't listen an' follows the *other* part. It leads to trouble. You best be listenin' right."

"I understand. I'm taking it slow this time. I want to do things properly."

"Just listen to your *heart.*" Elijah stood and rested his hand on Andrew's shoulder. "Let's see if we can hunt up Tobias. If he ain't around, you're gonna hafta stop bein' so nervous. Maybe you're seein' things."

"I don't think I am. You told me to listen to my heart regarding women. There's another voice that speaks to me —tells me when something isn't quite right. Well, that voice has been talking loud and clear. I'm not imagining this."

"You said you was lonely. Seems to me your voices keeps you in good company." Elijah's comment lightened their mood.

They looked all over Shanty Town for Tobias, asking everyone if they'd seen him. His old shack remained vacant and in disarray, but it appeared to have been occupied. Regardless of what they saw and heard, nothing convinced Andrew the man was gone. He'd probably been made aware they were hunting him and hid.

Sooner or later, there'd be a confrontation. Hopefully at Andrew's choosing, not Tobias's.

After thanking Elijah for his help, Andrew returned to his hotel room to freshen up. He intended to pay Victoria another visit. Since they were officially courting, he'd been told he was welcome anytime.

On the way to her home, he stopped at the mercantile and purchased a bar of chocolate. If she offered it to him again in the manner she had before, he might oblige her.

The thought of it caused his heart to race. How could he *think* with it, if he couldn't get it under control? Concerning Victoria, he found it difficult to think with anything but the *other* part of his body.

I might need to marry her soon.

He knocked on the now-familiar door and was greeted by Izzy.

"Doc Fletcher! I heard the good news. Come on in!" She grabbed him by the arm and yanked him inside.

"Thank you, Izzy." No longer nervous, he felt confident, believing he belonged here. "Miss Victoria is home, isn't she? She wasn't aware I was returning this evening."

"Yessa, she's here. In her room. But her folks is away. Had sumthin' at the church. I's shore it's fine for you to be here, bein' you're courtin' now. I hafta be leavin' myself. Gots to get home. Can I trust you here with her?"

"Of course you can, Izzy. I'll be a perfect gentleman." He meant it. Still, knowing he'd be alone with Victoria in her home made him uneasy.

Can I control myself?

"I'll get her for ya." Izzy went up the stairs.

Andrew paced.

I shouldn't be so nervous.

In minutes, Victoria glided down the stairway. Her hair fell soft again over her shoulders.

God, she's beautiful!

Andrew's heart thumped.

"Back so soon?" she cooed.

"Yes. Do you mind?"

"Course not. But my parents are out. Should you be here?"

Izzy scooted by them. "Behave yourselves now. I gots to go!" She bustled out the front door, leaving them completely alone.

Victoria stepped close and placed her hand flat against his chest. "Since we *are* courtin', what would you like to do?"

Breathing would be helpful.

His mind raced at the same rate as his heart.

I shouldn't have come. Why am I here? I don't love her, I simply want her. This is wrong.

A truly poisonous woman.

She guided him down the hall to a sitting room at the farthest end of the house. It had a large bay window with a cushioned bench. An upright piano stood to one side of the room and a settee on the other. She positioned herself on the upholstered settee and patted the spot beside her.

With a pounding heart, he took it. When he turned to look at her, she met his gaze.

Unable to help himself, he kissed her. He pulled her in, then caressed her while he brushed his lips along her neck and worked his way down.

She smells so good.

He paused to take in her beauty—memorizing every detail. Her rapid breaths dusted his face, and his eyes were drawn to the movement of her bosom, rising and falling with each breath.

He returned his attention to her eyes. Her incredible green eyes begged him to have her.

He reached into his pocket and produced the bar of chocolate. The corners of her mouth turned upward into a devilish smile. She blinked slowly, then moistened her lips with her tongue.

Yes, I know what you want. Much more than the candy.

After placing a small piece in his mouth, he moved toward her, offering it. Without a moment's hesitation, she took it from him with a deep kiss. Their lips joined and they shared the candy's sweetness.

I want this.

Locking eyes with her, he broke off another piece and set it in her hand. A low sinister laugh emerged from her and she tucked it into her delicious bosom.

He kissed her again fully on the mouth, firmly holding her arms. His lips glided over her chin, then moved to her neck.

A blissful-sounding moan escaped her as he worked his way down, lower and lower until he nuzzled her breasts and took the candy from its place. He quickly devoured it, then returned to her flesh and ran his mouth along her voluptuous mounds.

Every woman feels the same in the heat of lovemaking. Find a woman to satisfy your needs.

He shook his head. His father's words haunted him.

"No . . ." He stood. "I'm *not* my father."

"What are you talkin' 'bout?" She breathed hard, glaring at him.

"I can't do this. I want to, but I'm not in love with you. We've got to stop. Maybe if we slow down my feelings will change. But I won't have you this way. I'm sorry . . ."

He ran down the hall and out the door, slamming it as he left.

When he got back to his hotel room, he eventually fell asleep. But this time, his thoughts had returned to Claire.

* * *

After Andrew's second night at Mobile Hotel, he went home. If he saw Tobias again, he'd follow him wherever he led. Determined to face his fear of the man head-on, he'd put an end to this, one way or another.

He decided to keep his distance from Victoria for a while. If they were alone again, he feared he'd break the promise he'd made to himself. He would *not* have a woman simply for pleasure.

I won't become my father.

Two weeks passed. November came, bringing the coolness of the approaching winter. It'd been raining steadily for several days, making the whole world gloomy.

As he left work, the chill in the air made him shiver. He couldn't wait to get home to a roaring fire.

Victoria?

He sighed. She stood before him looking utterly miserable.

Am I ready to face her?

He'd never seen her in a coat. Of course it was a very *fine* coat, tailored to fit her figure. She wore white gloves and a scarf that covered her head and wrapped around her neck.

"Drew?" Her voice shook and she nervously twisted her hands together. "I hope you don't mind that I came. I just . . ." She stopped and turned her head.

Compassion gripped him. "Victoria, I'm sorry I left the way I did."

She faced him with tear-filled eyes. "I've missed you, Drew."

He wiped away the droplets on her cheeks with the tips of his fingers. "I didn't mean to hurt you. I left so I wouldn't."

"But—the way you kissed me. I know you wanted me. Why'd you stop?" She peered so deeply into his eyes that it pierced his soul.

"I stopped because it wasn't the right time—or place, for that matter. I'd like to see you again, but perhaps with a chaperone?" He grinned.

Her mouth twitched into a smile. "Don't be silly."

"I'm quite serious. I don't trust myself with you."

"Would you at least consider joinin' us for Thanksgivin' dinner? My parents asked what happened to you. I told them you've been busy." She looked down.

You shouldn't have to make excuses for me.

"I *am* supposed to be courting you," he said, lifting her chin. "I'm not doing a very good job of it."

"You could try a little harder."

"Very well, then. I'll join you for Thanksgiving. What time should I be there?"

"Three o'clock. Izzy likes to have plenty of time to cook the bird." She licked her lips.

Such a tempting mouth.

She'd come a long way since their first kiss.

Showing affection in such a public place wouldn't be wise, so he led her behind the building, out of sight.

He brushed her cheek with his hand and gazed into her eyes—green, shimmering, and inviting.

Pressing her against the side of the building, he encircled her with his arms and kissed her. Long and deep. His heartrate doubled. He'd managed to return to where he'd run from.

He backed away, breathing hard.

She leaned her head back against the building. "You're not being fair, Drew. You can't keep doin' this and not follow through. I can't endure much more."

"I'm sorry." His heart continued to thump. "I want you, but I know it's wrong. So here's what we have to do if we're to continue this courtship. I won't touch you—except to hold your hand. I can't kiss you, because when I do, I don't want to stop. And now isn't the time."

"I don't understand. This isn't how it's supposed to be."

"You're wrong. Ask your priest. We're *supposed* to be in torment until I put a proper ring on your finger." He forced a grin.

"Oh, Drew." She swatted his arm. "I don't want you to stop seein' me, so if those are your terms I'll do my best to abide by them. Though they don't sound like much fun."

"You *do* like to have fun, don't you, Victoria?" He circled her face with the tip of his finger, then tapped her on the nose.

"I've been *tryin'.*"

He guided her from behind the building, only to run into Sally. She glanced at their adjoined hands, then frowned and walked away.

"Poor girl," Victoria said in a manner displaying no sympathy whatsoever. "Seems you broke another heart, Drew."

"Be kind. Not every woman is Victoria O'Malley."

"A fact I'm certain makes you happy. You can scarcely handle one." Raising her chin in the air, she walked on, tall and proud.

He couldn't disagree.

They continued to the livery, and he took her home in his buggy, but didn't go inside. At the front door, he kissed her hand and told her he'd see her on Thanksgiving.

"You just kissed me, Drew," she said. "You're breakin' your own rules."

"I can resist your hand. It's your lips that get me into trouble."

He drove away quickly before thoughts of her enticing mouth overtook his good sense.

CHAPTER 10

When Claire received Beth's invitation for Thanksgiving dinner, she had mixed feelings. But since Beth seemed eager to entertain, they'd accepted.

They left home bright and early so they'd arrive at Beth's by dinner time. Beth had made arrangements for them to stay at the boarding house with Mrs. Sandborn. Some of her tenants had gone away for the holiday, so she had room. Apparently, the woman was thrilled at the idea of having them there. According to Beth, she couldn't wait to see the baby.

Why does everyone insist on seein' Michael?

Claire could handle Mrs. Sandborn, but not someone the likes of Lucy Beecham.

We simply won't go to church.

Walking through Beth's door, Claire inhaled deeply. The house smelled wonderful. In no time at all, they were enjoying the Thanksgiving feast. Roasted chicken, baked apple *and* pumpkin pie, green beans, cornbread stuffing, fried corn, and mashed potatoes.

With full bellies, they moved to the living room and pulled in extra chairs from the kitchen table so they could all be entertained by Michael. At seven months, he scooted across the floor, constantly babbling. He was a beautiful child with hair as black as night and eyes to match.

He said a few simple words—his favorite being *Dada*—but he'd mastered *Mama* as well, much to Claire's delight. His early vocabulary eased her, believing him to be quite smart. An answer to a never-ending prayer.

"I can't believe how big he is!" Beth exclaimed. "What have you been feedin' him?"

Gerald laughed. "Just Claire."

"Well, he *is* a baby." Claire glanced at Henry. Instantly, warmth filled her cheeks. He stared at her in a way that no man—aside from her husband—ever should.

"I'm goin' out," he said, then walked out the door.

"What's wrong with Uncle Henry?" Beth asked.

Claire knew, but wasn't about to say and remained quiet.

"I ain't sure," Gerald replied. "He's been actin' strange for some time now. I figgered maybe he was sick, but Claire thinks he's just needin' some space."

"That's silly," Beth said. "I know he's happy havin' you live with him. Least he's not lonely no more."

"No," Claire said. "I reckon he *is* lonely. Sarah's been gone a long time. He sees Gerald an' me happy together. It hasta be hard on him."

Beth wrinkled her nose. "Makes sense. You know, Mrs. Sandborn ain't never remarried. Reckon we need to do a little match-makin'?"

"There's an idea," Gerald said, rolling his eyes. "Us bein' all the way in Mobile. How'd that ever work?"

Beth frowned. "It was just an idea. You should try to find a nice single woman in Mobile for Uncle Henry. Ever think a that?"

"S'pose we could." Gerald shrugged. "What do you think, Claire?"

"Best idea I've heard in a while. Maybe Henry would stop mopin'." And *maybe* he'd lose his interest in her as well.

"Hope he comes back soon," Beth said. "We'll need to get goin' if we're gonna make it to church on time."

"Beth . . ." Claire tried to remain calm. "Would you mind so much if we stayed here an' didn't go to services?"

"But we always go to church on Thanksgivin'."

"I know. But it's been a long time since I've been here in my old house, an' I'm enjoyin' it. 'Sides, Michael will need a nap soon. I really don't care to go." Claire focused on the floor, unable to look at her friend.

Gerald gave her a little squeeze, but she couldn't even *force* a smile.

"Beth," he said. "Claire's right. It's nice bein' here, an' we don't have much time with you. Reckon we can stay here an' relax with the baby till it's time for us to go to the boardin' house?"

"What will I tell Reverend Brown on Sunday?" Beth pouted. "He's sure to miss me."

"Tell him the truth," Gerald replied. "You had family in and wanted to stay home."

"That's even more reason to go, Gerald. Everyone will wanna see you." Beth wasn't letting up.

"Church isn't s'pose to be 'bout seein' people," Claire whispered. "It's s'pose to be 'bout worshipin' God. I reckon He'll understand."

Beth didn't say another word about it and excused herself to clean up the dishes.

Henry had been gone for hours. Gerald was about to go out searching for him when he walked through the door, limping more than usual.

Gerald crossed to him and got right in his face. "WHERE'VE you been? Looks like you OVERDID it!" He pointed at his leg.

Henry looked away. "I was walkin'. That's all. Started gettin' cold so I figgered I better come back. Leg's hurtin', too."

Claire pitied him. Because of her, the man was in pain. How could she ever make things better with him? Perhaps Beth was right. They needed to find him a woman.

Gerald stoked the fire and Beth served another round of dessert. Once they all started talking and laughing again, Claire became more at ease about making Beth miss services.

After taking a long nap, Michael sat up tall on the braided rug in front of the fire, playing with a ball Beth had given him. The warmth from the flames seemed to be helping Henry. He no longer complained about his leg and appeared to be enjoying entertaining the baby.

Claire looked around her old home and breathed in the wonderful aroma of the wood smoke. Though at ease, she was far from content. She saw Andrew everywhere. Memories of him flooded her mind. The joy of those memories had been replaced with heartache.

It'd be getting dark soon, and she was ready to go to the boarding house. *A good excuse to leave.* She couldn't take much more.

"Now Beth," she said. "Gerald will come by and pick you up in the mornin' so we can all have breakfast together at the boardin' house."

"I'll be ready." She took hold of Claire's elbow. "You all right? You ain't quite yourself."

"I'm fine. Just a little tired." She faked a yawn.

"Tired? You ain't . . ." She stared wide-eyed at Claire's belly.

Gerald rushed over, with hope-filled eyes.

Claire laughed. "Heavens, no. Least, I reckon not."

"It'd be nice if you were," Beth said. "Michael'd like havin' a playmate."

Claire clung to him as they walked to the wagon. Gerald started to help her up, but she stopped him.

"Gerald," she said, holding back tears. "Can you give me a minute?"

"Sure can."

The worry in his reply didn't help. But she had to do this.

She wandered away from everyone else with Michael held close. Once she reached her mama's grave, she knelt down beside it.

"Mama, this is your grandson, Michael. Isn't he beautiful? I know you watch over me. You know things no one else does. You know 'bout Michael's daddy an' everythin' I've done. I wish you were here. I need you to tell me it's all right—that I did the right thing."

Tears streamed down her face. Michael's tiny hands gently brushed her cheek as though he understood her pain.

She smiled and kissed his forehead.

"Mama, I *do* love Gerald. More than I ever thought I could. But there's still a piece of my heart with *him*. You know who I mean. Bein' here has brought it all back to me. I miss him. I'll keep on lovin' Gerald an' Michael, but I can't stop lovin' him, too." After wiping away her tears, she kissed the tips of her fingers and touched them to the headstone. "I love you, Mama."

She took a large breath, stood, and returned to the wagon. Beth gave her a hug, then Gerald helped her and Michael take a seat. She glanced at Henry, who faced forward and didn't acknowledge her.

"I'm sorry," she said. She hated they'd seen her cry. "I didn't mean to spoil Thanksgivin'."

"You didn't spoil anythin'." Beth patted her knee. "It's fine to cry. I know you miss your mama. We miss ours, too."

Gerald nodded. "We'll see you in the mornin', Beth."

As Henry popped the reins, the wagon jerked. Claire held Michael even tighter.

Gerald draped a blanket around her shoulders. "You gonna be all right?"

"I feel better now. I just needed to talk to Mama."

They rode the rest of the way in silence.

Mrs. Sandborn greeted them with open arms. Chattering non-stop, she showed them to their rooms. After a brief time playing with the baby, she told them goodnight and let them go off to bed. They'd been given the room Gerald had occupied for many years.

"Feels kinda strange havin' you in my old room," he said, scratching his head. "But I'm glad you're here with me."

"I'm glad, too." She pulled back the quilt and fluffed the pillows. "Reckon we'll put Michael between us." He'd already fallen asleep in her arms, so she laid him down in the center of the bed.

"I don't mind," he whispered. "I like watchin' him sleep."

They put on their nightclothes and crawled into bed.

"Claire?" Gerald propped himself up on one elbow, whispering over the top of Michael. "I was wonderin' 'bout what you were sayin' to Beth. Are you gonna have a baby?"

"I . . . I don't think so." She knew she wasn't, but he sounded *so* hopeful. "But, I'll know for sure in a week or so."

"I hope you are. Best thing ever happened to me was you carryin' our child."

His words tugged at her heart and she couldn't help but smile at him through her guilt. "Goodnight, Gerald," she whispered.

"Night, Claire." He raised himself up over the top of Michael and kissed her. "I love you."

"I love you, too." Pushing her head back into the soft down pillow, she closed her eyes and let her body melt into the comfort of the bed.

I love you too, Andrew.

* * *

"You don't hafta tell everythin', Mrs. Sandborn," Gerald muttered.

Claire gave her husband an encouraging smile. The poor man's cheeks were beet red.

They were all gathered around the breakfast table and Mrs. Sandborn had decided to tell everyone about the time he got his arm stuck in the water pump. Claire prayed she wouldn't bring up the incident with the mule. *That* story needed to be left untold.

"He was the most accident-prone child!" Mrs. Sandborn tittered.

"The boy's come a long way," Henry said. "I'm might proud a him. He's a fine worker. Good at what he does." It was the first time Henry had said much of anything since they'd left Mobile.

"Thank you, Uncle Henry." Gerald beamed. The praise from Henry had made up for every bit of embarrassment he'd suffered. Claire couldn't be more proud of her husband.

"Gerald," Beth said. "Can you watch Michael for a spell? I'd like to steal Claire away."

"Course I can." He lifted Michael from Claire's arms, then winked at her. "Beth's upta sumthin'."

Claire followed her out of the kitchen, then up the stairs to their room.

"What is it?" Claire asked with a grin, expecting gossip.

Beth frowned and took her by the arm. She sat on the edge of the bed, pulling Claire down beside her.

"It's Henry." Beth's sour expression remained. "Sumthin' ain't right. He follows you with his eyes everywhere you go, lookin' like a lost puppy. Is sumthin' goin' on?"

"What do you mean?" Her stomach turned flips.

"Don't know. I just get this feelin'." She narrowed her eyes. "You watch yourself. I reckon Henry might . . . well . . . have feelin's for you. Understand what I'm sayin'?"

"Yes. But that's plum silly. He's Gerald's uncle. Yours, too."

"He's also a lonely man, an' you're a fine woman. Please be careful. I don't want you *or* Gerald hurt."

"Henry wouldn't do anythin' to hurt us. He's been good to us lettin' us live there an' all. But since you're so worried, I promise I'll be careful." She hugged her friend.

"I care 'bout you. You're my sister now."

It might have been the perfect time to tell Beth the truth, but she couldn't. Some things were best kept hidden.

They went back to the kitchen and immediately received a grin from Gerald. "Have some good gossip to share?"

"We're Baptists, ain't we?" Beth laughed. "Right, Claire?"

"Yes, we are," she said, taking Michael. "But we're also women. Some things aren't to be shared with you menfolk."

When it came time to go home, saying goodbye to Beth was harder than ever. She'd made her promise again to be mindful of Henry. As they drove away, the worry on Beth's face gave her every indication Henry could be capable of most anything.

CHAPTER 11

Andrew dressed in a navy three-piece suit for Thanksgiving. He even went so far as to put on a string tie, but refused to wear a hat. Though he wanted to make a good impression, covering his head made him feel restricted and confined.

He'd hated turning down invitations from both Alicia Tarver and Margaret Mitchell. But when they'd learned who he'd be having dinner with, they encouraged him to go, with no hard feelings.

Victoria had told him three o'clock. He had ten minutes to spare. Better he arrive early than late, especially since he assumed her parents might already be thinking poorly of him.

From what she'd said at their last meeting, she'd made excuses for his absence.

Hopefully they believed her.

When Izzy opened the door, he kissed her on the cheek. "Happy Thanksgiving, Izzy."

Her eyes opened wide. "Oh my, Doc!" She sounded giddy and rapidly fanned herself. "Come on in. We've missed your face 'round here."

She giggled as she led him into the house, but once Victoria's parents appeared, she excused herself to the kitchen.

"You look wonderful, Dr. Fletcher," Mrs. O'Malley said, with a gracious smile. "'Tis a fine suit."

"Thank you, ma'am."

Victoria drew their attention by clearing her throat. She posed at the top of the stairway, wearing a velvet blue dress. As she descended, it floated down the stairs. Her ringlets were gone, much to his preference. A cameo graced her neck, but as usual, the plunge of her neckline took his eyes elsewhere. Quickly, he shifted his gaze upward. When their eyes met, his heart pounded from her undeniable effect.

Once she reached the bottom, he took her hand, then raised it to his lips and kissed it. "Happy Thanksgiving, Victoria."

"And to you, Drew." She coyly bit her bottom lip.

"Patrick," her mother sighed. "Don't they make a fine pair?"

"Aye, they do." The man rubbed his hands together. "I'm hungry. Let's eat!"

Victoria giggled. "Daddy's been tortured all day by Izzy's cookin'. The smell alone makes his mouth water. He tried to sneak a few bites in the kitchen, but Izzy slapped his hand."

"Did she now?" Andrew asked.

"Aye," he chuckled. "It's her domain. I may employ her, but she takes her kitchen to heart." He leaned close to Andrew. "Without her, I'd have to live on Irish stew," he whispered.

Remembering Izzy's remarks about Mrs. O'Malley's stew, nothing more had to be said.

The dining room had been set with fine china trimmed in gold, atop an enormous table made from dark oak. The table's legs were sculpted and swirled and the tabletop had been covered with a white linen cloth. Even the utensils were gold and the drinking goblets were made of fine crystal.

It reminded Andrew of holidays in Connecticut. His father had always insisted on the very best since they frequently entertained important guests.

Mr. O'Malley sat appropriately at the head of the table, with Andrew and Victoria to one side of him and his wife on the other.

The far end of the table had been left open so Izzy could set the food there. She bustled in and out of the kitchen adding more and more. Finally, she brought out the turkey on a large silver platter—perfectly golden brown.

Izzy definitely knows what she's doing.

Once the food had been set, Mr. O'Malley folded his hands for prayer and everyone followed suit. "Lord," the man spoke with reverence. "We ask your blessings on this Thanksgiving day. We're thankful for all you've given us."

Andrew nearly jumped out of his skin. Victoria had unfolded her hands and inched one of them under the table and onto his leg. As the prayer progressed, so did her hand, moving further up his thigh. As inconspicuously as he could, he moved *his* hand under the table and pushed hers away, then gave her an admonishing sideways glance.

"Thank you especially this day, for bringing Dr. Fletcher to our family," the man went on. But the moment he'd said Andrew's name, Victoria's hand returned to his leg and gave it a little squeeze. "You blessed him with the gift of healing, and he saved our little girl. Bless this food and keep us safe. Amen!" He crossed himself, as did his wife.

Victoria batted her eyes and crossed *her*self in the most unchristian-like manner he believed possible.

Mr. O'Malley clapped his hands. "Now, let's eat!"

Victoria pursed her lips. At least now she'd have to busy herself with eating and stop the under-the-table torment.

The meal was fabulous. As they ate, they chatted casually. Andrew had finally relaxed. It appeared her parents didn't suspect anything was wrong with the courtship. However, they were most likely expecting an engagement soon.

I'm not ready for that.

"Dr. Fletcher . . ." Mrs. O'Malley smiled shyly at him. "I know you're older than me daughter, but exactly how old are you?"

Victoria's eyes widened, waiting.

"I'm twenty-four. Nearly twenty-five. My birthday's in a few weeks. December fourteenth."

"It is?" Victoria brightened. "Your birthday's just before Christmas." She turned to her father. "Daddy, may we throw Drew a party for his birthday? It'll give us all a chance to get together and exchange gifts." Once again, her hand went under the table to Andrew's leg.

He cleared his throat. "That's not necessary." He gave her another visual admonishment. "I appreciate the offer, but it seems like a lot of trouble."

"Oh 'twill be no trouble at all," her mother chimed in. "'Tis a fine idea. Besides, it'll make Victoria happy, being she won't be here to celebrate Christmas with you."

"I'll take care of everything!" Victoria looked directly at him, beaming with elation. "And I know *exactly* what I'll give you." Her lips formed a wicked smile. It was bound to be a party he'd never forget.

"So, Doctor," Mr. O'Malley said, as he helped himself to another slice of sweet potato pie. "When do you plan to move into the city?"

What? Where did that come from?

"I don't intend to, sir."

"You should give it some thought. I hear you live near the shanties. A wretched part of Mobile."

"It's convenient for my work." The mood at the table suddenly changed. Defensive, Andrew stiffened.

"But your work is at the hospital—in the city—isn't it?"

"Yes. Most of it."

"I've heard you do some doctoring in Shanty Town. Is that so?" The man glared at him.

Victoria giggled. "Daddy, you're bein' silly."

He ignored her and kept his eyes on Andrew.

Mr. Schultz must have told him.

Andrew sat up straight and returned his piercing stare. "Yes, I doctor them. And I'm proud to. They need my help as much as those who live in the city."

"Patrick," Mrs. O'Malley whispered. "'Tis not the place for such talk."

"I need to know what me daughter is getting herself into!" O'Malley slammed down his fork. "He's courting her, for God's sake! If his intentions are marriage, he needs to keep away from those people and stay with his own kind! I won't have her living with the Negras!" He pounded his fists on the table. "Move into the city!"

Andrew stood, biting back the words that wanted to fly from his lips. "Sir, what I do is important to me, but I can see you don't understand that. I care for your daughter, but if I'm not the kind of man you think she needs, then I'll leave."

"Daddy, don't do this!" Victoria cried. "You're ruinin' everythin'!" She ran from the room.

Her mother arose, and after taking the time to glare at her husband, went after Victoria.

"Sit down, lad," the man said, lowering his voice. "Please?"

Though he didn't want to, Andrew sat.

"I got ahead of meself," O'Malley said. "I've been doing some thinking since our last conversation. Didn't you wonder how I knew that the man who was after you was a Negra?"

"No, I hadn't considered it." His blood continued to pump hard. He wanted nothing more than to leave.

"Mr. Schultz has been concerned over your business with the Negras. Doesn't want you mixing with their kind. Neither do I. Izzy's the only exception. She's been with us a long time and I trust her. But you don't find many like her. She knows her place. They don't belong here and we don't want them here." He took a drink from his wineglass, then wiped his mouth with the back of his hand.

"Tell me about the man who's been following you," O'Malley went on. "I'll see to it he's taken care of. I can't risk me daughter being harmed because of your discretion. You're trying to protect him, aren't you?"

"I don't believe in what you want to do. I went after him myself and couldn't find him. I think he's left for good."

Though he'd lied to the man, he'd not have him going after Tobias with a lynch mob.

"You'd better be right," the man warned, pointing his finger. "If anything happens to me daughter, it'll be on your head."

"I see," Andrew said, coolly. "Am I still welcome here?"

"Me daughter thinks she's in love with you. You're welcome as long as she wants you. But if you decide to marry her, you'd best be planning that move." O'Malley's lip curled into a snarl.

He'd laid down the rules—now Andrew had to decide whether or not to follow them. Andrew stood there, saying nothing. What *could* he say? He wished he'd accepted a different dinner invitation.

"I'll get Victoria," O'Malley said. "You'll enjoy her company more than mine." He left the room.

Izzy bustled in from the kitchen. "I done heard every word," she whispered. "You listen to me, Doc. You're a good man and I knows how many a my people you've hepped. Don't you ever stop bein' the man you is just because he threatened you. If you loves Victoria, marry her an' move far away. You don't needs her daddy runnin' your life." Her head popped up like a nervous jackrabbit, then she scuttled away without waiting for a response.

He wanted to run out the door right then, but he was a better man than that.

He'd stand his ground.

* * *

"You *make* him see things my way, or you will never marry the man!" Victoria's daddy hovered over her. "Have I made myself clear?"

"Yes, Daddy," she replied through her tears.

It's not fair.

But why on earth would Andrew doctor the Negroes?

He escorted her mama from her bedroom. The woman had been no help at all, immediately becoming silent the moment her daddy had appeared.

Victoria dried her tears and freshened her face, getting ready to see Andrew again. After checking her reflection one last time, she made her way down the stairs.

"Drew," she said, entering the room. "I . . ." She looked down, searching for the right words. "Why don't we go to the sittin' room? We can have some privacy there."

He didn't reply, yet followed her down the hallway. They sat once again on the settee, but it was nothing like the previous time.

"I think I should go," he whispered. "I don't belong here."

She touched his face. "I want you here. Don't be upset by Daddy. He's used to gettin' his way. But he knows I want you, and what I want is important to him."

"No. This has been a mistake. We shouldn't continue seeing each other." He looked at his hands and not at her.

"Are you lettin' my daddy decide your feelin's? I know you feel sumthin' for me." She leaned toward him.

Please look at me.

"Yes, I feel *something* Victoria, but I'm not sure what it is." He stood.

"Maybe a little time will help? Like you said before . . ." She rose and placed her hand against his chest.

"I don't know. For now, I need to go." He headed for the door and she remained at his heels.

Once he'd opened it, the cold night air slapped her in the face. But she wasn't about to leave him. She stepped outside and shut the door behind her. Without a coat, she shivered.

"What are you doing?" Andrew finally looked at her. "You need to go back inside."

"No, Drew. I can't let you leave like this." She tilted her head upward to meet his gaze. "Please—hold me."

Without waiting for him to act, she encircled him with her arms and pressed herself into his warm body.

Within moments, he responded and pulled her tightly to him.

She lifted her face and closed her eyes, then received what she'd hoped for—a warm, soft kiss. More real than any they'd shared before.

As their lips parted, she slowly raised her lids and peered into his eyes. "Please, Drew. Think 'bout me. Don't let Daddy change everythin'. I love you." She brushed his cheek with her hand.

After saying *goodnight*, she went back inside.

CHAPTER 12

Andrew's stomach flipped. He could've sworn he'd seen Tobias out of the corner of his eye, but it couldn't have been him. Worry had gotten the best of him. Even so, he continued to look over his shoulder.

He drove Sam hard, anxious to get home, all the while thinking about Victoria and the whirlwind they'd been in. Thoughts of *her* helped remove those of Tobias.

Then it struck him.

I know what's missing.

Their relationship had no substance. No common values. She had no compassion and cared only for herself and personal gratification.

Why didn't I see it sooner?

Her beauty had blinded him. Physical desire had caused him to overlook everything else.

But she said she loved me.

He hadn't been able to say it back. His heart still ached for Claire. He'd learned more about her in the few days they'd been together, than in the months he'd known Victoria.

The following Saturday, he rode to the Tarver's. They always lifted his spirits.

In addition, he had a package for Clay. In lieu of a portion of the money he'd agreed to pay him for staying at his house, Clay had asked him to buy an ornament for his mother for Christmas. They didn't have any store-bought ornaments on their tree and the boy wanted to give her something special.

When Andrew had described the selection from Parker's, Clay stopped him when he mentioned the crystal snowflake. He'd shared a story his mother had told about being a girl in Mobile and a Christmas when snow had fallen from the sky. She'd said it was the most beautiful thing she'd ever seen and every year hoped to see it again. But snow was rare in Mobile. Clay believed the ornament would mean a lot to her.

As usual, the boy greeted him the moment he arrived. Since they were alone, Andrew handed him the carefully-wrapped ornament. "It's fragile. Take care not to break it."

"I will." Excitement radiated from the boy's face in the form of a never-ending smile. "I cain't wait till Christmas mornin'. Thank ya, Doc!"

Andrew laughed at his enthusiasm. "Your mother will love it." He ran his hand over Clay's head, then patted him on the back. "You're a good son. I know she's proud of you."

"Thank ya." He hung his head, his smile humbled. "I'm gonna hide it 'neath that oak tree back a the house. It'll be safe there." He hurried off.

They gathered around the familiar wood table, and Andrew stuffed himself with leftover dessert. Over pie and coffee he told Alicia and Elijah about his experience on Thanksgiving.

"Her father was being so unreasonable!" Andrew exclaimed, tightening his fists. But almost immediately, he calmed. Being among friends, he had no reason to be angry.

"I understan' him fearin' for his daughter," Alicia said. "But he had no business tellin' you to stop what you're doin' here. These folks need ya. Don't he see that?"

"No, he doesn't. But as far as Victoria's concerned, I feel she'd be better off without me. If Tobias is still after me, the further away from me she is the safer she'll be."

"You seen him again?" Elijah asked.

"No. Not for a long time. Maybe he *is* gone." He didn't want to mention his suspicions the other night. After all, it'd been more of a *feeling* than an actual sighting.

"Let's hope so," Alicia said and arose from the table. "I needs to put Betsy down for a nap."

"I should be going, anyway," Andrew said, rising. "There's a storm coming and I'd like to beat it home."

After thanking them once again, he rode away.

* * *

In a little more than a week, Andrew would celebrate his twenty-fifth birthday. Although Victoria had offered to throw him a party, undoubtedly those plans had changed.

He hadn't seen her since Thanksgiving. Believing he'd no longer be welcome at the O'Malley's, he wasn't about to call on her. He assumed her father had told her to forget about him, which would be for the best.

Oddly, he missed her attention. She could be annoying, but also stimulating. Selfish, *yes*, and sometimes childish, but she had a way of making him feel good about himself.

The woman's tormenting me with her absence!

Then suddenly—as though he'd willed it—she was there, waiting for him once again as he left work. He wanted to run to her, but kept his composure and walked briskly instead.

"Hello, Drew," she said with a smile.

"Victoria." He acknowledged her with a nod. "How have you been?"

"Miserable." She frowned and lowered her head.

He lifted her chin so she'd look at him. "Why?" He hoped he already knew the answer.

"I miss you. I wish we could try again. Daddy's feelin' awful 'bout Thanksgivin'. He's truly not all that bad. He's simply lookin' out for me."

"As any father should. I've missed you, too."

Her smile returned. "Truly?"

"Yes." Something came over him. No longer caring about being in public, or the rules he'd set down, he bent down and kissed her. After their lips parted, he held her tight against his chest.

Maybe Izzy was right. He should take her away somewhere.

Not fully grasping what he'd done, he believed he was following his heart. Or had he? Maybe she simply filled a void he couldn't overcome.

"Drew," she cooed, while brushing her fingertips across his chest. "'Bout your birthday. Would you be willin' to come to our house again? Just for supper? I haven't planned the party. I was afraid you wouldn't want it. But I can have Izzy fix you sumthin' special. Just tell me what you like."

Sitting down to a meal again with Patrick O'Malley wasn't a pleasant thought, but he'd do it for her. *Only* for her. "It's thoughtful of you." As he stroked her cheek, her green eyes sparkled. "I'll come."

He drove her home, but didn't go inside. They said their goodbyes in the buggy.

* * *

Saturday, December fourteenth. Andrew's twenty-fifth birthday.

Victoria bubbled over with excitement preparing for Andrew's arrival. As she walked to Parker's, she hummed to herself. Izzy was hard at work making roasted chicken with all the trimmings and the house would smell wonderful upon her return. She'd told Victoria about the importance of pleasing a man's appetite.

I aim to please more than his hunger for food.

She needed to check on the hat she'd ordered for Christmas. She'd already bought Andrew's birthday present—a stylish top hat—that she knew he'd love. She had it wrapped and waiting for him at home and would give it to him after supper.

Along with so much more.

She sauntered into the mercantile and gave Mr. Parker an enticing smile.

As she neared him, she unbuttoned the top buttons of her coat. Her Christmas-ribbon candy-striped dress lay beneath it. Since this would be their Christmas, as well as Andrew's birthday celebration, she wore the dress, hoping to impress him. Trying it out on Mr. Parker couldn't hurt. She just hoped the hat had arrived to complete her attire.

"Miss O'Malley!" Mr. Parker appeared more excited than ever to see her. "It's here! It came today!" He produced a box from behind the counter.

Victoria quickly flipped off the lid and held the hat in her hands. "Oh, Mr. Parker! It's exquisite!"

"Be careful, now. Them pins is sharp. Already stuck myself when I opened the box to make sure it was what we ordered."

The pins were about six inches long. She withdrew one of them and pressed her finger to the tip. The man was right. If she'd applied more pressure, she'd have drawn blood.

"Best not *poke* one of these into my head," she said with a giggle and bent toward him.

I love to watch you sweat, Mr. Parker.

Standing upright, she put the thing on with ease. The pins worked just as they should. She shook her head and the hat stayed firm.

She pushed the empty box toward him. "I'll wear this home." Posing, she batted her eyes. "Do I look fine, Mr. Parker?"

"Finest lookin' woman in all of Mobile, Miss O'Malley." His words came out in a growl, followed by a lick of his lips.

"You're more than kind, Mr. Parker." To repay him for the compliment, she unbuttoned her coat even further. "Shall I sign Daddy's bill?"

With trembling hands, the man produced the document and slid it toward her.

Bending low across the counter, she took her time signing. "Daddy's gonna love it, too." She shifted her eyes enough to see *his* glued to her bosom.

With the final swoop of her pen, the man groaned, then took the receipt and placed it in a drawer. "Thank ya, Miss O'Malley. You be sure and come back real soon."

She touched her hand to her breast and the man whimpered. "Oh, I will. I promise you."

As she walked away, she glanced over her shoulder one last time, delighted to see the man's tongue hanging from his mouth.

She went to open the door, but it was opened from the other side by a large Negro. She gasped and backed away.

"Ma'am," he said. "I'll hold the door for ya." He opened it wide.

She didn't speak to him, and not wanting to make eye contact, kept her attention focused downward. Her heart thumped so hard she could scarcely breathe. She inched out the door, staying as far away from him as possible.

What's a Negro doin' at Parker's?

She hastened to the alley.

Perhaps she'd been silly letting the man upset her, but aside from Izzy, she'd never been around a Negro. Especially not a *male*.

Rounding the corner past Parker's, her body was jerked from the path, forcing her breath from her lungs. A large dark hand clasped across her mouth. The man's other hand grabbed hold of her waist.

Oh, Lord!

She wanted to scream, but he held her from behind. He pulled her body into his with so much strength she couldn't move, let alone *yell*.

"Don't make a sound, or I'll snap your neck." His mouth touched her ear and his gruff voice made her shudder. His hot foul breath covered her neck.

While her heart raced, her mind whirled.

He must be that Negro who held the door for me. But how'd he get out here so quickly?

The tightness of his massive hand ground her corset into her ribcage. Disregarding the pain, she tried to find a way to break free.

He dragged her toward a storage building behind the mercantile.

No!

She wouldn't go in without a fight.

She bit down hard on his filthy hand. At the same time, she reached up behind her and raked her fingernails across his face.

"Damn, woman!" he cursed, loosening his grip.

She jerked free and tried to run, but he grabbed her by the arm and covered her mouth again so quickly she didn't have time to scream.

As hard as she struggled, she was no match for him. The wounds she'd inflicted only infuriated him and he held her even tighter.

He muttered obscenities under his breath and pushed her toward the building. While holding onto her with one hand, he opened the door with the other, then threw her in and closed it behind them.

She stumbled and fell onto the hardwood floor.

The man laughed.

How can this be happenin'?

Too scared to cry, she lay there, trembling. "Why?" She choked out the word, but then drew her legs to her chest, fearing the answer.

He touched his cheek, then looked at his fingers, showing traces of blood. "You're gonna pay for that!" With one large stride, he hovered over her, then smacked her hard across the face.

It stung, but she wouldn't cry.

I won't give you the satisfaction.

Frantically, she scanned her surrounding for an escape. Wooden crates were piled up high around her. The only way out was the door behind him. The tiny window at the top of one wall looked much too small. Light filtered through it, allowing her to see every wretched detail of him, from his dirty clothing, down to his rotting teeth.

She tried to back away, but there was no stopping him. He lay down on top of her, pressing her body into the floor. Breathing became even more difficult.

"You try anythin' again, an' I'll hurt you bad." His hand covered her mouth, but she dare not bite it again.

"Wanna know why I got you?" He glared at her and grinned. She was looking into the eyes of the devil; dark and piercing. "I know your man's Doc Fletcher." He put his face next to hers and his lips to her ear. "I been watchin' you struttin' all over town showin' yourself." His cold, raspy voice sent shivers across her skin.

"You think your man is good an' fine? Well, he ain't. He killed my wife. Took my woman from me." He grunted. "Now ..." He ran his tongue along her chin. "I'm gonna take *his* woman. It's my right."

Unable to hold back, tears rolled down her cheeks. And even with him weighing her down, she couldn't stop her body from shaking.

He wants to kill me.

His eyes moved to her bosom rising above her low-cut neckline and she scolded herself for not buttoning her coat. He breathed heavily and swirled his tongue around his lips. "I ain't never had me a white woman."

Grabbing the front of her dress, he ripped it to one side, exposing more flesh. He fumbled briefly with her corset, but with only one free hand, he cursed and gave up. Placing his hand atop her breast, he squeezed hard.

She whimpered.

He tightened his hold even more and chuckled at her agony.

Leaning down, his face came mere inches from hers. "Don't make a sound. If you do, I'll show ya *real* pain." He removed his hand from her mouth, then grabbed a fistful of her hair and yanked her head, holding it fast.

In a flash, his mouth covered hers. He devoured her like a hungry animal eating its prey.

No!

Her body tensed and became rigid. She choked and struggled to breathe. There'd been a time when a cruel boy had locked her in the outhouse. Now, not only did the rank smell fill her nose, but she tasted it as well. She retched.

His head jerked back. "What's wrong? Ain't I good 'nuff for ya?" Returning his hand to her mouth, he moved his face to her neck and licked her as though she was the last bit of tasty gravy on his dinner plate. From her neck, he made his way down toward her breasts, dripping saliva like a rabid dog.

He stopped, rose up, and the corners of his mouth curled upward, torturing her with his amusement. Until now, she'd never seen a smile formed from hate. So she closed her eyes and prayed it would end.

Please make him go away.

A sinister laugh erupted from him.

He dove at her neck and bit down hard, breaking the skin. Pain shot through her, and her eyes flew open wide. Her hands tightened into fists.

Oh, God!

He muffled her agonized cry with his hand, which she dampened with tears.

"Payback!" he jeered, then spit out a mouthful of blood.

While mumbling to himself, he rolled slightly to one side. She watched in horror as his free hand moved downward and unbuttoned his pants. With a moan, he removed himself from them.

His evil laughter made her cringe. "I'm gonna give you your Christmas present. Sumthin' you've been askin' for."

No! Not like this.

The excruciating pain from her neck caused her heart to pump even faster. But fear overshadowed pain. She had no doubt he'd only begun his torment.

Maybe if I lay still he'll stop hurtin' me.

Drawing air in through her nose, she filled her lungs full.

No! I'll be still when I'm dead!

She wriggled as hard as she could and attempted to kick him, but he rolled over onto her fully again. His firmness pressed into her like a rock.

As he struggled to lift her dress, he cursed louder, snarling and spitting. The full material stood in his way. With violent determined tugs, he swore and tore until he exposed bare flesh.

She took advantage of his distraction and squirmed even harder.

"Be still!" He slapped her hard across the face.

She whimpered, but then sucked in her breath and cleared her mind.

His calloused hand skimmed across her bare thigh. He chuckled and dangled his tongue out the side of his mouth.

Holding her breath, she jerked her body and tried to move out from under him. One final effort before the inevitable.

"You ain't goin' nowhere!" He forced her legs apart with his own, then grunted as he positioned himself to take her.

The hat pins.

Though he'd trapped one of her arms beneath his body, she moved her free arm up over her head and grabbed one of the long pins. Her hand shook, but her adrenaline surged. She plunged it like a dagger, forcefully into his back. It went deep. All the way to the bone.

"Damn you!" He jerked away and stood, contorting his body in an effort to remove the thing.

She hastened to her feet, then kicked him as hard as she could, squarely in the groin.

He fell back in pain, muttering and cursing.

Racing to the door, she flung it open, and flew toward the mercantile without looking back.

* * *

Andrew's spirits were high.

He walked into Parker's with the intention of purchasing something for Victoria, but was taken aback when he spotted Elijah at the counter.

Knowing Jake's feelings about the Negro population in Mobile, nothing good could possibly come out of this.

Why would Elijah risk coming here?

Elijah's demeanor didn't seem right. His shoulders were down, defeated. Not the confident man Andrew knew him to be. He hastened to the counter.

"Hello, Elijah."

"Hey, Doc." He stared at the floor.

Andrew placed his hand on Elijah's shoulder. "Is everything all right?"

Jake grunted. "We don't sell to no niggers here."

Elijah's head popped up, looking between him and Jake.

"Excuse me?" Andrew asked, glaring at the man on the other side of the counter.

"I said we don't sell to niggers!"

Andrew pointed to a nickel on the counter. "Is that yours, Elijah?"

"Yessa. But he won't take it."

Andrew picked it up and held it in front of Jake. "You see this? It's a nickel. It's good money. The man wants to make a purchase and you're going to help him."

"I ain't," Jake snarled, crossing his arms.

Andrew turned to Elijah. "What do you want to buy?"

Elijah hung his head. "Some candy for the children. For Christmas. Leesha warned me not to come. 'Fraid sumthin' like this would happen."

She'd probably *begged* him not to come into town. Andrew would've gladly done it for him, but knowing Elijah, the man wanted to stand on his own two feet.

I can still help.

"Jake . . ." Andrew couldn't help being cold, but remained calm. "I'd like to buy as much candy as I can with this nickel." He grabbed Jake's hand and pushed the coin into his palm.

"I said I don't sell to niggers!" He slammed the nickel on the counter.

"I'm not a nigger," Andrew sneered. "Now give me the candy."

Jake glared at him, but then grabbed a large bag and filled it with licorice and candy sticks. He handed it to Andrew, who in turn passed it over to Elijah.

"Thank ya, Doc," Elijah said, and turned to leave.

Andrew took hold of his arm. "I'm proud of you for trying. Someday things will be different."

With a sad nod, Elijah left the store.

Andrew wasn't done with Jake. "Elijah Tarver is one of the finest men I've ever known. You had no right to treat him the way you did."

"No right? I had every right. This is my store. *Mine!*" Jake pounded his fist on the counter. "I can choose *not* to help anyone I please. You're a nigger lover. You had no *business* interferin'!"

"I came here to buy a gift for Miss O'Malley. I'm having supper with them this evening." Andrew wanted to pound *his* fist into Jake. "I'll just take my *business* elsewhere!"

The moment Andrew mentioned the name *O'Malley,* Jake drew back. His body folded into itself.

Andrew was about to say something more when the jingling doorbell caught his attention. He turned to the sound and gasped.

Victoria?

She stumbled in, holding her coat tightly around her. Her tattered dress dangled beneath it, and she had blood near her face.

"Oh, God! Victoria!" Andrew ran to her side and tried to hold her.

She jerked away. "It's *not* what I wanted!" Hysterical sobs erupted from her. "It's *not* what I wanted!" Crumbling, she fell to her knees.

Andrew knelt beside her and again tried to touch her, but she backed away.

"No!" she screamed with wild, wide eyes. "Don't touch me!"

Jake ran out from behind the counter and squatted next to Andrew. "What happened to her?"

"Victoria!" Andrew tried to get her to focus on him without touching her. "Victoria, look at me. It's Andrew."

"No!" She acted crazed, waving her hands in the air. "He was on me!"

"Who? Who did this to you?" Andrew's stomach knotted, fearing the worst.

"A Negro—a large Negro!" Her body shook out of control.

Knowing he needed to get close to her, Andrew made another effort to hold her. Her body folded in, as if trying to remove herself from his touch.

"In the building!" Her voice trembled. "He's in the building!"

"No, Victoria. He's not here. You're safe. You're with me." Tears welled in Andrew's eyes, seeing her pain. Her blood dripped onto the floor.

I've got to get a closer look at her.

"Behind . . . the store . . . building behind the store." She could barely get the words out.

"Jake, get your gun," Andrew said as low as he could, making an effort not to upset her any further. "I know you keep one behind the counter."

Jake stared at Victoria and didn't move.

"Jake!" Andrew yelled, losing his patience. "Go out back. Check your storage building!" He had to shake him out of his entranced state. "Go! *Now!*"

Jake shook his head, then jumped up and ran to the back of the store. He shuffled around at the counter, then soon after, the back door slammed shut.

Andrew would've gone himself, but he wasn't about to leave her. "Victoria," he whispered, trying to calm her. "Please, try to tell me what happened." He took her hand and this time she didn't pull it away.

Thank God.

"Andrew?" She finally seemed to recognize him. "Andrew. He said . . . you killed . . . his wife." Her words came out between gasping breaths.

Tobias . . .

"He wanted to . . . hurt me. He *did* hurt me!" She sobbed, trembling in his arms.

Andrew had to get her home. Then he'd find Tobias and make certain he never harmed anyone again. Though enraged, he gritted his teeth, keeping his composure for Victoria.

The back door slammed a second time, causing her to shake and whimper.

Jake ran through the store to Andrew's side. "He ain't nowhere! But I seen where he broke the lock on my storage buildin'! I found her hat on the floor. She just got it from me, not long 'fore you came in. I found this by the door." He held up a hat pin. "Think there's blood on it."

Andrew wished Jake was wrong. But looking at the long pin, there was no doubt. Not only did it have blood on it, it was bent. Now more than ever he needed to get Victoria home so he could give her a thorough examination. If the blood was hers, the puncture wound could've caused an internal injury.

"Andrew?" Victoria's voice was barely audible. "I scratched him."

"What'd she say?" Jake asked.

"She said she scratched him!" Andrew's heart pounded.

For a moment, her gaze met his, but then her eyes closed and her head dropped backward. She'd passed out.

"I have to get her home." Andrew lifted her from the floor. "I believe I know who did this. Jake, help me with the door!"

He pushed it open and Andrew carried her to his buggy. Not wanting her shamed in front of Jake Parker, he'd pulled her coat around her and covered her bare flesh.

"What you gonna do, Doc?" Jake asked, following him. "You goin' after him?"

"Of course I am! After I get her home."

Jake rubbed his hands together, grinning. "I can get some men together that know how to take care of a nigger!"

"No! This is something I have to do by myself." Andrew glared at him. The man's eagerness disgusted him. Yes, he was angry, but what Jake suggested was exactly what Patrick O'Malley wanted to do. He wouldn't lower himself to it.

He popped the reins hard and drove off, preparing to face Victoria's father.

CHAPTER 13

Andrew raced the ten blocks to Victoria's home. He jumped from the buggy and lifted her down, then ran to the door with her in his arms and opened it without knocking.

Izzy instantly appeared. "Oh, Lawd! Miss Victoria!" She became frantic, waving her hands and screaming. "Mista O'Malley! Ms. O'Malley, come quick! It's Victoria!"

Andrew didn't wait for permission, and he wasn't about to stand there and be told by Patrick O'Malley to leave. He rushed Victoria up to her room and laid her on the bed.

After removing her coat, he tore away the remnants of her dress. It had nearly been torn in two.

O'Malley grabbed him by the shoulder, yanking him away. "What are you doin' to me daughter?" Bursts of air hissed from his nostrils, his wide eyes glaring.

Mrs. O'Malley ran to Victoria's side and threw a blanket over her. "How dare you look at her like this!"

"I have to examine her!" Andrew's anger had reached a boiling point. "I believe she's been raped!"

Izzy cried out and clung to Victoria's mother, who burst into sobs.

"No!" the woman cried. "Not me daughter!"

O'Malley sneered and shoved Andrew. "You have no business looking at her! Leave at once!"

"No business?" Andrew fired back at him, unmoved. "I'm her doctor!"

The man took a step back. The muscles in his face twitched as he shifted his gaze between him and Victoria. "Izzy. Shannon. Go out of the room. I'll let him examine her."

Mrs. O'Malley seemed reluctant, but Izzy put her arm around her and led her away.

Victoria's father hovered close.

"Do you mind?" Andrew sat beside her on the bed, looking up at him. "I know you're her father, but I also know she wouldn't want you to see her like this."

The man huffed. "Fine. Look her over. And when you're done, I'll see you in me study." With a snarl, he walked out.

Andrew took a deep breath and pushed aside his personal feelings.

He became her doctor.

A bruise had begun forming on her cheek.

He pulled the blanket away from her body and she trembled. Was she cold, or still in shock? He assumed the latter.

More than anything, he needed to find the puncture wound. Curious about the blood near her face, he brushed back her hair, exposing her neck. Fresh blood oozed from an open wound.

Odd . . .

He examined it closer.

Did he bite her?

The wound went deep. A piece of flesh hung loosely—ripped almost completely off. It would need stitches.

Her corset remained tightly cinched around her waist. He rolled her onto her side, painstakingly untied it, and carefully removed it. Then he lifted her chemise from her bare flesh. She was frail. Nearly lifeless.

He explored her body, searching for damage.

Another bruise. This one on her breast.

Sucking in air, tears filled his eyes.

It's all my fault.

Doing his best to remain professional, he continued the examination. His heart ached and guilt seeped into every part of his being. He shook his head, blinking away tears.

At least he discovered she'd not been defiled. Somehow, she'd stopped him.

Where did the blood on the hat pin come from?

He examined her back and found no wounds. Her body lay limp in his arms, as though she'd shut down, afraid to react.

Could it have been Tobias's blood?

With the examination complete, he pulled the blanket up around her.

"Izzy! I need your help!"

She ran into the room. "Yes, Doc? What can I do?"

"Go downstairs and boil some water. I'll need a towel—something I can clean her wound with. And my bag's in the buggy. Can you bring it to me?"

"Course, Doc. I already been boilin' water." She exited quickly. In no time at all, she returned to the room with Mrs. O'Malley behind her.

Tears flowed from the woman's eyes. "Has she been . . . *defiled?*" she whispered the word.

"No, thank God. But he hurt her." He turned Victoria's head to the side, displaying the wound. "I believe he bit her."

Mrs. O'Malley gasped. "Who would do such a thing?"

He wasn't about to address the issue of Tobias Lewis with the woman. Right now, he had to focus on Victoria.

After cleaning the wound, he opened his bag, then removed a needle and silk thread.

"I'm afraid it'll leave a scar. It's deep. I'll do my best to make it clean, but it'll need to be tended to. Do you understand?"

Izzy nodded, while Victoria's mother cried.

Holding the needle steadily in his hand, he pushed it through her skin. She whimpered, but didn't move. He worked meticulously, repairing her flesh to the best of his ability.

"Though she's bruised, aside from the bite wound, she appears to be unharmed. She's gone through an ordeal which will probably change her. Her behavior may not be what you'd consider *normal* for some time. She'll need a lot of love and . . . to feel safe." Guilt plagued him, but he had to set it aside.

He took her hand and checked her fingernails. They were long and sharp. If she'd truly scratched Tobias, she'd have left a mark.

He stood. "I need to go now. Look after her."

Her mother hadn't stopped crying, but nodded, affirming she'd heard him.

He motioned to the tattered pieces of her dress lying on the floor. "I'm certain she'll never want to see it again, so get rid of it before she's aware."

Before leaving her room, he bent down and kissed Victoria on the forehead. As his lips brushed her skin, she trembled, and tears welled in his eyes.

He descended the stairs one at a time, feeling physically ill. With every step, the pit in his stomach grew.

Why did this happen to her? It was me he wanted.

Then he understood. Tobias had succeeded hurting *him* by hurting Victoria. But the man hadn't accomplished everything he'd most likely set out to do. He hadn't killed her *or* shamed her.

Will he try again?

Did criminals on their way to the gallows feel as he did now? He found the hallway to O'Malley's study as intimidating as any death walk. He paused before entering the room and filled his lungs with air. Possibly his last breath.

O'Malley stood the moment Andrew entered. "Well? Did he have her?"

"No. She must have fought him. She'll be all right . . . In time."

With fire-filled eyes, the man strode across the room and shook his finger in Andrew's face. "You did this to her!" He spit out the words. "You were protectin' that man. This is your fault! *Your* fault! It was that Negra, wasn't it?"

Andrew looked away. The man had every right to be furious. "Yes, I think it was." He forced himself to look the man in the eye. "I'm going after him."

"You do that," O'Malley snarled. "And don't you ever come back here. You hear me? Don't come anywhere near me daughter ever again. Now, get out!" He shoved him toward the door.

Andrew stumbled, then composed himself and walked out. O'Malley could've done much worse.

Guilt wore him down. Finding Tobias Lewis would likely be the only thing that could heal his pain.

* * *

"No!" Victoria cried out, slapping at the man. "Don't touch me!"

"Shh . . . Victoria. It's Daddy," he whispered and stroked her hair.

She forced her eyes open. "Daddy?"

Latching onto him, she cried, while he rocked her in his arms.

"Hush now, child," he lulled. "Hush. Daddy will take care of everything."

The soothing way he touched her brought calm. She closed her eyes and managed to stop her tears.

"Victoria," he whispered. "Look at me."

She did as he asked.

He smiled. "That's my good lass. I know 'twill be hard, but you must tell me what happened."

"No. I can't!" She rapidly shook her head. *Please don't make me.*

"Shh . . . Hush, now. I can only help if you tell me. Do you know who did this?"

"He ... He . . ." Panting, her words came out in pieces. "He was large . . . A *huge* man! A Negro . . . He was at Parker's. He h-held the door for me!" She sobbed and buried her head into his shoulder.

"That's a good lass. You're doin' fine." He stroked her hair, allowing her to cry. "Shannon, hand me that glass of water."

Until that moment, she'd not been aware of her mama's presence. Even Izzy hovered close. If only the entire thing had been a nightmare. The expressions on their faces confirmed the opposite.

Victoria raised her head and her daddy lifted the glass to her lips. The cool water soothed her aching throat.

"How did you get away from him?" he asked, setting the glass on the bed stand.

"I hurt him! *Scratched* him!" She held her hand to her face and moved her fingers down her cheek to show what she'd done. "It made him angry . . . and . . . he . . . he hit me!"

Her daddy's hand tightened around the blanket covering her, but then opened and relaxed. "Then what did you do?"

"He . . . He was on me . . . had his mouth all over me . . ." Again, she panted. "He intended to have me . . . but I didn't let him. I st-stabbed him in the back . . . with my hat pin." Her body shook out of control. She didn't want to remember any of this—wanted it all to go away.

She took a long drawn-out breath, trying with all her might to still her body. "I kicked him hard as I could. He had no right! He hurt me, Daddy!"

He pulled her into his arms. "You did well, Victoria. Daddy is proud of you. You rest now . . ." He kissed her forehead, then lowered her onto the pillow and tucked the blankets around her. She hadn't stopped trembling.

He stood and took her mama's hand. "Izzy, you stay here with Victoria. Don't leave her side. Me and the Misses have some talking to do."

"I won't Mr. O'Malley," she replied, and sat down beside her.

Victoria closed her eyes. With Izzy close, she felt safe.

She tried to sleep, while listening to the sound of her parent's muffled voices in the hallway. Her lips curled into a smile.

Daddy will make it better. That man will never hurt me again.

Chapter 14

Andrew rode into the setting sun determined to find Tobias. He'd taken his buggy home and set out again on Sam.

First, he looked in the man's shanty. Someone had been there, evident by the partially eaten fresh food on the table.

He stopped at the nearby shanties and asked if anyone had seen him. They told him *no* over and over again.

The unstoppable pain in his heart intensified with every negative answer. He'd probably *never* be able to make things right with Victoria.

Will she blame me?

Things could've turned out worse. Tobias could've easily killed her. He'd become insane to the point of being criminal.

Unsure what Tobias was capable of; Andrew didn't know what he'd do once he found him. He'd never been faced with this sort of problem before. His job was to heal people, not *hurt* them. Could he take another man's life?

Tobias *had* to be stopped, one way or another.

He'd been going in circles. The air was frigid, and he wasn't accomplishing anything, so he decided to go home.

Eventually, *Tobias* would come for *him*.

Hours passed.

Andrew's head bobbed downward toward his chest, but somehow he had to stay awake.

Coffee . . .

He wandered to the stove and placed the coffee pot over the eye to heat it. There'd been a little left over from that morning. It would have to do. He didn't have the energy to make a new pot.

He was afraid to sleep, knowing Tobias was out there somewhere.

Why doesn't he come?

Visions of Victoria rolled through his mind. Her wound. The bruises. Her shame.

If I'd told O'Malley about Tobias, could he have stopped him?

He fought against every principle he held close to his heart. This had all gone too far and he blamed himself.

The doorknob jiggled.

With a rapidly beating heart, Andrew inched toward the door.

"Doc!" Clay screamed and pounded on the door. "Doc! Open up! It's Daddy! They gots Daddy!"

What?

Andrew lunged for the door and jerked it open.

Clay huffed, out of breath. His eyes were wide with fear. "They gots Daddy!"

"Who?" Andrew grabbed his shoulders. "Who has him?"

"The Klan! They's at our house! They gots him!"

No! Andrew grabbed his coat and bag. He flew out the door, grasping Clay by the arm.

They sped to the barn. After putting Clay on Sam, he mounted Charger. They dug their heels in and raced to Elijah.

As the hooves pounded the earth beneath him, the sick feeling coursing through Andrew's body, grew even stronger.

God, no. Please, not Elijah.

At least they didn't have far to go.

As they neared the shanty, several horses with riders sped away.

Andrew jumped from Charger and ran into the house. Clay headed in the opposite direction.

"Thank the Lawd!" Alicia yelled, and grabbed hold of him. "Doc, you gots to help Lijah!" She sobbed, gripping his coat.

"It'll be all right now. I'm here to help." He spoke with calm, trying to reassure her. "The men are gone. They rode away."

The door flew open.

"He's dead!" Clay screamed. "Daddy's dead!"

"No!" Alicia shrieked and raced out the door. "Not my Lijah!"

Andrew's knees gave way, but he caught himself on the edge of the table before falling to the ground.

God, no . . .

Clay had to be wrong.

He turned to Jenny, who sobbed and clutched onto Betsy. Samuel and Joshua clung onto Jenny between them.

"Jenny," Andrew said, stilling his heart. "Stay here with the children. Don't come outside."

Her chin quivered. She nodded without speaking.

Andrew went after Alicia, but stopped and froze when he saw Elijah.

He clutched his chest and dropped to the ground.

No, God. No . . .

I'm too late.

Elijah's limp body hung from the large oak tree, barely illuminated in the starlit sky. An eerie, despicable vision he'd never be able to erase from his mind.

Kneeling at the base of the huge oak, Clay wrestled with the rope, trying to untie it.

Andrew shifted his attention to Alicia, standing beneath Elijah, clinging to his body. She shook without control and her wailing cut through the chill in the air like a knife piercing his soul.

Breathing had to be forced. His heart wanted to stop beating.

I have to be strong. God, help me.

Andrew rose on shaky legs, denying his own pain, wanting to comfort her. He moved close to Alicia and reached out his hand, but she slapped it away.

Even in the darkness he could see the unmistakable glare in her eyes. "It's your fault! *All* you white men! You done this to him!" Sobbing, she faced him and beat on his chest with both fists. "I hate ya! I hate ya!"

Unable to move, he shared her pain. His chest tightened more than ever. If beating him eased her, he'd bear it. He found no fault in her actions, but swore he'd make someone pay.

Moaning, she backed away and put her face in her hands. Then her body jerked and she threw her arms upward and lifted her face toward the sky. "Elijah!"

Her scream filled the air.

The sound echoed around them.

Her lamentation soared all the way to the heavens.

She lowered her head and placed her hand to her breast. Turning, she approached Andrew. Her breathing slowed. "Oh, Doc. I'm sorry . . ." She moved into his embrace and allowed him to hold her.

He let her cry, pulling her as close as he possibly could. Being strong for her, he wouldn't cry now. It wasn't *his* time.

Lifting her head, she looked into his eyes. "We gots to get him down." She stepped away and returned to her husband.

Having focused on Alicia, Andrew hadn't been watching Clay. But now, Clay's pain increased his own. The boy continued to fumble with the rope. He blew on his cold hands, then yanked and pulled without success. The darkness of the night made it almost impossible for him to see, and the tears in his eyes—which he kept wiping with the back of his hand—obviously added to his difficulty.

Andrew ran back to the house and brought out a lantern, then knelt beside him. "Clay?" He rested a hand on his shoulder. "Help your mother. I'll untie the rope."

The boy pulled his trembling hands away, and without speaking, stood and moved to her side.

Andrew managed to loosen the knot enough so that Elijah's body began to lower to the ground. When his feet touched the earth, Andrew moved around the tree and helped them lay him down.

He cringed, but tried to hide his feelings. The man's body had been beaten—whipped horrifically. His back no longer resembled human flesh. More like raw, tattered meat. Butchered and beaten.

They laid him on his back so the wounds could no longer be seen, but blood oozed out onto the ground beneath him.

Oh, how he'd suffered.

Andrew's eyes welled with tears. He took a large breath through his nose and set his mind right.

I can't cry. Not now.

Even though Elijah could no longer *feel*, Andrew removed the noose with slow, deliberate care. But the moment it cleared his head, Clay wrenched it away and threw it as far as he could. He then knelt beside his father's body and stared at him. Heavy breaths came from Clay's nostrils, as he rocked back and forth.

Alicia draped herself over Elijah's body—held onto him and sobbed.

Slowly, her head came up. "Why, Doc? Why'd they do this to Lijah?"

He shook his head. "I don't know." He *needed* to understand why. Why this man? The kindest, most loving and giving man he'd ever known. The type of father he hoped he'd be one day.

Why him?

Holding the lantern close, Andrew gazed at Elijah's face. There were fresh, deep scratches across his cheek.

Why?

The truth hit him harder than Alicia's fists.

They killed him because of Victoria.

His mind raced, staring at the marks on his dead friend.

It couldn't have been Elijah.

Victoria had to have told her father what happened.

O'Malley knew a Negro hurt her.

He thought back to the incident earlier in the day. Jake had offered to help find the man. If Victoria told her father she'd been at the mercantile, then O'Malley would have gone to question Jake.

Elijah infuriated Jake. And I helped. Oh, God. I helped fuel the fire.

Andrew wiped away tears. His mind spun, piecing it all together.

In one of their conversations, Victoria had told him that her father had financed Jake's business.

Jake must be O'Malley's connection to the Klan.

Jake had never hidden his hatred of Negroes. And because of what had happened at the mercantile, Elijah topped his list.

Jake did this to him! He knew Victoria scratched the man who attacked her. He also knew Elijah wasn't the man they were looking for, so they marked him to make him appear guilty.

Fingernails could never have cut so deeply into his flesh. Examining the wound closer, he determined Jake must have used some kind of sharp instrument.

O'Malley wanted blood and he got it.

How could he tell Alicia the truth? He couldn't tell her about Victoria and what he knew Tobias had done to her. Victoria had been shamed—nearly *raped*—Elijah was dead, and Andrew blamed himself for all of it. He couldn't bear to have another soul blame him for what had happened, especially Alicia.

Alicia's face wrinkled with pain. "I told him not to get the candy! I told him to stay outta town—to stay home! I told him *you* could do it! Why din't he listen to me? He was so proud he got that candy!" The lantern light reflected off her tears.

Elijah didn't tell her I helped him.

Andrew chose his words carefully. "He wanted to show he's a free man, Alicia."

"He's free now," she whispered and laid her head on his chest.

CHAPTER 15

Carrying Elijah's massive body into the house required every ounce of their strength. Emotional *and* physical. Andrew and Clay worked together to lift him from the ground and Alicia held his head.

They laid him on the bed, then Alicia rushed to the water pitcher, dampened a rag, and began cleaning his body. His blood hadn't stopped seeping and soaked into the blankets.

"I gots to get him warm," she said, mindlessly moving the rag over his skin. "He's so cold."

Andrew could do little more than watch. He understood she needed to do this, but she appeared *entranced;* simply going through the motions. She'd stopped crying, and he believed her to be *numb.*

He pulled the curtain around the bed, so the children wouldn't be further upset. They undoubtedly understood their daddy had died, with the exception of little Betsy. She'd never know what a wonderful man he'd been.

Andrew stayed all night with them, not even considering being elsewhere.

They'd need to bury Elijah tomorrow. The cold hard ground would make it difficult, but it wouldn't take long for his body to start decaying. Dead bodies weren't a pretty sight and unfortunately he'd seen his share. But this one should've never died. Elijah had been young and strong, with much to live for.

Andrew woke early, after minimal sleep.

"I couldn't sleep neither," Alicia said. With a trembling hand, she extended a cup of coffee.

He'd heard her stirring through the night, between episodes of sobbing. With Elijah on *their* bed, she'd slept beside Jenny on her small bed. Betsy lay between them. Very little room, but it didn't seem to matter. They clung to one another.

He didn't believe his heart could ache any more than it already did, but seeing them that way had made it worse. What would they do without Elijah?

"You mind checkin' on Clay?" Alicia asked. "He's been outside for some time now. I's worried 'bout him." The pain behind her eyes stabbed into Andrew's already pierced heart.

How's she functioning at all?

He gave her a gentle hug, compelled to somehow ease her suffering. "I'll be right back. It's too cold for him to stay out long."

Bundling up in his coat, he wandered out into the crisp air and found Clay kneeling beside the oak tree, staring at the ground. He placed his hand on Clay's shoulder, but the boy didn't respond to his touch. Undoubtedly, he, too, felt numb.

"Look, Doc." Clay held up his hand. "It's broke." He sniffled, then wiped his nose on his shirt sleeve.

The crystal snowflake lay in pieces in his palm. Apparently, it had been trampled.

Andrew closed his eyes and shook his head. "I'm sorry, Clay. I'll buy another."

"No, Doc. I don't want it. I just want my daddy back!" His face scrunched tight, fighting back tears. Slowly, he stood and squared his shoulders. "Men ain't s'posed to cry."

Andrew drew him into his arms, remembering the night his mother had died and his father had told *him* not to cry.

He was wrong.

"It's all right to cry, Clay. You can let it out."

The moment he said it, Clay erupted into tears.

As if a dam burst wide open, Andrew joined him. No longer strong, but weak. He'd lost his best friend and he blamed himself.

* * *

Word spread quickly through the shanties about the hanging of Elijah Tarver.

In no time, men showed up to help dig the grave and women brought food. *Everyone* mourned. They'd not only loved Elijah, but respected him more than any other man living there. He'd taught many of them how to farm—how to work their land and make a living. They cursed over the injustice that had befallen him.

Somehow, Andrew had to make everything right again, but he couldn't bring a man back from the grave.

He went through the motions of the burial in a fog. Nothing seemed real. And then it occurred to him that it had happened on his birthday. Twenty-five now, but he felt like he'd aged a hundred years.

They gathered around Elijah's grave, beneath the oak tree. His blood had already stained the ground, now his body would lie beneath it.

A woman stepped forward and began to sing, "Swing low, sweet chariot, comin' for to carry me home." Other voices joined in the mournful song. They sung out for Elijah, but the melody haunted Andrew.

When the song ended, he studied the woman who'd started the song.

Izzy?

Having only seen her in the uniform the O'Malley's required her to wear, he hadn't recognized her. He'd forgotten it was Sunday; her only day off. Dressed in solid black, she also wore a hat with a veil that partially covered her face.

As the service ended, people wandered around comforting one another and offering to help Alicia.

Izzy walked up to Andrew, took him by the arm, and led him away from the others. "I don't believe what they say he done. I know it wadn't him. 'Twas Tobias. Wadn't it?"

Andrew looked at the ground. "Izzy, it's my fault. Elijah's dead because of me."

She lifted his chin, forcing him to look at her. "Doc, you din't do this. Nothin' you coulda done woulda stopped them men."

He couldn't face her and turned away. "Mr. O'Malley asked me who I thought was following us. I wouldn't tell him, because I knew he'd do *this*. I don't agree with this. But because of my principles, Elijah's dead!"

"Your principles is what makes you a good man. Don't you change! Stop beatin' yourself up. There's more you're gonna needs to do. Other folks what's gonna need your hep."

"You mean Victoria, don't you?"

"Mmm, hmm. She's hurtin' bad, Doc. Won't stop cryin'." Izzy hung her head. "I din't wanna leave her, but they told me to take my day off. Glad I did. Elst I couldn't a been here."

"Her father won't let me see her."

"I know. But she loves ya. Give him time an' he'll want you there again. They's leavin' t'morra for Birmin'ham. Decided to go early. Victoria may stay there awhile."

"It might be best for her to go far away."

"Maybe so. She had a fit last night after you left. Jumped outta bed an' yanked all her dresses outta the wardrobe. Started rippin' 'em to shreds. Took Ms. O'Malley a time to settle her down."

"I wish I could help her." How could he help anyone? It seemed every life he touched, he inflicted pain.

"In time." She patted his hand. "In time . . ." After letting out a loud sigh, she nodded toward the others. "I best be goin' home. Folks is leavin'. I knows you won't say nuttin' bout my bein' here. Miss Victoria's folks wouldn't understan'. They think Lijah was the one what hurt her, but you an' I knows the truth. Still, it's best she believes the man what did this be dead."

"I agree." No truer words could've been said.

She quickly hugged him, then walked slowly away, joining the rest of those departing.

Andrew's eyes shifted from Izzy, to a man cowering at the back of the crowd. His coat had been turned up high on his neck. His head bent low and his eyes were focused downward.

Tobias?

Andrew's heart raced and his fists tightened.

How dare he be here?

Tobias raised his eyes, meeting Andrew's. He sneered, then turned and walked away. His pace increased with every step.

Andrew didn't want to upset Alicia any further, but he wasn't about to let the man get away. Once he followed him into the trees, Tobias bolted.

Andrew broke into a sprint and easily overtook him. With a burst of angry energy, he sprung on the man's back and held on. They tumbled to the hard frozen ground.

"No!" Tobias screamed, then moaned in pain.

Not caring how much pain he'd inflicted, Andrew flipped him over and pinned his body into the rocky surface. The man's face contorted with agony.

Good! I want you to hurt.

The scratches on his face were all Andrew needed to see. They confirmed the truth.

He gripped Tobias's chin. "A good man is dead because of you!"

"Don't know what you're talkin' 'bout!" Tobias snarled, jerking his head away.

"You know very well what I mean!" Andrew grabbed his shoulders. "*You* should've been the one hanging from that tree! *You* were the one who hurt Victoria!" With every word, he pushed him harder into the ground.

Tobias groaned and wrestled beneath him.

"Does that hurt?" Andrew asked, breathing hard.

It must've been how Victoria freed herself. She had to have pierced his back with the hat pin.

To test his theory, he pushed again, harder than ever.

"Damn you!" Tobias yelled, then moaned in pain.

"*You'll* be damned, Tobias. You deserve to suffer."

The man chuckled. "Don't know what you're talkin' 'bout." He struggled, but Andrew's anger kept him strong, holding him firm.

With each breath Tobias exhaled, a foul odor drifted upward into Andrew's face. Picturing beautiful Victoria terrorized by this wretched man, intensified Andrew's emotions. Magnified his hate. "Where'd you get those scratches?" He spit out the question.

"Cat got me," Tobias smirked. "A feisty one!"

Andrew smacked him hard across the face. "I know it was you!"

"What you gonna do 'bout it?"

Andrew scanned their surroundings. A large rock lay within reach. He grabbed it and held it over the man's head. His hovering hand trembled.

"Go on!" Tobias spat at him. "Kill me. It's what you do!"

Andrew sucked in air. His words stung.

I can't do it.

He hurled the rock as far away as he could.

"What's wrong, Doc? Lose your guts?" He glared with a sadistic mixture of hate and pride. Taunting him.

"I'm a better man than you, Tobias. I'll take you into town and turn you over to the law. I'll tell them the truth."

It's the only way.

"You can't, Doc." He laughed hard, seemingly forgetting his pain. "Don't you see? They already hung the man what did it. You go tellin' 'em they's wrong, an' they ain't gonna like it none. You'll make 'em look bad. You can't win, Doc. This is *my* game."

Andrew stared at him. His stomach twisted into knots.

Oh, God. He's right.

From what Izzy had said, O'Malley had already been told they'd killed the man responsible for Victoria.

She couldn't bear it if she knew he was alive.

"Cat got your tongue, Doc?" Tobias's body jerked with laughter beneath him.

I have no choice.

Deflated, Andrew stood and jerked him to his feet, holding him by his collar. "I want you to leave. Go far away! Don't ever come here again!" He tightened his grip and brought the man forward. Mere inches from his face. "Stay away from Victoria! And if I *ever* see you again, I *will* kill you! Now go!" He pushed him hard.

Tobias tripped, then got up quickly and flew off deeper into the trees. But not before casting a hateful, victorious sneer in Andrew's direction.

Andrew leaned over and placed his hands on his knees, steadying himself.

Did I do the right thing?

The man's injury would most likely become infected. He wanted Tobias to suffer. If he developed gangrene, he'd die a slow, painful death.

Maybe he should've smashed his head with the rock. Yet, he'd never taken a life. It wasn't in his nature. Still, he chided himself for letting him go.

He searched his heart, but couldn't discern whether he'd been righteous or simply a coward.

* * *

On a day like today, Andrew had little to be thankful for. At least it was Sunday and he didn't have to go to work.

After leaving Alicia in the care of one of her friends, he went home, promising he'd return later that evening. He wasn't about to leave her alone.

Exhausted, he lay on his bed. Instantly, he envisioned Claire—the one person who'd ever given him *real* comfort. He drifted off to sleep, longing for her.

His body jerked, startled from deep slumber by the sound of breaking glass. A large gasp took his breath.

What?

Multiple sets of heavy hands gripped him hard. Before he could speak or lash out, a black hood covered his head. They cinched it tight around his neck. So tight, he could barely breathe.

His heartrate doubled and he struggled against them, knowing full well the methods of the Klan.

They laughed at his attempt, infuriating him further.

Stay calm. If they wanted to kill me, they'd have done it already.

Not only did the hood inhibit breathing, but also made it impossible to see. From the number of hands on him, he believed there to be three men. They jerked him upright and bound his hands, then tied him to the bed.

"Who are you?" Andrew rasped.

"We've got a message for ya," an unfamiliar voice answered.

"What?" Every time he spoke, the limited air around him heated, making him light-headed. It didn't help having his heart beating out of his chest.

"We came to tell you to stop helpin' the niggas. Start actin' like a white man, or we'll hang you like your friend, Elijah."

"You're all cowards! Let me see who you are!"

They laughed even harder. "Best you don't know. If you did, we'd *hafta* kill ya!"

"Move into the city!" a different voice yelled into his ear. *I know you.*

"Get outta Shanty Town, or else!"

Andrew's head flew back against the wall from the force of the man's fist slamming into his jaw.

Total darkness.

* * *

"Doc! Doc, wake up!"

Andrew's body jerked.

Clay?

With a pounding head, Andrew opened his eyes. Immediately, he began to breathe in rapid bursts, fighting against the black hood.

"I'll get it off, Doc. Whoever done this is long gone. Don't be scared no more." The boy tugged at the knot.

The constricting rope loosened. Andrew finally managed to calm, but the ache in his head didn't subside.

After lifting the hood, Clay leaned in, staring at him. "Your face looks bad, Doc."

It took him a while to recall what had happened, then it all came rushing back. "How'd you get in?" He yanked at the ropes binding him to the bed.

Clay switched his attention to Andrew's bindings. "Your winda was broke. I climbed in through there. 'Fraid you was dead when I seen you on the bed."

As soon as he had a free hand, Andrew rubbed his jaw. It throbbed with pain. "What time is it?"

"Nearly ten o'clock. Mama was worried sick." Clay stopped working on the other bound hand. "They after you too, Doc?"

"They gave me a warning. They know how to deliver a message." Again, he rubbed his jaw. At least they hadn't broken it.

"I think they want Mama, too." Clay's voice shook.

"What?"

"Jenny said right before we got there, them men was comin' to burn down the house. I heard their threats soon as they rode up. They was yellin' an' cussin'. Daddy was scared they'd burn us alive. That's why he went outside. Mama told me to come for you. I crawled out the winda and them men didn't see me." He swallowed hard. "Once they done killed Daddy, Jenny said they yelled for Mama to come out, but she wouldn't go. Figger we musta scared 'em off."

The horror of it all brought every detail to life. Andrew had to prevent anything further from happening. While Clay spoke, he'd finished untying the last knot. Andrew jumped to his feet and threw on his clothes. "Your mother's not safe. Is someone with her?"

"Lotsa folks keep comin' 'round bringin' food an' checkin' on her. Reckon it's keepin' 'em away."

"C'mon!" Andrew grabbed Clay's arm and headed for the door, avoiding the fragments of broken glass on the floor.

They sprinted to the barn and found the horses in their stalls where he'd left them. Safe.

Something else to be thankful for.

They mounted and sped away.

When Andrew told Alicia what had happened, she crumbled into a chair and started crying again.

"Please don't," he pleaded. "Don't cry over me. I'm fine. But I'm worried about you and the children. I'm going to the shanties to find someone to come and stay with you. Then … I have somewhere I have to go."

She didn't argue. Clay sat beside her and pulled her close.

It didn't take long for Andrew to find more than one person willing to watch over her.

With Alicia secure, he prepared for a confrontation with Jake Parker.

Jake lived in an apartment over the mercantile. Giving little thought to the late hour, Andrew pounded on the man's door. "Jake! Open up!"

He banged harder, until it opened.

"What you doin' here?" Jake snarled.

"We need to talk."

"It's a might late to be knockin' on someone's door." He eyed Andrew up and down, then stepped aside and let him enter.

"I believe you know why I'm here. You've been busy, haven't you?" Andrew glared at him.

"Business ain't bad. It's almost Christmas."

"You know I'm not referring to that kind of business!" Andrew tightened his fists, wanting to plant them into *his* jaw.

"Not sure what you mean." The man's passive shrug fueled Andrew's rage.

"I know you were involved with Elijah's hanging. Patrick O'Malley put you up to it, didn't he?"

"I ain't sayin' nuttin'." Jake backed away.

"You *know* you got the wrong man! You made it look like he was the one who did it, but you know the truth. You killed an innocent man!"

"Didn't do no such thing."

"So it wasn't you who came to my house with a warning that sounded like something Patrick O'Malley would have said himself?" Air hissed from Andrew's nostrils.

"Don't know nuttin' 'bout it."

"Call the dogs off Alicia! You got your *man* and I'm certain O'Malley is satisfied. Leave the woman alone." Andrew pressed his finger into Jake's chest.

"Why should I?"

Andrew shook his head. "There are laws in this country protecting those people." He gave Jake a push, causing him to stumble. He wanted to do much worse.

"You're in Alabama now, Doc," Jake sneered, attempting composure. "Alabama has its own laws."

"Did O'Malley order you to kill a woman?"

"No." Sweat beaded on Jake's brow.

"Won't he get angry if you do something he didn't tell you to do? Especially something as horrible as taking the life of a woman—or her children?"

"Never thought it through," Jake said, scratching his head. "You got a point." He glanced nervously around the room, then returned his attention to Andrew. "I'll leave the woman alone, long as you don't tell him we done the wrong nigger."

Andrew grabbed him by his collar. "Don't call him that! He was a decent man! You're more of a *nigger* than he ever was." He pushed him to the floor.

Unshaken, Jake smirked. "Do we have a deal?"

Andrew hesitated, breathing hard. "Yes." He strode out the door, slamming it behind him.

Alicia would be safe, but he swore he'd just made a deal with the devil.

Chapter 16

With Christmas approaching, Claire began to prepare her home for the holiday. It would be Michael's first Christmas and nothing thrilled her more. Of course, Gerald liked to remind her that Michael had been present the previous Christmas, but because he'd still been in her belly, she told him it didn't count.

Joyful laughter filled their home.

Claire had taken Beth's warning regarding Henry to heart. She kept her distance, but couldn't stay away from him entirely. After all, they shared the same home.

She continued to cook, clean, and care for Michael. A happy routine where everyone knew their place. At nearly eight months, he crawled all over the house, exploring everything. He especially enjoyed the kitchen and entertained himself by beating a wooden spoon against one of her cooking pots while she cooked.

"You'll be a fine musician someday," she said, scooping him into her arms.

He babbled and rambled off a few unrecognizable words.

"Oh, my!" She waved her hand in front of her face.

Gerald had come in from chopping wood; hot and sweaty. He snuck up behind her and kissed her neck, then turned her around and hugged her, along with the baby.

Though his affection made her giggle, his unbearable smell almost made her retch. "Gerald, I love you, but you need to wash up."

He grinned, released her, then went to the sink.

"You might need more than a face wash. Why don't you bring the tub in and have a nice bath after supper? Maybe I'll join you."

"I like the sound a that." He peered over his shoulder and jiggled his brows. "Reckon Uncle Henry would watch Michael?"

"I'm sure he would. It's time for a good bath anyway. I'd like to go to town tomorrow and buy a few things for Christmas."

They ate their meal, then Gerald pulled Henry aside, while Claire cleared the dishes and pretended not to listen to their conversation.

"Henry, do you MIND watchin' MICHAEL for a SPELL?" Gerald still assumed Henry's hearing was far worse than it truly was. She rarely had to raise *her* voice when she spoke to him.

"You goin' somewhere?" Henry asked.

"Nope. We'll be RIGHT HERE in the KITCHEN. Claire an' I just want a little PRIVACY!"

Claire covered her mouth, trying not to giggle.

"Oh. All right," Henry mumbled.

A short time after supper, Henry sat with Michael in the living room, while Claire and Gerald bathed.

They'd positioned the tub at the center of the kitchen floor. A swinging door between the kitchen and living room separated them from Henry. Knowing the man wouldn't dare walk in on them, Claire relaxed and leaned her head back against the edge of the tub, facing away from the door. With her hair piled high on her head, the steam soothed her. But as she closed her eyes and Gerald's hand moved up her thigh, relaxation changed to something else entirely.

"Oh, Gerald . . ." She'd taught him well.

As they finished their *bath* and were drying off, Gerald jerked his head up, looking in the direction of the swinging door.

"What's wrong?" she asked, buttoning her gown.

He pushed his glasses up on his nose. "Thought I seen Uncle Henry lookin' through the door. I reckon I was seein' things." He shrugged and finished dressing.

Claire eyed the door, still slightly moving.

Was he watchin' us?

Her stomach knotted.

Certainly not.

* * *

The next morning, they bundled up and drove the wagon into the city. Fortunately for Claire, Henry chose to stay behind. The thought he'd seen her bathing, and perhaps what she and Gerald had done together, made her cringe.

She focused on Michael, whose eyes were wide, taking in the decorations in the streets. The buildings were adorned with green boughs and wide red ribbons. The city square had a large Christmas tree that stood tall and majestic, decorated with hand-made ornaments. The ornaments sparkled, reflecting the light from the winter sun.

Gerald left them at the mercantile, while he went to find a Christmas tree. Their first family tradition.

As she entered the store, the bell jingled.

"Afternoon, ma'am," Jake said, from behind the counter.

"Hey, there," she replied, swaying with the baby in her arms.

Michael giggled and patted her face. "Mama," his little voice chirped.

"You've been busy since the last time I saw ya," Jake chuckled. "That's a fine lookin' boy."

"His name's Michael. He needs some new clothes, so I'd like to get some material. Grows like a weed."

"Let me know what you need, an' I'll get it for ya. It's fine seein' you again, ma'am." With a broad grin, Jake raised his eyebrows, then peered at Michael and wrinkled his nose.

A knot twisted deep in Claire's belly.

What's he thinkin'?

Trying to ignore her paranoia, she wandered through the store and showed Michael all the pretty things, avoiding the breakables.

The bell rang and three young women walked in. Claire glanced at them briefly, then continued browsing.

The women giggled, looking through a selection of dresses. As loud as they were, Claire couldn't help but hear them.

"That one dips much too low," one of them said. "Jake must have a lot of them in stock now that Victoria's gone."

They erupted into laughter. "She used to buy them all up, but now I'm certain she'll wear them up to her chin."

Are they talkin' 'bout Victoria O'Malley?

She'd never forget her low-cut dress. Claire scooted closer to the women, able to see them plainly, but still keeping her distance.

"She's away in Birmingham now," one whispered, but Claire could hear her plain as day. "I was told she's carryin' a colored baby."

The women covered their mouths as if in shock, but then giggled.

"No," one said, in mock surprise. "S'pose her daddy will let her keep it?"

"Patrick O'Malley?" the other woman blurted out. "With a colored grandchild?"

They broke into a fit of laughter.

"She was askin' for it!" one exclaimed, in a far more serious tone.

Her friend looked at her wide-eyed. "How can you say such a thing?"

The woman defiantly crossed her arms. "She flaunted herself all over town actin' like a dog in heat."

Once again, the women giggled, then made their way to the counter. In no time at all, Jake fell in with them, gossiping with more enthusiasm than the females.

"That's right," he said. "Ravaged by a nigger right behind this here store. But don't you ladies worry none." He stood up straight and pulled his shoulders back. "We strung him up. He won't be doin' it again."

They fanned themselves and thanked him for his bravery and ridding the city of such a horrible man. Jake grinned from ear to ear, chuckling as they left the store.

Appalling.

But could it be true? Had that beautiful woman been defiled by a Negro? Claire wasn't about to ask Jake. Such things were impolite to even mention, let alone go on and on about. She regretted having heard it. She quickly made her selections. Jake cut the material and packaged it up, then she walked out of the store and waited for Gerald.

Standing there, her heart raced, feeling completely vulnerable. This time last year Andrew had walked by on the street and she'd so desperately wanted to look at him. Part of her wished she'd see him now, but that would be dangerous. Secrets had to be kept—especially the one she held in her arms. She could only do that by *not* seeing the man.

Once again, Beth and Aunt Martha would be joining their Christmas celebration. This time they'd *invited* Martha and placed a gift for her under the tree.

I hope she behaves herself and doesn't talk too much.

The Saturday before Christmas, Gerald busily dressed, preparing to pick up Beth. Claire didn't want him to go.

"Gerald?" She moved up behind him and encircled him with her arms. "Could you ask Uncle Henry to get Beth?"

He turned to face her. "Why? I don't wanna impose on him."

"I don't reckon it'd be imposin'. Beth *is* his niece." Not wanting to be alone with Henry, she *had* to convince him.

"He's expectin' *me* to go."

"But I want you here. The baby's still sleepin'. We have at least another hour. I thought maybe we could try workin' on another one." Once again, seducing him seemed like the only way to accomplish what she wanted.

He looked at the floor. "I hated it was a false alarm last time."

"Me, too. So . . . let's try again. Go ask Henry to go. Please?" She raked her fingers through his hair and placed soft kisses across his face.

He smiled and wiggled his brow. "I'll go ask him." He covered her mouth with a passionate kiss. "Hold that thought," he said and raced down the stairs.

Claire positioned herself on the bed, waiting for him to come back.

Surely, Henry won't refuse.

Within minutes, Gerald returned and frantically ripped off his clothes the second he closed the door.

He pounced on the bed. "Henry's gone to get Beth."

"I coulda guessed that." She giggled, finally able to relax. "So . . . what do you wanna do now?" Seductively, she bit her bottom lip.

"What I always wanna do, Claire. Let's make a baby."

She closed her eyes and did something she hadn't done in a very long time.

Andrew . . .

She envisioned his touch—his body pressed to hers. Tingling at the thought of him, her lovemaking ignited, fueled by the fire of desire.

What am I doin'?

Opening her eyes, she gazed up at her husband. *Gerald, not Andrew.* A man who loved her wholeheartedly. *Unconditionally.* She focused on him alone. Exactly what she should've been doing all along.

"I love you, Gerald," she whispered and he covered her lips in a tender kiss. She held on tight and poured her love into him.

When they finished, he hovered above her. "That was amazin', Claire."

Unable to speak, she merely nodded. Maybe in time, even the tiny corner of her heart Andrew still held would be filled completely by her husband.

* * *

On Christmas morning, Claire woke early to prepare the holiday breads and hot cocoa; another new Alexander family tradition.

Peering out the kitchen window, she smiled. Frost covered the ground, resembling snow. It glistened in the sunlight. The day couldn't have been more beautiful. Not only were they celebrating the wonder of Christ's birth, but they were all together. One big happy family.

A family with countless secrets.

Beth joined her in the kitchen. Martha was still sleeping and the men had gone out to tend the horses. Claire enjoyed the time alone with Beth, but then Michael woke up and started to cry.

"I'll get him," Beth said. Without waiting for a response, she headed out the swinging door.

Claire bustled around the kitchen, grateful for her help.

Beth reappeared, jostling Michael. "I think he's grown since Thanksgivin'!" She sat at the table. "I changed him. He was awful wet."

"Thank you. Reckon I'd better feed him. There's just still so much to do."

"Well, I can't do *that*." Beth laughed. "*You* feed him. I'll get the turkey goin'."

Claire thanked her and took Michael. She draped a blanket over him, so as not to expose herself. "I never know when Henry might walk in."

Beth gave her a sideways stare. "Nothin's happened, has it?"

"No. But the way he looks at me sometimes makes me uncomfortable."

"Does Gerald suspect anythin'?"

"No. And I can't tell him. You know how angry it'd make him. Hopefully, by next year, we'll have enough money saved so we can get our own place."

"You need to. The sooner, the better." Beth laid her hand on Claire's shoulder. "I worry 'bout you."

"I know. I worry 'bout me, too." She switched Michael to her other breast and readjusted the blanket.

"How long you gonna nurse him?"

"Till he bites me, I reckon."

"Can't comprehend all that," Beth mumbled, shaking her head.

After Claire finished nursing, Michael perched on a blanket in the kitchen, happily playing, while they finished preparing the food. The bread was about done and the cocoa steamed, piping hot.

"We should get everyone together to exchange gifts," Claire said.

The kitchen door swung open. Martha appeared, wearing a bathrobe. "Much too early to get all gussied up!" She set her spittoon on the table. Seemed it was never too early to chew.

When Henry and Gerald finished their chores, everyone gathered around the Christmas tree.

Martha handed out jars of preserves. "Can't go wrong with food!" She grinned, then promptly turned her head and spit.

The clothes Claire had sewn were well received by everyone, but Michael. He showed more interest in the shiny ornaments on the tree. It didn't take much to entertain him.

Gerald gave Claire a new sewing basket. Overwhelmed by the beautiful gift, she hugged his neck and thanked him with a sweet kiss.

While everyone enjoyed their cocoa, Claire had her eyes on Gerald, who beamed with an enormous smile.

"I saved the best for last!" he exclaimed and rushed out the door.

What?

He'd already given her so much.

He returned carrying a large wooden rocking horse.

"It's for Michael," he said, setting it on the floor.

Claire giggled. "Course it is."

He lifted Michael onto it, rewarded with grins and baby giggles. "Daddy's gonna get you a real horse one day."

It warmed her heart watching the two of them together. "Not too soon, Gerald. I don't want my baby growin' up so fast."

"We'll just hafta have us another one. That way you can have a baby, an' I can have Michael to do things with me."

Claire forced a smile. How could he ever understand they couldn't have any more children? Eventually, he'd wonder why. They frequently accomplished everything necessary to create a new life, and in Gerald's mind, it should've already happened.

"We missed one," Beth said, lifting a small unopened box from beneath the tree. "Who's this for?"

Henry cleared his throat. "It's for Claire."

Beth hesitated, but handed her the box, her eyes filled with concern.

Claire took it, though her hands trembled.

"You all right, Claire?" Gerald asked.

"Course. I'm fine. Reckon my hands are a little cold." She untied a simple red ribbon, then cautiously opened the box.

A weddin' ring?

She gulped and stared at the gold band centered with a golden rose that held a sparkling ruby. As she pulled it out, Beth's eyes grew wide.

"I—I don't understand," Claire said, holding up the ring.

Henry met her gaze. "I want you to have it. It was Sarah's."

Last year, she'd wanted to give back the necklace he'd given her, but had been told to keep it.

I can't wear this ring.

"But . . ." She had to make a stand. "I ALREADY have a WEDDIN' RING." She looked directly at Henry, emphasizing her words more than ever. She wiggled her finger in the air, displaying the simple gold band wound with yarn.

"That ring ain't good enough for ya!" Henry yelled. "You need sumthin' better!" The look he gave her caused her stomach to flutter.

Gerald tapped her shoulder. "It's much nicer than the ring I gave you. You should wear it."

"I *love* the ring you gave me, Gerald'." She fought back tears. "I don't want another one."

"Claire's right," Beth said. "The ring you gave her is special."

"But it's got yarn on it!" Gerald crossed his arms over his chest. "Aunt Sarah's ring even has a stone. I want Claire to have it. She deserves sumthin' fine like that."

"Heck!" Martha threw up her hands. "I'll take it if she don't want it!" She reached for the ring.

Henry grabbed Martha's arm. "No! If Claire don't want it, I don't want no one to have it." While taking the ring from Claire, he made a point to brush her skin with his fingertips. He paused and looked her in the eye. "Maybe someday you'll change your mind. I'll keep it for ya." He put it back in the box.

She swallowed hard.

We've gotta move. Another year will be too long.

CHAPTER 17

Andrew gripped his glass of wine and gazed at the sparkling Christmas tree. He certainly didn't feel like celebrating.

I shouldn't have come here.

"Let's go sit down and talk," Dr. Mitchell said, coming up behind him.

Andrew followed him to the library, where they sat comfortably enough in leather chairs. He'd eaten little. At least Mrs. Mitchell hadn't taken offense.

"I'm sorry," he said, then took a sip of wine. "I'm afraid I'm terrible company."

"Don't be sorry. You lost a good friend. I understand what a difficult time you've been going through."

I can't tell him everything.

Even though Harvey Mitchell had become a friend, as well as a mentor, some things needed to be kept inside. He'd deal with the pain alone.

"Andrew?" Dr. Mitchell leaned in. "You can't change the world all by yourself."

"Maybe not. But what they did to Elijah was inhumane. The man was innocent."

"You're certain?"

He nodded. "I knew him well. He'd never have laid a hand on Victoria. Besides, I know who did it."

"What? Why haven't you gone to the authorities?"

"I can't." He trusted his friend, but if he told him details, he'd risk involving him. His family didn't need the Klan showing up on *their* doorstep.

Dr. Mitchell sat back, drawing in a long breath. "Someone's pressuring you to remain silent."

Andrew nodded, twisting his wineglass through his fingers. "Staying quiet will protect Elijah's wife. *And* Victoria needs to believe that the man who hurt her is dead."

"O'Malley thinks they hung the *right* man, doesn't he?"

Another nod. His friend had a better grasp on the situation than he realized.

Dr. Mitchell leaned in, shaking his head. "Did you fully comprehend what you were getting into when you decided to court his daughter?"

"Maybe not."

"When you declined our Thanksgiving invitation and said where you were having dinner, I should have warned you then. I could have told you about his connections. The man uses his money for despicable things." His eyes narrowed. "I know I don't have to tell you that this conversation should go no further than this room."

"Of course. And since we're speaking openly, can I assume that by *connections* you're referring to the Klan?"

The man's head moved slowly up and down. "They're dangerous. I wish you'd reconsider and move into town."

"No. I won't be bullied." The bruise on his face had finally started to fade. The pain in his heart would never heal.

Dr. Mitchell peered at him over the top of his glasses. "I don't want you *dead*."

"Lately, I've felt I have little to live for."

"You'll get beyond this. But it might be wise for you to go away for a time, until things settle down. Perhaps a trip to see your father?"

Andrew grunted. "It wouldn't help. Besides, I'm trying to assist Alicia as much as I can. And Clay's tending their farm and no longer works for me. So that gives me even more to do. Honestly, the hard labor helps clear my head."

Nearly every night he rode to the Tarver's to check on Alicia. She'd dealt with her loss as best she could, determined to continue being a good mother. Jenny helped her with chores and tending the children. Even Samuel did what he could to help Clay, but the others were too little.

Dr. Mitchell cleared his throat and brought Andrew out of his thoughts. "I wish you'd taken interest in Rachel. My daughter's quite smitten."

When Andrew didn't respond, the man cocked his head to one side. "Or Elizabeth. She's younger than Rachel, but she, too, has had her eyes on you."

"I'd be better off running far from women. No offense to your daughters, of course," he quickly added. "But it seems every time I become involved, my life gets overly complicated."

"Maybe so." His friend grinned. "Still, there *are* benefits. My opinion is you've not found the right women."

No doubt Harvey still respected him. A man would never offer his daughters to someone he didn't hold in high regard. But the man couldn't be more wrong. He'd found the *perfect* woman, but she'd decided she didn't want him.

Andrew polished off the remaining wine in his glass and stood. "I'd best be getting home."

Dr. Mitchell rose. "Yes, it's getting late and we have to be at the hospital quite early." He led Andrew from the library and they returned to the living room where the women had been waiting.

Rachel's face lit up, but Andrew couldn't encourage her. "Goodnight," he said, dipping his head. "Thank you for a lovely evening and a splendid meal." He addressed his final comments to Mrs. Mitchell.

Shouts of *Merry Christmas* echoed behind him.

Merry? I'm far from it.

* * *

Somehow, Andrew managed to go to work every day as he should. On time and professional.

The New Year came with little festivity.

As he passed the front desk, he looked for the smile he always counted on from Sally—one of the only things lately that lifted his spirits.

"Dr. Fletcher?" The girl appeared timid, with no trace of a smile.

"Yes?"

Her brow wrinkled. "I . . . I wanted to wish you a happy New Year."

"Thank you. Happy New Year to you as well." He started to leave.

"Dr. Fletcher!" she yelled, stopping him. "I also wanted to say I'm sorry about what happened to Miss O'Malley. I heard horrible things."

He crossed his arms, facing her. "What did you hear?"

"Well . . . I know you care for her. I saw you together . . ." She paused, seeming to struggle with what to say. "I heard about the Negro and what he did to her." Her eyes pooled with compassionate tears.

He'd heard some of the rumors as well. Everything had been blown out of proportion. Nothing could've been more unfair to Victoria. She didn't deserve it.

"Don't believe everything you hear, Sally."

"Then it's not true?" She leaned in. "About the baby and all?"

"Baby?" His stomach churned. "What baby?"

"When he had her." The girl's cheeks turned a bright shade of red. "They say she was sent away because he . . . well . . . made a baby with her."

He unfolded his arms and moved closer to her. "Sally, I took care of her after it happened. He hurt her, but he *didn't* have his way with her. Do you understand me?"

"Yes, Doctor. But that's not what everyone's saying." She raised her wide eyes.

"As I said, don't believe everything you hear."

He walked away.

Just when he thought things couldn't get worse, Victoria's reputation had become the main topic of conversation for the city of Mobile.

I hope she stays away a long time. Maybe by then, the rumors will have ended.

* * *

When Andrew arrived for work the next day, Sally told him Mr. Schultz wanted to see him in his office.

This can't be good.

He knocked on the door. After being invited, he stepped inside.

Not good at all.

He stood face-to-face with Patrick O'Malley. Not what he'd expected.

"I'll leave you two alone," Mr. Schultz said and exited, shutting the door behind him.

Instantly, the air in the room became stifling. Andrew loosened his collar.

"I know you're surprised to see me, Dr. Fletcher," the man said. He moved behind the desk and sat, then pulled out a pipe and lit it. "Sit down." He pointed to a chair.

Though Andrew had no respect for the man, he wanted to hear what he had to say, so he complied.

"You made a real mess a things," O'Malley sneered and puffed on his pipe.

Andrew considered leaving. No one had to remind him of the *mess* he'd made. Deeming a response unnecessary, he listened.

"Me daughter will be coming home in a few weeks. She's doing better, but not much. I imagine you've heard some of the rumors going 'round the city? *Everyone* has, and that's why I'm here." He stood and moved toward Andrew.

"I blame *you* for what happened to her." O'Malley hovered above him. "If you'd listened to me, I could have taken care of the man. I know now why you were protectin' him. He was your friend. How you could befriend an animal like him, I'll never understand. But I made certain he'll never harm another woman. *I* took care of what you wouldn't!"

Andrew wanted to scream—to tell him Elijah would've never harmed a soul, and that they'd hung the wrong man. But in order to protect Alicia, he'd have to keep his word to Jake. He remained silent.

"Victoria still loves you," O'Malley said, lowering his voice. He moved away and began pacing. "Shannon sent word that she can't stop talking about you. Victoria will want to see you when she returns. You *will* see her, and you will ask her to marry you. And I don't give a damn whether you love her or not." He stopped in the middle of the floor, glaring. "You *owe* this to her! No other man will have her now. Not with all the talk."

Marry her?

Andrew had to speak. "She wasn't defiled. You know that. Regardless of the rumors."

"Aye. I know it, and you know it. But no one else believes it! She needs a husband. And since she loves you, you'll marry her and make it right!"

"I have no say in the matter?" Why bother asking? He already knew the answer.

"You lost your say when you remained silent about that man. You *will* marry her. Understood?"

"Does Victoria know you're making this demand?"

"No! Certainly not. *Never* tell her I asked you to do this. You're to profess your love to her. Make her think it was your idea and give her back her pride!" O'Malley thumped Andrew's chest.

"Yes, sir," Andrew said, squaring his jaw. What other choice did he have? She deserved dignity.

It's the only way to make it right.

"You behave as though it's a horrible thing! Me daughter is the finest woman there ever was. You're getting a prize, Dr. Fletcher, and I'm giving it to you."

"Yes, sir. I know she's a fine woman. I'll marry her and love her as you requested."

"You'd better. I've taken the liberty of ordering a ring from Parker's. Me daughter deserves the best and that's what she'll get. I've arranged to have the money withdrawn from your pay. A little each month. And one more thing—you must convert to Catholicism."

"Is that all?" Andrew asked, dryly.

"Don't be fresh with me, lad! One word from my lips and you'd find yourself unemployed. I don't play games. I make the rules. You will meet with Father O'Meara one day a week starting next Tuesday evening. He'll instruct you in the Catholic faith. Me daughter deserves a church wedding and she'll have it." O'Malley folded his hands in front of himself. "You may go now. Remember, next Tuesday at St. Mary's, six o'clock sharp."

Andrew stood to leave.

"Oh . . . There *is* one more thing." The hatred in the man's eyes made Andrew cringe. "Move into town!"

Andrew couldn't get out of there fast enough.

"I'm going out," he said to Sally, but didn't wait for a response.

After walking hard and fast, he found himself on the beach. With thoughts racing, he paced up and down the shore.

How did I get into such a mess?

Not only did he have his father telling him what he should and shouldn't do, but now he'd also have a father-in-law far worse.

At least Claire didn't have a father I had to worry about.

He and Claire had made their own choice to love each other. Not forced, but real. He wanted *her.*

He raised his face toward the sky. Was Elijah watching over him now, along with his mother?

"What do I do?" He tightened his hands into fists. "Claire!" He screamed from the depths of his being. Knowing exactly where she was and not being able to go to her, made her absence even more painful.

Jumping up onto the smooth rock where he'd placed Victoria so long ago, he sat and gazed out at the water sparkling in the cool winter sun.

I'm trapped, so I might as well make a plan.

He'd marry Victoria, move into town, have some children, and work at City Hospital. She'd spend all of his money and hire a nanny to raise their children. Eventually, she'd tire of him and begin flirting with other men. He'd work late at night and try to ignore where she might be.

It would be his punishment, his retribution. And he'd have to live with it.

He returned to work and set about his business. Once again, with an empty heart, he simply went through the motions.

* * *

As promised, Andrew attended class with Father O'Meara and began learning about the Catholic faith. He listened to the best of his ability, but his mind wandered. He'd only gone to satisfy Patrick O'Malley, not to save his soul. He learned about their core beliefs and the priest spent a lot of time discussing the sanctity of marriage. He spoke of fidelity and honor, and the proper way for a husband to respect his wife.

Andrew showed *him* the respect he deserved. Always being polite and kind. He didn't let on that he didn't want to be there. In turn, Father O'Meara expressed how happy it made him knowing Victoria had found a man willing to adopt her faith.

The classes would last for six weeks, then Andrew would be a Catholic.

O'Malley made another brief stop at the hospital to inform Andrew of Victoria's homecoming. She'd be home on Sunday, and he insisted Andrew be there for supper. In addition, he told him to bring flowers and arrive at six o'clock. *Sharp.*

It appeared even their courtship would be orchestrated by the man.

Andrew would finally have the pleasure of Mrs. O'Malley's Irish stew. Her *loving husband* demanded that Andrew like it and even insisted he compliment her on her fine cooking, even if it wasn't so fine.

Since flowers weren't easy to come by in January, he bought Victoria a box of hard candy, *not* chocolates. It would be best not to display any kind of implications.

It had been six weeks since she'd left town. Strangely, he looked forward to seeing her, though he wished it wouldn't be in her parent's home. But her father made the rules and Andrew had no choice but to follow them.

Though asking Victoria to marry him had been rule number one, he hadn't been told *when*. The ring had been ordered and he'd have to check with Jake to find out when it would arrive. Maybe he could at least make the decision on the day and location of his proposal. O'Malley had to give him *some* choices.

As he approached their home, Andrew's heart fluttered, not knowing what to expect of Victoria. Would she be well?

O'Malley answered the door and shook Andrew's hand as if they were old friends.

"Glad you could make it, lad!" he said, patting Andrew on the back.

Mrs. O'Malley joined them. "Dr. Fletcher, we're so happy to have you here again. I hope you'll like me Irish stew."

"Thank you for having me, Mrs. O'Malley. I'm certain I'll love it."

O'Malley smiled with approval. "I'll get Victoria." He ascended the stairs.

Mrs. O'Malley took Andrew by the arm. "She's still having a difficult time, but she's doing better. Be patient with her. She loves you, you know."

"She's a wonderful woman, Mrs. O'Malley. I promise to be patient *and* understanding."

"You're a fine lad. We're blessed to have met you." She gave him a kiss on the cheek.

Andrew turned his head, drawn to Victoria being escorted down the stairs by her father. Her appearance made his heart ache.

She wore a plain blue dress with a high neckline. No bustle. No corset. Her hair hung loose around her shoulders, covering her neck. With shattered confidence, her head bent low, but she was still stunning.

O'Malley placed her hand into Andrew's. He raised it to his lips and kissed it lightly, then offered her a smile. "Hello, Victoria."

After meeting his gaze, she returned the smile, though the corners of her lips barely rose. "Hello, Andrew."

What happened to Drew?

"You look lovely," he said, then handed her the box of candy. "This is for you."

"Thank you," she whispered.

"Well now," her father said, rubbing his hands together. "I believe supper's ready."

They went to the dining room and sat. O'Malley at the head of the table, Victoria to one side of him, and Andrew to the other. After Mrs. O'Malley served the soup, she sat at the far end of the table opposite her husband.

"Now . . ." O'Malley said. "Isn't this fine? All of us together again?"

Victoria stared blankly at her bowl of stew.

"Yes, sir," Andrew said. "I'm glad to be here."

Victoria lifted her head enough to look at Andrew. "I was surprised when Daddy told me you asked to come over."

The man gave him a warning glare.

"I wanted to see you," Andrew said. "I've missed you, Victoria."

O'Malley's dirty look transformed into a smug smile.

"I've missed you, too, Andrew." Again, her lips scarcely lifted. Her smile didn't light up her face as it used to.

"How's the stew?" Mrs. O'Malley asked.

"It's delicious, ma'am," Andrew truthfully replied. At least he didn't have to lie about something else tonight. Izzy's caution had to have been in jest.

"I'm thrilled you like it. It's an old family recipe. I'll teach Victoria how to make it. We need to keep our traditions going." The woman beamed.

"I can't cook, Mama," Victoria muttered.

"Oh, but you can learn. Can't she, Dr. Fletcher?"

"Of course she can. If that's what she wants." Andrew kept his eyes on Victoria, wishing he could take her away somewhere.

She locked eyes with him, and her smile broadened. A spark of the old Victoria.

They finished eating, and her father suggested they spend some time alone in the sitting room.

Andrew gladly obliged and took Victoria by the hand. He led her to the very familiar settee. They sat side by side.

"I'm worried about you," he said, taking her hand.

"I'm fine. You don't need to worry."

"I know it's been hard for you, but I'm here now. I want to help you." He simply touched her face, afraid to kiss her.

"I know he's dead." Her words caught him off guard. "But I still get afraid. I don't even want to go out anymore. I feel like he took sumthin' from me I can't get back."

"Victoria . . ." He struggled to find the right words. "Don't be afraid. Let me take care of you."

Her chin quivered and tears trickled from her eyes. "Truly? You still want to be with me even after what he did?"

"Of course. Please don't cry." He wiped away her tears.

"What will we do, Andrew?"

"We'll take one day at a time and figure it out as we go." He smiled. "Is that all right with you?"

"Yes. So . . . you'll be patient with me?"

"I'm *very* patient." The tides had turned.

She grinned. "A patient doctor. That's kind of funny."

He chuckled.

"Andrew?" She slowly blinked. "I'm tired. Would you mind so much comin' back again another time?"

"Not at all." He stood and helped her to her feet.

She's so frail.

She walked with him to the door and told him good-night. The instant he stepped through, she closed the door behind him.

Walking to his buggy, he couldn't stop tears from filling his eyes.

* * *

Even though it had been good seeing Andrew, Victoria hadn't stopped second-guessing his intentions.

Why would any man want me now?

She found comfort sitting on the sofa in the living room doing needlepoint. But even with a fire burning brightly in the fireplace, she still shivered. It helped having a blanket draped over her knees.

"Miss Victoria," Izzy said, clearing her throat. "Miss Penelope is here. You up to company?"

Victoria remained focused on her work. "I s'pose so."

When Izzy returned with Penelope, Victoria looked up, only to watch the girl tiptoe across the floor as if afraid of waking someone.

"Hello, Victoria." She bent down as though speaking to a child, then sat across from her in an over-stuffed chair and folded her hands in her lap.

Victoria continued sewing. "Hello, Penelope. It's kind of you to come by."

"I missed you. You've been away a long time."

Victoria sighed. Perhaps she should have refused her guest. Unimportant conversation no longer mattered.

Penelope cleared her throat. "Are you cold?"

"Yes." Since it seemed she'd have to talk to her, she set the sewing aside. "Penelope, you've been my friend a very long time, and there's sumthin' I need to know. What are folks sayin' 'bout me?"

The girl twisted her fingers together. "Well . . . I . . . They're sayin' many things." She shook her head and looked upward, mumbling something incomprehensible.

Victoria sat upright. "What sort of things?"

"Oh, Victoria!" Penelope held her hands against the sides of her face, then set them once again on her lap. "*Horrible* things! I can't believe they're true." She leaned in. "Are you goin' to have a baby?"

Victoria gaped at her, body trembling. "A baby? How could I have a baby?"

"From that Negro—the one who had you. It must have been terrifyin'!" Penelope placed her hand on Victoria's knee.

"Leave!" Victoria's outburst brought Izzy flying into the room. Victoria latched onto her arm. "Izzy, make her go away!"

Izzy frantically nodded. "I'm sorry, Miss Penelope, but you'll hafta leave. You've upset her." Izzy shooed her toward the door.

"I'm sorry!" Penelope yelled over her shoulder. "I didn't mean to! I just needed to know!" The girl ran from the house, slamming the door as she left.

"It's all right, baby," Izzy said, then sat beside her and drew her close. "Izzy's here for ya."

Victoria couldn't stop quivering and burst into tears. "They all believe he had me? They're sayin' I'm with child. I don't understand. Why would they think that?"

"Folks talk what shouldn't. We knows the truth." Izzy squeezed her a little tighter. "I'm gonna make you some nice hot tea. Make you feel better." She kissed her on the forehead, then went to the kitchen.

Victoria vacantly watched the fire, mesmerized by the dancing flames. She wanted to run away, but couldn't move.

"Here's your tea," Izzy said, handing her a cup.

She pushed it away. "I want to see Andrew, but I'm afraid to leave the house. Will you get him for me?"

"I can't leave you here alone. Your daddy's at work, an' your mama's at Miss Stacey's. I's shore Doc Fletcher will be by to see you again real soon." She set the tea aside and sat.

"He's the only one who knows the truth." Victoria grabbed Izzy's hands. "How will I ever walk down the street again? Folks are sayin' such horrid things 'bout me."

"You'll walk down that street with your head held high. That's how. You did nuttin' wrong. Don't you never forget it. Don't let that man ruin your life." She stared straight into her eyes. "I know what's goin' through your head. But you listen. It wadn't your fault what happened. Hear me?"

Tears trickled down Victoria's cheeks. "He said I was askin' for it. You always told me the way I acted would get me in trouble. You warned me, and I didn't listen."

"No man has the right to try an' take sumthin' from a woman she ain't willin' to give. You din't ask him to hurt ya, or to *have* ya. He was a bad man. What *he* did was wrong. *You* did nuttin' wrong!"

Her words went directly to Victoria's heart. She sat a lit-tle more upright. "Thank you, Izzy."

"I loves ya, baby."

Comforted, Victoria nestled into the warm body of her dearest friend.

CHAPTER 18

Alicia poured Andrew a cup of coffee, then sat across from him at the table. "You've got sumthin' on your mind, Doc. I can tell."

He sipped his coffee. "I have many things on my mind, but I won't trouble you with my problems. You have more than your fair share."

"Doc, we *both* lost someone we loved. I knows you loved Lijah, too. I don't expect you to keep comin' by here to look after me. I appreciate your company, but I'm shore you have other things you gots to do."

Unable to bear it any longer, he had to tell her. "Alicia . . ." He swallowed hard, then took her hand. "It's my fault Elijah died."

"Don't even say such a thing." After giving his hand a squeeze, she released it and sat back. "How could it be your fault? He was your friend."

Andrew couldn't look at her. "If I'd saved Mrs. Lewis, none of this would've ever happened."

"What's Emma got to do with it?" Warily, he shifted his gaze to look at her. Her eyes had narrowed. "You sayin' Tobias had sumthin' to do with all this?"

"Yes. *Tobias* should've been hung." He closed his eyes.

The silence surrounding him couldn't have been more painful. Then the sound of Alicia's breathing eerily filled the space between them.

He raised his lids to her expressionless face. He owed her a full explanation.

"Victoria's father asked me who'd been following us. I wouldn't tell him it was Tobias. The day they came here for Elijah, Tobias had tried to have his way with Victoria. I believe he would've killed her, but she fought back and got away."

Alicia gasped and clutched her chest. "Oh, Doc. Is she all right?"

"She will be. In time." He choked out the words and looked away.

I hurt everyone I touch.

She tapped his arm. "I still don't understan' how Lijah fits into all this."

Andrew twisted his fingers around his coffee cup. "All Victoria could remember was that the man who hurt her was a large Negro. She told her father she'd scratched him. Because Elijah had been seen in town that day, they mistook him for the man that did it. *Tobias.* So, they came after Elijah."

"But they shoulda known it wadn't him. He had no scratches when he came home from town." Her brow wove, obviously piecing it all together. "They put 'em there, din't they? They knew it wadn't him, so they put 'em there." She covered her mouth and slowly blinked, causing tears to drip onto her face. "I still don't understan' why you say it's your fault. *They* did it to him. Not you."

"I blame myself because I kept my mouth shut and didn't tell Victoria's father who'd been following us. I knew they'd send the Klan. Men shouldn't take the law into their own hands. But my silence killed Elijah." He lowered his eyes and let out a long breath.

"Doc, look at me." She sniffled. "You did what you thought was right! You *always* do. That's what makes you a good man. It's why you was Elijah's friend. He respected you." She took hold of his chin and forced him to face her. "I don't blame ya! Hear me? Elijah woulda stood by you no matter what you decided to do 'bout Tobias. So will I."

Never had words comforted him more.

"You're a good friend, Alicia. A *very* good friend."

"So are you, Doc." She patted his face and sighed. "Look what we's been through together. I don't understan' why things happen the way they does. S'pose God has a plan. But I shore wish He wouldn't make it so hard."

A plan? Why would God want Elijah dead?

He recalled something his mother had always said. "Bad times make us appreciate the good times."

"Mmm . . ." She nodded. "We shore did have some good times. That's what I wanna remember 'bout Lijah. If I went 'round angry all the time over what happened to him, I'd get ate up inside. Wouldn't be any good for the children. Lijah wouldn't want it that way."

Alicia stood and hugged herself. "I gots me an angel lookin' over my shoulder now, an' it warms me inside. I won't lie. I ache every day missin' my man, but I knows someday I'll see him again." She wandered around the table and stood beside Andrew, placing her hands on his shoulders. "I don't never want you to worry 'bout this again. It's done."

Like a rush of warm water cascading down his torso, relief covered him.

Alicia had always tried to give him advice. Maybe if he'd listen to her, his heart could start to heal.

* * *

Andrew faithfully attended all of his instruction with Father O'Meara, making certain Victoria wasn't aware of it. He'd also faithfully had supper with the O'Malley's on both Friday nights and Sundays since Victoria's arrival. He'd learned to appreciate good Irish stew.

Each visit with Victoria became easier. She talked more —though still not herself—and spoke with a soft voice and lowered head.

Her father continued to be overly jovial, pushing them together. After Sunday stew, he requested Andrew's presence once again in his study. They excused themselves from the ladies and walked down the familiar hall. O'Malley shut the door.

"Is there a problem, sir?" Andrew asked.

"Aye, there's a problem! It's high time you ask for her hand. Jake told me you already got the ring. Came in a week ago."

"I was waiting for the proper time." Andrew calmly folded his hands in front of himself.

"Proper time? Me daughter needs to know your intentions. I want her to regain her dignity!" He shook his finger in Andrew's face. "Far as I'm concerned, you need to march out there right now and ask her!"

"No." Andrew stood his ground. "I won't propose to her in your home."

"Where then? She won't leave the house!"

"I believe she's ready, and I know where I want to do it. At least give me that. You've planned everything else."

"Are you getting fresh with me again?" He glared, nostrils flaring.

"No, sir, just speaking my mind. I want this to be meaningful for her. I want to take her somewhere that was special for us before everything happened."

"Special? Did you *have* me daughter?"

"No, sir. I'm saving *that* for our marriage bed."

"Good. Father O'Meara must be teaching you well. So when do you plan to take her to this *special* place?"

"Thursday. For her birthday. I'll have finished my classes with Father O'Meara by then. I'll ask her to marry me and surprise her with my newfound religion. I'll tell her we'll be able to marry in the cathedral. I'm sure it'll please her." Andrew spoke automatically, with little emotion.

"It had better please her! It'll do you well to make her happy."

The plan was set.

* * *

The week flew by. Thursday arrived and Andrew knew what he had to do.

Am I ready?

Unfortunately, he had no choice.

I don't love her.

He cared for her a great deal, but caring wasn't true love. Perhaps forcing the feelings would make them real.

He patted his pocket, which held the ring inside a small box. 18 karat gold, sculpted into the shape of a heart. The gold heart encircled a ruby and there were tiny white pearls to each side. Jake had bragged that the purchase of that one ring equaled a full two month's business. Andrew felt its burden in his salary.

When supper ended, Andrew asked Mr. O'Malley if he could take Victoria for a short ride in his buggy.

The man's face lit up. "Of course! Doesn't that sound fine, Victoria?"

Her mother beamed and clasped her hands to her breast.

"I don't know, Daddy." Victoria didn't sound as enthusiastic.

Andrew took her by the arm. "You're ready, my dear. It'll be all right. " He smiled, receiving one from her in return.

"All right, I'll go."

"You'll need to bundle up good!" Mrs. O'Malley exclaimed. "Izzy, bring Miss Victoria's coat!"

Izzy rushed in with it and Andrew helped Victoria put it on, buttoning it up tight. After putting on his own coat, he escorted her out the door. He lifted her into the buggy and climbed in beside her. He then draped a heavy blanket over her lap. "Are you warm enough?"

"Yes, I'm fine."

As they neared the beach, her body trembled beside him. Maybe it hadn't been wise to bring her to the place where they were first aware they'd been followed.

He put his arm around her, pulling her close. "It's all right, Victoria. I'm here for you."

When they reached the beach, he helped her down and wrapped the blanket over her shoulders. He tried to hold her, but she backed away.

Fortunately, she didn't refuse his hand and allowed him to hold hers. They walked to the smooth rock and he lifted her upon it.

"Why did you bring me here, Andrew?" She stared out at the water.

He turned, following her eyes. The sky looked brilliant, boasting colors of orange and red with wisps of soft white clouds. Breathtaking. Like Victoria herself.

He knelt down before her on one knee, then pulled the box from his pocket and opened it.

Her eyes shifted to him and widened.

He removed the ring. "Victoria, I'd like you to be my wife. Will you marry me?" He extended the ring, waiting for an answer.

"Do you love me, Andrew?"

He hesitated. His dry mouth kept the words stuck somewhere deep inside him. So he thought of Claire, swallowed, and took a breath. "Yes, I love you." Though he looked at Victoria, he envisioned his *true* love.

"Then, yes, I'll marry you." Her face softened with a smile. "I love you, too."

The ring fit her perfectly. Patrick O'Malley had done well.

"Oh, Andrew! It's so beautiful. It's exactly the ring I'd have chosen for myself. How did you ever know?" Her eyes sparkled. A strong glimmer of the old Victoria shone through. Perhaps O'Malley had been right. She needed this.

"I thought it might be something you'd like. I'm glad I was right." She didn't need to know the truth. It would break her.

This would've been an appropriate time for a kiss, but he didn't feel compelled to. Instead, he lifted her from the rock and took her by the hand. They wandered along the beach.

"We'll be able to marry in the cathedral," he said as they walked.

"How?" She stopped and tipped her head. "You aren't Catholic."

"I am now. I've been instructed by Father O'Meara for the past six weeks. My final class was this past Tuesday. I'm a Catholic now."

"Six weeks? You've been plannin' this for some time, haven't you?" She grinned.

"Yes. I've known for quite a while that I wanted to marry you. I knew you'd want to have the ceremony in the church." Seeing her so pleased made it easy to return her smile.

She laid her hand against his chest. "It means a lot to me that you did this. Thank you, Drew." Wrapping her arms around him, she squeezed tight.

She called me Drew. She's starting to heal.

They stood locked in an embrace. She gave no indication she wanted to let go. But when the sun dipped lower on the horizon, he led her back to his buggy.

Once at her home, he walked her to the door, told her goodnight, and kissed her on the forehead.

One step at a time.

Chapter 19

Claire awoke from a restless sleep. *Valentine's Day.*

Gerald lay sleeping soundly beside her.

She got up and dressed as quietly as she could and crept out their door.

As she made her way to the nursery, she stumbled in the darkness. Michael turned over in his crib, but continued to sleep, so she tiptoed down the stairs. Everything had been dead quiet, but then the stair creaked. The second stair from the bottom *always* squeaked and now seemed louder than normal.

She wanted to be alone. Didn't want anyone to be aware of her. She wanted to be invisible for just a short while.

Though she wasn't hungry, she went to the kitchen. A place she felt comfortable. A place to sit for a moment. She'd grown tired; tired of all the secrets. Tired of looking the other way when she caught Henry's eyes on her. Tired of pretending to Gerald there was nothing wrong. He'd been good to her—better than she deserved—but he didn't complete her.

The sun would soon come up, the rooster would crow, and she'd start another day in her existence. Today celebrated lovers and she thought of hers. *Both* of them. She had one, but longed for the other; the one she had no business having. It was a sacrilege. Her heart had been split in two—shared by different men. One side beat strong, the other waited to be resuscitated.

Michael kept her mind busy most of the time. He was active and steadily growing. He'd been transforming before her eyes; becoming more and more like his daddy. No wonder she couldn't let go of Andrew. His presence remained right before her every day of her life.

The door to the kitchen swung open. Henry stood in the doorway and stared at her. "You all right?"

Her heart raced. She wanted to run, but remained calm. "Yes, I'm fine." Not wanting to wake anyone else, she didn't raise her voice. Perhaps she should have.

He nodded at her and retreated.

Odd . . .

Why didn't he come in?

She breathed a sigh of relief.

A few moments later, he returned holding something in his hand. He set it down in front of her and took a seat.

She glanced at it, but didn't touch it. The small box he'd tried to give her at Christmas that held Sarah's wedding ring.

She looked directly at him. "What are you doin', Henry?"

"I figgered maybe you changed your mind by now." He gazed at her, slowly blinking.

"No!" she said in a loud whisper. "I'll never change my mind! I don't want your ring!"

"Claire, I'm tryin' hard, but it's killin' me bein' so close to ya." He reached his hand across the table to hers. She jerked away.

"Then I'll tell Gerald and we'll leave. Then you won't hafta worry 'bout me any longer!" How could he ever think she'd want anything from him? Anger overwhelmed her. It was all she could do to remain seated.

"No! I don't want you to leave. I *never* want you to leave."

"Then get hold of your feelin's. Stop bein' so foolish!"

"I'm a fool for you, Claire." He stood and picked up the box. "Happy Valentine's Day." He pushed the kitchen door open and went back to his room.

She sat there vacantly watching the sunrise out the window. The rooster crowed. Gerald stirred overhead.

Inhaling deeply, she stood and gathered what she needed to make coffee.

Another day.

* * *

Andrew awoke, got out of bed, and dressed for work. He'd become an engaged man; betrothed to a woman he didn't love. Was it fair to her?

He'd come to despise Patrick O'Malley, but wouldn't let Victoria know his feelings. He owed her a comfortable life and intended to provide it for her. If he didn't, O'Malley would make him even more miserable.

No doubt about that.

He'd been invited to have supper with them tonight. Izzy had promised something special for the holiday. On his dinner break he'd go to Parker's to purchase something special for Victoria. Though he didn't like to shop there,

O'Malley had made it clear he expected him to give Jake his business.

Deciding to be bold, he purchased some chocolate for her. Buying it didn't give him the same excitement as it had on the previous occasion. Everything had changed.

"You give Victoria the ring yet?" Jake asked, scratching the back of his head.

"Yes, I gave it to her last night. She accepted my proposal. We're to be married." Andrew spoke matter-of-fact —*unfeeling*—but he didn't like talking to Jake.

"Congrats, Doc! You're gettin' the finest woman in Mobile."

"Yes, I am." Andrew picked up the chocolate and walked toward the door.

He'd nearly gone out when he overheard Jake speaking to another customer.

Did he just mention Victoria?

Andrew could've sworn Jake said something about her ring. O'Malley hadn't been wise putting his faith in Jake Parker. The man was the biggest gossip in all of Mobile, but he'd be a fool to cross O'Malley.

Shaking his head, Andrew quickly left the mercantile.

* * *

Conversation at the supper table revolved around the upcoming wedding. Seeing the spark in Victoria made it worthwhile. Andrew smiled, watching her discuss the arrangements with her mother.

Mrs. O'Malley had secured the use of the church and would have invitations printed as soon as they chose a date. They decided on May seventeenth, a Saturday, at one o'clock in the afternoon. It would be the event of the year.

Patrick O'Malley had the money to pay for it and he would certainly see to it that it was a wedding never to be forgotten.

"Oh, Drew, you *must* invite your daddy!" Victoria exclaimed, wide-eyed.

"My . . . *daddy?*" Andrew hadn't considered him being there.

"Of course. I'm dyin' to meet him." Victoria turned to her father. "Drew's daddy is an attorney in Connecticut. He's a very important man."

"Is he now?" O'Malley asked, looking at Andrew. "You'll need to write him. Tell him to come."

Not a suggestion, the man's words were an order. Victoria wanted it and Andrew would have to deliver.

"I'll write him as soon as I return home this evening," Andrew said coolly.

"It will be lovely to meet a member of your family," Mrs. O'Malley chirped. "I was sad to hear about your mother. Victoria mentioned that she had passed."

"Yes." Andrew lowered his eyes. "It was a long time ago."

"Izzy!" O'Malley bellowed. "Time for cake!"

Izzy came out from the kitchen carrying a heart-shaped cake. She placed it on the table, then brought out plates and a knife. "Want me to cut it Mista O'Malley?"

"No. Shannon may cut the cake." He winked at his wife. "She already has a piece of me heart, now she can cut me a piece of another."

Mrs. O'Malley tittered, took the knife, and began to cut. As she passed the pieces around, Izzy brought out coffee to complete their dessert. When they'd finished, Andrew took Victoria by the hand and led her to the sitting room.

She seemed more relaxed and walked taller than she had. She wore a red dress with a high neckline that covered her scar, but still had no corset or bustle.

He handed her the bar of chocolate. "Happy Valentine's Day, Victoria. I know it's not much, but since I gave you your ring yesterday, I hoped this would suffice."

"May I eat it later? The cake was sweet. I'm not in the mood for chocolate right now."

He understood. Things were very different.

He held her hand. They stared out the window. It had become dark outside, so they could see very little. The light from the lantern in the room gave off an eerie glow. His heart beat steadily, unmoved by her. He simply sat beside a woman he now called his fiancée. Neither spoke.

He needed to break the silence. "Are you tired, Victoria?"

"A bit."

"I should go then." He stood to leave, then helped her to her feet.

"You may kiss me if you'd like, Drew." She raised her face toward him.

After a brief hesitation, he bent down and kissed her, but felt nothing.

She smiled. "That was nice. Thank you."

Forcing a smile, he walked with her to the door, then told her goodnight. She shut the door behind him.

When he returned home, he did as promised and wrote a letter to his father.

February 14, 1873

Dear Father,

For once in my life, I have done as you suggested. I am to be married.

You would approve of her. She is beautiful beyond words, young, and from the most prominent family in Mobile. Her father, Patrick O'Malley, owns the bank and comes from a long line of money. He and his wife, Shannon, are exactly the sort of family you would want me associated with. They have but one daughter, Victoria, and it appears I have stolen her heart.

We are to be married on Saturday, the seventeenth of May. They have requested your presence and I would like you to be there as well. You will receive a formal invitation. However, I wanted to write to you immediately, so you can make your plans.

The Mobile Hotel is a fine place to stay, and if you would like me to reserve a room for you, I would be happy to. I will reserve it in the name of John Fletcher, to protect your name.

I hope you can come a few days early, so we may spend some time together and attempt to settle our grievances.

I look forward to your reply,

Your son,

Andrew

He mailed the letter the following day. Would his father take time out of his busy schedule to attend the wedding? He despised Alabama, but Andrew hoped he cared enough for *him* to make a small sacrifice.

CHAPTER 20

Completely naked, Victoria stared at herself in her full-length mirror. She tilted her head from one side to the other. She then turned sideways and gazed at her curves. What she saw pleased her, until she moved her hair to one side, revealing the scar on her neck. It would always be a reminder of that horrible day.

When Andrew kissed her, something had changed. There'd been no passion or fire as there had been before. She blamed herself.

What's wrong with you? Will you let some disgustin' man ruin your life?

Standing up straight, she placed her hands under her breasts and pushed them upwards. Her lips curved into a smile and she grabbed her underclothes.

"Izzy! Izzy, I need you!"

The woman scurried into her room. "What's wrong, Miss Victoria?"

"Where's my corset?" Victoria dug into her bureau, flinging garments over her shoulder. "I need my corset!"

"Yes, Miss Victoria. It's in the bottom drawer."

Victoria yanked it open and giggled as she removed her beloved undergarment. "Help me with it, Izzy!"

Izzy placed it over her waist. "Mmm, mmm." She shook her head.

"Pull it real tight!" Every breath Victoria took came out in rapid bursts.

Izzy pulled and pulled. "You goin' somewhere?" She tied off the strings and stepped back.

"Yes. I'm goin' shoppin'." Victoria raised her head high and strode to her wardrobe. "I need new dresses. If I'm to be a doctor's wife I need to look like one." She grimaced at her ugly clothes. But since they were all she had, she put on the plain blue dress, then went to her vanity and started fixing her hair. After pulling it up on her head, she positioned a blue bonnet on top of it.

"I'll need my coat, Izzy." She proceeded down the stairs.

"You shore you're ready for this, Miss Victoria?" Izzy bustled behind her, holding her coat.

Victoria stopped on the staircase and turned, taking Izzy's hands in her own. "Yes, I believe I am!" She grinned, put on her coat, and in no time headed out the door.

As she walked down the familiar street to the mercantile, she remembered Izzy's words, *Hold your head high,* and she did.

Folks on the street whispered as she passed, but she didn't care. She'd grown tired of feeling sorry for herself. After all, she had a ring on her finger, and a man who loved her, and no one could take that from her.

She pushed the door open at Parker's, and her heart beat so hard she lost her breath. It all came rushing back to her and stung like a slap of cold water in the face. For a brief moment, she looked at the floor, then inhaled deeply and stood up straight. She walked tall and proud to the counter.

Jake's mouth dropped. "Mornin', Miss O'Malley."

"Good mornin', Mr. Parker." Why not be cheerful and shock him even more? "I'd like you to order some scarves for me—*silk* scarves—one in every color of the rainbow. Can you do that?"

"Yes, Miss O'Malley." He grabbed a catalog. "Whatever you need."

"I also want to look through the catalog for some dresses. The very latest fashion of course." She pursed her lips. "Have you any in stock?"

"Yes, Miss O'Malley. Right where I always keep 'em. I think you might find sumthin' you like." He grinned from ear to ear.

She rushed to the dress rack and her eyes lit up. "Mr. Parker! It's as though you ordered these just for me." She thumbed through, tingling from head to toe. "Imported . . ." Unable to control herself, she tittered. "The fabric is exquisite!"

"Glad you like 'em." Jake beamed.

She selected five in an assortment of colors, then flipped through the catalog and ordered half a dozen more.

Until the silk scarves arrived, she intended to sew some and selected material for that purpose. She would make her own fashion statement; a scarf at her neck and a plunging neckline.

Brilliant! Hide her scar and show her assets.

Victoria O'Malley had returned.

* * *

Victoria went home with her arms loaded down. Izzy met her at the door.

"You wadn't foolin' when you said you was goin' shoppin'." Izzy helped her with the packages.

"I bought a few dresses and some material to make scarves." She flitted off into the living room, pulled the material onto the floor, and got out a pair of scissors. She cut away at it, then began to sew.

Izzy stood back with her hands on her hips, shaking her head.

Victoria ignored her stance, with no desire to know her thoughts. "I want to go and see Drew. I want to surprise him." She frantically pulled the needle in and out of the material.

"You gonna go to the hospital? He'll be comin' by tonight to see ya."

"Well, I want to see him right away, as soon as I finish this." She continued sewing on the red fabric. She'd purchased a red dress trimmed with white lace, much like the one she'd worn last Valentine's Day but had torn to shreds. "This will look fine!"

"You best slow down or you might stick yourself."

"You worry too much, Izzy." Almost instantly, she pricked her finger. She put it in her mouth, blinking at Izzy.

The woman grinned, then chuckled. "I ain't gonna say it."

"I should always listen to you. I'll slow down. Unless— Izzy—will you help me sew? Please?"

"I was wonderin' when you was gonna ask." Izzy took the needle and thread, while Victoria sat and watched, nursing her finger.

When she'd finished the scarf, Victoria took it and went to her room. She removed her plain blue dress and cast it aside, never wanting to wear it again. She pulled the red dress over her head and it pleasingly plunged. A slight adjustment of her bosom created the perfect image in the mirror. At least . . . from *below* the neck. But after she tied the newly made scarf around her wretched scar, nothing showed that she didn't want seen.

While gazing in the mirror, she noticed Izzy walk into the room behind her.

"You look fine, Miss Victoria." Izzy placed a hand on her shoulder. "How do you feel?"

Victoria turned from side to side evaluating her reflection. "I feel like . . . *me*. Will you help with my hair?"

"Course I will. It's what I do." Izzy grabbed the brush and pulled it through her hair. She then rolled it and shaped it into soft curls. After pinning it partially up on her head, she placed a white cap hat on top. The hat tied under her neck with a wide white satin bow. The red and white together at her neck matched the dress to perfection.

"You're a picture!" Izzy exclaimed.

"Thank you." Victoria kissed her on the cheek.

With her head held higher than ever, she strolled through town once again on her way to City Hospital. It was late afternoon and Andrew would soon be getting off work. She wore a coat, but left it unbuttoned, wanting him to see every part of her.

What's takin' him so long?

Yes, she could have gone in, but didn't want to disturb him. Besides, she wanted to surprise him. So she paced with determined anticipation outside the front door of the hospital.

* * *

Victoria?

Andrew stopped and stared, then blinked several times making sure she was real. Before him stood the old Victoria whom he'd hoped would one day emerge. Tipping his head, he continued to stare. It seemed too soon.

She ran into his arms. "Drew, I missed you!"

"Victoria? I can't believe you're here."

"Do you like my new dress?" She coyly bit her bottom lip and backed away from him, then turned in a circle.

"Yes, I do very much." She looked amazing and as beautiful as ever, but something didn't seem quite right.

"I still have that chocolate bar at home, Drew. Why don't you come over and help me eat it?" She stepped toward him, then kept her eyes on him while moving her hand over her breast.

"I'll take you home, Victoria."

"I like chocolate!" She puckered her lips and moved in for a kiss.

"Not here," he scolded. Glancing around, he hoped no one had been watching. "Let me take you home." He took her by the arm and led her to his buggy. As he put his hands on her waist to lift her in, she bent down and kissed him.

"I want you, Drew," she said, licking her lips.

"Not now." He put her in the buggy and drove her home. He found her abnormal behavior disturbing. She'd gone from introverted to overly aggressive, and he hoped she'd land somewhere in between.

"I can't stay," he said, helping her from the buggy. I have somewhere else I need to go this evening."

She stuck out her bottom lip. "But . . . what about the chocolate?"

"Why don't you save it for later? You need some rest. You look a little tired."

"When will I see you again?" She continued to pout.

"Tomorrow for supper. Irish stew."

"Until then." She wrapped her arms around his neck and gave him a deep, sensual kiss. "Think about chocolate," she whispered, then walked into her house.

Andrew watched her go. It was as though she'd become drunk on herself. He felt sorry for her. But nothing more.

* * *

Andrew arrived the next evening at precisely six o'clock for Irish stew.

"Good to see ya, lad!" O'Malley chimed.

This had become routine and most likely the way their lives would be forever; always going to the O'Malley's on Sunday evenings for Irish stew. Could he endure it?

His eyes moved to Victoria, who stood statuesque at the top of the stairs. She'd dressed in a lavender gown trimmed in deep purple lace. It appeared she'd permanently returned to her former style. A corset had her pushed up and prominently displayed, and she carried herself in a way that showed pride in her protruding bosom.

As she cascaded down the stairway, she held her shoulders back and her head high. She'd tied a deep purple scarf around her neck. Her hair had been left down and flowed over her shoulders.

When their eyes met, she seductively bit her bottom lip. She then brushed one hand across her neckline and slowly moved it down toward her breasts.

Andrew swallowed hard. She took his breath.

Mrs. O'Malley grabbed his hand and squeezed it. "Isn't she beautiful?"

"Yes, she is," he replied and took Victoria's hand.

Once again they seated themselves in the dining room, while Victoria's mother served the stew.

Victoria gazed across the table at him. Each bite she took furthered the seduction she'd started on the stairway. Her eyes affixed to his as she placed the spoon in her mouth, then drew it out slowly. Her tongue flicked the corners of her mouth, while her eyes penetrated him even further.

Sweat beaded on his brow. After dabbing it away with his napkin, he loosened his collar.

Victoria pursed her lips, then formed them into a wicked smile.

"So, how's the guest list coming?" Mrs. O'Malley asked, apparently oblivious to the game at play.

Andrew cleared his throat. "Mine's done. I wrote to my father."

Victoria's father gaped at him with raised brows. "That's the sum of your list? Your father?"

"There are a number of people I work with whom I'll invite. But not many. I doubt you'd want me inviting some of my *other* friends." Andrew continued eating, trying *not* to look at Victoria.

"Those in Shanty Town?" O'Malley asked with a grunt.

"Yes. I was quite certain you wouldn't approve."

"You're learning lad," the man said almost under his breath, then grabbed a roll from the center of the table and bit into it. "Victoria will have plenty to invite."

"Nearly the entire city," she said, grinning.

The entire city?

The thought of entertaining so many people made Andrew's stomach uneasy. But a flashback of Claire turned his uneasiness to ache.

I'll put a notice on the church door and invite the whole town.

The excitement in her voice remained in his mind. He closed his eyes, attempting to erase the memory, then returned his attention once again to Victoria. Her grin hadn't disappeared, but she now accompanied it with slowly batting eyes.

Her mother laughed. "That's far too many, Victoria. How will we ever fit them into the cathedral?"

"I'm not serious, Mama," Victoria said. "I'll narrow the list to two hundred." She dipped her finger in her water glass, then glided it leisurely below her scarf. Water dripped toward her cleavage.

Andrew shut his mouth tight to keep from gaping.

"Are you warm, dear?" Mrs. O'Malley asked her.

"No, Mama. I'm *hot*." Victoria's tongue swirled around her lips.

Mrs. O'Malley fanned her hand in Victoria's direction. "Perhaps you need to step outside a moment and get a breath of fresh air?"

"That's a very good idea. Drew, would you like to join me?" Victoria stood and moved around the table behind him.

"Yes. I just finished eating. Fresh air sounds . . . *refreshing*." He rose and took her arm and they hurried out the front door.

The moment it shut, she leaned against it and yanked him to her.

"What are you doing, Victoria?" Why did he bother asking?

"You know what I'm doin'. I want you." She kissed his neck while letting her hands wander over his chest.

"We still need to wait." He wouldn't even consider having her in this state.

"Kiss me!" She grabbed hold of him and kissed him hard and deep.

He felt nothing.

"What's wrong?" She backed away.

"This . . . this just doesn't feel right. I'm sorry."

"It's because of *him,* isn't it?" Her eyes lowered.

"No. *No.* You just need to slow down. I want you, but when the time's right. That's not now. We'll be married in a few months and we'll have plenty of time for *everything.*"

"I don't believe you. You don't want me anymore." She sighed, then put her arms around him and leaned her head against his chest.

He stroked her hair, then gave her a soft kiss on the top of her head, grateful she'd calmed. "I want you to be my wife. How much more could I want you?"

She raised her head and peered into his eyes.

The look she gave him prompted him to kiss her. A *real* kiss. Sweet and sincere. It felt right. "Let's go in. I don't want you to get cold." He put his hand on the doorknob, but she stopped him from opening it.

"Wait," she whispered. "Just one more kiss."

Obliging her with a more passionate kiss, she seemed satisfied.

At least for the time being.

Chapter 21

Spring had come and in one month Michael would be a year old. He'd crawled the knees out of his pants and Claire wanted to go into the city to buy material for him. Sewing something for herself also appealed to her. She hadn't made a new dress since he'd been born.

Since Gerald needed to get supplies for the shop, he gladly agreed to take her. The roads were muddy from the thaw, but the warmer air and sunshine made up for the inconvenience of the mud.

As usual, Henry insisted they charge their purchases to him at Parker's Mercantile. Gerald tried to convince him it wasn't necessary, but Henry persisted, stating it was the least he could do for all the hard work Claire did around the house.

She wished Gerald would have argued the issue, preferring not to take anything from Henry. But Gerald accepted his offer and they went to Parker's.

Jake acted as cordial as ever and more jovial than usual.

"You're in a fine mood, Mr. Parker," Claire said as she made her selections. She perched Michael on her hip.

"Can't help myself. Business is good. Town's all abuzz with the big weddin' comin' up."

"Weddin'?" she asked with a polite smile. "What weddin's that?"

"Victoria O'Malley an' Doc Fletcher. Can't believe y'all haven't heard 'bout it."

Claire's heart stopped and her throat instantly cinched tight. "The young redhead?"

"Yep. Since her daddy owns the bank, it's gonna be the biggest weddin' this city's ever seen. Folks is buyin' all kinds a things from me for weddin' gifts. Not to mention all the things her daddy's buyin' for the weddin' itself." He grinned from ear to ear. "Business ain't never been this good."

Gerald stepped up beside her. "Are you talkin' 'bout Dr. *Andrew* Fletcher?" He piled his supplies on the counter.

"Yep. You know him?"

"I met him a while back. Shod his horse. Seemed like a nice fella." He put his arm around Claire and grinned, then looked at Jake. "So he found him a bride? I'm glad. Every man needs a good woman." He gave her a squeeze.

Jake bent low over the counter. "Folks is surprised Doc wanted her after what that Negro done to her. You know he ravished her right out behind this here store." He'd lowered his voice but seemed to enjoy telling them.

Claire looked down, appalled. The first time she'd heard him talking to those young women about what had happened to Victoria, she'd been disgusted by the conversation. And now, Jake had repeated the horrid tale. Had he told everyone in Mobile? How could he speak so openly about something so private?

Gerald shook his head. "Poor woman. Doc's a good man for marryin' her."

Even though Gerald gave Jake a look that she knew begged him to be quiet about the matter, *she* couldn't remain silent. "It's not polite to talk 'bout folks that way. Regardless of what happened. It's not sumthin' you should be discussin'."

Jake stood upright and twisted his mouth. "Sorry, ma'am, if I offended ya. But you don't need to worry 'bout that Negro. We took care a him." He smiled as if what he'd said would make everything all right.

Wanting to leave as quickly as possible, she pointed to another bolt of cloth. "Just two yards of that one, please?"

It took great effort making the request. She could scarcely breathe. As wrong as it might be, she was jealous. Just thinking about Andrew with another woman brought tears to her eyes, but she couldn't let them fall in front of Gerald.

Why wasn't she happy for Andrew? Victoria was a lovely girl, but if Jake had spoken the truth, Andrew might be getting himself into a difficult situation.

Jake's cheerful disposition had been squelched and she blamed herself. However, he might think twice about revealing such intimate details in the future. And though he'd upset her, she never felt good about making someone feel bad. Perhaps getting him talking again would ease his discomfort.

"When's the weddin'?" she asked.

"May seventeenth," Jake replied with a hint of a smile. "It's gonna be sumthin'. Too bad you wasn't invited."

"We don't really know 'em," Gerald said. "But I hope they'll be as happy as Claire an' me. If you see the doctor, tell him I'm real happy for him, all right?"

"I'll do that." While Jake tallied their purchases, Claire walked away and moved to the window, holding Michael closer than ever.

May seventeenth is so soon.

Her entire body ached. Keeping herself from crying wouldn't be easy.

"Claire?" Gerald's voice startled her out of her depression. "You need anythin' else?"

Taking a deep breath, she faced him. "No. I've got everythin' I need." She shifted toward the glass and stared blankly down the street.

Could he be close? *Is he with her?* Her chest tightened. She kissed Michael's cheek and raked her fingers through his hair, thinking of his daddy.

"Mama!" his little voice chirped and he patted her face.

"I love you," she said and drew him in even closer.

Gerald laid his hand on her shoulder. "Let's go home."

Jake followed them out and placed their packages in the wagon, then nodded to Claire. She couldn't say a word, but forced a smile. Gerald helped her into the wagon, then lifted Michael up onto her lap.

"You all right, Claire?" He hopped up beside them. "You look kinda pale."

"I'm not feelin' very well."

"Just come on all of a sudden?"

"Yes. Just get me home." She said nothing more and he didn't prod her. The concern in his eyes broke her heart, but she couldn't tell him what troubled her. Her head reeled. She wanted to cry or yell, or do most anything to make the pain in her heart stop.

Least I have Michael. The only part of Andrew she could *ever* have. Victoria would have the rest. Envy had made her miserable and tore at her insides. The moment she walked through their front door, she wanted nothing more than to lie down.

"Go on," Gerald said and took Michael from her arms. "You look like you're comin' down with sumthin'."

"Thank you." She trudged up the stairs to their room and shut the door.

As she laid her head on the pillow, tears fell. She couldn't have Andrew, but she couldn't bear the thought of someone else having him. How could she deny him the kind of love she had with Gerald? She shouldn't feel this way, but her broken heart couldn't be mended.

Maybe sleep would give her peace. In her dreams, she hoped to be with him.

The only way she could be.

* * *

"Claire!" Gerald jostled her shoulder. "Claire! Wake up! You gotta see this!"

She jerked upright. "What is it? What's wrong?"

"Come quick! It's Michael!" He took her by the hand and raced with her down the stairs. Her heart pounded, fearing the worst.

Henry sat on the living room sofa holding Michael's hands with his fingers. A broad grin stretched across Michael's chubby cheeks. He giggled and cooed.

Gerald knelt down on the floor. "All right, Michael. Do it again. Come to Daddy." He stretched out his hands.

Henry released Michael's hands and he walked step-by-step toward Gerald. His plump little legs wobbled to and fro, but he took five steps and didn't fall.

"He's walkin'!" Claire exclaimed, holding her hands to her face. She rushed to Michael and scooped him into her arms. "You're such a big boy!"

After kissing Michael out of utter joy, she turned to Gerald, not quite so joyful. "Gerald Alexander don't you ever scare me like that again! I thought sumthin' was wrong."

"Sorry, Claire." He encircled her with his arm. "I was excited. Do babies usually walk at eleven months?"

"I don't know. But ours does." She giggled, then sighed. "Now he's really gonna start gettin' into things."

She set him on the floor, hoping for a repeat performance.

Henry put his arms out. "Come to Uncle Henry." He waved him in and Michael toddled back to him. "I love ya." Henry lifted him up, then kissed him on the head.

Michael bent over backward reaching for Gerald. "Dada!"

"Reckon he wants *me*," Gerald said and took him from Henry.

"He's a daddy's boy," Henry said. "One day you'll hafta teach him how to shoe."

"Slow down," Claire said, waving her hands in the air. "Why do y'all want him to grow up so fast?"

"I don't," Gerald said. "I just love watchin' him grow."

He set Michael on his rocking horse, then stood beside him, laughing and talking. The two of them had become inseparable.

Claire felt ashamed for the tears she'd shed. She'd been wrong to envy Victoria. Everything she ever needed in life lay right here before her. Andrew deserved the same joy.

She'd prepare supper and do her best to forget about her trip to the city.

CHAPTER 22

Andrew lay awake staring blankly toward the ceiling. Tormented by Victoria, he couldn't sleep.

Though he'd cautioned her parents that her behavior would be different because of her ordeal, he didn't expect this. Calming her had been difficult, and he could never compel her to simply converse with him. Whenever they were alone, she didn't want to talk. She only wanted him to hold, kiss, and caress her.

Worst of all, she kept pushing him to take her completely. But he didn't want her and she knew it. She'd said it, and he'd lied only to appease her.

Out of obligation, he'd marry her and take her to his bed. O'Malley had trapped him, and it made him resent her.

A terrible way to start a marriage. I need to overcome my resentment and learn how to love her.

The letter from his father added to his insomnia. He'd read it more than once, surprised that the man planned to come a full two weeks before the wedding. He'd be arriving by train on Saturday, the third of May, stated that he hoped they *could* settle their grievances and he looked forward to meeting Victoria. Would he be able to see through the façade?

How can I explain to him that I'm marrying a woman I don't love?

And why was he coming so early? He assumed he'd be too busy to take such time away from his work.

Perhaps he cares more for me than I realized?

Thinking about how he'd make amends with his father, he finally slept.

* * *

Victoria huffed. Andrew wasn't behaving like a devoted fiancé. On the contrary, he'd become distant. Even when they were together, his mind was somewhere else.

Why did he ever propose?

She blamed her tarnished image on his lack of affection, but wouldn't let it ruin everything for her. She was determined to find out if her suspicions about Andrew were correct.

It was a Friday in the middle of April—just one month until their wedding day—and she set her plan in motion. It started with supper at her home. This had become a part of their weekly routine, so he wouldn't expect anything out of the ordinary. However, he had a tendency to leave shortly after the meal, scarcely giving her more than a simple kiss goodnight. Their routine couldn't have been more boring.

They'd finished their meal. *Time to go to work.* "Drew, I'd love to go for a ride this evenin'. It's been such a long time." She looked at him across the table and batted her eyes. Then she tipped her head ever-so-slightly to one side.

His brows narrowed, then his face softened into a smile. "That sounds like a fine idea."

"I agree," her mama said. "You two need to get out more. I know it can't be enjoyable to sit here with us old folks."

"Aye," her daddy chimed in. "'Tis a fine evening. Weather is suitable for a nice ride."

Andrew stood and moved around the table to help her from her chair. She took his arm and they went out the door to his buggy. Her heart fluttered with anticipation.

As he lifted her in, she squeezed the bulging muscle in his arm. If only he wanted *her* as much as she wanted *him*. When he took his place beside her, she set her hand on his leg and began a slow, sensual caress.

Might as well get things started.

He glanced at her, then immediately faced forward. "The beach?"

"No. I want to see where you live."

He stopped the buggy and turned to face her. "Your father wouldn't like it. You know I live by the shanties."

"I don't care. I want to see your home." She kept her voice soft, but firm. "Please, Drew?"

After letting out a long breath, he shook his head. "Very well." He snapped the reins. "Let's go home, Sam."

The sun would be setting soon. Just in time. She muffled a giggle, thinking about what she planned to do.

As they drove further from town, her heart fell, but she quickly recovered, not wanting anything to spoil her mood. The buggy jerked to a halt in front of a very small house. Several shanties could be seen further up the road. Her stomach knotted.

I'll convince him to move.

He let out a loud sigh and helped her down. Then he led her to the door. Without saying a word, he opened it and motioned her inside.

She stepped through and nearly gasped at the sparsely furnished place. "You like it here?"

"Yes, I do. It's home. Would you like to see the land before the sun sets? It's very beautiful."

She forced a smile. "Not tonight."

"Would you like to sit?" He pulled out a chair.

"No, Drew." She couldn't have imagined a home worse than this. "Drew?"

"Yes?"

"Do you still love me?" She couldn't look at him.

He pulled her into his arms. "Yes, Victoria, I love you." He kissed her forehead.

Raising her face to his, he kissed her lips. Much better, but she wanted more. They were alone—far away from anyone else—and she intended to have him. No more excuses.

She took him by the hand and easily found the bedroom. At least he had a bed. She crossed to it and lay down. Doing her best to ignore his poor quality furnishings, she focused on him. His eyes moved over her, then he lay down beside her.

No doubt she'd succeed.

Still the most handsome man she'd ever laid eyes on, she longed to see all of him and started by unbuttoning his shirt. His broad, smooth chest beckoned her and she couldn't resist kissing every inch of it. The sensation awakened her passion and caused her to breathe harder and harder.

Her hands wandered. Her kisses intensified. She snaked her fingers further down his body. Though she wanted his hands on her, she didn't mind being the aggressor. But when her hand came to rest between his legs, her passion turned to frustration. *No arousal?*

She jerked upright. "What's wrong with you?"

He rolled away from her, then sat on the edge of the bed with his head in his hands.

"Why don't you want me?" She couldn't hold back her tears. "I've done everythin' I can think of, and yet I know you don't want me."

"Please . . . don't cry, Victoria." He faced her. "It's not you. I just can't do this now."

"When? Do you think sumthin' special will happen on our weddin' night that'll change the way you feel 'bout me? I *know* I'm desirable! Even that Negro wanted me!" She shifted her body away from him, so angry that she couldn't look him in the eye.

Andrew took her chin in his hand, forcing her to face him. "You don't *ever* want a man to want you the way he did."

"I just want *you* to want me." She blinked hard and droplets trickled down her cheek. He wiped them with his fingertips and his gentleness calmed her. "You used to want me. Before he did what he did. I don't understand what changed. You know he didn't have me." Her unstoppable tears flowed.

"I know. But he still hurt you and I don't want to rush you. I want to wait until the time's right and I know we're both ready. We have our whole lives ahead of us." He cradled her in his arms and let her cry.

For some reason, it felt good to cry. And his soft words gave her comfort. Though this wasn't the night she'd planned, maybe it was what she truly needed.

"Victoria . . ." He brushed his lips across her damp cheek. "You need to start talking to me—let me know what you're thinking about—how you're feeling. I still don't know who you are."

She sniffled. "I'm simply what you see." Slowly, she raised her eyes to meet his. "I'll still marry you, Drew. I don't think anyone else would have me."

Before he could respond, she stood and faced away from him. "Drew? I need to know if the rumors are true."

"What rumors?"

She turned around. "Did my daddy choose the ring you gave me?"

His eyes opened wide, then his head dropped, shaking. His silence pierced her heart.

"You don't need to answer," she whispered. "I can tell by your actions that he did." She walked toward the door. "I'd like you to take me home now." *The sooner, the better.*

"Of course," he mumbled, buttoning his shirt. He then opened the door and helped her into the buggy. They were silent until they reached her home.

After he helped her down, he attempted to give her a goodbye kiss, but she turned her head. "Goodnight, Andrew." She walked up the pathway to her door, opened it, and went inside.

She didn't look back.

* * *

Andrew returned home, lay down on his bed, and once again stared at the ceiling. His life seemed hopeless. He never should've brought her here, but she'd been so eager and now he knew why. She thought she'd get him to bed her.

Why'd I let her take me into the bedroom?

As her doctor, he saw a troubled woman—manic one minute, then dour the next. She was struggling to find herself and trusted him to help her. He'd let her down, but couldn't remove the thoughts of the last woman who'd shared his bed.

Claire. The woman he'd intended to share his life with. Victoria didn't belong there.

How'd she ever find out about the ring? Jake Parker had to have told. He was the only one other than her father who knew.

Damn him.

Seeing her pain tore his soul in two. He'd have to do better.

Rolling over, he closed his eyes. The smell of her perfume lingered on his pillow.

I'll wash it tomorrow.

* * *

Andrew had been attending Sunday Mass with Victoria ever since his *conversion* to Catholicism. After his evening with her, he didn't feel like attending this week and chose to stay in bed and sleep. The only relief he had from the frustrations of his day-to-day life.

It was nearly ten o'clock in the morning and he was still in bed when a knock on his door forced him from the sheets. Assuming someone must need a doctor; he jumped up and went to answer it.

"Miss Izzy?" Not at all who he expected.

"Hey, Doc. Mind if I come in?" She wore a simple blue dress, Sunday hat, and a glum expression indicating she might be ill.

"Of course. Please do." He stepped aside so she could enter. "Have a seat while I get dressed." He motioned to a chair at his table and exited quickly, wishing he'd taken time to grab a shirt. His flannel pajama bottoms were not exactly appropriate attire for a reputable doctor.

"No need on my account," Izzy yelled after him, chuckling.

Her response made him grin and relax as he threw on his clothes. She was undoubtedly *not* ill.

When he returned, he found her nervously drumming her fingers.

"Are you all right, Miss Izzy?" He placed his hand on hers, stilling her movement.

"I knew you wouldn't go to services this mornin'. Seems sumthin' happened 'tween you and Miss Victoria Friday night. She cried all day yesterday. Worst of all, she wouldn't talk to me 'bout it."

"I hate to hear that."

"Doc, I know she ain't been right since what happened to her, but I'm even more worried now. Did the two a you have words?"

"You could say we did." *Maybe she can help.* "Izzy, you know her better than anyone. I feel like I don't know her at all, and I'm going to marry her in a month's time. Her emotions are so frail. She goes from giddy to gloomy with the turn of a head. I don't understand her." It felt good to have someone to talk to.

"She's still very much a child in many ways, Doc. But she has desires like a woman. She just ain't learned how to control 'em." Her eyes opened wide.

"She's always been very forward with her intentions." He'd not meant for the conversation to go in *this* direction. Talking about intimacy seemed highly inappropriate, but since Izzy brought it up, he'd try. "I tried to make it clear to her that it was best to wait until we're married."

"As it should be." Izzy smiled and patted his hand. "But if you know Victoria at all, then you know she don't like to wait for nuttin'."

"I know." He cleared his throat. "But after what happened to her, I thought it was an even better reason to wait. I feel sorry for her. I blame myself for what happened."

"Pity ain't love, Doc. Blamin' yourself won't do her no good neither. If you love her, then start actin' like a man an' take control."

"Alicia Tarver told me almost the same thing. She's been worried about me. Afraid I'm getting myself into something I don't want."

"Are ya?"

"Maybe so. But I don't have a choice. Just ask O'Malley." The words came out of his mouth and he wished he could take them back.

"Mista O'Malley put you up to this?" Izzy frowned. "Don't you *wanna* marry Miss Victoria?"

"I *have* to marry her. I'll do all I can to learn how to love her." He stood from the table and paced the floor.

"That ain't the way it's s'pose to be, Doc. It ain't right for you *or* her."

"But that's the way it is, Izzy. Sometimes choices are made for us. We have no control over them."

"I don't like it!" Izzy pounded her fist on the table, startling him. "I've raised her since she was a child. Watched her become a woman. She deserves *love,* Doc!" Tears welled in her eyes, tugging at his heart.

"Izzy." He put his hands on her shoulders. "I promise you. I won't hurt her, I *will* love her."

"I'm countin' on it." She sat silently for a moment, then wiped tears from her eyes and took a breath. "Now you listen. Be shore to go for stew this evenin' an' be gentle with Miss Victoria. I din't love her so much at first neither, but now she's like my own child. Never could have one a my own." She lowered her head, whispering her final words.

"I'm sorry." He took his seat, then reached for her hands.

"It's a'right. I'm long over it. My man died years ago. Folks never understood my wantin' to care for white folks, but it gave me a purpose. I wouldn't have it any other way."

"They're lucky to have you. Especially Victoria." He caressed her hand. "I'll go to supper this evening. I'll clear my head and do whatever I can to try and please Victoria. I promise."

"Thank ya, Doc. Always said you was a good man." She touched his cheek, then lightly patted it. "I best be goin'. Looks like you gots some work to do 'round here. Want me to find someone to hep ya?" She gazed around his little house and frowned. It spoke volumes. He'd never been a good housekeeper.

"Thank you, Izzy. I think I can manage." He helped her to her feet and walked with her outside.

"Your property's beautiful, Doc." Tipping her head back, she smiled into the sun, then scanned the area. "Shame you gots to leave it."

"I know." He sighed. He hated the thought of selling his home and would wait until the last moment possible to do it. "I'm glad you came by, Izzy."

"Me, too, Doc." She waved to him as she walked down the road toward her home.

For a moment he stood and watched her, then went back inside. He had a lot to do.

* * *

Andrew arrived on time for Irish stew that night at the O'Malley's. He was greeted with the usual handshake at the door from Victoria's father and a warm smile from her mother.

He'd barely gotten through the door when Mrs. O'Malley pulled him aside. "Victoria's been a might glum lately."

O'Malley called her down for supper, but she didn't come. His wife urged him to try again, but she still didn't respond.

"Shall I look in on her?" Andrew asked, and they readily agreed to let him go to her room.

When he went in, he found her lying on the bed. She had her back to him and had curled up in a ball with her head on the pillow. She was fully dressed—right down to her shoes—but she lay there not moving.

"I know that's you, Andrew," she whispered. "I know your footsteps."

"Yes, it's me. Are you well?"

"Why didn't you come to Mass this mornin'?" She didn't move.

"I—I didn't think you'd want me there after the other evening." He kept his distance at the far side of her room.

"Why wouldn't I? You're my fiancé." Her words sounded unemotional and matter-of-fact.

He pulled a chair up beside her bed and sat. "Victoria, we've both been through some difficult times. You more than I. I'd like to suggest something." He'd given this a lot of thought since his talk with Izzy. Victoria deserved a man who would love her, and he had to try harder.

"What, Andrew?"

"I want us to start over. Forget everything that has happened over the past few months and start fresh. You deserve that from me." He put his hand on her shoulder.

Her body relaxed beneath his touch. "Is it possible? To forget *everythin*?"

He cleared his throat. "Miss O'Malley, I'm Dr. Fletcher. *Andrew* Fletcher. But I'd be happy if you called me *Drew*."

Finally, she turned toward him. A smile warmed her face. "Drew, I'm Victoria, and you can call me . . . *Victoria*."

"It's a pleasure to meet you, Victoria." He bent down and gave her a tender kiss on the lips.

"That's some introduction. I'm very happy to make your acquaintance . . . *Drew*."

He wrapped his arms around her and kissed her again. They'd started over.

This time it felt right.

Taking her by the hand, he led her to the supper table. After they took their respective seats, she looked at him with warmth he'd not seen in some time. Her parents also appeared pleased, much to his relief.

"Have you heard from your father?" Mr. O'Malley asked.

"As a matter of fact, I have, sir. He'll be arriving by train on the third of May. In plenty of time for you and Mrs. O'Malley to get to know him before the wedding."

"That will be lovely," Mrs. O'Malley said. "I'll have him join us for me stew."

"I'm certain he'd enjoy that," Andrew said with a grin, then he winked at Victoria.

She coyly tipped her head.

When they finished eating, Andrew suggested he and Victoria might spend some time in the sitting room. Again, he received no objections from her parents. He escorted her down the hall to the settee. He sat first and tapped the seat next to him, then she sat. Things had definitely changed.

"Victoria," he said, as he pulled a box from his coat pocket, "I have something for you." He handed it to her.

"What is it?"

"Open it," he laughed. "I picked it out just for you."

With quivering hands, she opened the small box and pulled out the gold heart-shaped necklace that he prayed would help set things right between them. The golden heart encircled a small ruby. "Oh, Drew. It's beautiful. Please put it on me."

The joy on her face warmed him and he happily fastened the chain around her neck. It fell beneath her ever-present scarf and graced her bosom.

"I give you my heart, Victoria." He took her hand in his. "Will you take it?"

"Oh, yes. I will." With renewed eagerness she slid her arms around his body, then kissed him slowly. Her mouth moved with his as though she'd found something she'd been searching for. Possibly because she knew this gift had been one *he* chose; not something her father had. They'd truly started over.

CHAPTER 23

In one week, Michael would be a year old. Able to walk steadily now, Claire chased him around the house trying to keep him out of things. He'd become an exhausting joy.

In the mood for a glass of sweet tea punch, she tucked him in the crib for his afternoon nap and went down the stairs to the kitchen. It would be nice to relax for a brief moment.

Gerald was in the shop shoeing a horse and she thought Henry was with him. But as she passed by his bedroom, she heard him.

Is he cryin'?

She'd never gone into Henry's room in all the time she'd lived here. It was his personal space. And though she'd wash and dry his bedding, he always brought it to her and would put it on the bed himself. He did the same with his laundry. After she laundered his clothes, she'd leave them on the sofa for him to put away. It was almost like an un-written rule of the house: Henry's room was his alone.

Her heart ached, listening to his pain.

Regardless of their situation, she felt compelled to help him and knocked on the door. When he didn't answer, she assumed he couldn't hear and knocked louder.

"HENRY? Are you ALL RIGHT?" She probably shouldn't yell. It could wake Michael.

"No. I'm not." His voice trembled.

She built up courage and opened his door.

He sat perched on the edge of the bed cradling a photograph. Her eyes shifted around the plain dark room.

Reckon he never opens the curtains.

He glanced up and wiped his eyes, then lowered his head as if he felt ashamed she'd seen his tears.

Stepping forward, she cupped his chin in her hand and raised his face, forcing him to look at her. "Henry, is there anythin' I can do to help?" The moment their eyes met, she dropped her hands to her sides.

He blinked several times and shook his head. "It's been seven years today." He touched the photo, then traced around the edge with his fingers. "Sarah died cuz I sent her away. I made her go there. Do you know what horrible things they did to her in that hospital?"

Claire sat down beside him on the bed. "No."

"I won't tell ya. Would give you nightmares. I had no idea till years later, an' then I heard rumors. I looked into it and found 'em to be true. Know what it's like havin' that hangin' over your head?"

"Gerald said she had an awful time dealin' with your boys dyin'. You did what you thought was best at the time." She wanted to ease his pain. *Losing someone you love is never easy.* That she knew well. Without giving it a second thought, she rested her hand on his leg, then realized almost immediately it was a bad idea.

He covered her hand with his own and held on tight. Because her intent had been to offer comfort, she didn't pull away.

"Sarah was everythin' to me." He sniffled. "Some folks used to think she was plain-lookin', but not me. To me, she was the most beautiful woman that walked this earth. Took good care a me an' the boys. I loved her more than you can imagine. Then she was gone." He paused, then looked directly at her. "Do you know how lonely I've been?"

"Reckon I do. Fact is we've talked 'bout tryin' to find someone you could spend some time with." She swallowed hard and her stomach flipped. What was she thinking coming into his room?

"I don't want just someone, Claire. I never thought I could feel the way I felt 'bout Sarah ever again. Then you came along. You know how I feel 'bout ya." He took his other hand and moved it to her face with a soft caress.

"Henry . . . *don't*." She tried to stand, but he pulled her back down, dropping the photograph on the floor.

"Please, Claire. Just hear me out."

He continued to firmly hold one of her hands, then positioned his free hand at her waist. She felt trapped.

Her instincts told her to bolt, but she sat there hoping they were wrong, until he looked at her the way a lover would.

I'm not wrong.

She had no idea what to do.

He leaned toward her. His face came within inches of hers. "Do you know why I never have a hard time understandin' ya?" he whispered. "It's because I've memorized every line of your mouth. I watch it move as you smile, an' speak, an' even when you kiss Gerald." He released her hand and traced her lips with his fingertips.

She trembled, unable to speak.

"I've been watchin' every move you make for a very long time. Do you know when I like you best? In the mornin' 'fore you do your hair. You have it soft over your shoulders. Then I watch you go to the sink and twist it up on your head, exposin' your neck." He brushed his hand along it. "Just like you did that night when you was bathin' with Gerald."

Oh God . . . he was watchin' us. Her mouth became dry as cotton and her heart raced.

"An when I lay here at night, sometimes I can sense the movement of your bed. An' I know what he's doin' to ya. Claire, I love ya. You do everythin' for Gerald an' me. Everythin', but one thing. You only do that for him. Can't you give it to me, too?"

Her hands gripped the bedspread. "Gerald!" She screamed as loud as she could, no longer afraid of waking Michael. Her eyes filled with tears.

"Don't, Claire. He can't hear you and you'll only frighten Michael. Is it so horrible to think of sharin' yourself with me? All I want is one time. That's all. I swear it. Just once." He pushed her body back against the bed and held her down, gripping her with strength she didn't know he had.

"Gerald!" She screamed even louder, all the while struggling to free herself.

He'd gained control over her and lay atop her. Still pressing her arms against the bedding, he moved his mouth to her neck.

"Don't do this, Henry!" She arched her body and pushed against him, but it only encouraged him. "This can't be what you want!"

"Just once, Claire." He released one of her arms and clutched a fistful of her hair. His mouth covered her ear. He nibbled and licked.

"Henry! You've lost your mind!" With her free hand she hit him, but he grabbed her arm again and pressed it into the bed.

Michael's cries filled the air.

"Don't ever say that again!" Henry yelled. "I know what I'm doin'!" He kissed her all over her face and neck, then looked at her as though he couldn't understand why she didn't return his affection.

"Gerald! Gerald!" Tears erupted from her. Somehow he had to hear her.

And like an angel of mercy, Gerald flew into the room.

Henry's hand covered her breast and Gerald's eyes filled with fire.

"Gerald!" she cried again.

"What are you doin' to my WIFE?" he yelled and grabbed Henry by the shoulder, flinging him across the room. Henry stumbled backward. His already injured leg twisted beneath him. He cried out in pain. Gerald hovered over him ready to take a swing. His breath hissed out of his nostrils like steam.

Cowering in the corner, Henry put his hands in front of his face and sobbed. "Don't, Gerald. Please don't hit me. I'm sorry!"

She hopped from the bed and wrapped her arms around her husband. Anger rippled out of his body, making it shake against her. "Gerald, don't do it! Let's just go!"

"Go get Michael and pack a bag!" Gerald spit the words out. "We're leavin'!"

She scurried out of the room.

"You HEAR me?" Gerald's voice boomed through the house. "We're LEAVIN'! You ain't NEVER gonna see HER again!"

She quickly stuffed clothing into bags for the three of them. Gerald came in the room long enough to tell her he was hitching up the wagon, then left her to finish packing. She'd never seen this side of him before.

With their mare, Cocoa, pulling the wagon, they loaded it up and set out for Beth's.

Gerald had fallen completely silent. Did he blame her? Maybe it *was* her fault. If only she'd told him long ago about Henry's advances.

She comforted herself by clinging to Michael, who slept peacefully in her arms. He'd replaced her need to bite her nails.

"Claire," Gerald finally spoke. "You gotta tell me what happened."

Shamefully, she lowered her head, then raised it slowly and looked at him. "Oh, Gerald. I don't know what woulda happened if you hadn't come in." With a will of their own, tears came again.

He released one hand from the reins to wipe them away. "Sumthin' inside a me just told me I needed to come inside." His brows knit with worry and pain. "Please don't cry. I hate it when you do. I don't blame you. I just wanna know what happened."

She grabbed his hand and scooted closer to him. "I heard Henry cryin', so I went to his room. And 'fore I knew it, he was on me."

"Why would he do that? It don't make no sense."

The truth tore her up inside. She had to tell him. "Gerald," she whispered. "It's not the first time he tried sumthin'."

"What?" He frowned and his head drew back.

Why'd this have to happen? She didn't want to hurt him. "He . . . he kissed me. Over a year ago. It was our first Christmas together. He caught me when I stumbled down the stairs, then kissed me." She closed her eyes, then gasped when he pulled his hand away and returned it to the reins.

"Why didn't you tell me?" The sorrow in his voice crushed her heart.

"I couldn't. Henry promised it would never happen again. I believed him. I didn't wanna upset you. I knew you'd wanna leave and we needed a home for the baby." How could she make him understand?

"Haven't you learned you can tell me anythin'?" He shook his head. "How've you kept this inside so long? How could you stand bein' 'round him after what he done?"

"I held it in so you wouldn't have to be hurt by it. I love you . . ." She laid her head on his shoulder. When his arm encircled her, her heart rested.

"I love you, too." He kissed her on the head and they rode on for a great distance in silence.

Her mind spun, turning around all the events that had led up to this. "What are we gonna do?"

"I don't know." He pulled her closer. "For now we'll see if we can get a room at Mrs. Sandborn's. I can do some work for her."

"I can sew again." She attempted to smile.

"We'll figger sumthin' out. Long as we're together. I'll give Henry a little time to stew, then I'll go back there and deal with him an' get our things." Spite filled every word. Talking about Henry refueled his fire. "Haven't decided yet what I'm gonna say to him."

"He's still your family."

"Family ain't s'pose to do each other like that. I trusted him." He raised his head and breathed deeply. "Guess I need time to cool off. Best that way."

"What are we gonna tell Beth?"

"The truth. Truth is always the right thing to tell, even if it hurts." He faced forward, then clicked to Cocoa, encouraging her to go faster.

His words stung. She could never tell him everything. Never would she put him through that kind of hurt. Some secrets were best left hid.

They decided to see Beth before going to the boarding house. But before they arrived, she had to tell him one more thing. "Gerald, I think you should know . . . Beth warned me 'bout Henry."

"Beth suspected sumthin' an' she didn't tell me?" His voice rose and he frowned.

"Don't be angry with her. Please? She was lookin' out for me in a woman's way. She thought he had feelin's for me. Please don't blame her. This is hard enough."

"My own sister," he huffed. "She shoulda told me." He stared straight ahead and she decided to let him be to gather his thoughts.

When Beth opened the door, she couldn't have looked more shocked. Her mouth dropped to her chin. "Gerald? Claire?" Shock turned to concern and she pushed the door wide. "Come in."

Claire set Michael down on the floor and he toddled around taking in his new surroundings. Then she wrapped her arms around Beth and hugged her tight. "You were right, Beth."

"Henry do sumthin?" Beth took a seat at the table. Claire sat beside her and Gerald paced the floor.

He raised his hands in the air. "Why didn't you tell me?"

"What was I s'pose to tell ya? I only *thought* he might have feelin's for Claire. What'd he do?" Beth's brows wove with worry.

"He was on her!" Gerald yelled. "Tried havin' his way with her!"

Beth's hand shot to her mouth. "Oh, no. *No.* Claire, I'm so sorry!"

"It's all right." Claire reached across the table to her. Saying things were *all right* couldn't be further from the truth, but it seemed the natural thing to say. "Gerald came in an' stopped him. He didn't hurt me."

"I wanted to hurt *him* worse than I did!" Gerald raged. "I shoulda!" He fisted one hand and punched it into the other, mumbling something unrecognizable.

"We left right after," Claire said. "We just packed our bags an' left. Henry was on the floor. He fell when Gerald pulled him off me."

"Is he all right?" Beth asked, staring at her brother.

"You're worried 'bout Henry after what he done to Claire?"

"He's our uncle. He was lonely. He . . . he needed someone." Beth crossed her arms over her chest.

"Not my WIFE!" Gerald stomped across the floor and turned his back on Beth, then rested his forehead against the mantel of the fireplace.

Claire stood and went to him. She rubbed his shoulders, attempting to draw out his tension. "It's all right, Gerald."

She'd said it again. Maybe if she said the words enough, she'd turn them into truth.

Beth cleared her throat. "What are you gonna do now?"

"Don't know yet," he snapped. Claire patted him on the back and he let out a long breath. "Know if Mrs. Sandborn has a vacant room?"

"She might. Why don't y'all stay here tonight an' we can go see her in the mornin'? I can make a bed on the floor for myself, an' you can have the bedroom. Bed's big enough for the three a ya." The softness of Beth's voice proved how badly she'd felt about upsetting them. She'd certainly meant no offense in asking about Henry's well-being.

"Thank you," Claire said with a smile. "That fine with you, Gerald?" She squeezed him and gave him a peck on the cheek.

"Yep. Thank you, Beth." He pulled Claire in a little closer. "Reckon we can take a walk on the beach a little later? Help me clear my head?"

"Course we can. It'll help us both."

While Beth prepared their room, they wandered down to the beach. They held Michael's hands and laughed at his expressions when he felt the sand between his toes. Then he giggled when they took him to the water and it lapped at his feet. Being there gave them a new sense of freedom.

Claire finally felt free of Uncle Henry's watchful eye. Thankfully, Gerald understood and put no blame on her. Truthfully, she wished she'd told him sooner.

As night fell, they crawled into the bed that had once been hers. The bed she'd shared with Andrew. Michael nestled down between them and Gerald rubbed his tiny back, helping him drift off to sleep.

"He's gettin' so big," Claire whispered. "This bed's nearly too small for all of us."

"It's sure nice and cozy. Claire . . ." He sighed. "I promise you everythin' will be all right. I'll take care a you."

"I know you will." She lifted herself up over the baby and kissed Gerald on the lips. They laid their heads down on their pillows and in no time fell asleep.

CHAPTER 24

Mrs. Sandborn gave Gerald his old room and told them they could stay as long as they'd like. She even found odd jobs for him to do around the house to earn their keep. Claire planned to buy material to start sewing again.

That evening after supper, they sat at the table making other plans.

"Claire . . ." Gerald folded his hands on the table and leaned toward her. "I've managed to save a bit a money. I figger we could get a small loan and I can start my own blacksmith shop. I know the trade well enough an' I reckon I can make it work."

"Do you truly think so?" It would take a lot of money to start a business.

"We'd probably hafta move back to Mobile. That's where all the work is."

She blew out a breath. "You sure 'bout that?"

"I reckon it's the only way. You could try sellin' your dresses at the mercantile. Mr. Parker seems to like ya."

"But where would we live?" Her stomach turned flips just thinking about it.

"We can find a boardin' house there till we can buy our own." His lips formed the brightest smile she'd seen since they'd left Henry's. "I know we can do it."

Seeing him so eager, she wasn't about to express her doubts. "All right. But when?"

"I figger next week I'll go into Mobile—to the bank— an' see 'bout that loan. Then we'll go from there. And, Claire . . . I'd like it if we could go to services tomorrow. I know it'd make Beth happy. I was kinda hard on her last night."

Could she go to the Baptist church? Now she truly felt ill. What if someone said something about Michael? But then again, she was tired of being afraid.

"That sounds just fine," she said, sitting upright. "It *would* make Beth happy."

Mrs. Sandborn came into the dining room and sat down at the table with them, holding Michael. "I can't believe the way he's walkin' all over the place. He had me runnin'." She dabbed at her face with the bottom of her apron. "I think he's hungry, Claire. Which makes me wonder . . . You ever gonna stop nursin'? Ain't he gonna be a year old next week?"

Claire took him from her arms. "He's still my baby. I'm not ready to stop yet and neither is he. 'Sides, the price a the food is just right." She grinned at Mrs. Sandborn, then carried Michael up to their room to nurse.

A large overstuffed chair was the perfect spot. Michael nestled against her and she stroked his cheek as he suckled. It had always been a special time for them. Knowing it would only last a short while, she intended to cherish every moment.

A soft rap on the door turned her head. Gerald tiptoed into the room. Taking a seat on the bed, he kept completely quiet as he watched her feed their child.

After several minutes passed, he reached out and placed his hand atop Michael's head. "I want another baby, Claire. I can't explain it, but it means a lot to me to give you another child."

"Maybe it's not the best time. We don't even have our own house now." It tore her heart in two every time he mentioned having another baby.

"I don't care. I wanna do it." His eyes glistened, piercing into her soul.

He stood and went to the bureau, then pulled out one of the drawers and placed it on the floor. Taking a blanket from the bed, he folded it neatly into the drawer, making one end a bit thicker to form a pillow.

As Michael nursed, he fell asleep, so Gerald lifted him from her breast and placed him in the drawer. A perfect comfortable bed for him. He curled up and continued sleeping.

Gerald shut the bedroom door and lifted her to her feet. After pulling the pins from her hair, he watched it fall over her shoulders. "Claire, I'm sorry 'bout what Henry did." He sensually drew his fingers through her hair. "I shoulda seen it comin'. I knew from the start he cared for you, but I never thought he'd do what he did."

"I felt sorry for him." She lowered her eyes. Would he understand? "I knew he was lonely, but when he told me he wanted you to share me with him, I knew his mind wasn't right. He had no right to ask that a me."

"Claire, I don't ever wanna share you with anyone. Call me selfish, but I want you just for me." He pressed his lips to hers as he moved his hands down her back and pulled her close. She thought about their first kiss. He'd come a long way.

He undressed her, then himself, and they slipped into the bed between the soft cotton sheets. He made love to her, not sharing her with anyone. Not even the invisible guest who so often made his way into their bed.

* * *

Beth's eyes popped open wide when Gerald and Claire arrived at the Baptist church for Sunday services. Gerald walked in proudly carrying Michael and sat beside her. When Claire looked in Beth's direction, she beamed.

Claire wished she could share Beth's enthusiasm. Looking around the congregation, she hoped Lucy Beecham would remain absent, but she was sadly disappointed.

A visibly pregnant Lucy took her seat in the front pew along with her children in tow. They'd still not learned to bathe, and though Claire found it sad, she didn't feel as repulsed as she'd been before. She had a new understanding for Lucy. If Lucy truly loved her husband, it would be difficult to refuse him. Her children were either an indication of true love, or an insatiable sexual appetite on the part of Frank. This would be their sixth child.

Lucy's head turned. She stared at Michael, then shifted her eyes to Claire and smirked. Claire forced a smile. Had Lucy guessed the truth?

Reverend Brown asked them to stand, face the congregation, and introduce their son. Everyone smiled and nodded, but Claire thought she might vomit. Why did she ever agree to come here? She hadn't attended worship for over a year.

Their wedding had been the last time she'd been here and she'd not found a place to worship in Mobile. She missed the fellowship, but in many ways she'd been hiding from God and the untruths she lived with every day. Her silent prayers always asked for forgiveness and sought approval. But all the while, she knew what she'd done could never be condoned. In her mind, she continued to sacrifice herself for the sake of her son.

She sighed with relief when they sang the final hymn. Her feet couldn't carry her out of there fast enough.

Gerald walked away to talk to a few old friends and Beth held her by the arm as they exited. Claire clutched Michael close.

"Claire?" *Oh, God! Not Lucy Beecham.* "Claire, I wanna get a closer look at your baby."

No, you don't.

Claire plastered a smile on her face and turned around. "Hey, Lucy. You look well." The lump in her throat felt larger than a pond frog.

Lucy rubbed her swollen belly. "Thanks, Claire. As you can see, Frank's been at it again." She grinned. "I figgered you'd be carryin' another one by now."

Feeling defeated, Claire looked at the ground. What could she say?

Beth stepped between them. "She an' Gerald are tryin'."

"Must not be any good at it," Lucy said, smirking.

"That ain't a very nice thing to say," Beth scolded.

Lucy shrugged. "Well, maybe your next baby will look like his daddy."

Claire held Michael even tighter.

"Then again . . ." Lucy scowled. "Maybe this one already does."

Claire's heart stopped. Lucy knew. But before she could come up with something to say, Beth slapped Lucy hard across the face accompanied with a hateful expression that caused Claire to step away.

Lucy rubbed her cheek, but didn't strike back. She pushed Beth to the side and faced Claire square on. "The truth hurts, don't it Claire?" She scowled, then walked away with her children at her heels.

Ready to cry, Claire held it in.

Beth took her by the arm and rushed her to Gerald. "Gerald, you need to take Claire home. Lucy Beecham was horrid to her!"

"What happened?" he asked and put his arm around her.

"Gerald, please don't ever make me go back there again!" Claire almost sprinted to the boarding house and didn't bother to wait for him to follow. Yes, the truth hurt and she never wanted Beth or Gerald to know it.

* * *

Claire snuggled down into Gerald's arms. The day had improved. After a nice meal with Beth and Mrs. Sandborn, they'd gone on a long walk with Michael. Even with the pleasant afternoon, Claire couldn't shake Lucy's words. But now, she lay in bed with her husband, comforted against him.

"What exactly did Lucy do to make you so upset?" Gerald asked, and tenderly stroked her arm.

"First of all, she implied you and I don't know what we're doin' in bed." They whispered to each other, not wanting to disturb Michael, who had once again been placed in the bureau drawer.

Gerald chuckled. "You know *that* ain't true." He nuzzled her neck and rubbed her belly.

"Oh, Gerald." She giggled. He'd always been able to make her feel better.

"Seriously, though. It ain't none a her business. What we do in private is . . . *private*."

"I know. She's always flaunted what she does with Frank. What with all those kids it's hard *not* to know." She buried her head in his shoulder, muffling another giggle.

"Least you're not upset no more. I like hearin' you laugh." He lifted himself up on one elbow and stared at her. "You're the most beautiful woman I reckon ever walked this earth. Did you know that?" He touched her nose with his finger, then ran it down the side of her cheek and under her chin.

"You haven't seen all the women on this earth. You've not ever been much further than Mobile." She took his hand and kissed his fingers one by one. Love for him poured over her like a warm spring rain.

"I don't need to go further than Mobile. God created an angel when he made you, an' there ain't nothin' more beautiful than an angel." His hand moved tenderly down her neck and around to her back, melting her body into the bed.

"I kinda miss *our* bed. You put so much work into it and it sure has held a lot of love. And memories."

"I'll get it back. I promise you. All our other things, too. Thought I was ready to go to Mobile, but I reckon I'd like to wait one more week. If that's all right with you."

"That's fine. Go when you're ready. We can stay here as long as we need to. Mrs. Sandborn's glad to have us. Just promise me I don't hafta go to church again. Not there. I can't explain it, but I don't feel right there anymore. When we get back to Mobile, let's find a new church. All right? Do you think I'm horrible?"

"Course not. It's just a little hard to understand. We've always gone there. But if it's upsettin' you, then we don't hafta go." He kissed the tip of her nose. "Why don't we go to Beth's next Sunday and spend a day at the beach? Michael loved the water when we took him the other day. How would that be?" He gave her a smile warm enough to melt butter.

She hugged his neck. "Perfect. Thank you."

"You're welcome." With a grin she knew well, he removed his glasses and set them on the bed stand. "Now then, wanna prove Lucy Beecham wrong?" He wiggled his brows and pulled her to him, all the while allowing his hands to roam.

"Oh, Gerald," she said, breathlessly.

Lucy had been horribly mistaken.

* * *

The following week, Mrs. Sandborn found plenty of work to keep Gerald busy. So much in fact, that she paid him extra. Not just room and board. The house had been in need of major repairs and Gerald had a gift for woodworking. Mrs. Sandborn took advantage of it.

They threw a simple birthday party for Michael that Friday, the twenty-fifth of April, and gave him a set of building blocks Gerald carved and Claire painted. Michael loved stacking the brightly colored blocks and they enjoyed watching him do it.

Mrs. Sandborn baked him a cake and they let him bury his tiny hands into it and eat as much as he wanted. He was nearly weaned—but not quite—mostly because Claire wasn't ready to give up that special time with him.

Aside from the ordeal with Lucy, Claire could honestly say she felt happy. She and Gerald discovered a new spark in their relationship and a sense of independence being away from Henry. He'd brought them their livelihood, but also a feeling of dependency. They'd been set free.

The sun shone bright as they rode to Beth's, laughing and talking about their plans for the following week. Gerald would go to Mobile and talk to the bank and Claire fully supported his decision. They were ready to move back to the city. As long as they were together, they could accomplish anything.

Beth made a picnic dinner that they packed in a basket and carried to the beach. Claire's special beach. The one accessed only by her secret pathway. They placed a blanket on the sand far from the shoreline. April was the perfect month to spend time here. The sand was warm, but not hot. A natural rock embankment gave them some needed shade. The ideal place for their picnic.

Beth and Claire wore light cotton dresses and no stockings, which allowed them to stick their toes in the sand. Michael also enjoyed the feel of the sand. He laughed while he pushed it around with a spoon and tried to pile it up.

Claire sat back and marveled at her husband. His spirits were exceptionally high and he hadn't stopped talking about his upcoming trip to Mobile. His confidence had built over the past year working with Henry. She couldn't remember the last time he'd pushed his glasses up on his nose. She'd enjoyed watching the transformation and admired his strength of character.

He wore a white cotton shirt and light-weight tan pants,

which he rolled up to his knees. When he rolled up the sleeves of his shirt, a brief flashback of Andrew crept into her mind. She quickly cast it aside and focused solely on her husband.

He stood in front of them and flexed his muscles.

"What are you doin', Gerald?" Claire asked with a laugh.

"Nice muscles," Beth chimed in. "You need some work on that one though." She poked him in the belly. She and Claire both erupted with laughter.

He continued to pose for them, obviously paying no mind to their teasing. He sucked in his belly, then turned sideways and raised his arms over his head. "How 'bout this one?"

Claire fanned herself. "Oh, Gerald, you hafta stop! I can't take much more a this." She stood and wrapped her arms around him, then kissed him. One she hoped would spark something more for later.

"If you two are gonna start that, I'm gonna hafta leave," Beth said and rolled her eyes.

Claire grinned at Gerald, then kissed him again.

"Where's Michael?" Beth asked. The fear in her voice took Claire's breath. She and Gerald instantly turned their attention to where he'd been sitting.

"Michael?" Panic pumped Claire's blood hard and her throat went dry. She couldn't see him anywhere. "Gerald, where's Michael?"

Gerald's head shifted back and forth looking up and down the shoreline. "Michael!" The terror in his cry intensified her fear.

"Oh, God!" Beth shrieked and pointed at the bay. "He's in the water!"

Gerald sprinted for the water with Claire and Beth trailing behind him. Claire fixated on the rippling waves, but then Michael's tiny body disappeared below the surface.

"Hurry, Gerald!" she screamed. *No, God, no!*

"Gerald can't swim, Claire!" Beth shouted and burst into tears.

Gerald fanned his hands through the water, wading out deeper and deeper. He kept grasping and searching, bending down into the waves.

Michael's tiny head bobbed above the surface further out. He'd somehow gotten to where the seabed dropped off. "He's there!" Claire pointed.

Gerald glanced at her, then turned toward where she'd indicated and continued on further into the water.

Claire reached the shoreline and moved through the never-ending waves toward them. Beth stayed right behind her.

"Gerald, be careful!" Claire yelled. The second the words left her lips, Gerald disappeared. He'd reached the drop-off. "Gerald!"

His arms flailed in the water.

Beth shrieked, but Claire pressed on, moving deeper. She had to reach him. Pushing through the lapping waves, her hand caught Michael's tiny arm. She pulled his limp body up out of the water and passed him behind her to Beth.

He's not moving . . .

"Get him outta the water!" she yelled, then felt a tug at her leg.

Gerald?

In a flash, he yanked her under.

CHAPTER 25

Andrew arrived at work uplifted. Things had progressed with Victoria. She no longer pushed herself on him and was allowing their relationship to slowly develop. He'd been enjoying his time with her and had actually gotten to know her a little better. High time, since they'd be married in a few short weeks.

When he walked through the main hospital entrance, Sally stopped him. "Dr. Fletcher, Mrs. Stevens needs you immediately on the second floor. Mr. Schultz said you should go to her."

Ann Stevens—the hospital matron. She ran the women's floor of the hospital and oversaw all of the nurses. She made certain the women received the delicate handling they needed.

Whenever Andrew treated a female patient, he was required to report to her regarding their progress. Though strict, Mrs. Stevens wasn't as stern as Mr. Schultz.

He hastened up the stairs to the second floor. This wasn't uncommon. He had many female patients. At the top of the stairs he hurried past the waiting area and proceeded to the nurses' station right beside it.

"I was told Mrs. Stevens asked to see me," he said to the nurse on duty.

"She's in the common room, Dr. Fletcher," the nurse replied.

"Thank you." He hurried to the large room.

The *common room*, as she'd called it, accommodated up to twenty women. A room where those less fortunate were always sent. A private room could become quite expensive with an extensive stay. Since the war, more and more people had little money. Sadly, the large room frequently filled to capacity.

He walked in and Mrs. Stevens came right to him. She was middle-aged, tall, and had light blond hair she kept twisted on top of her head. Her wire-rimmed glasses fit her face, but didn't add to her appearance. She wasn't the attractive sort of woman who would make a man look twice, but one whom he respected.

Her sad eyes reflected concern. "Dr. Fletcher, a young woman was brought in last night. Dr. Mitchell had been attending her, but was called away on an emergency. Mr. Schultz suggested you take over for him."

"I understand. What's wrong with her?"

"She's unconscious . . . nearly drowned. Her sister-in-law brought her here." The woman's brow furrowed. "Dr. Mitchell feels there isn't much hope."

"There's always hope, Mrs. Stevens," he said with a soft smile. "What's her name?"

"It's Mrs. Alexander. *Claire* Alexander."

Andrew clutched his chest. "Claire Alexander?"

"Yes. Do you know her?"

"She's a friend." His heart pounded faster and faster.

"I'm so sorry."

She reached her hand out to him, but the sudden panic that swept through his body dismissed her compassionate gesture. "Where is she?"

"At the far end on the right." Her brows wove with incredible concern, intensifying his distress.

With a quick nod, he turned and walked briskly to Claire's bed.

Dear, God.

Her pale face made her appear nearly lifeless. Her hair lay tousled about on the pillow, tangled into knots.

Stifling his feelings, he became her doctor and pulled a chair up beside her.

He placed his stethoscope against her skin, finding a weak heartbeat. She lay completely still, with her eyes closed and her hands folded across her stomach, as though ready for the grave. He'd longed to see her for nearly two years . . .

Not like this.

He lowered his head. "Oh, God. No . . ." Tears worked their way into his eyes.

A touch on his shoulder startled him and he gasped.

"Are you all right, Dr. Fletcher?" Mrs. Stevens asked.

No, I'm not.

"Yes, I'm fine. Do you know how this happened?" He couldn't take his eyes off Claire.

"Her sister-in-law is in the waiting area. Perhaps she can tell you." She hovered over him, but he couldn't move. "Dr. Fletcher? Wouldn't you like to talk to her?"

"Of course." He turned from Claire and reluctantly followed Mrs. Stevens out of the room.

"Over here," she said, pointing to the waiting area.

When Andrew saw her, he knew Beth instantly.

"Miss Alexander," Mrs. Stevens said to her. "This is Dr. Fletcher. He'll be taking care of your sister-in-law."

Beth's eyes opened wide. "Dr. Fletcher?" She jumped to her feet and without any restraint wrapped her arms around him, tears flowing.

"I see you know each other," Mrs. Stevens said. "I'll leave you to talk." She excused herself.

"Oh, Beth . . ." Andrew held onto her. "I'm so sorry. Can you tell me what happened?" He led her to a sofa and sat beside her. As he placed an arm over her shoulder, she laid her head against his chest and sobbed.

She gasped several times, then raised her head and looked at him. Her swollen eyes indicated she'd been crying for a long time. "We . . . we went to the beach. We was . . . laughin' and havin' such . . . such a good time. Then Michael . . ." She sniffled. "Michael was gone." Her sentence came out in pieces between heavy breaths.

"Who's Michael?"

"My nephew . . . Claire's baby. He'd . . . gone into the water. We went after him. Gerald . . . Gerald didn't know how to swim!" Her sobs erupted and she laid her head down again, trembling. He could barely console her. "He couldn't swim!" She buried her face into his white coat.

His own emotions had him reeling, but he needed to keep her talking. It was the only way to help Claire. "Then what happened?" He spoke low, hoping to calm her.

"Claire . . . Claire . . . got hold a Michael an' she handed him to me. Told me . . . to get him outta the water. So I did. He wasn't breathin'." She looked straight at him. Tears trickled down her cheeks. "I laid him on the sand and patted his little back. An' then . . . He started spittin' up water an' started cryin'! I thanked God he was cryin'! I held him close, then I turned an' looked for Claire an' Gerald . . . But they weren't nowhere . . . I couldn't see 'em!" Panic overtook her and she gasped for air.

"Shh . . . Beth. It's all right. Take a deep breath."

"No! It ain't all right! I . . . I couldn't save him! I couldn't save 'em both! I had to choose. Why'd I hafta choose?" Her body folded into Andrew's lap.

He knew what she meant. Her pain pierced his heart.

He stroked her hair as she lay on his lap. Claire's husband had died and Claire lay at death's door. He wouldn't stand by and watch their son become an orphan. Not if he could help it.

"Beth, you did what you could. That's all any of us can do." Would his words give her comfort? Or did he sound like an unfeeling doctor trained to say the right things? If only she knew just how much he cared.

"I pulled her outta the water, but I couldn't get her to wake up! I went back in for Gerald ..." Her shoulders jerked and she struggled over every word. "I couldn't find him!" She sobbed even harder.

"Where's the child?"

She lay there for what seemed an eternity while he gently stroked her hair. She took a deep breath. "I ran with Michael in my arms up to the house. I got the wagon and put him in the back. I told him to stay there. He's just a little baby . . . I . . . I didn't know if he'd understand. He was cryin' an' I was afraid he might try to get out, but I had to go back for Claire.

"I drove far as I could down the road to where we was. I don't know how I had the strength to carry her up the hill to the wagon, but somehow we made it. Her body was limp! She was barely breathin', but I knew she wasn't dead. I knew I had to get her *here* . . . Oh, God!" Her face tightened with pain as she pointed into nothingness. "I looked back down at the shoreline an' saw Gerald's body washed up on the beach. I wanted to go to him, but I knew he was dead. My brother's dead!" Her long mournful cry made Andrew shudder.

"Beth . . ." He had to reassure her. Comfort her. "You did the right thing bringing Claire here as quickly as you did."

She sat up and looked him in the eye. "I . . . took the baby . . . to Mrs. Sandborn. At the boardin' house. She was gonna send someone ..." Her face scrunched tight. "To get Gerald. Then I brought Claire here. Oh, Dr. Fletcher . . . I can't believe he's dead!"

Mrs. Stevens approached them with one of the young nurses by her side. "Dr. Fletcher, I'm going to let Miss Elliott take Miss Alexander downstairs for a bit of fresh air. I think she could use it."

Beth sucked in a long breath. "I don't wanna leave."

"Beth," he said gently. "I think it would be good for you to walk a bit. You've been sitting here a long time. I'll take care of Claire. I promise you." He lifted her to her feet and kissed her on the forehead.

"All right," she mumbled. Having calmed, Miss Elliott took her by the arm and led her down the stairs.

Andrew hurried back to Claire's side and sat down.

He took her hand.

So cold.

He raised it to his lips and kissed it, fighting back tears. She'd become his patient and he had to start acting like her doctor. But how could he remain professional when his heart had been ripped from his chest?

He got up to find Mrs. Stevens, then spotted her going over the chart of another patient. "Mrs. Stevens," he said, standing beside her. "I'd like to start intravenous fluids for Mrs. Alexander."

"Dr. Fletcher." Her eyes narrowed. "You'll only prolong the inevitable."

Damn the inevitable!

"She's not dead yet." He'd spoken a little too loudly, so he lowered his voice. "The fluids will help her. It's the least we can do." Standing tall, he gathered his composure. "I'd also like to have her moved into her own room."

"That's out of the question," she whispered. "There's no money."

"I don't care what it costs. *I'll* pay it!" Without even observing her reaction, he walked away.

So much for composure.

He took his seat beside Claire once again. Being near her eased his frustration, however his worry was another matter entirely. The rise and fall of her chest appeared so minor that he frequently listened to her heartbeat. But as long as he heard even a trace, he had hope.

"Dr. Fletcher?" He looked up into the face of a young nurse.

"Yes?"

"Her room's ready. I'll get someone to help move her." She turned to leave, but he stopped her.

"No need," he muttered and lifted Claire from the bed. "I'll follow you."

The nurse gaped at him. "Y-Yes, Doctor." She led him from the room and he chose to ignore the eyes that followed him. None of what they thought mattered. He only cared about Claire.

He placed her limp body onto the bed and secured the blankets around her. As soon as the nurse left the room, he ran his hands through Claire's hair, attempting to untangle it. Then, he arranged it on the pillow. Lying down beside her and holding her was out of the question. But, oh, how he wanted to.

He went to the nurses' station and ordered supplies for the intravenous treatment. Though uncommon to use, he'd studied it in medical school and had used it several times before. The fluids would prolong her life, but she'd still die of starvation if she didn't wake soon.

Luckily, they quickly delivered what he needed.

Her veins were small and receded and he had some difficulty placing the needle. Determination pushed him on. The saline had to be administered slowly and with great care. The infusion pump was sensitive and if the vacuum wasn't properly used, he could push air into her veins and kill her. But without the fluid, she'd certainly die.

The liquid seeped into her veins. Time-consuming. A slow, tedious task.

Quite a few minutes had passed when Mrs. Stevens appeared in the doorway. "Dr. Fletcher, Miss Alexander wants to speak with you again. She'd also like to see Mrs. Alexander. Would that be all right?"

"Yes, she may come in," he replied with a sigh. "I'm almost finished here."

"Very well. One other thing . . . Mr. Schultz wants to see you in his office after you speak with Miss Alexander."

Just what I need.

"I'll go. As soon as I'm done."

Mrs. Stevens walked away, then Beth entered the room.

She inched close to the bed. "How is she?" Her face wrinkled at the sight of the needle, but at least she'd calmed down. The walk must have been good for her.

"She's doing as well as she can. Don't worry about the needle. It's not hurting her. It's helping." He continued pushing the fluid into her arm.

With a grimace, Beth turned her head.

"If this bothers you, you may want to wait outside the room."

"No. I just need to sit down." She stumbled to a chair and turned her back to them.

He finished administering the saline, then removed the needle and wrapped Claire's arm with a bandage. The treatment would have to be repeated every four hours, and *he'd* have to do it. He didn't trust anyone else with this procedure.

After he folded her hands once more across her stomach, he couldn't help but caress her skin.

Good thing Beth wasn't watching.

"I'm finished now."

She turned around. "I don't understand all this. Why would God take my brother away, and leave Claire like this?"

"I don't believe God does those things." He took a seat beside her. "We live in an imperfect world. Sometimes bad things happen to good people." The deep-seated words came out easily. He'd said them many times and believed them. More so now, than ever.

"My brother was the best. If you'd only known him."

"I *did*. He put shoes on a horse for me. He seemed like a fine man and I could tell . . ." He cleared his throat and looked at Claire. "He loved her very much."

"He did. An' little Michael, too. He gave his life for that baby." Once more her eyes filled with tears. "He loved him more than anythin'."

Beth glanced at Claire, then crossed to her and took her hand. "It's gone."

"What?" He stood up beside her.

"Her weddin' ring. It's not on her finger." Beth's chin quivered. She looked utterly defeated. "It musta come off in the water. We'll never find it again. It belonged to my mama."

Losing *his* mother so long ago, instilled his doctor's compassion. But this situation weighed heavier on him than anything he'd experienced in his career. He put his arm around her shoulder. "Do you have any other family that could be with you now? Perhaps your uncle?"

"I don't want him here." Her body tensed beneath his arm. "If it weren't for him, this wouldn't a happened."

The implication perplexed him. "But your uncle should know. They worked together."

"I s'pose you're right. Still . . . I can't see him. I don't *wanna* see him now." She stared off toward the wall.

"I can tell him. I know where he lives. Would you like me to do that for you?"

"Thank you." She fidgeted with her fingers. "Would it be askin' too much if you were to have Uncle Henry go an' tell Claire's Aunt Martha? He knows where she lives. I know Martha would wanna be here for Claire."

"Yes, I'll take care of it. I can go this afternoon. It won't take me long. Claire will be fine while I'm gone."

"Can I stay in here with her?" Beth's puffy red eyes pleaded.

"Of course. But, you look tired. When I return, you should consider getting a room at the hotel. You'll need your rest."

"I can't sleep. Not now. But I might check into it later." She sat down once again beside Claire and held her hand.

He walked out of the room and went down the stairs to the first floor. Then he headed for Mr. Schultz' office and knocked on the door.

Time to get this over with.

"Come in," the man said.

Andrew took an enormous breath and pushed the door open.

Mr. Schultz sat behind his desk with papers in his hands. "Mrs. Stevens tells me you're paying for a private room for one of our patients. Is this true?"

"Yes, sir." He faced the man with his hands casually folded in front of him, determined to remain calm.

"She also tells me you're administering intravenous fluids for this woman, yet she'll likely not live. Can you explain *why* you're wasting your time and energy providing these services for a woman on her deathbed?" He rose to his feet.

"She's not dead yet, sir." *Calm* wasn't possible. "I'm trying to prolong her life. Little is known about the reasons for sustained unconsciousness. She could wake up at any moment." He'd probably raised his voice a little too loud, but he had to convince him. Otherwise, Mr. Schultz could instruct him to terminate her care.

Mr. Schultz frowned and sat down. "She's dying a slow, cruel death. She'll starve. You can't save her."

"I can try. Her heart's beating and she still breathes. Give me some time." Andrew leaned on the desk and looked him in the eye. "All I'm asking for is *time*. I'll pay for her care."

"What does she mean to you?"

The question clamped onto his heart like a vice. "She's a friend and she just lost her husband. They have a child. I don't want their little boy to lose both of his parents." Yes, he held concern for the boy, but the thought of losing Claire brought tears to his eyes.

The man raised his chin, studying him. "I give you a week. At the end of that time she'll likely be dead. However, if she's still breathing, you'll allow her family take her home and bury her next to her husband. It's the right thing to do."

"Bury her while she still breathes? That's inhuman!"

"Death by suffocation or death by starvation—either way—she *will* die." Mr. Schultz picked up his papers and rummaged through them, showing no compassion.

"Not if I can help it!" Andrew stormed away, slamming the man's door.

Though tempted to curse, he chose to pray.

CHAPTER 26

Andrew left the hospital and rode to Alexander's. He'd always hated this part—telling the family their loved one had died. He promised Beth he'd give her uncle the news, but dreaded it.

When he arrived, the place seemed unusually quiet. He expected to find Mr. Alexander in his shop, but he found the barn door shut. The shop door had been pulled to, and a handwritten sign simply stating *closed* had been posted on the door.

So he went to the house and knocked, but got no answer. Remembering the man's impairment, he knocked again. Louder this time. Someone shuffled to the door.

"Who is it?" The voice sounded gruff.

"Mr. Alexander? It's DR. FLETCHER! I need to speak with you!"

The door opened a crack. Mr. Alexander peered out, squinting at the sunlight. "What you want?"

"May I COME IN?"

The man glanced over his shoulder, then frowned at Andrew. "Reckon so." He stepped aside and let him enter.

The scent of liquor wafted through the air as Mr. Alexander spoke. He stumbled across the room even though he used a cane.

He's drunk. In his condition I can't tell him about his nephew.

"Do you have any COFFEE?" If Andrew could get him drinking something other than alcohol—and perhaps get some food in him—he might sober up.

Maybe he already heard about Gerald. It would explain his intoxication.

"Yep." Mr. Alexander nodded to another room. "In the kitchen."

When he turned to show Andrew the way, he nearly fell over. Andrew grabbed his arm and led him through the door to the kitchen, then helped him sit in one of the chairs at a small wood table.

Dirty dishes were stacked high on the counter. The entire house was in disarray. At least Andrew managed to find the coffee pot and coffee and busied himself fixing it. Searching for food, he found a loaf of partially eaten bread. He tore some off and handed it to the man.

"You need to EAT this."

Mr. Alexander looked up with eyes half-closed. "Why you here?" He slurred his speech. "If you need a shoein'— sorry—my nephew don't work here no more."

He doesn't know.

Time pressed him. He needed to get back to the hospital to administer another treatment to Claire, so he couldn't stay long. But he had to tell him. The coffee wasn't ready, so he poured him a glass of water.

"Drink this. You need to SOBER up."

"Why should I? It helps the pain." He reached into his shirt pocket and pulled out a flask.

Andrew yanked it out of his hand. "No more ALCO-HOL! I need you SOBER! If your LEG is hurting you, I can GIVE you some MEDICINE for it."

"Ain't my leg what's hurt. It's my heart." He laid his head down on the table.

His heart?

"She's so beautiful . . . an' she's gone," the man rambled. "I love her, you know. *She* left me, too."

"Who left you?"

"CLAIRE! Claire left me! I kissed her an' they left. Why'd they hafta leave?" His head bobbed as he squinted at Andrew.

"You kissed CLAIRE? Why? She was GERALD'S WIFE!"

"I know it! DAMN IT! But I love her." His head fell against the table. After shaking it, he slowly raised it. "You know Claire? She's the most beautiful woman ever was." He smiled a crooked smile.

"YES, I know her and she's part of the REASON I'm here." He looked directly at Mr. Alexander, hoping he'd grasp his words. Between his hearing difficulties and his stupor, Andrew doubted he could make him understand anything. And what did he mean, *he loves Claire?* He had no business loving her.

"I only wanted her once. Just once." The disgusting man waved a single finger in the air. "I wanted to feel her. Is that so wrong?" Had he not been drunk, Andrew doubted he would've been talking so openly. And if he'd been sober, Andrew would've likely punched him.

"YES! It was WRONG! She wasn't YOURS to HAVE!" Perhaps a hard slap across the face would sober him up. He tightened his fists. What had he done to her? Probably the reason Beth didn't want to see him.

"Don't yell at me!" He fired back, then held his head in his hands. He was most likely getting a headache, but Andrew felt no sympathy for him.

The coffee had finished brewing, so Andrew poured a cup. "Drink this!"

Henry took it from his hand and sipped, then nibbled at the bread. It would take him a good deal of time to reach full sobriety and Andrew didn't have that long.

"Mr. Alexander, I have to tell you about YOUR NEPHEW and CLAIRE!"

"Please don't yell. It hurts. I'll watch you speak and I'll understand." Though his head still bobbled, he looked at Andrew.

Andrew took a deep breath. "There was an accident. I'm sorry, but your nephew drowned. He *died*."

Mr. Alexander stared blankly, then tears formed in his eyes. "Gerald's dead?"

"Yes. I'm so sorry."

The man's body jerked, then shook. "No! He can't be dead!" He hunched over the table and sobbed without control.

Andrew went to his side and knelt down. "I'm very sorry, Mr. Alexander. I know he was a good man."

"It's my fault! If I hadn't done what I did they never woulda left." His face went blank and his tears stopped. "W—Wait. You said you came to tell me 'bout Gerald *and* Claire. Is she . . . Oh, God! Is she dead, too?"

"No. She's in the hospital. But she . . ." He swallowed hard. "She may not live." The words had been almost impossible to say.

"NO! NO!" He beat his fists on the table. "I have to go to her! She needs me!"

"She doesn't need you like this. You have to pull yourself together!"

"No! I gotta go now! You hafta take me to her!" He tried to stand, but teetered. Andrew put him back in his chair. Even in his drunken state, the man managed to feel grief and obviously remorse. Tears flowed from his eyes.

"You come to the hospital when you're able. I have to go back now. *Alone*. And one more thing . . . Beth wants you tell Claire's Aunt Martha what happened and where to find Claire. Can you remember all this?" Andrew grasped the man's shoulders. "Can you remember?"

"Yep. I can." He glanced up, then laid his head back down on the table and cried. "It's my fault. Gerald's dead. It's all my fault."

In his drunken state, Andrew doubted he'd remember *anything*, so he decided to find something he could write on to leave instructions. Unable to find what he needed in the kitchen, or the downstairs bedroom, he went upstairs.

Their bedroom.

He froze, staring at the pine bed. *GERALD & CLAIRE ALEXANDER, SEPTEMBER 2, 1871. The bed they shared.*

His stomach twisted into knots, feeling a new kind of pain. He couldn't stay in this room, thinking of her with him. He crossed the hall to a room even more difficult to bear. The crib stung his heart; more proof of her love for Gerald.

Spying a desk in the corner of the room, he found paper and a pen and wrote instructions for Mr. Alexander. After leaving the nursery, he had his foot on the top step when something compelled him to go back to their bedroom. He lifted a pillow from their bed and pressed it to his face.

Honey. Claire's scent. His heart thumped. He had to get back to her.

He flew down the stairs and went to the kitchen. Henry had passed out face down on the table, so Andrew tucked the note under one of his hands. Surely, he'd find it there.

* * *

When Andrew returned to the hospital, Sally stopped him. "Dr. Fletcher!"

"What is it? I'm in a bit of a hurry." Claire needed her treatment.

"Miss O'Malley was here." Sally leaned toward him with wide eyes. "She was looking for you. She said you were supposed to have dinner with her and you didn't show up. I didn't know where you'd gone. She's very concerned."

He rubbed his temples. His worry over Claire had caused him to forget his plans to meet Victoria at Sylvia's. "Did she go home?"

"Yes. She said to tell you to come by for supper this evening. I told her you must have been called away on an emergency." She smiled sweetly, but because of her past encounters with Victoria, the ordeal had to have been uncomfortable for her. Victoria could be quite demanding.

"As a matter of fact I was. Thank you, Sally. " After returning her smile, he went up the stairs to tend to Claire.

Beth hadn't budged. She looked up at him and sighed. "I'm glad you're back, Dr. Fletcher." She frowned. "Claire hasn't moved."

"Well then, we'll need to do something about that." He went to Claire's side. "I'll need to give her more fluids. I know you don't like seeing the needle. Why don't you go and stretch your legs again?"

"All right. How long?"

"Give me thirty minutes." He rested his hand on her shoulder, prompting a smile. Then she dutifully left the room.

Before starting the fluids, he moved Claire's legs and arms to stimulate her circulation. He intended to instruct the nurses to do the same on a regular basis. Her muscles needed to be kept active.

A bruise had formed on her arm where he'd previously put the needle, but it couldn't be helped. He inserted another needle and started the slow process of administering the saline.

If only I could give her food.

Miss Elliott stepped into the room. "Mrs. Stevens told me to bathe her, change her, and freshen her bedding."

"Yes, thank you. I'm about done." He didn't take his eyes off Claire. *Please, wake up.*

"I'll come back in five minutes," Miss Elliott said.

He finished the treatment, removed the needle, and bandaged her arm. Then he bent down and kissed her on the forehead. "Wake up, Claire," he whispered. "Come back to me."

Resting his cheek against hers, he smelled her hair. It no longer held its sweet honey scent. It had the unpleasant odor of Mobile Bay.

He sat up just in time. Miss Elliott returned and stood over his shoulder.

"When you bathe her, could you please wash her hair?" Andrew asked.

She tipped her head, questioning him with her eyes. "Yes, Dr. Fletcher. I'll take care of her." Perhaps it had been a strange request, being she'd only been there one day, but he didn't care.

As he left the room, he met Beth in the hallway. "The nurse is going to bathe her. You should wait a bit longer before you go back in."

"Oh, all right." She blinked hard. The puffiness in her eyes hadn't diminished.

She's exhausted. "You were up all night, weren't you?"

"I couldn't sleep."

"Have you eaten?"

"No. Couldn't do that neither." She hung her head.

"You need to eat something. Why don't I buy you some dinner? There's a café next to the hotel. It's just around the corner. The food's good and I *want* you to eat." He lifted her chin and emphasized his doctor's orders with a firm stare.

"You're gonna buy me dinner?" Her voice quivered.

He extended his arm. "I missed my dinner break and I'd love to buy your dinner." Otherwise, she could end up in the bed next to Claire. "Wait here a moment." He went down the hallway to the nurses' station. Mrs. Stevens was there speaking to one of her staff. She abruptly stopped her conversation.

"Good," she said, looking at him over the top of her glasses. "I was hoping to see you, Dr. Fletcher. You left un-expectedly. How is Mrs. Alexander?"

"I had to leave to give the news of her husband's death to their uncle. Her condition hasn't changed. I'll continue to administer saline treatments every four hours."

"That demands a lot of you. Are you certain it's necessary?"

"It'll keep her hydrated if nothing else. I have to do *something*. I can't just let her lie there." He stood firm.

"Don't let your care for her interfere with the rest of your patients. Mr. Schultz would *not* be pleased."

Mr. Schultz is never pleased.

"I'll finish the remainder of my rounds after dinner. I haven't eaten yet today and want to keep my head clear. I'm going to take Miss Alexander with me to Sylvia's. She needs to eat *and* sleep. I hope to convince her to get a room and get some rest."

"That's kind of you, Doctor. Her family must mean a great deal to you." The woman finally smiled.

"Yes, they do. I'll be back in one hour." He returned to Beth.

Aside from being tired, Beth appeared timid when they sat down to eat. She picked at her food and only ate few bites. He understood grief. It's impossible to do much of anything when grieving, but there seemed to be something more to her behavior.

It struck him upside the head.

How could I have been so blind?

Angry that he hadn't realized it sooner, the way she kept gazing into his eyes told everything. She believed their meal to be more than just a friendly gesture. What could he say to her that would make her understand without hurting her feelings?

He dabbed at his mouth with a napkin, then smiled at her. "I was supposed to have met my fiancée here for dinner today, but I forgot. She came by the hospital while I was at your uncle's. Hopefully, she'll forgive me. I appreciate you accompanying me for the meal."

Beth stared at her plate. "Your fiancée?"

"Yes, I'm to be married on the seventeenth of this month. Her name is Victoria O'Malley." Had he been gentle enough?

New tears formed in her eyes. Obviously *not* gentle enough.

She set down her fork. "I'm happy for you."

"Thank you." He regretted telling her, but having her misinterpret his intentions would be far worse.

She turned her head and wiped her eyes. "Got sumthin' in my eye," she muttered without looking at him. When she faced him she blinked hard. "So, you seen Henry? How'd he take the news?" She lifted her fork and prodded at her food.

"Not well. He was intoxicated. Does he drink often?"

"Uncle Henry was drunk? Don't sound like him." Her mouth twisted and she gazed upward. "Well, he *did* hit the bottle after Aunt Sarah died. That was 'bout seven years ago. But he gave up drinkin' since then."

"He's back at it again. He kept saying that it was his fault. He didn't make a lot of sense—something to do with kissing Claire?" Maybe she could tell him more.

"He done more than just kiss her!" Beth's eyes lit on fire, then she shifted them around the café, breathing hard. "He was on her," she whispered, leaning in. "Tried havin' his way with her. Gerald got there just in time. My own uncle. Makes me sick."

I should've punched him.

Pushing aside his anger, he focused on Beth. "So that's why they left? They went to the shore to get away?" Claire's house on their beautiful beach.

"Yep. Gerald wanted to get far away from him. And he did, didn't he?" Her chin quivered and she lowered her head.

"It seems you're about done eating. Would you like me to walk you to the hotel?"

"No, I'll go myself. Wouldn't look right for an engaged man to accompany a single woman to a hotel." She stood. "Thank you for dinner." She walked out of the café and left him sitting there.

No, he had *not* helped her grief.

* * *

Andrew went back to work, saw to all of his other patients, then returned to Claire to give her a saline treatment before he left to have supper at the O'Malley's.

His head reeled. How would he split his time between obligation and desire? If he'd been able, he wouldn't have left Claire's side. Even though things were going well with Victoria, he didn't look forward to seeing her tonight. After seeing Claire, he had no doubt she still held his heart.

Izzy had prepared a wonderful meal, but all the while he watched the clock, knowing he needed to get back to Claire. With his mind elsewhere, he paid little attention to conversation at the supper table.

"Drew?" Victoria patted the table. "Did you hear what I asked you?"

"I'm sorry, Victoria. What did you say?"

"I asked what time your daddy will be here on Saturday.

I know you told me, but I don't remember." She tilted her head and batted her eyes.

"One o'clock. His train arrives at one."

"I can't *wait* to meet him." She tittered and wiggled in her chair.

"What?"

"Where are you tonight, Drew? You've not joined in on any of the conversation. Are you all right?"

"Yes. I'm fine. But I have a patient I need to see to. She's unconscious and I have to administer treatments to her every four hours."

"Can't someone else do it for you?" her father asked.

"No. It's a new procedure and is quite delicate. One small mistake and the woman would die."

"That's horrible!" Mrs. O'Malley exclaimed. "The poor woman."

"I just hope I can help her," Andrew said, staring at his food. "Please don't think me rude, but I need to get back to the hospital. I'll likely get a room at the hotel. It'll be easier for me."

"Yes, stay in the city," O'Malley muttered. "It's what I've been telling you to do all the while."

"Do you truly have to go now, Drew?" Victoria pouted. "We haven't had our dessert yet."

"I need to make arrangements for someone to watch my house so I can stay in town. I need to go." Disregarding her disappointment, he stood.

"I'll walk with you outside." Victoria rose to her feet.

He knew what she wanted. This had become routine. The moment they were out the door, she wrapped her arms around him. "I hate that you have to leave so soon. I've missed you."

"I'm sorry. But I'm a doctor and these things happen sometimes. You're going to be my wife, so you need to understand."

"I do, but I don't like it." She lifted her face to his and puckered her lips.

He bent down and lightly kissed her.

"That's all?" she whimpered.

"For now. I'll see you again on Friday night. And soon you'll have me *every* night."

"It can't come soon enough for me." She pouted again, then hugged him one more time.

Every night.

He shook his head and left.

* * *

Before returning to the hospital, Andrew went to see Alicia Tarver. He had to tell her about Claire.

She poured them some coffee and sat with him at the table. "You mean to tell me that woman what left you is in your hospital an' you're treatin' her?" Alicia sighed. "Lawdy, Doc. You have your hands full. Your weddin's in a few weeks and now you have that woman messin' with your head again."

"Why do you say that? I'm trying to help her." He cradled his coffee cup. "Claire's unconscious. How could she mess with my head?"

"She may be unconscious, but I can tell by the way you talk 'bout her you's still in love with her."

He said nothing. Alicia was right. How could she read him so well? He put his head in his hands. "Yes, I'm still in love with her. There. I said it. Are you happy?"

Alicia laughed.

He glowered at her. "This situation is nothing to laugh at."

"I'm sorry, Doc. I know you're hurtin', but you shore do know how to get yourself into a mess. It was never that hard for Lijah an' me. We always knew we was in love. Never tried to hide it. Least not from each other." She'd sobered and reached across the table, taking his hand. "What happens when she wakes up? Her husband's gone, Doc. You love her. You gonna tell her? An' what 'bout Miss Victoria?"

"I don't know *what* I'm going to do. I don't know if Claire *will* wake up. But I *do* know I want her to. I don't want her to die."

"Then you'd best do some prayin'. You're gonna need hep. You just follow your heart, then you'll know what you needs to do." She released his hand and gave it a pat.

"Elijah told me the same thing once." The memory of his friend calmed him and he managed to smile.

"My Lijah. Always knew 'bout love." She closed her eyes and her face warmed.

"I miss him," he whispered and she nodded her agreement. He couldn't understand how she managed to live each day without him. Even though Claire was no longer his, he had no idea how he'd cope with her dying.

After thanking her for the coffee, he arranged for Clay to tend the horses and chickens while he stayed at the hotel. Alicia assured him she could manage without Clay for a while.

He returned to the hospital and followed his heart. Right back to Claire's bedside.

CHAPTER 27

Andrew managed to get a small amount of sleep at the hotel. Per his instruction, the nurses sent someone to wake him every four hours. He'd jump right out of bed, go to Claire, administer the treatment, then return to his room and try to sleep again. It made for a difficult night, but he'd do anything for Claire.

Morning came too early. He trudged to Claire's room and found Beth by her side.

"Good morning, Beth," he said as he walked up to her. Hopefully, she'd overcome her disappointment about his upcoming marriage.

"Mornin', Dr. Fletcher. Looks like she ain't changed none."

"Don't lose hope. Keep saying prayers for her. God will hear you."

"I will. I don't wanna lose her, too."

Neither do I.

There would probably be more visitors today. Once Mr. Alexander woke from his stupor, he'd read the note and likely everything would come back to him . . . *painfully.*

"Beth . . ." He almost laid a hand on her shoulder, but pulled back. "I need to speak with Mrs. Stevens, but I'll be back soon for Mrs. Alexander's treatment. And Beth—it's possible your uncle will come to see her."

"I don't want him here!"

He shared her feelings, but that wouldn't keep the man away. "He's not a blood relative." He whispered the words, thinking aloud. "I agree with you. He shouldn't see her."

Beth gave him a satisfied nod.

"I'll let the staff know he's not allowed in her room. As for her Aunt Martha—"

"That's different," Beth jumped in. "Claire would want her here. Even though I don't 'specially care for her, Claire loves her."

"You don't like her?"

She wrinkled her nose. "It ain't polite to say bad things 'bout people. All I can say is—she's rubbed me the wrong way a time or two. She's a might outspoken."

"Well then, I'll look forward to meeting her." He grinned. *Outspoken just like her niece.*

"Oh, don't worry none. She'll like *you*. Likes good-lookin' men." The moment the words left her mouth, her cheeks flushed a brilliant red. Her hands flew up and covered her face.

He decided to ease her discomfort with a simple, "Thank you."

Still using her hands to hide behind, Beth turned her back on him. She didn't say another word.

"I'll be back soon," he said and left her to her embarrassment.

Keeping Mr. Alexander away from Claire would be best for everyone concerned. It shouldn't have taken Beth to make him realize it. Regardless of whether or not the man wanted to see Claire, the mere mention of him made his blood boil.

If it came down to the possibility that she may not recover, he'd allow him to see her—only to say his goodbyes. But he quickly cast the thought aside. Mr. Alexander would have to keep his distance, and he certainly wouldn't be left alone with her.

God forbid.

After checking on his other patients and warning the staff about Henry Alexander, Andrew returned to Claire's room. Beth wasn't alone.

He assumed the woman with her to be Claire's aunt, but she looked *nothing* like Claire.

They must be relatives by marriage, not blood.

She stood upon seeing him, then turned and winked at Beth. "You was right."

"I'm Dr. Fletcher," he said, smiling.

"Yes, you are. I'm Martha Montgomery. You takin' good care a my niece?" Her eyes narrowed as she leaned in with her hands on her hips.

"Yes, ma'am. I'm doing everything I can for her. It's up to her now." He gazed at Claire and smiled, then absentmindedly stroked her hand.

"Hmm," Mrs. Montgomery mumbled.

What was I thinking? His gesture hadn't been that of a doctor and he knew Claire's aunt noticed. He pulled his hand to himself and crossed his arms.

"You an Indian?" Mrs. Montgomery asked, weaving her eyebrows.

Odd question. "I'm *half* Indian. Cherokee." A nervous chuckle came from his throat. "Why do you ask?"

"What you say your name was?"

"Dr. Fletcher. *Andrew* Fletcher." He smiled, but something about the way she studied him made him uneasy. *What's she thinking?*

The woman stood on her tiptoes and peered into his eyes. Her mouth dropped open wide.

Beth stepped in front of her. "I didn't know your given name was Andrew." She shook her head and grinned. "That's my nephew's middle name. Imagine that."

Mrs. Montgomery hadn't taken her eyes from him. "Yep. Imagine that."

His stomach twisted and he had to turn away from them. Why would Claire give the baby his name?

"You should see that boy," Mrs. Montgomery went on. "Has the darkest hair an' eyes I ever seen. Almost like yours."

Andrew tried to clear his dry throat. His heart raced. "Must take after his mother."

"He don't look like his daddy. That's for sure," Beth said. "Gerald always said he was glad a that. He never liked his own appearance, but *I* thought he was handsome."

"You all right, Doc?" Mrs. Montgomery asked. "You're lookin' a little pale. No offense."

"I'm rather tired—haven't had much sleep lately—but I'm fine. If you'll excuse me, I have other patients to see. I'll be back soon for her treatment." He nodded. "It was nice to meet you, Mrs. Montgomery." He hurried from the room.

Is it possible? Could Claire's child be mine?

He had to find out the truth. But how?

"Dr. Fletcher!" Sister O'Casey rushed toward him. Of all of the Sisters of Charity, Mary Margaret had always been his favorite, even though she could be a little overwhelming.

She fanned her face with her hand, winded. "I hear you're tendin' Mrs. Alexander. Such a shame about her husband. And if she dies, the poor child will have no parent at all."

"Do you know her?"

"Aye! 'Twas I who helped bring her babe into the world. I was her midwife. I never forget any of the little ones I deliver. This one was special to me."

"How is that?" Could the answer to his questions have fallen into his lap?

"Such a lovely couple. They were so certain the babe was premature, but he was the most healthy, beautiful lad I ever delivered." She lowered her voice, put her hand beside her mouth, and shifted her eyes from side to side. "He was full term. They hadn't been married long enough to warrant it. She asked me not to say a word to the uncle. Didn't want him to know of their—well—premature passion." Her eyes grew wide and she nodded her head.

"I see." More than she'd ever know. "When was he born? Do you remember the date?" His heart pounded, waiting for the answer.

"Aye. 'Twas one month before me brother's birthday. I was knittin' him a sweater." She grinned. " 'Twas April the twenty-fifth sure as anything."

The calculations weren't difficult. He couldn't move. Aside from his thumping heart, his body had gone numb.

He's mine.

Mary Margaret tipped her head. "Your face is a wee bit pale, Doctor. You should get some air. Mind if I look in on the lass?"

"Of course. Thank you, Sister. She could use your prayers."

"She has them." Mary Margaret scurried away and left him standing alone.

Yes, he needed air.

A lot of it.

In a daze, he walked out the front door and stood on the steps of the hospital. The sun shone bright and the sky was clear, like many days before. But everything had changed. Placing his hands on the concrete wall, he steadied himself. He closed his eyes and breathed in the fresh air, trying to keep his self-control.

I have a son!

How was it possible to burst with joy and simultaneously hurt?

She knew he was mine. Why didn't she tell me?

Perhaps he didn't know her as well as he thought and had completely misjudged her character. Regardless, he had to contain his feelings. If she didn't wake up, he'd never be able to claim the child. He had no legal rights to Michael. Only Claire's word could reveal the truth. Aside from that, he couldn't shame her memory be telling her family that *he'd* fathered her son.

I'd never do that to her. I love her too much.

But one day soon, he wanted to see the child.

Regaining his composure, he went back to Claire's room and carried on as if nothing had happened. Her aunt kept looking at him as if she knew. Maybe she did. Beth seemed oblivious to everything, focusing solely on Claire's recovery.

"I told Martha 'bout Uncle Henry," Beth said, holding Claire's hand. "She wondered why they wouldn't let him come to Claire's room with her. She an' Henry came here together, but now she feels like me. She don't never want him 'round her."

Mrs. Montgomery grumbled something he couldn't make out and twisted her face. "Damn! Forgot my spittoon. Be right back." She bustled out of the room.

"She ain't too happy," Beth said.

"None of us are." He glanced over his shoulder, still in awe of Mrs. Montgomery's behavior.

"Good thing is, our preacher came by while you was gone." Beth brightened talking about someone other than her uncle.

"I'm sorry I missed him."

Mrs. Montgomery came back in the room, wiping her mouth. "Didn't wanna spit on the hospital floor."

"Thank you," Andrew said. A very unique woman, to say the least.

Beth sighed. "I was just startin' to tell him 'bout Gerald." She frowned at Claire's aunt, then returned her attention to him. "They done buried him next to Claire's mama. Reverend Brown said they're gonna have a memorial service on Sunday. I wanna go, but you reckon I should leave Claire—I mean—if she ain't awake yet?"

"*I'll* be here," Mrs. Montgomery said. "You need to go to your brother's service. Doc an' me can take care a Claire. Right, Doc?"

"Y-Yes." The look the woman gave him confirmed his gut feeling. "You should go to the service."

"They couldn't find his glasses," Beth muttered. "But Reverend Brown said he don't need 'em in Heaven. He's seein' just fine without 'em." Tears glistened in her eyes.

Mrs. Montgomery swung her arm over Beth's shoulder. "Now don't you cry. Your brother's in a better place. But I know you miss him."

"Reckon he's watchin' over us?"

The woman shuddered. "That idea always gives me the willies. Thought a someone invisible watchin' everythin' I do. Some things I don't want no one watchin'. Reckon Doc feels the same. Don't ya, Doc?"

"Yes, Mrs. Montgomery, I do. Some things are private." Their eyes met and she offered him a warm smile. *What did Claire tell her?*

"Heck! Call me Martha."

He liked her more every minute. "Very well, Martha."

* * *

Martha booked a room at the hotel and told Andrew that as long as Claire was in the hospital, she wasn't going anywhere. He wasn't either. It would be impossible for him to continue Claire's treatments without being close by. Besides, he *wanted* to be close to her.

Claire had been in the hospital four days and her condition hadn't changed.

Andrew paced the floor in her room, as if his presence alone might wake her. Beth and Martha had gone to eat, so he was once more alone with her. Every time he got near her, he wanted to hold her, but remained professional and sat beside her, keeping his distance.

"Claire, there's so much I need to know. Please come back to me." Scooting in closer, he kissed her cheek.

She's so cold.

He breathed in her sweet scent. The nurses had washed her hair more than once and he couldn't resist nestling his face into her neck.

What am I doing? He sat upright and stared at her, then took hold of her hand and caressed her fingers.

"Drew?" Victoria's voice startled him and he jerked free from Claire.

"Victoria?" He stood and kissed her cheek. "I'm surprised to see you."

"I can see that," she fumed, glaring at Claire. "Who is she?"

"She's the woman I told you about. Mrs. Alexander." He lifted his chin and smiled. Would she see through his feelings?

"The one whose husband died?"

"Yes. The one I've been caring for all week. She's no better." He couldn't mask his disappointment.

"She looks dead. Why don't they take her away and bury her?" Her tone flowed with jealousy.

He held back what he wanted to say and remained calm. "They've given me a week. I have until Monday. Hopefully she'll wake up by then."

"Hmm . . . Seems like a waste of your time. Besides, we have a lot to do to get ready for the weddin'. Your daddy will be here in two days. Have you reserved a room for him?"

"Yes, I have. Don't worry. We'll have everything done in plenty of time for the wedding." He took hold of her hand, gently caressing her skin.

Her demeanor softened. She batted her eyes, gazing at their adjoined hands. "Have you eaten? I thought we could go to Sylvia's."

"That would be fine. I need to report to Mrs. Stevens, then we can go."

"Good." She kissed his cheek. "I've missed you, Drew."

When they walked into Sylvia's, Andrew spotted Beth and Martha and took Victoria to their table.

"Beth, Mrs. Montgomery, I'd like you to meet my fiancée, Victoria O'Malley." He smiled as he presented her, then had to restrain a chuckle when Beth's eyes popped wide, staring at Victoria's protruding bosom.

"Pleased to meet ya," Beth said, wrinkling her nose.

Andrew immediately recognized Victoria's forced smile. She tilted her head and opened her mouth to speak, but before she uttered a sound Martha lifted a cloth napkin from the table and placed it over Victoria's cleavage.

"Beth here was tellin' me you was gettin' married." Martha peered into Victoria's face. "Hope your weddin' dress is a might larger than this here dress ya have on. Seems you're fallin' outta this one."

Andrew covered his mouth. Victoria would never forgive him for laughing. *Outspoken* didn't come close to describing Martha.

"Oh!" Victoria huffed, threw the napkin on the floor, and pulled Andrew to another table. "How rude! How do you know those people?"

"They're the family of the woman you saw me with at the hospital. They're staying in town until she's better." He spoke with calm reassurance.

"Backwoods country folk! They have no sense of fashion." Victoria waved her hand in their direction. "About that *woman*. Why were you holdin' her hand?"

"I wasn't. I was . . . taking her pulse."

"Then why'd you pull away so quickly when I called out your name?" Her lips pursed with tight confrontation.

"You startled me. I lost count." Her expression hadn't softened, so he decided to say more. "She's my patient, Victoria. You needn't worry about her."

"She's also a woman. An *attractive* woman. First time you ever found me attractive was when *I* was unconscious. Maybe you like that sort of thing."

He grinned, remembering her in the ice bath. She was right. He'd first become fond of her then. "I prefer you conscious. You're much more fun that way."

"I can't wait until we can have some *real* fun. I'm countin' the days."

She hadn't been pushing herself on him, but often made sexual insinuations. And though she'd agreed to wait, he knew she didn't like it. She overflowed with desire—long overdue for personal gratification.

After they finished their meal, he returned to work and Victoria went home. Would Martha or Beth comment about her? He had no doubt what they must be thinking. He often thought it himself.

CHAPTER 28

The time had come for Claire's midnight treatment. Andrew trudged toward her door, not fully awake.

Why is it closed?

Her door was never closed. Even when the nurses changed her, they left it ajar. Worse yet, when he attempted to open it, it was locked. His heart pounded as he rapped on the door and worsened when no one answered.

He sped to the nurses' station, completely awake. "Why is Mrs. Alexander's room locked?"

The night nurse furrowed her brow. "It shouldn't be. We never lock the doors." She dug into a desk drawer, then handed him a key. "This should work."

He fled down the hall and inserted the room key. The door still wouldn't open, so he beat on it. "Who's in there?" he yelled.

Pressing his ear to the door, he could've sworn he heard someone jump from her bed.

Damn it!

Sweat beaded on his brow. He jiggled the key until finally, the lock clicked and the door opened.

Mr. Alexander?

Andrew glared at him. "What are you DOING HERE? And why did you LOCK the DOOR?"

The man backed into the far corner of the room. "You don't understand. I had to see her!" His face puckered as though he might cry. "Please, let me stay."

"No! You need to LEAVE." Andrew's eyes shifted to Claire. Her blankets were rumpled and her hands weren't across her stomach as they'd been when he left. His chest heaved with anger. Fuming, he shifted his focus back to Henry. "What did you DO to her?"

"Nothin'! I just talked to her." He inched closer to Claire. "Reckon she heard me?" He'd lowered his voice, but wouldn't look at Andrew.

Andrew wanted to believe him, but the wrench in his gut warned him otherwise. Not wanting to yell, he took the man's chin in his hand and forced him to look his way. "I don't know. No one knows what a person is aware of when they're unconscious." He couldn't mask his anger. Even with a hearing impairment, Andrew had no doubt the man read him loud and clear.

Mr. Alexander took a step back and stared at the floor. Andrew gave Claire his full attention. He wanted to examine her and affirm the man hadn't touched her, but he'd have to do it later. For now, he repositioned her hands over her stomach.

A ring encircled her finger. It hadn't been there before. "Where did *THAT* come from?"

"Don't know. It's her weddin' ring. They musta found it."

In a brief moment of calm, Andrew lifted her hand and fingered the ring. "It's beautiful. I'm certain she'll be happy it was found."

Mr. Alexander scratched the back of his head. "I reckon I'll be goin' then. Don't tell Beth I was here."

"It would be best if you STAY AWAY, Mr. Alexander. Best for everyone." Andrew crossed his arms and watched the man limp out of the room. Once the tapping of his cane grew faint, Andrew pushed the door nearly shut.

He moved to Claire's side and ran his fingers through her hair. "I hope he didn't hurt you. I'm sorry I wasn't here." After tucking the blankets around her, he kissed her cheek, then sat and prepared the saline.

Once he finished the treatment, he'd give her a thorough examination. He wouldn't leave her again. Not tonight.

* * *

Sleeping in a chair in Claire's room had been uncomfortable, but Andrew would endure anything for her. After administering her morning saline treatment, he reluctantly left her to see to another patient.

"Dr. Fletcher," Miss Elliott said, coming to his side. "Miss Alexander is asking for you. She's in Mrs. Alexander's room and is very upset."

He'd only been gone from her room for thirty minutes. What could have possibly happened in such a short amount of time? Had her uncle come back?

"Thank you," he said and hastened to Claire's room.

Beth stood beside her. Her head jerked up when he entered and she greeted him with anger-filled eyes.

"What's wrong?"

She lifted Claire's hand. "How'd he get in here?" She spit the words out and pointed at the ring.

"Who?"

"Uncle Henry! He put this on her finger and I can't get it off!" She yanked and pulled.

"Please . . . *don't*." He took Claire's hand and returned it to a comfortable position. "Isn't it her wedding ring?"

"No! That ring was my Aunt Sarah's. Henry tried to give it to Claire at Christmas. She didn't want it because she knew he wanted her. This just ain't right!" She broke into tears.

"Please don't cry." He rested his hand against her back. "Yes, your uncle was here last night. I don't know how he got in, but I'll make certain it doesn't happen again." He examined Claire's finger, wishing he hadn't failed her. "I'll try to remove it later. Her hand is swollen right now. He must have forced it on her." And it certainly didn't help having Beth try to yank it off.

"I hate him!"

"I'll have someone watch her room at night and tell the front desk to watch for him as well. A man limping with a cane should be easy to see. I'm sorry this happened." More than she'd ever realize.

"She's helpless right now! He coulda done things to her. I don't even like to think 'bout it."

"Then don't. And I can assure you, he didn't harm her."

"He ain't himself," she said, calming. "I know he loved Gerald, an' I know he's hurtin', but he still had no right. She's not *his* wife."

Miss Elliott came in to give Claire a bath and change the bedding, so Beth moved toward the door. They'd become used to the routine. The only one missing was

Martha, who he assumed slept in. She'd been exhausted with worry.

"Dr. Fletcher," Miss Elliott said. "I thought you should know. Her milk is finally drying up."

"What?"

"Her milk. She'd been nursing a baby before she came here. Mrs. Stevens was concerned her milk would back up and cause infection. Didn't she tell you about it?"

"No, she didn't. I wonder why?" He tipped his head, questioning Miss Elliott with his eyes.

Blushing, she looked down. "Maybe it's because it's a woman's problem. She may have thought you didn't need to know. We took care of her."

"I'm her doctor. I should know everything." He spoke sternly, but then smiled at the nurse. "Thank you for telling me." He left her to tend to Claire and joined Beth in the hallway.

"That poor baby," Beth said. "He wasn't even weaned. Claire didn't wanna stop. Said she liked the closeness with him. I hope he likes cow's milk or Mrs. Sandborn is gonna have an awful time. All he ever had was his mama."

He gaped at her, and his heart began to race.

Of course! "Why didn't I think of it before?" He grabbed Beth and hugged her, lifting her off the floor.

Her eyes popped. "Why'd you do that, Dr. Fletcher?"

He laughed and set her down. "I'm sorry. But what you said made me realize something. I never considered cow's milk. We need to get a milk cow."

"Who needs a cow?" Martha walked toward him. "I got one. Tessie's a good cow."

"No, you live too far away. I need a cow I can bring to the hospital." He paced the floor, thinking hard.

"Uncle Henry has a cow," Beth mumbled.

"Your uncle Henry might be able to do something good after all." He never imagined he'd be excited about seeing the man again. "I need to go there right away."

"What you gonna do, Doc?" Martha asked.

"Feed Claire!" He ran down the hall and out the door and didn't even stop to tell Mrs. Stevens he was leaving.

* * *

Andrew beat on Henry Alexander's door, and the moment he opened it, grabbed him by the arms. "Mr. Alexander, we need your COW!" He had no time for formalities.

"Rosie?" he asked, scratching his head. "Why you need Rosie?"

"I need her MILK—for CLAIRE."

"Claire can't drink milk. Claire can't do nothin' right now." He scowled at Andrew as if he'd lost his mind.

"She's not going to DRINK it. I'm going to put it in her VEINS."

"You're crazy! You tryin' to kill her?" Sneering, he waved his hand in Andrew's face, then turned and walked away.

Andrew hurriedly followed him and stopped him, looking directly at him. "No. I plan to feed her. It hasn't been tried many times before, but I'm almost out of time and options. I'm willing to try anything. I read about the procedure in a medical journal about two years ago. It's been done, but the milk has to be fresh and clean. Straight from the cow to the patient. We'll have to take Rosie to the hospital."

"You *are* crazy! 'Sides, there are plenty a cows what provide milk to the hospital. You don't need mine." Mr. Alexander waved his cane and pointed to the door.

"I need one no one else will be using! I need *YOUR* COW!" Andrew gripped the man's arms and stared into his eyes.

"I'll do it long as you let me see her again. You can be in the room when I do, but I wanna see her!"

Andrew had no choice, so he released him and did his best to calm down. "Fine. Can we put ROSIE in the back of your WAGON? We need to get her there as QUICKLY as possible."

Mr. Alexander mumbled the entire time they loaded Rosie into the wagon, but Andrew ignored him. He tied his horse to the rear so he could drive and Mr. Alexander could hold Rosie steady in the back. Mr. Schultz would probably call him to his office again, but he didn't care. This could be Claire's last hope.

When they reached the hospital, they parked the wagon around back and led Rosie into the grass, where she immediately started grazing. Mr. Alexander stayed with her while Andrew went inside to get a sterile bottle and Aunt Martha. Since Martha wanted to help in any way she could, he'd trust her to do the milking rather than Beth's uncle.

"Martha, I need you to milk the cow. I've got a clean bottle to put the milk in." Andrew rushed around getting the supplies he needed to take care of Rosie. He then showed Martha where to wash up and took her to the cow.

"Good thing I hadn't milked her this mornin'," Mr. Alexander said. He positioned a stool for her that he'd brought along and smiled with a nervous, crooked smile. "She's got plenty."

Martha scowled and sat. The tension in the air could've been cut with a knife. None of them had any respect for the man, but they endured him for Claire's sake.

Andrew knelt beside Martha to clean and sterilize Rosie's udders. Then Martha squeezed out the milk while he held the bottle. Even with all the tension, he beamed. He finally had hope. More hope than he'd had since Claire first arrived at the hospital.

When the bottle became half full, Andrew raced with it up the stairs. He mixed it with saline and prepared to administer it.

Beth left the room.

"Claire," he whispered. "This will give you some of the nutrients the saline doesn't carry. I want to keep you strong." After glancing over his shoulder, he put his lips to her ear. "Our son needs you."

Her body had become weak and he had difficulty finding a vein. But he persisted and was able to release the milky fluid. Slow and steady. It had to work.

* * *

Andrew had barely tapped on the door, when Mr. Schultz told him to come in.

As he stepped inside, he noticed Dr. Mitchell standing by the man's desk.

What?

He gave Andrew an encouraging smile.

"Dr. Fletcher," Mr. Schultz said. "You never cease to surprise me. Now we have a cow on hospital property. What in God's name do you think you're doing?" He glared at Andrew with his arms folded across his chest.

"I'm trying to save my patient," Andrew replied with forced composure. "She needs nourishment and I'm giving it to her."

"It's barbaric!"

"It's modern medicine! And it's been done before. Until we can develop a way to feed the unconscious, this is the best thing we can do for her." He looked toward Dr. Mitchell for help.

"Dr. Fletcher is correct," Dr. Mitchell said. *Thank you.* "But it hasn't always been successful."

"Maybe not," Andrew said. "But it's better than nothing." He wouldn't give up.

Mr. Schultz breathed heavily. "You have until Monday, then her family takes her home. Keep the cow tended and cleaned up after. Are we clear?"

"Yes, sir." Andrew said.

"One more thing. If you hear that elephant's milk is even better for her, you will *not* bring one to the hospital!" He slammed his fist on the table.

Andrew didn't reply. He grinned and headed for the door.

Dr. Mitchell followed him out. "Dr. Fletcher?"

"Yes, sir?" Andrew turned to his mentor.

"I don't want you to think I was opposing your means of caring for your patient." They stopped in the long corridor, facing each other. "Mr. Schultz called me to his office questioning your interest in this woman. He feels your behavior with her is out of line. That you're spending too much time with her."

Andrew squared his jaw. "I won't stop."

"Andrew?" Dr. Mitchell grasped his arm. "She's special to you, isn't she?"

Andrew swallowed hard. "Yes. Very much so. Please trust me on this, Harvey. I won't let my other patients suffer from lack of care. I can handle this."

Dr. Mitchell studied him, then slowly nodded. "I'll help you as much as I can."

"Thank you." He shook the man's hand, then hurried back to Claire.

CHAPTER 29

Uplifted, Andrew arrived at the O'Malley's door with a smile on his face and flowers in his hands.

"These are for you, Izzy," he said, handing her a bouquet. "And these are for Victoria." He produced a second bunch of flowers and held them close to his heart.

"What's gotten into you, Doc?" Izzy laughed and took her bundle from his hands. "They's right pretty!"

"What's gotten into me?" He beamed. "*Hope.*"

Victoria came down the stairs looking lovelier than ever. He bowed low and presented the flowers. Not wanting her to be jealous, he'd made certain her bouquet was larger than Izzy's.

Victoria's face lit up. Before she could say a word, he grabbed her around the waist and kissed her on the lips. "You look beautiful tonight."

She staggered backward. "Thank you, Drew."

Izzy laughed aloud, then took both bouquets to put in water.

For the first time in a long time, Andrew felt his life was

looking up. He wouldn't even allow Patrick O'Malley to burst his bubble.

As the man passed the food at the supper table, he eyed Andrew. "You're in a good mood tonight, lad. What's the occasion?"

"Am I normally that glum?" he asked, raising his brows.

"No," Mrs. O'Malley said. "You just seem more chipper than usual."

"I had a very good day today. I tried something at the hospital that we've never done before. I believe it may work."

"Truly?" Victoria batted her eyes. "What did you do?"

Andrew puffed up his chest. "I put cow's milk in a woman's veins."

"Cow's milk?" Victoria's parents exclaimed in unison.

Victoria scowled. "Disgustin'."

"Yes, cow's milk. Crazy as it may sound. It's been done before and I decided it was needed for my patient—the woman who's unconscious. I'm trying to save her life." Finally having an appetite, Andrew helped himself to more food.

"I thought she'd be dead by now," Victoria mumbled.

"No, she's not, thank God. But I only have until Monday, so I hope this will work. I'll need to return to the hospital after we eat. It takes even longer now that we have to milk the cow prior to each treatment."

"You have a cow at the hospital?" O'Malley bellowed. "I never heard of such a thing."

"The milk has to be fresh," Andrew said, undaunted by their obvious disapproval.

"Are you certain someone else can't give her those treatments?" Jealousy oozed from every word Victoria spoke.

"Why not Dr. Mitchell? He's been a doctor much longer than you. You shouldn't have to be doin' this all by yourself."

"Dr. Mitchell has other patients to tend. In fact, he's been helping me with some of *my* other patients to free up my time. He trusts *me* to administer this treatment. Besides, it's only a few more days." His chest tightened. *Oh, God. Only a few more days.* Claire could be gone forever.

"Good!" Victoria bubbled. "Now don't forget . . . you need to pick me up at twelve-thirty tomorrow so we can meet your daddy at the train station."

"I won't forget. Hopefully the train will be on time." He dreaded seeing his father, but maybe things would be better. "I should be on my way." He stood to leave, then nodded to her parents. "Thank you for a wonderful meal."

"It's our pleasure," Mrs. O'Malley said. "Don't forget Irish stew on Sunday. And bring your father."

"I won't forget." He walked around the table to Victoria. She hadn't finished her meal yet. "Please don't get up on my account. I'll see you tomorrow." He bent down and kissed her on the cheek.

Pouting, she raised her lips to him.

"Go on and kiss her, lad," O'Malley said. "We don't mind."

Andrew obliged and kissed her on the lips.

She smiled, then looked at her father. "Thank you, Daddy."

"That was so sweet," her mother said. She folded her hands together and grinned at the two of them.

Before leaving, Andrew stopped by the kitchen to thank Izzy. "You're the best, Izzy."

"No, *you* are, Doc. Thanks for the flowers." She hugged him and he walked out the door.

A mixture of emotions tore at his insides. Happy about what he'd accomplished today, but distressed over how little time he had left.

* * *

Andrew's fondness for Aunt Martha grew each time she milked Rosie. Since Mr. Alexander had gone home, Martha not only milked her, but also cared for her. She never complained. And though they did Claire's treatments every four hours, she got up the first time he knocked at her door.

They both loved Claire.

"Looks like Claire has more color in her face," Beth said. She'd just come in the room after Claire's most recent treatment.

"I hope you're right." Andrew found her words encouraging. He'd thought the same thing, but had been afraid to speak it aloud. "Her heart's still beating strong and the movement you've been doing with her has certainly helped."

"I'm glad." Beth sighed. "Them nurses was happy to show me what to do. Breaks my heart seein' her lie there like that."

He couldn't reveal *his* heart to Beth and simply nodded. "I couldn't have done this without you and Martha. I'm glad she went back to the hotel this morning. She needed more rest."

"Least she'll be back before I hafta leave."

"Yes, she will. Oh, and *I* need to leave after the midday treatment. I have to pick up my father at the train station.

But I'll be back by four o'clock. I imagine you'll be gone by then."

"Yep. Takes 'bout four hours to get home. I hate to go, but I hafta be there for Gerald." She let out a long breath, looking at Claire. "I don't wanna dig another grave, Dr. Fletcher."

"I don't want that either, Beth."

"I'm glad you're her doctor." She smiled at him. "I think you really care 'bout her. Not every doctor would do all you've done."

"I *do* care. She's a special woman."

"How well'd you know her?" Beth stared into his eyes.

"Not well enough."

* * *

Andrew changed into a suit before picking up Victoria. When he arrived at her home, she came out—smiling from ear to ear—and handed him a box.

"What's this?"

"It was your birthday present," she whispered, pouting. "I forgot to give it to you—what with everything that happened." She shrugged, then brightened again. "So—happy birthday!"

"Thank you." He kissed her on the cheek and opened the box. *A top hat.* He lifted it, dreading the inevitable.

"Isn't it a handsome hat?" She beamed with excitement. "Put it on, Drew. It's very much in style."

He reluctantly obliged. How could he not?

"It's perfect. You look dashin'." She nuzzled his neck and he snapped the reins.

Undoubtedly, she wanted him to dress properly in order to impress his father. But he could tell she'd taken even greater lengths grooming herself today. *Stunning* couldn't fully describe her. She wore a dark green gown, plunged as only Victoria would have it. Few women had breasts like hers and his father would certainly appreciate the view. Appropriate? Perhaps not. But he'd never attempt to change her.

White lace offset the low neckline, adding a *touch* of sophistication. Her matching parasol shaded both of them. And aside from her signature perfume, a white satin scarf around her neck completed her attire. Her scar had been well hidden.

He smiled when he noticed one final item; the heart-shaped necklace he'd given her.

Whether or not top hats were in style, he couldn't wait to remove it. He'd wear it for her, but nowhere else.

She cuddled closer. "Will your daddy love me?"

"Yes, Victoria, he'll adore you."

She giggled like a little girl.

* * *

As the train neared the station, John gazed out the window. After all these years, he still hated the south, but curiosity brought him here. He'd always been proud of what his son had accomplished in his career, but he needed to see the woman he planned to marry.

How did he ensnare the daughter of the wealthiest man in Mobile?

Most southerners would never approve of a half-breed.

The train came to a stop. He stood and smoothed his clothing. His three-piece suit had been tailored to fit his form, and as he positioned his top hat, he smiled. The woman in the seat across from him had her eyes on him.

She'd been flirting throughout the journey. Had there been time, he'd have given her a night to remember.

"Enjoy the rest of the ride," he said to her, tipping his hat. "This is my stop."

She tittered and fanned herself. Her approval gave his esteem an unnecessary boost. No one had to tell him he was good looking.

As he stepped from the train, he breathed deeply, then coughed.

Damn humidity.

He loosened his collar, plastered a smile on his face, and scanned the waiting crowd. It didn't take long before he spied Andrew. Though it had been three years since their last encounter, he hadn't changed. When his eyes shifted to the woman at his side, his pulse quickened.

Good God.

He licked his lips and moved from the platform.

* * *

Victoria gasped and clutched her bosom. "That's your *daddy?*" Andrew had just pointed to a tall, well-structured man. *So handsome.*

She'd always considered Andrew to be the best-looking man she'd ever seen, but this man had something more. He walked fully upright and proud. To be old enough to be Andrew's daddy, he'd certainly aged well. He was clean shaven, but had long sideburns. He'd retained his hair and wore it in a stylish manner. In addition, his attire exceeded all expectations. *The epitome of fashion.*

"Yes, that's him." Andrew sighed.

Her heart fluttered and unexpected warmth spread

through her body. Truly improper thoughts came to mind. "My, oh my," she muttered.

She grasped Andrew's arm and allowed him to lead her to the man. She donned one of her best smiles.

"I'm glad you're here, Father," Andrew said and shook his hand.

"It's good to see you, Andrew." He smiled at his son, then shifted his gaze to her. "And this must be your lovely fiancée." She felt his eyes on her bosom like liquid heat, so she took a deep breath to accentuate his view.

"Yes, Father, this is Victoria." Andrew stepped aside.

The man removed his hat, then bowed low. As he raised his head, he continued to study her breasts. His eyes finally lifted, meeting hers. Then he smiled. The most gorgeous smile and blue eyes she'd ever seen. Coyly, she bit her bottom lip.

"Andrew told me you were beautiful," he said. "But words can't describe what I'm seeing."

"You're too kind, Mr. Fletcher." Her heart raced. She hadn't felt this way in some time.

His attention flattered her.

She wanted more.

"Please . . . call me John." He raised her hand to his lips and kissed it. As he let go, he brushed over it with his fingers. She pursed her lips, tingling all the way to the tips of her toes.

"I'll get your bags, Father," Andrew said and walked to the platform where they'd been unloading the luggage.

John extended his arm to her. "Shall we?"

"Shall we *what*, John?" She raised her eyes slowly to meet his.

"Go to your buggy? I assume you have one waiting. We

aren't *walking* to the hotel, are we?" His deep voice made her tremble.

"Not yet." She licked her lips.

She had to be completely out of her mind flirting with Andrew's daddy. But she hadn't had this much fun in a *very* long time. Andrew returned with the luggage and followed after them. Had he been aware of her behavior? And more than that, did he notice the way his daddy had looked at her?

They drove to the hotel and she waited in the buggy while Andrew helped him take the bags to his room. Before they went inside, John looked over his shoulder and winked at her.

She squirmed in the seat.

Andrew took his place beside her and John hopped in on the other side.

"Where to now?" John asked.

Andrew took a deep breath. "I'll need to get back to the hospital soon. But—"

"Yes." She cut him off short. "He has a demandin' woman to tend to."

"Oh?" John raised his brows. "I'd hoped to see more of the city."

"*I'll* show you," she said without hesitation. "I don't mind."

"Thank you, Victoria," Andrew said. "Do *you* mind, Father?"

"Not at all." John looked directly at her. The smile he gave her made her blood boil.

Andrew stopped the buggy at the hospital, then handed the reins to his daddy. "I'll meet you at Sylvia's for supper at six. Victoria can show you where it is."

She batted her eyes. "I'll be happy to. It'll be good for the two of you to have some time alone together. But for now, *I'll* entertain your daddy."

Andrew stepped down and backed away from the buggy. She wiggled her fingers at him and John clicked to the horse. The time had come to get well acquainted with her future father-in-law.

* * *

John took Victoria home after a long ride around the city. She'd chatted nonstop and he let her. But something about her had him in knots. Though she was his son's bride-to-be, she'd been flirting with *him*. Had the situation been different, he would've already taken her to his bed. He wanted her, but he had *some* respect for Andrew. She undoubtedly wanted him, too, which made it even more difficult to resist her. *All* women wanted him.

He chuckled. *I haven't lost my touch.* Not even with someone as young as Victoria.

He'd taken Andrew's buggy to the hospital livery, then walked to Sylvia's. He flipped open his pocket watch. Six o'clock sharp. Pushing open the door, he spotted Andrew at a corner table. *Early? Impressive.*

Andrew stood upon seeing him. "I hope your day was enjoyable," he said and motioned to another seat at the table.

"Yes. *Very.* Your fiancée is fine company." He sat and placed a napkin across his lap. "I must say, you look well, Andrew."

"Thank you. So do you. I can assume your business is thriving."

"Yes. Extremely successful. My partner's handling my

clients while I'm away. He's a good attorney, who I trust completely."

They ordered the daily special and the waitress brought it quickly to their table. John stared at the mound of potatoes and roast beef, then speared a small amount on his fork and forced it into his mouth.

Is this the best Mobile has to offer?

"Don't you like the food?" Andrew asked.

"Not what I'm used to." *Another reason to hate the south.* "The *food* lacks quality, but I have to tell you—I'm *quite* impressed with Victoria. You did well for yourself." He picked at his food. At least he had *some*thing pleasant to think about.

"Thank you. She's a fine woman."

"Fine? She's more than fine. She's exquisite." He leaned toward his son. "Have you bedded her?"

Andrew wrinkled his brow and drew back. "No, I haven't. But that's not your concern."

"Why? You wrote of the other woman you had a go at. How could you not bed Victoria? If she was mine, I doubt I could keep my hands off her." His hands and *other* parts of his body.

"I'm waiting for our wedding night. Isn't that what I'm supposed to do?"

"I find it surprising, that's all." He took a sip of his coffee. "You'll have an incredible wedding night. She radiates sensuality. I'm rather jealous." The frown on his son's face indicated his disgust. Victoria had been much better company.

"She's to be my wife. I wish you wouldn't speak of her that way." Andrew's face tightened as he spoke.

"I'm only speaking the truth. You're not a *boy* any longer. Can't I speak to you like a man?"

Andrew looked away and cleared his throat. "Would it be possible for you to draw up the papers to permanently change my name?"

"Of course. It's rather simple. Not a bad idea, since you intend to remain in Alabama. I have to admit, it was odd hearing Victoria call me Mr. *Fletcher*. I suppose I'll have to endure it while I'm here."

"Is it so terrible using Mother's name? I happen to like it." Andrew sat up and defensively crossed his arms.

"No, but it's not *my* name. I'll draw up the papers. You'll have it done before the wedding. I can file them here." He stood to leave.

"Are you finished eating?"

"Yes. I've had enough of this . . . *food*." *More than enough.* "I'm tired. I think I'll go to my room."

"I'll walk with you." Andrew paid for their meal and they walked to the hotel without speaking.

Andrew hesitated at the door to his room. "I've got to go back to the hospital." His brow wove as if he had something more on his mind.

"I understand." John was tired and ready for decent sleep. He hoped the bed measured up to his standards. The food certainly hadn't. "I'll see you tomorrow then."

"Father?" Andrew laid a hand on his shoulder.

"Yes?"

"You need to know something about Victoria. It's important." Andrew's tone piqued his interest.

"I'm listening."

"She went through an ordeal not long ago. She was attacked—nearly raped. He savagely bit her. She wears a scarf to hide a scar. I wanted you to know so you'll understand. Her behavior can be erratic at times. I've been trying to help her through it."

"I see." John nodded. It explained a few things.

"I just thought you should know. Goodnight, Father."

"Goodnight."

John shut the door and readied himself for bed.

Nearly raped?

The thought disturbed him. A woman like Victoria deserved an exceptional time in bed, not something horrific. With that thought in mind, he crawled between the sheets.

* * *

Andrew returned to Claire's bedside. He brushed his fingertips along her cheek. Did it hold more color? He could only hope.

Soon he'd need to administer fluids, so he sat back and waited for Martha. The room seemed strangely quiet. Claire's shallow breath gave every indication that at any moment it could be gone forever.

He took her hand and held it to his face. The room was warm, but her hand felt icy cold. He breathed on it and tried to warm it, then held it against his chest. "Claire, my father's here. I don't know why, but I don't care to be around him. I feel no love from him. I miss *you*. You need to come back. Wake up, Claire, please wake up."

* * *

Victoria watched John drive away, then raced through the door and went straight to the kitchen. "Oh, Izzy!" She dropped into a chair in the corner of the room. "I've had the most incredible afternoon." Happier than she'd been a long time, she felt like singing.

Izzy glared at her. "What you doin' in my kitchen? I'm tryin' to fix supper."

"Is Mama home?"

"No. Your mama's havin' tea with Miss Stacey. She'll be home by the time your daddy gets home from work. Why?"

"I need to talk to you and wanted to be sure we're alone."

"You're upta sumthin'. Ain't ya?" Izzy's eyes narrowed.

"I met Andrew's daddy." Victoria tipped her head, envisioning the incredible man. "Oh, Izzy, he's the most handsome man I've ever seen."

Izzy crossed her arms and tapped her foot. "Andrew, huh? What happened to *Drew*?"

"I've come to realize he's more of an *Andrew* than a Drew." She didn't want to talk about him. She wanted to talk about John. Sitting upright, she returned Izzy's accusatory gaze. "John Fletcher is sophisticated, rich, and successful. *And* he's gorgeous. Oh—and Izzy—I felt sumthin' with him I've not felt in such a long time." She glided her hands down her own body, imagining what it would feel like if they were John's.

"Don't be doin' that in my kitchen!"

Victoria giggled. "I feel so good, Izzy! I'm happier at this very moment than I've been since . . . well . . . since before it happened." She didn't even want to think about it.

"You're gonna send me to my grave, child. What you gettin' yourself into?"

"I don't know. All I know is John makes me feel . . . *alive*."

"John? You already callin' him by his given name? I don't like it." Izzy beat her fist into the bread dough she'd been kneading.

"He *asked* me to call him John. Wait till you meet him. He's . . . He's . . . a *real* man." She leaned her head against the wall, closed her eyes, and sighed.

"What 'bout Doc Fletcher? He's a real man, too. One whose heart you're gonna break if'n you keeps actin' like this over his daddy."

Victoria didn't want to hear it. "I don't know 'bout Andrew anymore. Everythin' changed after what happened. Sometimes I feel he doesn't *want* to marry me." Her enthusiasm had been squelched. "I don't think he loves me, Izzy."

Izzy mumbled something she couldn't hear.

All of the energy Victoria had when she'd entered the room vanished. She slumped down in the chair and stared at the floor.

But then her thoughts returned to John. "Izzy, I'm goin' to my room. I have some thinkin' to do." She stood to leave.

Izzy took hold of her arm. "You do that. Don't do nuttin' you're gonna regret."

After Izzy gave her a kiss on the forehead, Victoria went to her room. She stood in front of the mirror and smiled at her reflection. John wanted her. Had things been different, she would've given herself to him. The simple thought had her trembling with desire.

How can I love Andrew, but want his daddy?

She *did* have a lot to think about.

CHAPTER 30

John pulled his door shut and stretched, doing his best to remove the wrench from his back. He'd have to speak to the hotel manager about the poor quality of the beds in this establishment.

"What the . . .?" A large woman nearly bowled him over. He brushed off his clothes.

"'Scuse me," she chirped. "I'm in too big a hurry."

"You should watch where you're going!" He stepped back and leered at her.

No, it can't be.

Martha Montgomery. One of his least favorite people in the south.

"John Martin?" Martha snarled and glared at him. "What the *hell* are you doin' here?"

He wasn't about to let on that he knew her. "I'm sorry, madam, but you have me mistaken for someone else." He smoothed his clothing and stepped away from her.

"I'd know your face anywhere. You haven't changed much. Still look like a snake in the grass!"

Why did I ever come back?

"Madam, I assure you I don't know who you are." Again, he tried to walk away.

She grunted. "Never thought you'd step foot again in Alabama! You here cuz a Claire?"

He stopped dead in his tracks and turned to face her. "What about Claire?"

Martha scowled and shook her finger at him. "Knew it was you!"

"Yes, Martha. I never could fool you, could I?"

"Nope. I seen your true colors 'fore Ruth ever did."

"That was a long time ago. We've all moved on, haven't we?"

She mumbled something under her breath. *She's undoubtedly the most revolting woman in the country.* Her lip protruded as he'd always remembered it. Full of chaw. *Disgusting.*

But, he had to know. "Now, what were you saying about Claire?"

"Surprised you remember her. Since it was such a *long time ago,* figgered you forgot you *had* a daughter."

"I didn't forget her. How is she?"

"Nearly dead, truth be told. She's in the hospital." Martha's eyes scrunched tight, glaring. "That's why *I'm* here. Why are *you* here?"

He stood up straight and pulled at his lapel. "For my son's wedding. Andrew's marrying one of the *finest* women in all of Mobile." He lifted his chin proudly in the air. He'd made more of his life and prodigy than Martha would have ever expected. He happily threw it in her face.

"You got a son named Andrew?"

"Yes, he's a doctor. He's done quite well for himself."

"Doctor, huh?" Martha gulped. "Andrew Martin?"

He'd accomplished exactly what he'd intended. She looked like she'd swallowed a whole chicken. "No. He's taken the name, *Fletcher*. His mother's name." Gloating had never been more enjoyable.

Martha stumbled backward. Her face turned ashen.

"What's wrong, Martha? You act as though you've seen a ghost."

"I'm fine. I just need to get to Claire. You gonna look in on her?"

"No. I doubt it would be wise. Besides, if she's as close to death as you say, what sense is there in my seeing her?"

"You haven't changed, have you, John?"

He smirked. "Thank you, Martha. I'll take that as a compliment." He walked down the hall with his head held high.

Thank God I got away from that family.

* * *

Andrew looked up as Martha entered the room. "Her hands are so cold, Martha."

"Well then, let's get her some milk." She crossed the room and laid her hand on his shoulder, then gave it a gentle pat. "I ain't givin' up hope."

They had the routine down and in no time Andrew started feeding Claire the precious fluid. The needle didn't seem to bother Martha as it had Beth. She sat beside him while he administered it.

"You care 'bout my niece a great deal. Don't you, Doc?"

"Yes, I do." He hadn't been able to hide his feelings from her. Maybe he didn't want to.

"Doc, I know she's more to you than a patient."

He swallowed hard. "What do you mean?"

"I reckon you're in love with her."

"I'm her doctor . . ." He kept his eyes on Claire, watching the fluid flow into her veins.

"You're more than that. Beth don't know, an' I ain't gonna tell her. I ain't gonna tell no one. It's just you an' me here—an' Claire—an' I want you to know." Her eyes filled with tears. "I reckon she loved you, too."

His throat dried, but tears came. Slowly, he faced her. "How do you know?"

"She came to me broken-hearted, but wouldn't tell me why. She led me to believe it was over Gerald, but I found out different when Michael was born. They brought him to my house so I could see him. I could tell by lookin' at him he wasn't Gerald's. When Gerald was outta the room, I pressed Claire to tell me who the daddy was. Told her the baby looked like an Injun. Figgered she'd been defiled by a savage. She told me it was nothin' like that. Said *Andrew* is nothin' like that."

His heart pounded. "But why did she leave me?"

She turned away and mumbled something inaudible. Almost as if she was arguing with herself. "Don't know. But I do think she loved ya. Loved Gerald, too. Wish I could explain it better, but I can't."

"So Michael *is* my son?" He had to hear it, though he knew it to be true.

"Yep. He's yours." Martha hung her head.

"Why'd she give him my name?"

"I asked her the same thing. Said it was a long story, but it was Gerald's idea. I reckon we'll never know the answer to that neither. Till she wakes up." Martha leaned toward Claire. "I wanna believe we'll have a miracle."

"I've never stopped believing." Relief flooded over him. He could speak openly with her now. "What can you tell me about my son?"

"I only seen him a few times. Last time was Christmas. He's a beautiful child. Healthy an' strong. She was a good mama, too. An' I hafta say . . . Gerald was a good daddy. He woulda done anythin' for that boy. Never once doubted he was his son. Never knew Claire'd been with anyone but him. You understand what I'm sayin?"

"Yes. If I try to see him, it'll hurt the family. But I *want* to see him."

"I know. I'll help ya. In time. But we *gotta* give it some time." She gave him a sad smile.

"They're going to take her away tomorrow," he whispered.

"Then we need that miracle soon. I'll say some extra prayers tonight." She grasped his hand and they both fell silent.

* * *

Not knowing what to do, after the four o'clock treatment, Andrew rode to see Alicia.

He admired her strength. Ever since Elijah's death, she'd grown even stronger. She cared for her children and the farm, and had found a way to laugh with them again. She kept Elijah in her heart and his spirit alive for their children.

Her table had become a place of counsel. She had a way of making sense of things, serving coffee *and* advice.

"I wish they'd give me more time." Andrew stared at the contents of his cup.

"She can't go on forever like she is, Doc."

"I think the milk's helping, but it's hard to know for certain. She's so frail." He set his cup down and ran his hands back through his hair. "I don't want them to take her. I've considered taking her away myself. Taking her to my home."

"You'd hurt her family if you do. It ain't right."

"I know. But I can't bear the thought of them burying her while she still breathes. It gives me nightmares."

"What more can you do?"

"Nothing. And that's what's tearing me up inside. I can't help her." He stood and paced the floor. "There's something else. Something I just found out."

"What?"

"Her child is mine." He dropped back into a chair and put his head in his hands.

"Oh, Doc."

He looked up at her and beheld pity. "You don't have to say it."

"But I *do*. I wanna say I'm sorry, but the only thing I feels sorry 'bout is knowin' the pain you're in. This baby's a blessin'. If she dies, you'll still have a part of her."

"I don't want her to die. Our son needs her."

"Course you don't. But it's in God's hands now."

He studied his own hands. "I just wish He'd show me what to do."

Alicia moved behind him and rested her hand on his shoulder. "I'm sorry I laughed at you before. You're in the kinda mess no one deserves. I'm here for ya whenever you need me. You gots a lot a thinkin' to do, Doc."

"Yes, I know. And now I have to go have supper again with my father *and* the O'Malley's. That's even more difficult to deal with." He stood to leave.

"You come back an' see me t'morra night. Let me know what happens. I'll be prayin' for ya."

He needed all the prayers he could get.

* * *

Victoria primped in her room, preparing for Sunday supper. Irish stew had never been so stimulating. Of course, the anticipation of being in the same room with John again made her temperature rise.

"Mama!" she yelled. "Mama, I need you!"

The woman appeared in her doorway. "Victoria, I have to watch me stew. What is it you need?"

"Help me with my corset. Please?" At times like this she wished Izzy worked every day of the week.

"You're beautiful without this, my dear," her mama said, but helped her regardless.

"Thank you, Mama. I need it to make everythin' just right." John deserved to see her at her best.

"You're a smart lass. You've done well with the gifts God gave you." She tied off the strings and placed her hands on Victoria's shoulders. "I remember when I had a shape like yours. Your father couldn't keep his hands off me." Her mama's soft laughter filled the air.

"Mama!" Victoria gaped at her. She'd never spoken about such things. "But what happened? Why'd it change?"

Her mama sat on the edge of Victoria's bed and sighed. "I got older. But before that, I was losin' too many babies. Patrick feared he'd lose me, too."

"So you just stopped . . . bein' together?"

"We *had* to. 'Twas difficult at first, but after a time, me desires faded. But your father—well, 'tis different for men. They never lose the desire."

Victoria sat beside her. "What did Daddy do?"

"He loved me, but I couldn't take care of him so he found other means." She took a deep breath. "He was always discreet and he paid them well. I looked the other way. I loved him enough to allow him his pleasures."

"I can't believe Daddy would do such a thing. How could you let him?" All this time and she had no idea what had been going on in her own home.

"I loved him. I still do. I used me wiles to get him as me husband. He was the finest catch in Mobile. Being Irish helped, but I used me looks to make him me husband. I've never wanted for anything. Had plenty of money and all I could ask for. He saw to it.

"You'll have everything *you* ever want. Just use what God gave you. While it lasts. I know that is how you got your doctor. Why do you think I always let you dress so? I knew you could catch a fine lad. One who will take care of you and give you whatever you want. Enjoy being young. It doesn't last forever."

Thoroughly depressed, Victoria's body deflated and she let out a heavy sigh.

"I'm sorry, dear . . ." Her mama grasped her hands. "I didn't mean to upset you. You're about to be married, so I wanted you to know what to expect. Passion won't last forever, I'm sad to say. But the money does. Use your gifts to persuade Andrew to give up his charity work. He'll do far better in the city where people have more money.

"You can change him. A woman can control her man. I know you have what it takes. You think I haven't been watching you? I see the way you look at him. I'm not that naïve. I know what you've been up to. You have a talent you haven't fully realized. Use it, Victoria. Use it to obtain all the riches you could ever imagine." She gave Victoria the same wicked smile she'd often used herself.

Victoria tilted her head and bit her lip. "I think I understand. I had no idea. Thank you." She gave her mama a warm hug, realizing she'd never truly known her until that moment. They were a great deal alike.

"One more thing, Victoria."

"Yes?"

"I'm proud of you for standing up to that Negra. It would have been your right to kill him for what he tried to do. Fortunately, your father took care of him. 'Tis an ugly thing killing a man. But remember—never let a man *take* from you. You may give yourself to whomever you choose, but no man has the right to take it. I know 'twas hard for you to endure, but you did well. I knew you'd find yourself again.

"You can find pleasure with a man in many ways. The best kind of man is one who cares more for pleasing you than himself. He'll make certain you're satisfied before reaching his own gratification. Never forget that." She kissed Victoria's forehead, then stood to leave.

"Mama?" Victoria stopped her. "What if there's someone who can give me more than Andrew? What would you suggest I do?"

The woman smiled. "You already know the answer to that, my dear. Take the one who can give you more. The most important thing about a man is the size of his *wallet*."

Victoria beamed. "Thank you, Mama."

Once she left, Victoria let her words sink in.

She put on her finest royal blue dress. Without Izzy, she fooled with her hair until she got it just right. She left it down on one side, swept it up on the other, and tucked a silk flower into it. Then she tied a matching silk scarf in a bow at her neck, with Andrew's necklace gracing the center.

Tonight would be the final test. She'd watch her two men together and see which one she truly desired.

As she applied perfume at the center of her bosom, she closed her eyes. Her hunger stirred. Not for Irish stew, but for another form of fulfillment.

A knock at the front door made her heart pound. Moving to the top of the stairs, she watched and waited.

When her daddy opened the door, she couldn't help but wonder how many women had serviced him over the years. She'd never look at him the same way again.

Andrew walked in with John right behind him. "Mr. O'Malley, I'd like you to meet my father, John Fletcher."

Her daddy extended his hand to John. "Welcome to our home, Mr. Fletcher."

"Thank you." John shook his hand. "It's kind of you to have me."

Her mama came out of the kitchen and eyed John up and down. A sting of jealousy twisted in Victoria's belly when John took her hand.

"You must be Mrs. O'Malley," he said, then raised her hand to his lips and kissed it. "I see now where Victoria acquired her beauty."

"Oh, Mr. Fletcher!" She fanned herself.

"Please, call me John." He kissed her hand again.

Victoria fumed. But then he turned his head to the stairwell and their eyes locked. He winked.

He'd redeemed himself.

Ready to join the party, she descended the stairs. Andrew walked toward her to take her hand, but John stepped in front of him. "Allow me," John said, extending his arm.

Victoria willingly looped hers through it.

"Seems your father is one step ahead of you," her daddy said to Andrew.

Victoria glanced over her shoulder. The frown on Andrew's face affirmed he wasn't amused.

She and Andrew sat side-by-side at the table and John sat directly across from them. Her daddy had his regular place at the head of the table. Her mama served the stew, then sat at the opposite end.

Once everyone was settled, Victoria smiled at her mama. They now shared a secret. Could it be possible her mama knew John was the man she'd referred to?

"Your stew is delicious, Mrs. O'Malley," John said.

"Please, call me Shannon." She beamed. "We're nearly family."

"It's a lovely name, *Shannon*." John raised his glass. "I'd like to propose a toast to Andrew and Victoria. May they remain as much in love as they are at this very moment."

Her daddy raised his glass. "Here, here!" He touched it to John's.

Her mama slowly raised hers. She and Andrew followed last. Victoria forced a smile, then clinked her glass to the others.

John's hunger-filled eyes were on her. A chill ran down her spine, knowing he looked further than the fabric of her dress. She could play this game. It hadn't been long ago that she'd played it with Andrew.

Taking a bite of stew, she drew the spoon slowly out of her mouth, then licked her lips. John watched every move she made and swallowed hard. He lifted his napkin and dabbed at his forehead.

"Father, are you all right?" Andrew asked. "You look flushed."

"It's a bit warm in here. I'm not used to the Alabama heat." He stared at Victoria as he spoke.

"Tell me more about where you live in Connecticut, John," her mama said, breaking the spell. *Why?* Was she enamored with him as well?

"I live in Bridgeport, not far from the water. Of course the Atlantic is much different than Mobile Bay."

"Do you have a large home?" Victoria asked, wanting to regain his attention.

"Two stories. Six bedrooms." John raised himself up in his seat. "It's large, but I do enjoy entertaining."

"Entertainin'?" Victoria's eyes widened. "Do you have parties?"

"Yes. Dinner parties. Business gatherings. A great deal of social affairs." He wiped the corner of his mouth with a napkin, his eyes once again focused on her. Exactly where she wanted them.

"Oh …" She almost purred, just thinking about it. "I've always wanted to go to fancy parties. Are they wonderful?" She wanted to know everything about him. As for Andrew, he didn't appear to be interested in anything other than eating. *What did I ever see in him?*

"Victoria, I've taken you to social gatherings," her daddy said. "The bank has thrown some fine affairs."

"Daddy, they were borin'. I imagine the parties John's speakin' of are spectacular." She held her hand to her breast. "John, do the women dress splendidly?"

John chuckled. "Yes, they do. Though I must say, none are as lovely as you are tonight." He raised his glass to her, nodded, and took a drink.

Victoria coyly tilted her head. "Have you ever met any important people?"

"I know *many*. I even had the opportunity to meet the President—*Lincoln*, that is. He gave a speech in Bridgeport in—let me see—it was 1860. I was thirty-four at the time. I had the honor of meeting him after the speech. I always admired the man. Even modeled my law practice after him." John sat back in his chair, with his head held high.

"Lincoln?" Her daddy snarled. "Damn republican."

"Patrick," her mama scolded. "Not at the supper table." She turned to John. "We try to refrain from talking politics and religion while we eat. It's not good for the digestion."

"Forgive me," John said. "I enjoy politics. I've even considered running for office. I believe I'd do well in the senate."

"A senator?" Victoria asked. "That sounds excitin'. Doesn't it, Andrew?"

"What?" Andrew's brows wove.

Victoria scowled at him. "Are you with us? Or is your head still at that hospital?"

"I'm sorry, Victoria. I have a lot on my mind."

"It's that woman again, isn't it?" Victoria huffed. "The one who should be dead by now?"

"Please don't say that." Andrew sighed. "But I *do* need to get back to her. Tonight's the last night. Her family will be taking her home tomorrow."

"Those backwoods folk? Well—good riddance is all I can say!" *The sooner the better.*

"Leave now?" John asked. "You can't be serious, Andrew. You're not being cordial to your hosts. The O'Malley's went to a great deal of trouble preparing this meal. At least you could participate in the affair, not go off with your thoughts elsewhere."

"Forgive me. But it's difficult to leave my work behind." Andrew frowned at his daddy. "This woman may die."

"Every doctor loses patients. You knew that when you chose your profession. Be a man, Andrew." John spoke with little emotion.

Andrew stood. "Perhaps I should go and tend to my business. It seems I'm putting a damper on the evening. Father, why don't you stay? Enjoy the company and I'll return for you later."

"If you need to leave, *Doctor*," her daddy snapped. "*Go*. I'll take your father to the hotel m'self."

Andrew gazed around the room. "I'll go then. Thank you for the meal, Mrs. O'Malley."

He walked out, but Victoria remained seated. "I don't know what's gotten into him. He's been different since that woman came to the hospital."

"What woman is that?" John asked.

"Some *country* girl." Victoria scowled. "She's unconscious—nearly dead. I wish she'd died already."

"Victoria . . ." The way John said her name, calmed her. "You're more beautiful when you smile. Don't let my son upset you. I'll speak with him later."

His soft voice melted her face into a smile.

"There's my lass," her mama said, beaming.

Her daddy clapped his hands together. "What's for dessert? I'm in the mood for something sweet."

"So am I," John said and locked eyes with Victoria. She instantly dismissed all thoughts of Andrew.

"Izzy made a wonderful dessert," her mama said. "I'll get it." She stood from the table and went to the kitchen.

"Who's Izzy?" John asked.

"Our servant," her daddy muttered. "Used to be a slave. Now we're required to *pay* her thanks to your President Lincoln."

"Daddy," Victoria said, "Mama said no politics."

"It's all right, Victoria," John said with a smile. "I take no offense."

Her mama returned with a platter full of tarts and a bowl of whipped cream. "John, I hope you like cherry tarts." She set them on the table, then got out dessert plates from the china cabinet. "They're Patrick's favorite. Aren't they, dear?"

Victoria locked eyes once again with John. "I like mine with whipped cream." She bit her lip, then dipped her finger in the bowl and drew out a large dollop. After showing it to him, she placed it in her mouth, then slowly withdrew her finger.

"Yes, Victoria *loves* whipped cream," her mama said to John. "So, how many would you like, John?"

"I'd better start with one," he replied. "One *tart* is about all I can handle. Please, put a dab of whipped cream on mine as well." He hadn't shifted his gaze.

"Here you are, John." Her mama handed him a plate. "I think you'll enjoy it."

"Yes, Shannon. I believe I will." He looked up briefly, then returned his attention to Victoria.

"What about mine?" Her daddy's loud voice *almost*

broke the sensual tension in the air. "I would like two. No whipped cream."

"Yes, dear. Guests are always first." Her mama smiled at John and dished up the dessert for her daddy.

* * *

John finished the tart on his plate, but it hadn't been the one he truly desired. The luscious woman who'd teased him throughout the entire meal would certainly be even tastier.

He'd enjoyed the game at the supper table. Victoria had certainly put Andrew in his place. Not only was she beautiful, she had spunk. Something he admired in a woman. But even without it, she had the most desirable body he'd seen in a great while. He wanted to see more of it. *The time will come.*

After dessert, Patrick invited him to his study for a smoke. Aside from women, a good cigar had always been one of John's favorite vices.

Patrick handed him one. "One of me finest." He grinned and motioned for John to have a seat in an expensive-looking leather chair.

"So, you're a republican?" Patrick asked as he puffed the cigar.

"Yes, I am. However, I judge a man by his character rather than his politics." *Time to impress the man.*

"Politics *make* a man's character." His brow wove like a slinking caterpillar. "I don't know what to think of you. I admire your success, however. You *do* have money, don't you?"

"Money makes the world go around, doesn't it, Patrick?" John took a long drag from his cigar.

"Yes, it does." Patrick chuckled. "Especially in *my* business."

"My world is spinning fast," John boasted, blowing out smoke. "I lack for nothing."

"What about a good woman? Your son's a lucky man capturing Victoria's heart." Patrick leaned forward. "I was sorry to hear your wife passed on."

"That was a long time ago. And . . . I plan to alleviate my loneliness soon." *If you only knew.*

"Someone special in your life? 'Tis a good thing. There's nothing like having a good woman to come home to." The man took another puff on his cigar.

"I couldn't agree more. And speaking of the ladies, shouldn't we get back to them?"

"Aye. I assume you enjoy their company more than mine. I must say me lassies are fine to look at. Don't you agree?"

"I couldn't agree more. You see, we *do* agree on some things." John laughed heartily and Patrick joined in. He patted John on the back as they walked down the hall.

John was satisfied. He'd made the impression he'd intended.

* * *

As soon as the men walked away, Victoria rushed to her mama's side. "How'd I do, Mama?"

She took Victoria's face in her hands. "Very well, dear. But be careful not to draw *too* much attention to yourself. Your father wouldn't approve."

"Why? John has money. That's what matters to Daddy, isn't it?"

"You're still his little girl. I'm certain he'd find the idea of his baby girl with an older man disturbing. He'll see things our way when the time is right." She brushed her hand across Victoria's cheek. "One other thing—and this is *very* important. Don't give yourself to him before he vows to marry you. Understand?"

"Yes, Mama. I do." She grinned. "This is fun."

"That's my lass." Her mama hugged her, then kissed her on the forehead. "Speaking of marriage. If you don't intend to marry Andrew, entice John quickly. Your father spent a great deal of money on this wedding."

Victoria nodded. No more needed to be said.

The men returned and John explained that he had to get back to his hotel room.

"I'll bring me buggy 'round," her daddy said and left to get it. Her mama excused herself to the kitchen.

Victoria pulled her shoulders back and leaned against the wall in the hallway.

John crossed to her and left almost no space between them. He leaned close. His mouth nearly touched her ear. "Don't toy with me, Victoria." His words made her tremble. "I expect you to follow through." His hand cascaded down her arm.

Hardly able to breathe, she managed to speak. "I always play with my toys, John. Sometimes they may sit on a shelf until I'm ready for them, but I promise you . . . eventually I play."

"I'm counting on it." He stared into her eyes.

She gazed back at him, heaving her breasts with every breath.

His lips hovered inches from hers, then his mouth curled into a grin.

"In time," he whispered and backed away.

CHAPTER 31

As Andrew walked up the steps to the hospital entrance, relief flowed over him. Even with what he'd likely face here, anywhere would be better than where he'd been.

How could he have been raised by that man and still have compassion for other people? His father thought only of himself.

Thank God for Mother. The love she'd given him when he was a boy formed him into the man he'd become. Without her, he could've become like his father. And in many ways Victoria acted just like him.

I don't want to marry her, but I have no choice.

All the way to the hospital he prayed he'd find Claire sitting up in bed and smiling. But his prayers weren't answered. She hadn't moved. Martha had fallen asleep in the chair next to her. Her chin had dropped to her chest and her loud snoring filled the room.

Andrew tapped her on the shoulder. "Martha, wake up. It's nearly time for her treatment."

Martha raised her head, yawned, and rubbed her eyes. "Doc? Sorry. Seems I dozed off."

"You're fine. We still have time. I think I'll try full strength and not dilute the milk. Only three more treatments before they take her. I have to feel like I've done something, *anything* to help. " He sat on the bed beside Claire and held her hand. Bruises ran up both of her arms along the vein line. Her face had become sunken in and shallow. He couldn't mask a frown. Seeing her this way tormented him.

Martha stood. "Let's go see Rosie!"

They milked her by lantern light.

"I'm gonna miss ol' Rosie," Martha said, patting her side. "She's a good cow."

Her words pierced him like a nail in Claire's coffin. Sending Rosie home meant sending Claire . . . *home?*

"Henry will be by tomorrow to tell her goodbye." Andrew swallowed, attempting to moisten his dry throat. "I told him he could come."

"Much as I don't like it, you did the right thing. But *I* ain't ready to tell her goodbye." Finished with the milking, Martha rose from the stool. "She ain't dead yet, Doc."

He couldn't utter a word.

Lantern light pulsed eerily in Claire's room for her eight o'clock treatment. He worked the needle into her shallow vein and allowed the full-strength milk to flow into her body.

Martha sat beside him. "You're a gifted man, Doc. Quite handy with a needle."

He managed to smile. "That reminds me of something Claire said to me when we first met. We realized it was something we had in common."

"Yep. I know what you mean. She always made the finest clothes in town. Her mama taught her."

"It's not right. We're talking about her as though she was already dead—remembering what she was like. I don't want to do that. I want more memories with her. Martha, I want Claire."

Martha mumbled something he couldn't understand, then loudly cleared her throat. "Doc, you mind if I go out for a spell? I'm kinda hungry. Didn't have no supper. I figgered maybe I'd give you some time alone with her."

"Of course. And after you eat, if you're tired, go on to your room. I'll send someone to get you at midnight."

"All right, then. I am kinda tired. It's been a long week." She patted him on the shoulder and walked out.

Slow and steady, the milk flowed into Claire's veins. He finished the process, then removed the needle, bandaged her arm, and sat back in his chair. The room felt like a prison. A place she was trapped in, but far better than the casket she'd be in tomorrow night.

He stood. After looking out the doorway and down the hall, he determined there was no one anywhere close. Thoughts raced through his mind. His heart pounded and his mouth became drier than ever.

Moving to Claire, he gazed down at her face and recalled how she'd looked at him when they'd first met. Her eyes had glowed with life, now they were closed and lifeless. Her arms had reached out and held him, now they lay limp at her sides. Her lips had met his with passion, now they barely passed breath.

He scooped her still body into his arms and held her close. Her arms dangled as though death had already claimed her. His body shook and tears streamed down his cheeks. Sobbing, he took her face in his hands and pressed his lips to hers. Could he breathe life into her with a kiss?

She didn't move.

Why won't she move?

With great care, he laid her back down on the bed and put his ear to her chest. Her faint heartbeat broke him.

"Claire, we don't have much time! Please wake up!" Unable to stop his tears, he let them flow.

His chest heaved, passing streams of breath through his nose.

No. I won't let them take you.

Once again, he checked to make certain the hallway was clear, then went to her side and lifted her into his arms.

Clutching her to his chest, he walked toward the door. He'd take her home.

"What you doin', Doc?"

Martha? Why'd she come back?

Though she'd folded her arms across her chest, her expression seemed sympathetic. Maybe she'd understand.

"I can't let them take her." He held Claire even tighter. "I want to take her home."

"She ain't yours to take, Doc. I know you love her, but we love her, too. You gotta put her down. Put her back in bed." Martha gestured toward it. "She's dyin'. We can't help that now. We've done everythin' we can. You gotta let her go." Martha's eyes misted over with tears.

He didn't want to accept it, but she was right. Reluctantly, he laid Claire back in the bed.

"I just want to hold her," he whispered. "Is that so wrong?"

"No, it ain't wrong." Martha peered out the door, then pushed it so it was barely ajar. "It's just the three a us here. I ain't gonna tell no one. You go on an' hold her, Doc. Be close to her one last time." She placed a chair on the far side of the room by the door, and sat, facing away from him. "I'll make sure no one comes in."

One last time.

He removed his shirt, then pulled back the blanket on Claire's bed and lay down beside her. The bed was small, but he turned her body and laid her upon his chest, cradling her.

"I love you, Claire," he whispered, and kissed the top of her head. *Oh, God, how I love you.* The memories of their love wrenched his heart. How could he ever let her go?

With his fingers entwined in her soft brown hair, he laid his head against the pillow and drifted off to sleep with her body pressed to his.

* * *

"Gerald?" *Why's it so hard to speak?*

Claire tried again. "Gerald?" Her raspy voice barely made a sound.

My throat hurts.

Something felt terribly wrong. The room was dark and she could feel his body, so why didn't he respond? She brushed her fingers across his chest.

What happened to his hair?

Her body trembled. *This isn't my bed!*

"Claire? Claire, are you awake?" His body rose to a sitting position beside her.

"Gerald?" It hurt to speak.

"Shh . . . don't try to talk." He climbed out of the bed and laid her back against the pillow. Then he took her hand in his and stroked it. "Claire, you're going to be fine."

I'm not fine. Gerald didn't sound like Gerald and this wasn't her room. Every part of her body felt strange. Her head pounded. Why couldn't she remember what happened?

Someone mumbled. She squeezed her eyes shut. Maybe she'd been dreaming.

"Claire Belle? It's Aunt Martha. I'm here for ya, baby." She stroked Claire's hair.

"Aunt Martha?" Claire whispered. "Gerald . . . Where's Gerald?" She tried to open her eyes. "I can't see."

"Claire . . ." The man spoke again. "Don't try. Not yet. Your eyes need to adjust. You've been asleep a very long time."

Her heart thumped. She recognized the voice. Why him? Her body shook and she couldn't breathe. "Where's Gerald?"

"Claire Belle, it's all right. You're with Aunt Martha. You're gonna be just fine."

She was far from fine.

Why do they keep sayin' that?

Martha's fingers brushed across her skin as if she'd never touched her before. And why was Andrew in her room?

A shuffling of feet and clothing made her even more anxious. For a brief moment, she believed they'd left her. But she didn't want to be alone and her throat felt too sore to call out.

"Claire . . . you're gonna be fine." Martha tucked the blankets in around her. "I promise ya, Aunt Martha ain't goin' nowhere. I'll stay right here."

Andrew's heavy footfall confirmed he'd left the room, but having Aunt Martha close gave her comfort. Still, nothing made sense.

"Where's Gerald?" Claire rasped. "I want Gerald."

Martha sighed, then muttered something under her breath.

"Martha, please get Gerald. I need him." She tried to lift her arm, but didn't have the strength.

"Baby . . ." *Martha sounds so sad.* "Gerald's gone. I'm sorry."

"What? Where'd he go?"

The woman sniffled.

Is she cryin?

"You was in the water, Claire Belle," Martha whispered. "Gerald . . . *drowned*. He died. I'm so sorry." She pulled Claire into her arms and held her against her breast. "We almost lost you, too."

Though too weak to cry, tears formed in Claire's eyes. "No. God, no . . ." It couldn't be true.

The beach.

Claire gasped as the memory rushed in. Instantly, she panicked and tried to push against Martha. "Where's Michael? Where's my baby?"

"He's fine, Claire. He's with Mrs. Sandborn. Beth pulled him from the water. He's just fine." Martha held her even tighter, then rubbed her back and swayed.

"Thank God. My baby . . ." Claire's body went limp from exhaustion. She couldn't say another word.

Martha laid her back against the pillow and stood from the bed. Within moments, she returned and put a glass to Claire's lips. "Take a drink. You need this." She tilted the glass.

The cool water soothed her parched throat, but nothing could ease the ache in her heart.

Gerald.

"Not too much. She needs to start slowly." She and Martha were no longer alone. He'd come back in the room.

"Andrew?" Claire had to know.

"Yes, Claire. It's Andrew." He sat beside her and took her hand. Though weak, she managed to pull it away from him. He had no business holding her hand.

"It's not time for that," Martha scolded in a whisper. "I told her 'bout Gerald."

"Where am I?" Claire asked.

"You're in the hospital, Claire Belle," Martha said. "Doc Fletcher is carin' for ya."

"Andrew?" Claire struggled with every word. "Is it really you?"

"Yes. But you have to stop talking. You need to give your voice time. You've been asleep for a week." He let out a long, loud sigh. "Martha, give her a little more water."

Martha supported Claire's head while she helped her take another drink.

The light from the lantern hurt her eyes, so she kept them shut. Though a part of her wanted to see Andrew. But she couldn't accept he was there. Nothing seemed real.

"Dr. Fletcher?" Another voice hovered in the air. "I brought the broth."

"Thank you, Nurse," Andrew said. "Claire . . ." He touched her arm and she gasped, so he pulled his hand away. "Claire, you need to sip this broth. Start with just a bit."

An unfamiliar hand cradled Claire's head.

"I'll help you," the nurse said.

"We'll be back in a moment," Andrew whispered. The shuffling of feet indicated he'd led Aunt Martha from the room.

* * *

Andrew took Martha into the hallway just outside Claire's room. He could hardly contain himself. "I still want to do her treatment at midnight." He kept his voice low. "We aren't out of danger yet, but Martha . . . I know Claire's going to live. I believe we've had our miracle."

Martha grabbed his arms. Her eyes narrowed. "What were you doin' tryin' to hold her hand? She just lost her husband!"

"You know how I feel about her. I won't push her. But you've got to understand how much hope I have now."

Martha took a step back and folded her arms across her chest. "You forget 'bout your fiancée?"

"N—No. Of course not." How could he? "But Claire came back to me—*us* . . ."

Martha's mouth twisted. "Us. She ain't yours, Doc. No matter what happened in the past, you'd do best to forget it. That bein' said . . . I can't thank you enough for bringin' her back. She'd a died without ya."

Maybe it was selfish wanting Claire when he'd soon be marrying Victoria. But he couldn't ignore what they had together. They had a son. It would be impossible to forget. *Why did Martha suggest it?*

The excitement he'd felt hearing Claire's voice had been doused. He hadn't even cared that the name she'd spoken had been her husband's. As long as she spoke.

"Martha . . ." He let out a long breath. "I *can't* forget what we had. But I'll mind my manners and be her doctor."

Martha gave him a satisfied nod. "We best be gettin' back to her. I know she's scared."

When they walked back in, the nurse was laying Claire's head against the pillow. "She drank a bit, Dr. Fletcher. But she's very tired."

Andrew thanked her and she left the room. Claire had fallen asleep. He studied her breathing. Weak, but in a normal sleep. No longer unconscious.

He needed to give her the midnight treatment. Her body could use the vital nutrients from the milk. It would be a while before she could digest regular food.

Though hard to leave her side to milk Rosie, he knew she wouldn't go anywhere. Still, he didn't want to miss a moment with her. And once he believed her to be strong enough, he'd have the answers to his questions.

When he inserted the needle, she whimpered. His heart simultaneously ached and rejoiced. He didn't want to hurt her, yet the fact she felt pain meant death no longer beckoned her.

"You should get some sleep, Doc," Martha whispered as he finished.

"I don't want to leave her."

"Doc? What 'bout Victoria?"

He lowered his head and sighed. "I have to marry her. It's hard to explain, but I have no choice."

"There's always a choice. That woman don't seem right for ya."

"I want Claire. I know she just lost her husband, but I can't deny my feelings for her. I've never stopped loving her." He wanted to lie down beside her again, but knew he no longer could.

"She loved Gerald. She'll need time to grieve. Don't push yourself on her. Probably best you marry Victoria—if it's as you say."

Martha had him even more confused. First, she told him to forget Claire, then she told him he had a choice. And now she indicated it would be best for him to marry Victoria, even though she knew they weren't right for each other.

Maybe I'm too tired to see anything clearly.

"Even so," he finally said. "My heart tells me otherwise."

"Go get some sleep, Doc. I'll stay with Claire. I don't mind sleepin' in this here chair. I'll look for you in four hours." She patted his shoulder.

"All right. I have a lot on my mind, but my body's begging for rest." He stood to leave.

"G'night then. You done good, Doc. You saved my girl."

"You helped. I couldn't have done it without you." He kissed her on the cheek, then left the room. Before leaving the hospital, he instructed the night nurse to send for him in four hours.

Climbing into bed, Claire filled his thoughts. Victoria had been long forgotten.

CHAPTER 32

Andrew had barely laid his head on the pillow when a knock came on the door. He mindlessly got out of bed, dressed, and returned to the hospital.

After rousing Martha, they went one more time to Rosie. Both exhausted, they simply went through the motions.

"I know this hurts her," Andrew whispered as he started Claire's treatment. "We should be able to get some soft food into her."

"Beth'll be here by ten o'clock. You know she's expectin' to take Claire home in a casket."

"She'll be happily surprised." He couldn't help but frown. "But it'll be hard on her. She'll have to relive all the pain with Claire."

Claire stirred. "It hurts," she whimpered.

"Shh . . . don't try to talk," Andrew said. "I'm almost done. I won't do it again."

"Andrew?" Claire rasped. "Is Gerald really gone?"

"Yes, he is. I'm so sorry." His heart ached for her pain. "You're getting better, Claire. But it'll take some time."

She didn't respond.

He removed the needle and bandaged her arm. Unable to help himself, his hands lingered on her arm.

She attempted to open her eyes, but squinted against the lantern light.

Andrew dimmed it. "Is that better?"

"Yes, thank you." Her voice remained barely audible.

Martha raised a glass of water to Claire's lips and she eagerly drank.

"More," she rasped as Martha started to pull it away.

A very good sign.

Even though there would be no more treatments, he decided not to go back to his room. He made himself comfortable in one of the chairs and remained with Claire and Martha. They all dozed in and out of sleep.

* * *

Sunlight seeped in through Claire's half-open lids. Even through blurry eyes, she sensed his presence. She'd missed Andrew for such a long time, yet now she could only think about Gerald. What would she do without him? More importantly, how would she go on without a daddy for Michael? It could never be Andrew.

Andrew.

Even in the stillness of his breathing, she felt his love. She'd heard it in every word he'd spoken to her. He still loved her, making her pain even greater. Sooner or later he'd ask the question she dreaded. It would cause both of them more heartache.

"Mrs. Alexander?" Miss Elliot entered the room and shrieked. "Oh, my goodness!" Her loud cry woke the others. "Dr. Fletcher, when did she wake up?"

"I thought the night nurse would have told you," Andrew said, stretching. "She woke during the night."

"I came in to change her. To . . . to get her ready to leave. I guess she won't be leaving now. Isn't that right, Doctor?"

"Yes. She'll need to stay until we can build up her strength. Go ahead and tend her. She'll need a clean gown and bedding. Martha . . . how about some breakfast?"

"Sounds good to me, Doc. Reckon I got an appetite now." Martha kissed Claire on the forehead. "We'll be back real soon."

Claire tried to smile, but couldn't.

Miss Elliott lifted the blankets and began to undress her.

Claire's eyes opened wide.

"Don't be embarrassed, Mrs. Alexander. I've been caring for you ever since they brought you in."

Miss Elliott sounded very young. Younger than her. Even through her clouded eyes, Claire could tell she had a sweet face. The nurse obviously cared, but she felt ashamed knowing she'd been tended to like a baby—diapers and all. No one should ever have to care for her that way.

But since she couldn't even raise her arms—let alone dress herself—she let Miss Elliott do her job. The woman handled her with the same gentleness Claire had with her own son. She missed Michael.

I need to hold him again.

Tears began to form.

She'd never again hold *Gerald*.

"Don't cry, Mrs. Alexander," Miss Elliott said with a voice as soft as her down pillow. "I don't mind helping you. You'll be caring for yourself again in no time. Dr. Fletcher has done something amazing with you. Something no other doctor has ever done here before. He fed you milk through your veins. That's what kept you alive. He's a very good doctor." She washed Claire's body, then dressed her in a fresh gown.

Somehow, Miss Elliot managed to change the bedding beneath her without removing her from the bed. She put a clean case on her pillow and fluffed it up. "There you are, Mrs. Alexander. All better."

"Thank you." With great effort, Claire reached out and touched Miss Elliott's arm.

"I'm so glad you're better." Miss Elliott sniffled, wiped away some tears, then hugged her. "I have a feeling you'll have a lot of visitors today. You're a miracle." She left the room.

Claire lay there as still as ever. Even though her body wouldn't cooperate, her mind had become active again. Thoughts raced through it. She did her best to piece together what had happened. She remembered Michael being gone. Everything else was as blurry as her current vision. Maybe she didn't *want* to remember everything, but she longed to see clearly again.

When she'd first heard Andrew's voice, her heart had jumped. There'd been so many times she'd wished she could see him. But not like this. Not ready to answer his questions, she prayed he'd let her be for now. Her body couldn't digest food let alone all the horrible things that had happened to her. Surely, being a doctor, Andrew would understand and not push her.

"Mrs. Alexander?"

Claire looked up and blinked hard. She didn't recognize the voice.

"I'm Dr. Mitchell. I'd like to have a look at you."

Another doctor? She managed to nod.

He scooted a chair close to the bed. He proceeded to take her pulse, then placed a cold stethoscope against her skin. Lastly, he placed his hand to her brow. "Incredible . . ." he mumbled. "You're a fortunate woman."

No, I'm not. My husband's dead. The thought prompted her tears to return.

"I'm very sorry." He took hold of her hand. His words sounded sincere. "I know you've lost your husband. Your heart must be broke in two. But you're alive. I was told you have a young son. Your love for him will keep you strong."

"Michael," she whispered. "His name."

"A very good name." He stood and took a step back. "Dr. Fletcher will be in soon to check on you. He never gave up. I've never seen a doctor so determined."

He loves me.

"You're going to be fine, Mrs. Alexander. I'll let you rest now."

He left.

How many times had she been told she'd be fine? It couldn't be further from the truth.

* * *

John forced down another mouthful of scrambled eggs.

How hard can it be to cook a decent egg?

He was about to call the waitress to his table when his eye caught Andrew's. But then he nearly choked when Martha met his gaze.

Good Lord.

Andrew smiled and strode across the café. After dabbing at his mouth with a cloth napkin, John stood and faced his son. He'd learned a long time ago how to wear a convincing smile.

"Father, I'd like you to meet Martha Montgomery. She's the aunt of the patient I've been tending—the woman I spoke to you about at supper last evening."

John nodded at Martha. "It's nice to meet you, Mrs. Montgomery." Would she reveal their familiarity?

Martha's upper lip twitched. "Mr. *Fletcher.*"

"Father, the most wonderful thing has happened. Mrs. Montgomery's niece woke up last night. She's going to live." Andrew beamed brighter than he had when he'd received high marks in school and seemed oblivious to the animosity between him and Martha.

John sat down.

My daughter's going to live.

"That's wonderful news, Andrew." He patted him on the back. "Would you like to join me?" He motioned for them to take a seat, though he would've much rather booted Martha out the door.

"Looks like you're 'bout done," Martha said, staring at his plate. "We wouldn't wanna keep you if you got somewhere to go."

Yes, Martha, I know you despise me.

"Actually, I *do* have some things I need to see to. Andrew, why don't we dine this evening at some *other* restaurant? Just the two of us. I know we haven't had enough time to talk since my arrival. Now that you won't be tied up with that woman at the hospital, perhaps we can have an enjoyable evening together?" Did he sound convincing? Anything would be better than sharing a meal with Martha Montgomery. The sight of her alone made him retch.

"That sounds wonderful, Father. I'll come to your room at six. Thank you for suggesting it."

John stood to leave. "It was a pleasure meeting you," he said, nodding to Martha.

"Pleasure's all mine."

As he exited, he glanced over his shoulder and met Martha's glare. With a satisfied smirk, he left.

* * *

Andrew sat with Martha at another table. He was glad he'd run into his father. It was the first time they hadn't parted on strained terms. Everything seemed to be looking up.

"I'm so hungry!" he exclaimed, rubbing his hands together. "I didn't realize how much. The last few days haven't been easy."

"Not for any of us. 'Specially Claire, poor thing. I don't wanna leave her alone too long. I promised I'd stay close."

"I feel the same. I know I have no rights to her, but I can't help how I feel. I'm just glad I can talk to you about it." He smiled, then placed their order. "I'm glad you met my father," he went on once the waitress left their table. "You probably noticed I look nothing like him. I take after my mother."

"Be glad a that," Martha mumbled and stared at her lap.

What an odd thing for her to say. Martha was probably the only woman he'd ever met who didn't seem to find his father attractive. He decided to ignore her comment. After all, Martha had never acted *ordinary*.

"Oh . . ." He tapped his finger to his forehead. "I almost forgot. I need to tell Alicia that Claire's all right."

"Who's Alicia?" Martha asked with a frown.

He proceeded to tell her the story of Alicia and Elijah. Martha listened intently as he told the details of Elijah's death and Victoria's involvement. "And that's why I have to marry her. I owe it to her *and* her father. He's never forgiven me for it."

"Poor girl." Martha sounded genuinely empathetic. "Horrible thing to go through. But you still have a choice. If you don't love the girl you won't be happy. Always follow your heart. I told Claire the same thing once . . ." Martha's voice drifted away.

They ate their meal silently, then returned to Claire. They found her sitting upright in bed, with Miss Elliott beside her, helping her drink some broth.

The nurse smiled at him as he entered the room. "Mrs. Stevens said I could give her the broth. I know you gave her some last night. I hope you don't mind, Doctor."

"You've done well. Why don't you ask the kitchen staff to puree some fruit and vegetables? Warm oats would be good also. We need to go easy on her stomach."

"I feel like a baby," Claire whispered.

"You're doing fine," Miss Elliott said. "We'll have you eating solid foods in no time. I'll come back in a little while and we'll see about getting you on your feet. How does that sound?"

"Frightening."

"I'll help," Andrew added. "You may need my strength. She's going to be a little wobbly at first."

"Thank you, Dr. Fletcher," Miss Elliott said and left the room.

Claire turned her head and partially opened her eyes. He could tell she struggled.

"Here, I have something that should help." He produced a small bottle of eye drops. Putting his hand on the side of her face, he gently tilted her head backward. "I'm going to drop a bit of this into each of your eyes. It should soothe them." With great care, he pulled one eye open and dropped the liquid into it, then repeated the treatment for the other.

He could almost swear he saw a trace of color in her cheeks. Her face felt warm against his hand.

"Is that better?"

She nodded, blinked a few times, then slowly opened her eyes wide.

He sat on the edge of the bed. *So close to her*. He studied her eyes, attempting to remain professional, but then she met his gaze and made his heart thump. He didn't want to move away.

Martha cleared her throat so loudly that both he and Claire were startled.

He'd try to do better.

"Beth should be here soon, Claire," Martha bellowed. "Won't that be nice?"

After acknowledging Martha with an, *I'll behave myself* look, he turned back to Claire. "Yes, she'll be very happy to see you sitting up in bed. Truthfully, *overwhelmed* might be a better way to describe it."

"It must've been horrible for her." Claire's voice had become stronger. "Gerald . . ." She stopped. Instantly, a pool of tears covered her eyes.

Miss Elliott walked in. "Dr. Fletcher, Mr. Schultz would like to see you in his office."

"Thank you, Nurse, I'll be right there." He nodded to Martha. "I'll be back soon." Knowing Martha would comfort Claire, he left the room and went down the stairs to the first floor.

When he got to the man's office, the door had been left open, so he walked in.

Mr. Schultz crossed the room and shook his hand. "Dr. Fletcher, in all my time at this hospital, I've never seen such unusual practices. Yet your innovative means saved that woman's life. I commend you for your fine work."

Andrew nearly fell on the floor. "Thank you, sir."

"Don't look so surprised. You did a fine job. Now, please have the cow removed from the premises as soon as possible."

"Yes, sir. I'll see to it right away." Andrew started to leave.

"One more thing. You should take a few days off to prepare for your wedding. You've worked long hours this past week. Take some time." He waved Andrew out of the office.

Andrew shook his head and went back toward the stairs to the second floor. Before he got there, he noticed Mr. Alexander sitting in the hallway.

"They wouldn't let me go up," he said, sadly shaking his head.

The strict instructions Andrew had given the workers at the front desk had been taken seriously. He couldn't help but feel sorry for the man, regardless of what he'd done.

"Mr. Alexander . . ." Andrew looked directly at him. "I'll take you up myself. She's awake."

He gasped, then put his head in his hands. "Oh, God." His head jerked up. "She'll live?"

"Yes, sir." Andrew understood his feelings. "But I'm not sure she'll WANT to see you. We can TRY, but she hasn't lost her memory, and she *has* lost her husband. Her emotions are fragile." Andrew spoke slowly and emphasized every word.

"No, you don't understand." Mr. Alexander tried to stand and wavered against his cane. "Claire needs me now. I can take care of her. Michael, too."

That'll be my job.

Andrew placed a firm hand on his shoulder. "It's probably best you see her before Beth arrives. If you upset her, you'll HAVE TO LEAVE. Do you understand?"

"Yes."

"Also, they want you to take ROSIE home. Will you need help with her?"

"No. I can tie her behind the wagon. Let her walk home. It'll do her good. An' don't you fret. I won't go fast." He smiled, obviously trying to appeal to Andrew's soft side.

They ascended the stairs and went down the hall to Claire's room. Martha stood beside her.

"What's *he* doin' here?" Martha scowled.

"Since he let us use Rosie, I promised him he could see her. But since Claire's awake, it's up to her. In any case, I told him I'd have to stay in the room."

"I don't like it!" Martha walked toward the door, stopped, and shook her finger in Andrew's face. "You keep a good eye on him. *I'll* wait down the hall."

"I will, Martha." He led Mr. Alexander into the room.

When Claire saw him, her body stiffened.

Andrew rushed to her. "He wanted to make sure you're all right, Claire. I'm not going to leave you alone with him."

"Can I sit by her?" Mr. Alexander asked and nodded to the chair beside the bed.

"Claire, do you mind?"

"Long as you stay in the room, Andrew." When her eyes met his, he witnessed fear. He wished he hadn't made the promise to the man.

He motioned for him to take the seat and stepped away.

"Claire," Mr. Alexander's voice broke. "I'm sorry 'bout what happened. I never meant to hurt ya . . . or Gerald neither. I'll never forgive myself for what happened to him. But I have sumthin to tell ya." He hesitated and looked at Andrew, then raised his chin and faced Claire again. "You know how I feel 'bout ya, an' I know you need to be cared for. Michael, too. I want you to be my wife. I love ya."

Claire didn't say a word. She tried to grasp the blanket with quivering hands.

Helplessly, Mr. Alexander shifted his gaze to Andrew, then back to Claire. "I brung your ring. I—I put it on your finger. You gotta know how much I love ya an' want you to come back home. Please say you'll marry me."

Claire lifted her hand and froze, staring at the ring. "Take it off!" Her body shook. "Take it off!" She tried to pull it from her hand. Tears streamed down her face. "Where's *my* ring? I want *my* ring!"

Andrew wasn't about to let this continue. "You need to leave, Mr. Alexander. Please? GO."

The man stood, but bent close to Claire. "I'm sorry. I only done it cuz I love ya!"

"Go *NOW*!" Andrew grabbed him by the shoulder and moved him toward the door.

Mr. Alexander flashed a look of utter defeat, limped out the door, then before he walked away, beat his fist against the wall. Andrew stood in the doorway until he knew for certain the man wouldn't turn around. Then he returned to Claire.

Fighting the urge to hold her, he sat in the chair beside the bed. "I'm sorry." The words seemed empty. He wanted to say so much more.

The moment he reached his hand toward her with the intent of wiping away her tears, Martha walked in.

He jerked his hand to himself.

CHAPTER 33

Andrew paced the floor, chiding himself for allowing Mr. Alexander into the room. The look Martha gave him didn't help. He should've listened to his gut and kept the man away from Claire.

Martha spoke soothingly to her, trying to get her to leave the ring alone. Claire kept pulling at it, but it wouldn't budge.

"Claire?" They all turned to face Beth. She wobbled and Andrew prepared to catch her. But she quickly regained her composure and ran to Claire's bedside. She wrapped her arms around her and nearly smothered her. "I can't believe you're all right! When I left, you was nearly . . . Oh, Claire!"

After holding onto her for several long minutes, Beth stopped and sobered, looking at Martha. "Does she know?"

Martha nodded. "I'm goin' out for a spell. You sit here, Miss Beth. I'll give you some time alone with her."

"Beth," Andrew said. "I have some other patients to see. I'm glad you came back to find her well. She's a real fighter."

"She had a good doctor." Beth's smile warmed the room. "Thank you for all you done." Her arms encircled him and she hugged him tight.

"You're welcome."

He followed Martha out the door. He had every intention of talking to her about the incident with Claire's uncle, but she walked away without giving him another thought. She had every right to be angry, but he hoped she knew he never intentionally wanted to hurt Claire. Maybe Martha needed some time to herself. When the moment was right, he'd speak with her about it, but for now, he had patients to tend.

* * *

Claire scooted up in the bed as best she could. She missed the comfort of her own mattress, the cheerful colors in her room, and more than anything—*Gerald.* Though she was grateful to see Beth, the reality of Gerald's absence grew. She'd never again see his sweet face or run her fingers through his curly hair.

Beth's head tipped to one side and her chin quivered. She perched on the edge of the bed. "I don't know what to say, Claire. It's all been so horrible. I wanted to save Gerald, too." Tears emerged and instantly dotted her cheeks. "But I couldn't."

"I can't believe he's gone . . ." Claire finally had the strength to cry. Her body shook and tears streamed.

Beth embraced her. They wept together, finding comfort in each other's arms. Time became non-existent while they held one another and grieved.

"I loved him so much," Claire said, sniffling. "I didn't even get to tell him *goodbye.*"

"Me, too. I miss him." Beth sobbed. "But I thank God I didn't lose you, too."

Claire raised a weak hand to wipe the tears out of her eyes. "How's my baby? How's Michael? I need to see him."

"He's fine. Mrs. Sandborn has been takin' good care a him. But he misses his mama." She sucked in air. "And his daddy." She cried even harder.

"It's not fair. He'll never know what kinda man Gerald was. He loved him so much . . ." Claire's voice started to fade.

"You sound tired. We can talk more later. I'm just thankful you're alive." After giving her one more hug, she helped her lay back against the pillow.

While patting Claire's blankets into place, she took her hand and glared at Henry's ring. "I still can't believe he snuck in here and did this."

"He was here a little while ago. Asked me to marry him."

Stepping away, Beth clinched her fists. Her face twisted and fire replaced the tears that had been in her eyes. "Why'd they let him in? He had no right. I can't believe Dr. Fletcher let him near you!"

"Don't be angry with Andrew. He didn't leave us alone." She hadn't meant to upset her. They had enough to feel badly about without her worrying over Henry.

"Andrew?" Beth's brows dipped. "You callin' him by his first name? Why you doin' that? It ain't appropriate."

"He told me his name." *What was I thinkin*? Hopefully, Beth would accept the explanation. "After all we've been through, he thought it was appropriate."

Beth's face softened. "I reckon you're right. He *has* taken good care a you. He's a good man." Once again, she lifted

Claire's hand and stared at the rose ring. "I hate that you lost Mama's ring. Gerald lost his glasses, too. They buried him without 'em. But like Brother Brown told me, he won't need 'em in Heaven."

"He *is* in Heaven, isn't he Beth? Never was such a good-hearted man." A man she certainly hadn't deserved.

Beth sighed. "They buried him next to your mama. Brother Brown held a real nice service for him yesterday. Everyone was there. They was all worried 'bout you. Said lotsa prayers. Fact is, Brother Brown's here. He's waitin' outside the room. Would you like to see him?"

"Yes, I would." The time had come to stop running from God and make amends. Gerald deserved it.

Beth left the room and returned with the reverend.

He walked to Claire and patted her hand. "God answered our prayers, Claire. We're so grateful."

She managed to smile, but felt too weak to do much more. She wanted to know why she'd lived and Gerald had died. Could Brother Brown explain it?

"You don't need to speak. When you get stronger, come and see me. I know this'll be a difficult time. I'm here for you when you need to talk." He lightly tapped her hand again, then nodded toward Beth. "I best be headin' home. Can you find a way back? I'm sure you'll want to stay here with Claire until you can bring her home."

"I'll figger sumthin' out, Reverend," Beth said. "Sorry you came along for nothin'."

"I'm not. I'm thankful it turned out as it did. I'll let everyone know back home. Mrs. Sandborn will be overjoyed." He turned to leave.

"Reverend?" Beth said. "Please tell Mrs. Sandborn we'll be home soon."

"I will." He nodded to both of them, then went on his way.

Though they hadn't said it, Claire knew Reverend Brown had accompanied Beth for the sole purpose of taking *her* home in a casket. The thought made her shudder. Somehow she had to find a way to make her life meaningful again. Stop the deceit and properly raise Michael. But how? She couldn't do it alone, and she'd never tell Beth the truth about Andrew. She sank deeper into the pillow wishing she could find a simple solution.

Miss Elliott entered the room, followed by Andrew. Claire's heart skipped a beat. Her eyes had finally focused properly, giving her the ability to see him clearly. *More handsome than ever.*

I should be ashamed of myself! She had to dismiss her sinful attraction.

"Ready to get on your feet?" Miss Elliott asked with a cheerful ring.

"I'll try," she rasped. "I still feel like a baby."

Andrew handed Beth a glass of water. "Give her a little. It'll help her throat."

The cool water soothed, but the heat building inside her couldn't be squelched. What was she going to do? Having Andrew so close made everything complicated.

Beth set down the water glass, then stood back so Andrew could help Claire to her feet.

He put his arm behind her back, then Miss Elliott helped her swing her legs around and onto the floor. Andrew eased her fully upright.

His arms feel so good . . .

She looked up into his eyes, but stopped herself amidst the vision of the two of them on that stormy night. She couldn't let Beth see her feelings.

"Easy now," Andrew said.

She put her full weight on her feet and her legs shook. Her knees buckled and she dropped down.

Andrew tightened his grasp. "I've got you." He lifted her again.

She took a step.

Miss Elliott beamed. "You're doing well. You'll be running after that baby in no time."

Maybe Claire had imagined it, but it seemed Andrew's body jerked slightly at the mention of her baby. One day she'd tell him about Michael. But not now. And certainly not around Beth.

Andrew helped her walk across the room and then back to the bed. "We'll do more later. Beth, when she's ready, you can help her walk again. And it would be helpful for you to do the exercises with her that you did while she was sleeping. The more she works her muscles, the better."

"I can do that. You reckon I really helped her?"

"Yes, you did. You're a good friend."

"I'm her sister. I love her!"

My sister.

Claire rested back in bed and looked around the room at all the smiling faces. Smiling for her. Smiling for her miraculous recovery. Love surrounded her, but she felt lost. She had no idea where she'd call *home*.

* * *

Andrew couldn't wait to tell Alicia the news about Claire. He had plenty of time for a visit before he had to pick up his father for supper.

When he arrived at the Tarver's, he found Clay working in the fields. No longer a thin awkward boy, his body had filled out from all the hard work. He grew taller and more like Elijah every day.

Jenny stood by him holding Betsy on her hip. She ladled some water for Clay to drink. When they noticed Andrew, they smiled and waved.

He waved back, then knocked on the door. It opened a crack. Joshua's dark eyes blinked at him in the sunlight. "It's Doc, Mama!"

"Let him in, Josh!"

Joshua stepped aside so Andrew could enter. Alicia stood at the stove stirring the contents of a large pot.

"Where's Samuel?" Andrew asked. "I saw the other children in the field."

"That boy will be the death a me!" Alicia fussed and shook the wooden spoon in the air. "He runs off all the time. Needs to be heppin' Clay, but I cain't get him to stay 'round long enough to lift a finger! One day he's gonna hafta learn to do a hard day's work!"

Andrew chuckled. Though Alicia fussed, her animation always tickled him. "Want me to say something to him?"

"No. I'll be turnin' him over my knee soon enough. Times like this I shore do miss Lijah. He could make the boy mind just by lookin' at him. But that's enough a my troubles. I knows you got enough a your own. Have a seat an' tell me what happened."

After giving the pot another good stir, she sat with him at the table.

"She's alive, Alicia," he said with a generous smile. "She woke up last night. God answered our prayers."

"Praise be!" Alicia exclaimed, but then sighed. "Now the hard part's a comin'. Ain't it, Doc?"

"It already has. I have so many questions I want to ask her, but she's still weak. It's difficult for her to speak. And . . . she's mourning her husband. It's tearing me up inside."

"She hasta mourn. If she don't, I'd wonder what kinda woman she really was."

"I know she loved him. But I can tell she loves me, too. I see it in her eyes. I want to tell her how I feel—let her know I still want to be with her. But how much time do I need to give her?"

"Now wait one minute, Doc! Ain't you supposed to be marryin' Victoria? You're in a mess. If you ain't gonna marry her, you needs to tell her."

Hearing Alicia say it made it sound simple, but it was anything but that.

"You know I have to marry her. O'Malley will see to it. He's never forgiven me for what happened. I haven't forgiven *myself* either. I don't love her, but I *will* care for her."

"It ain't right!" Alicia shook her head. "It just ain't right. How can you be happy if you're with the wrong woman?"

"Maybe I won't be, but maybe in all this craziness I'm supposed to be with Victoria. I still don't know why Claire left me to begin with. Maybe she doesn't want me and I'm imagining her feelings." He stood and paced, clenching his fists. "God, this is killing me!"

"Know how many times you walked my floor? Reckon you wore it out there." Alicia pointed at his feet and chuckled, but her attempt at soothing his pain wasn't working.

"I don't understand why life has to be so difficult." He continued pacing, hoping the floorboards would render some sort of revelation.

"That's life. It's the way it is." Alicia stood and moved to the stove. "I needs to finish supper. Wanna eat with us?"

"I can't. I'd love to. Believe me I enjoy your company more. But I'm having supper with my father."

"Still havin' a hard time talkin' to him?"

"We have nothing in common—except blood. Sometimes I wonder how I could ever be his son." He thanked her for listening and hugged her.

"You just keep prayin', Doc. You still need it." Alicia walked with him out the door.

"There's Samuel," Andrew said, pointing down the road. The boy kicked at the dirt as he walked.

Alicia huffed with her hands on her hips. "You get your tail in here this minute, boy!"

Andrew grinned. Knowing how soft-hearted she was and that she'd never strike her children, he wondered what punishment Samuel would face. She'd likely scold him and sit him in the corner for a while, then hug him and tell him she loved him. Then they'd all have a pleasant supper together.

Somehow she'd learned to cope without Elijah. But he didn't want to have to live without Claire.

* * *

John pulled his pocket watch from his jacket and flipped it open. Six o'clock. A knock on his door made him smile.

"I have to say this for you, Andrew. You *are* punctual." John put on his top hat and followed Andrew to his buggy.

"My father taught me the importance of being on time," Andrew said, grinning. "I know of a restaurant on the pier. I seem to remember that you're fond of oysters."

"Very fond. Thank you. Anything but Sylvia's." If he *never* ate there again, it would be too soon.

Even for Mobile, the weather was pleasant. John managed to ignore the horrid smell of the water and instead set his mind to eating oysters. Hopefully, they had the sense to cook them properly. After all, it wasn't difficult.

Lack of elegance seemed abundant in the south. The restaurant had simple wood chairs and tables. Nothing elaborate. At least he'd been given a cloth napkin for his lap. When the food came, he was surprisingly pleased. Andrew had been right about this establishment after all.

"This is good, Andrew," John said. He took another bite of soup.

"I'm glad you like it. Victoria brought me here the first time I offered to take her to supper."

"She likes oysters?"

"Not especially." Andrew leaned toward him. "She thought they might arouse my desires for her," he whispered.

John smirked. "I take it they didn't work. I still don't understand why you haven't taken her to bed."

"Please, Father. Let's not speak of that."

"You brought it up. Why do you find it so difficult to speak about women?" John pressed him. *Women* had always been his favorite subject.

"I don't care to speak about them the way you do. We don't view women the same way."

"What other way is there?" John took another bite and waited for his son's response. He'd spent many years trying to teach him, and he still didn't seem to comprehend the pleasures of having a woman.

Andrew shook his head. "Did you ever love my mother? *Truly* love her?"

"Of course I did. She was beautiful. She made me quite happy . . . while she lived." John buttered a slice of bread and ate heartily. This could be the only decent meal he'd have until he returned home.

"But did you love *her*? Did you make *her* happy?"

"I gave her you. *That* made her happy."

"She was a good mother." Andrew smiled and sighed.

"Then she died." John scowled at the memory. "She just *had* to have that baby."

Andrew's expression instantly changed. His smile disappeared, replaced by scorn. "She wanted to give you another child. How can you fault her for that?"

"She was too old. I'd arranged to take care of the baby so she wouldn't have to carry it. She refused. And then she died. I never forgave her for that." He glared at Andrew. How dare he challenge him on something he knew so little about?

"How can you say that? Not forgiving her for *dying*? Sometimes we have no control over death."

"*I* had it under control." John gripped the table with both hands. "The pregnancy would've been terminated and your mother would've lived. Wouldn't that have pleased you?"

Andrew swallowed hard. "Yes, of course I wanted her to live. But I'd *never* ask a woman to do that."

"Don't say *never*, Andrew!" John hissed his words. "You don't know what you'd do if you were faced with the same situation. Don't judge me!" He slammed his fist against the table.

Andrew motioned for him to calm down. "Why must we always argue? I was happy until we started talking."

"Happy? Oh—because of your success with that woman?" The woman he'd never reveal as his daughter. Andrew could never know.

"Yes, because of Claire." Andrew whispered her name. "About Claire . . ."

John's heart began to race. "What about her?"

"Do you remember my letter about the woman I met? The one I fell in love with? The one who left me?"

"Yes, of course I remember." Racing became pounding.

Andrew took a large breath. "That woman was Claire. She's the woman who I've been caring for. Mrs. Montgomery's niece. I'm still in love with her, Father."

Disgusted, John looked away from him. Andrew's eyes revealed extreme pain. Regardless, he wouldn't have him make a mess of everything.

He had to set him straight, so he faced him again with a look his son knew well, demanding obedience. "Get yourself together! You have a fiancée and a wedding in less than two weeks! Victoria's the perfect match for you. Forget that little whore!" His loud voice caught the attention of others in the restaurant. They gaped at him, horrified.

"Don't you *ever* call her that again!" Andrew yelled. "I love her! And if she'll have me, I'll find some way to be with her!"

"No!" John pounded his fist on the table. "Marry Victoria! You owe it to her!"

A man in a suit approached their table. "This is my establishment. You'll have to keep your voices down or leave the restaurant."

"I'm ready to leave," Andrew snarled and handed money to the man. "This should be more than enough for our meal." He stormed out.

John smirked, tipped his hat, and strode after him. Andrew had waited for him, already in the buggy with reins in hand. He hopped up beside him.

"I imagine I should never have come here," John said coldly. "I thought we could settle our differences, but it seems that will never happen. We're much too different."

"Can't you *try* to understand me? Try to listen to what I have to say? You're so opinionated. You never hear me."

John chose not to reply. He crossed his arms and sat back in the buggy, anxious to return to the hotel. Once they came to a stop, he decided to speak. "We're supposed to have supper with the O'Malley's tomorrow evening. Do you suppose you could try not to hate me for one more night?"

"I don't hate you, Father. I just don't understand you."

"Well then, let's try to put all that aside and make an effort to enjoy a meal with your future in-laws. You still intend to marry her, don't you?"

"Yes. Whether I like it or not."

"Good. You have to trust me on this. It's for the best. That other woman doesn't suit you."

Andrew stared forward. "I need to go back to the hospital to check on her."

"You're asking for trouble."

"She's still my patient." Andrew left him standing at the hotel.

He doesn't know the half of it.

John sauntered to his room. It was still early. Perhaps he could find some company for the night. Someone to ease the tension between his shoulders.

Among other things.

CHAPTER 34

Every bit of frustration toward his father melted away when Andrew reached Claire's room. She was sitting up in bed, with Martha to one side and Beth to the other. Her lips turned slightly upward as he walked in. But then as quickly as she'd smiled, she looked down and away from him.

"How are you feeling?" he asked.

"Stronger."

"Heck!" Martha chimed in. "She's doin' great! We had her walkin' part way down the hall."

"You did?" Andrew couldn't be more pleased. "That's incredible. You have good nurses." He nodded toward Martha and Beth.

"We like to help her," Beth said. "She wants to go home."

Home?

She couldn't leave. Not yet. "She'll have to get stronger first."

"Maybe tomorrow?" Claire asked. Her pleading eyes tugged at the core of his heart.

"We'll see." If it were up to him, he'd keep her there indefinitely, though he knew she longed to see their son. He did, too. "Have you eaten anything?"

"She had applesauce just a bit ago," Beth chirped. "Ate it all, too."

"That's good." He tipped his head and grinned at Claire. "How about a steak?"

Her soft laugh sounded more beautiful than music. "Very funny, Andr . . ." She caught herself. "Dr. Fletcher."

Out of the corner of his eye he noticed Beth nod and smile with satisfaction. Had Beth noticed their familiarity? "Well, I think *I* may actually go home tonight," he said. "I miss my own bed. That hotel is fine, but there's nothing like home." He gazed at Claire. Had she read into his words?

"I miss mine, too." Martha said. "But I ain't ready to check out yet. I won't leave till Claire does."

"Me neither," Beth added. "Don't worry, Dr. Fletcher. We'll look after her tonight. You go on home an' get a good night's sleep. You deserve it."

"Thank you. I'll see you all in the morning." He walked toward the door, then paused and looked at Claire one last time. Her eyes met his briefly, then shifted. How could he ever get her alone? He'd never have his answers with Martha and Beth constantly by her side.

When he arrived home, he should've done some packing, but was much too tired. He'd been procrastinating as long as possible. Completely exhausted, he lay down on his bed and fell asleep thinking of Claire. They needed to talk soon. Otherwise, she'd slip out of his fingers once again.

* * *

Since Mr. Schultz told him to take a few days off, Andrew allowed himself to sleep in. He wasn't expected at work; however, he had to confront Claire. He dressed casually and rode to the hospital. It was nearly time for dinner.

When he arrived at her room, an unfamiliar man hovered in the corner.

Odd.

Martha let out a laugh. "This here's George. He's my hired hand. Was worried 'bout me since I'd been gone so long."

George hung his head and clutched a straw hat. The poor man appeared more uncomfortable than anyone he'd met before. It seemed unusual for such a shy man to work for someone as outspoken as Martha.

"I'm pleased to meet you, George." Andrew extended his hand. "I'm Dr. Fletcher."

George removed one hand from his hat, shook Andrew's hand, then grasped the hat firmly again with both hands. "Doc." He nodded, then stared at the floor.

Martha chuckled. "I reckon he wants to take us home. What do you think, Doc? Can we take her home today?"

Claire's eyes pleaded just as they had yesterday. How could he let her go?

"I don't know. I'll need to take a good look at her and make a decision. I don't want her to leave if she's not strong enough."

"I walked a few steps by myself this mornin'," Claire said. "I feel much better . . . *Doctor.*"

Martha gave Andrew a little nudge. "Tell you what. We'll all go down to Sylvia's an' have us a bite. Give you a chance to check her over. Maybe when we get back you'll let her leave."

"That sounds like a good idea," Beth said. "I'm hungry, too."

As they left the room, Martha met his gaze and he thanked her with his eyes. She shook her head and frowned, then walked away.

A strange response.

He shut the door tight.

"Why'd you do that, Andrew?" Claire's voice trembled. Was she afraid to be alone with him?

"I need to talk to you. I don't want anyone disturbing us." He sat down beside her. He'd ask her the one question he needed an answer to, but he'd leave it up to her to tell him about Michael. She owed him that much.

She stared at him. "Please . . . don't do this."

He tried to take her hand, but she pulled away. "Claire, I know you feel something for me. I can see it in your eyes."

"No. I can't do this right now. I just lost my husband. You have no idea how that feels."

"Don't I? I lost my wife nearly two years ago. I've been grieving for her ever since."

"I was *never* your wife." Her harsh tone cut him like a knife.

"We had everything but the piece of paper, Claire. You wore my ring and you lay in my bed. In my mind, you *were* my wife. I have to know why you left." Tears started to form, but he refused to cry.

"You don't wanna know. Trust me." She looked away.

"I *have* to know. It's never made sense. I know you loved me."

Tears rolled down her cheeks "Yes. I did."

"Then why? Why leave?"

The ache in his heart grew with every second she hesitated. But he'd push her until she answered.

She took a large breath. "I had no choice. You aren't gonna like what you hear, but if you insist on knowin', I'll tell you." She fidgeted with her blanket, staring at the thing.

"Please, I'm *begging* you." What could be so horrible?

"I . . . I was so happy that mornin'. I cleaned your house. Fixed it up for you. I wanted to make it real nice for you when you got home." She smiled and for a brief moment met his gaze. "Then I saw what a mess your desk was. I thought I'd tidy it up, too." She looked down and her shoulders slumped as if she wanted to hide from him. "I found the photograph of you with your mama. And . . . your *daddy.*"

"I don't understand. If you were happy, why'd you go?"

"I thought your daddy looked familiar. I didn't understand why, so I read the letter that was with the picture. Then it all made sense. I knew who your daddy was."

Anger boiled up inside him, heating his face. "You left because you found out my father's John Martin? He warned me there'd be people like you. People who'd judge me for what he'd done. I never imagined *you* would be one of those people! Why'd you judge me by my father?" Wanting to distance himself from her, he stood and stormed across the room. All this time he thought he knew her. He'd been wrong.

"I didn't judge you! I loved you, Andrew!" Her chin quivered and her tears fell as droplets onto the blankets. She sniffled. "Your daddy told you he'd had another wife, but he didn't tell you everythin'!"

"What do you mean?" Though angry, he moved to her bedside. He couldn't bear seeing her so distraught.

"Your daddy never told you he also left behind a child. A little girl. A girl named *Claire*. I'm your sister, Andrew!" Her tears flowed freely down her face. She sobbed without control.

Andrew's heart seemed to stop beating and he slumped down into the chair. He shook his head. "No. No. It can't be true. Your name's *Montgomery*."

"My mama changed it. It was her maiden name. I didn't know my daddy's real name until years later. I made Martha tell me."

"He couldn't have known there was a child. He wouldn't have done that." His head dropped into his hands and he covered his face. She had to be mistaken.

"I was a year old when he left, Andrew. He knew. He *chose* to leave us." She reached out to him and raked her fingers into his hair. "It's true. John Martin's my daddy. You can ask Martha. She'll tell you. That's why I left. I found out and was ashamed of what we'd done. I didn't want you to know. I loved you so much I didn't want you to hafta bear the shame. I hoped you'd forget me and go on with your life."

He couldn't move. How could he when his heart had been ripped from his chest? "He didn't have the nerve to tell me. He had every opportunity last night . . . and he didn't tell me."

"What do you mean last night? Is our daddy here?" She nervously pulled the blankets up around her.

"*Our daddy.* God, it can't be true. How can I love you this much if you're my sister?" Tears cascaded down his face and he made no attempt to stop them.

She reached for him and he didn't hesitate embracing her.

"Maybe we can learn to love each other as family," she said, holding him tight. "I still love you, too."

* * *

Victoria had had enough. Only two weeks until their wedding and Andrew still spent all his time with that woman.

She didn't even have the decency to die.

She intended to seek him out and make her feelings known. She deserved better treatment.

"I remember you! Ain't you Doc Fletcher's fiancée?"

Victoria turned sharply and looked down her nose at the despicable woman. "Yes, I am. I'm here to see him. I was told he's in that woman's room. Seems she didn't die."

"She's my niece, an' yes, she's still breathin'. Ain't that nice?" The woman snarled. *How dare she?*

"Nice for you. She took a great deal of Andrew's time. We have a weddin' comin' up, you know?" Victoria proceeded up the stairs, then down the hallway toward the resurrected woman's room. If she had her way, she'd send the little homewrecker six feet under.

To her dismay, the woman's ugly aunt followed right behind her. When they got there, the door was shut.

"I wouldn't open it if I was you." The wretched woman stood in front of the door, wrinkling her nose. "He might be examinin' her."

Victoria stood upright and threw her shoulders back. "Well!" The thought of him *examining* another woman infuriated her.

"Let *me* check on 'em. She's my niece after all. I've seen it before."

The woman gave her a wry smile, then squeezed through the door, shielding her from whatever was going on inside the room. The door shut tight behind her, then the lock clicked.

"Oh!" Victoria leaned against the wall and waited. Her mind reeled wondering what they were doing. Even if she didn't want Andrew any longer, he had no right to treat her this way.

* * *

Andrew raised his head from Claire's embrace as Martha entered the room. Taking the corner of the blanket, he wiped Claire's eyes and then his own.

"Damn," Martha muttered and dabbed *her* eyes with the sleeve of her dress.

"Why didn't you tell me, Martha?" he asked.

"Wasn't my place. You don't know how sorry I am, Doc. I've grown quite fond a you. Tore me up knowin' eventually you'd learn the truth." She looked at Claire. "I understand now what you done. Wish you woulda told me. I woulda listened. Don't know how you could bear keepin' it inside so long." Martha moved to the other side of Claire and stroked her hair. "Doc?" She paused and sighed. "Your fiancée is outside the door. She wants to see ya. I stopped her from comin' in."

Andrew sat upright and shook his head. "I don't want to see her now. I can't handle any of this. I don't know how to feel."

Martha moved to him and put her arm around his shoulder. "You hafta face her. She's waitin'. You don't want her to get suspicious."

"I know you're right." He stood. He needed to act like a man and deal with this. "Claire, I'll come back later. We have more to talk about." He walked from the room to face Victoria.

* * *

"Everything hurts, Martha," Claire said. She breathed deeply and tried to regain her composure.

Martha sat beside her. "Time will make things better. Won't be easy, but it'll happen. Sorry you had to tell Doc 'bout bein' his sister."

"How'd *you* know?"

"I put the pieces together. Well—that and I ran into John Martin at the hotel." She turned to spit, but stopped herself.

"So, he *is* here?" Claire's stomach flipped.

"Yep. For Doc's weddin'. He was all puffed up an' proud he's marryin' a rich girl. Makes me sick."

"I don't wanna see him. I don't want any *chance* of seein' him. Can you get George an' Beth an' take me home? I wanna leave before Andrew comes back."

"Why?"

"Seein' him makes my pain even worse."

"You up to goin'?"

"Yes. I can travel. If George can take Beth an' me home, then you can go back home, too. I'm sure you're tired of this hospital."

"Matter a fact, I am. Hope I never have to come back here again. What 'bout Michael? You gonna let Doc see him?"

"I didn't tell him Michael's his son. He doesn't know. I can't do that now. It would hurt Beth."

Martha stood with her back to her, muttering something she couldn't make out. Martha cleared her throat, then turned to face her. "I'll go get Beth an' George. We'll get you home." She left the room without saying another word.

Though she'd grown accustomed to Martha's odd behavior, sometimes it still confused her. So rather than worry, Claire laid there and thought about Andrew, relieved he finally knew the truth. It had hurt him, but it had been for the best. Perhaps now he could marry Victoria and be happy. And somehow, she'd find her own way.

CHAPTER 35

When Andrew left Claire's room, Victoria grabbed him by the arm and reminded him they were all having supper that evening. Not wanting to deal with her now, he told her he wasn't feeling well and needed to lie down.

Oddly, she didn't argue and left to return home. But rather than lying down, he went where his anger led him—to the hotel to confront his father.

He pounded on the door, releasing some of his fury, but plenty more remained for the man on the other side.

The door swung open, but before his father could say a word, Andrew drew back his fist and punched him square in the jaw. "You BASTARD!"

The man stumbled backward and fell to the floor. At the same time, Andrew slammed the door behind him. He lunged for his father ready to take another swing.

His father rapidly shook his head, jumped to his feet, and grabbed Andrew by the arm, stopping the blow. "What the hell is wrong with you?"

"I despise you! You've ruined my life!" Boiling anger allowed him to say the words he'd longed to ever since his mother had died.

"You'd better calm down and explain yourself!" He pushed Andrew backward onto the sofa.

Andrew steadied himself on the cushions, but his anger wouldn't subside. "Why can't you ever tell me the truth? I'm your son! Last night you could've told me about Claire!"

"What about her?" his father snarled and clinched his fists.

"What about her? What about your *DAUGHTER*?"

"Oh. That. Is that what this is all about?" The man rubbed his jaw and casually took a seat in a chair as though they were having an ordinary conversation.

"You called her a whore! Your own daughter. You knew I was speaking of her and you still didn't tell me. My God, Father! I bedded my sister!" Andrew held his face in his hands, ashamed of what he'd done.

"You didn't know at the time, Andrew. How *could* you have known?"

"I could've known if you'd told me I *had* a sister! How could you leave a child that way? Leave her and never look back?"

"I met your mother. I wanted *her*. Besides, Ruth was in the way of my career. She was a simple girl. Nothing like your mother. I didn't love her. I was young and she was beautiful. She seduced me and I bedded her." His father leaned back in his seat and unconcernedly crossed his legs. "Those stupid people would've shot me if I hadn't married her. So, I did. Only to regret it. I began to despise her and the child she bore. I would never have done anything with my life if I'd stayed with her. Don't you understand that?"

"No, I don't. Claire's the most wonderful woman I've ever known." For a brief moment his fury calmed, but then it flared again. "She bore me a son! My *sister* has given me a son! Do you know what that means?"

His father stared blankly at him. "Claire had your son?"

"Yes. You're a grandfather. From *both* of us." Andrew took a deep breath and tried to still his pounding heart.

His father stood and paced the floor. Andrew watched and waited, while the man rubbed his chin and seemed to be perplexed by the news. After several moments of silence, he faced him. "The boy will be fine, Andrew."

"I'm a doctor. I know what can happen to children whose parents are blood-related. Don't tell me he'll be fine." Andrew ran his fingers back through his hair and shook his head.

"Stop moping!" His father snarled. "You're *not* blood-related!"

Andrew sat up straight. "What do you mean? You *are* Claire's father, aren't you?"

"Yes. Of course I am! But I'm not *yours*!" The man sat, breathing heavily.

"I don't believe you. Mother would never have done that!"

"Your mother was faithful to me," his father muttered. Almost as if he faulted her for it.

"Then you make no sense." Andrew kept his eyes glued to the man. Over the years, he'd learned to tell when he was lying. He needed the truth now more than ever.

"When I married your mother, she became pregnant

within weeks of our marriage. She miscarried after only three months. She was heartbroken. Several months later, she conceived again. This time she only carried for five months.

"She retreated into herself. She became depressed and withdrew from me. She wasn't the woman I married." He paused, letting out a long sigh. "I wanted my wife back. I wanted the lover she once was. So I went to the orphanage. I saw a baby boy there with black hair and deep black eyes. I knew he was perfect. . . . *you* were perfect, Andrew. The matron told me you were Cherokee. Just like your mother."

He stopped speaking and looked at Andrew, obviously waiting for a reaction. But how could he react? His life had been a lie.

Andrew turned away. His heavy breathing and thumping heart made it difficult to speak. "Why didn't you tell me?"

"I promised your mother I wouldn't. She loved you as her own. I took you home from the orphanage and placed you in her arms. Her face lit up and she became alive again. You meant everything to her. She told everyone you were ours and she grew to believe it. You gave me back my wife. You were tiny and didn't know it, but you made our home happy again."

"Then she died and everything changed, didn't it?" Andrew snapped. "You never loved *me*! I finally understand. I'm not your blood! You only wanted me so your wife would come to your bed again!"

Without warning, John slapped Andrew hard across the face. "I gave you everything! I put a roof over your head and food in your mouth! I gave you your career! Don't you ever forget it!"

The sting in his cheek relit Andrew's rage. "It was mother's money that did it all! *You* wouldn't have had a career if it hadn't been for her!"

"You'd better thank God I took you from that orphanage!" John stood and hovered over him. "No one else wanted a *dirty* little Indian!"

"Mother was Cherokee! How can you speak like that?" Andrew thought he couldn't hate his father any more than he already did, but he'd been wrong. *He's not even my father.*

"Your mother was special."

"And her parents were rich!"

John raised his hand to strike, but Andrew grabbed it. "You won't do that again!" Andrew held his wrist tighter than any vice.

Hot air streamed from their nostrils. They faced each other without speaking. Hatred surrounded them like a thick black fog.

John jerked his hand from Andrew's grasp, smoothed his clothing, and sat.

Andrew needed to know more. "What do you know of my *real* parents? Since you're finally telling me the truth, I want to know everything."

"Fine! I'll tell you," John snarled. "I can only tell you what the matron told me." He repositioned himself on the chair, then grabbed a pipe from an end table, filled it, and lit it. All the while Andrew waited as patiently as he could.

John took a long drag from the pipe. "Your mother brought you to the orphanage. She begged them to take you. She was a Cherokee who'd been raped by a white man. He'd held a knife to her throat. He was drunk and passed out after the deed was done. So she took the knife from him and slit his throat.

"In no time, the law went after her. She ran and hid. When she realized she was pregnant, she remained hidden until you were born. Then she took you to the orphanage. They wouldn't take you—said they only took orphans. She begged and pleaded, explaining what had happened to her, but they wouldn't give in.

"She knew she couldn't stay in hiding with a child. So, she laid you at the feet of the matron and ran out the door into the alley. The matron sent someone after her. But when they found her, she'd taken her own life. Stabbed herself through the heart. So they took you in. You'd become an orphan."

John recanted the story without emotion. Cold and matter-of-fact. Did he feel nothing at all? Andrew wouldn't allow himself to cry in front of the man. He couldn't imagine the pain his real mother must have felt. He'd seen Victoria after Tobias tried to take her. The thought of his mother going through the same ordeal tore at his soul.

"There!" John slapped his hands against his legs. "Now you know everything. So, what are you going to do? Run back to Claire?"

Andrew had been so caught up in learning the truth about himself that the realization of Claire hadn't sunk in. *She's not my sister.*

Oh, God . . . Claire's not my sister!

His heart raced. No longer from anger—from hope. But he had no intention of sharing his feelings with John. "Why should *you* care anymore what I do, John? You're not my father. You've *never* been my father."

"*John*, is it? I raised you!"

"You *paid* for me! Mother raised me!"

"She *wasn't* your mother," John sneered. "I just told you about your *real* mother."

"Elizabeth Fletcher will always be my mother. She loved me. You never did." Andrew stood to leave. "I don't know what I'm going to do, but it'll be far away from you."

"What about supper? We're supposed to dine this evening with the O'Malley's. You haven't forgotten Victoria, have you?" John's words were smug, in an evil, sadistic way.

"You go. Tell them I'm ill. Besides, I believe they prefer *your* company."

John smirked. "Fine. I will. But how shall I get there?"

"Rent a buggy!" Andrew snapped and slammed the door as he left.

* * *

Even after the ordeal with John, Andrew's heart raced with joyful anticipation as he fled to the hospital. Finally he had good news for Claire. She could stop condemning herself. And perhaps in time she'd come back to him.

When he reached her room, he found the bed stripped and empty. He raced down the hall to the nurses' station. "Where's Mrs. Alexander?"

"Mrs. Stevens released her. The family wanted to take her home. We knew you were off today, so Mrs. Stevens signed the papers." The nurse was as matter-of-fact as John had been.

"How long ago did she leave?"

"'Bout an hour ago."

His heart sank. Bursting with the news, he had to tell *someone*. So, he went to Alicia and told her everything.

And even though she helped calm his fury toward his *father*, she reminded him that his troubles were far from over.

CHAPTER 36

John rented a buggy, dressed in his finest suit, slapped on some expensive cologne, and headed to the O'Malley's. He was more than ready to play with Victoria again. Unable to find a companion last night, he needed something to relieve his frustrations.

His discussion with Andrew had given him indigestion. He hoped Izzy was a good cook.

When he knocked on the door, it was opened by a large Negro woman. She stared at him, taking him in from head to toe. "You must be Mr. Fletcher."

"Yes, I am," he replied, looking down his nose. "And you must be Izzy . . . the *servant*."

"Hmph," Izzy grunted, then stepped aside so he could enter. He'd make a point to speak with Patrick about his rude employee.

Shannon appeared, improving the view. "John, it's so good to see you again. But where is Dr. Fletcher?"

"My son is ill. He insisted I come." He smiled and kissed her hand.

"I hope 'Tis nothing serious. I'm so happy you decided to come regardless."

"I wouldn't have missed it for anything."

"Victoria will be surprised to find only you at our door. She may be disappointed."

"I'll try to appease her." He kissed her hand once again. *And hopefully she'll appease me.*

"You are a charming man, John Fletcher. Patrick! Mr. Fletcher has arrived!"

Patrick came into the hallway and shook John's hand. "What? No son? Where's the doctor?"

"As I was telling your lovely wife, my son is ill. I imagine he's been working too hard and became run down."

"Well, he'd best heal quickly. The weddin's not far off."

Victoria made a grand entrance down the stairway. John licked his lips watching her cascade down each step. She wore a deep red velvet gown with even darker red lace. A white scarf adorned her neck, but his eyes were drawn to her bosom, which floated a heart-shaped necklace. With her hair piled high on her head, exposing her long neck, he couldn't help but envision his lips gliding along her soft skin.

"Did I hear y'all correctly? Andrew won't be here tonight?"

John extended his arm. "No, I'm afraid he won't. I'm sorry, Victoria."

She took his arm. "I hope it's nothin' serious. Is it, John?"

"Nothing a good night in bed won't cure." He gazed into her eyes.

"Yes, a good night in bed can help most anythin' that ails a man." She squeezed his arm. The game had begun.

"I hope you're hungry, lad," Patrick said. "Izzy made quite a feast."

"I'm getting hungrier by the minute," John replied. He brushed his hand over the top of Victoria's.

She pursed her lips. The game had quickly advanced.

They walked to the dining room where Shannon motioned to a chair. "John, why don't you take the seat beside Victoria? Izzy will be serving us this evening. We can leave the end open for her to serve, since Dr. Fletcher isn't here. I'll sit across from you."

John nodded to Shannon, pulled out a chair for Victoria, then sat beside her.

Izzy brought out the food; roast beef, potatoes, carrots, fried corn, green beans, baking powder biscuits, and preserves. It looked promising.

"Pass that around!" Patrick instructed. He rubbed his hands together and lit up like a starving orphan. "Nothing like Izzy's cooking."

John tipped his head slightly to one side and gave Victoria his most inviting smile. "What's for dessert this evening? More *cherry* tarts?"

She responded with a seductive grin. Exactly what he'd hoped for.

"No!" Izzy snapped. "I made devil's food cake. Seems appropriate."

John scowled at the woman who returned his look with ice of her own, then went to the kitchen, muttering under her breath.

"I love chocolate. Don't you, John?" Victoria asked, licking her lips.

"Yes, I do. I've had some of the finest chocolates from Europe."

"Well, so have I," she said, wide-eyed. "Mr. Parker orders them for me. Did you know there are many ways to eat it?"

"How's that?"

"I'll have to show you some time" She bit her lower lip. *What I could do with those lips . . .*

"Yes, my child loves chocolate," Shannon said. "So does her father. Don't you, Patrick?"

"Why are we talkin' about dessert?" Patrick scolded. "Pass the potatoes!"

"Yes, dear," Shannon said and handed him the bowl. "John, I hope that whatever Andrew has isn't contagious. 'Twould be a terrible thing, everyone ill for the wedding."

"I don't believe you'll have to worry about that. He became run down caring for that woman. The one who'd been unconscious."

"Yes, Mama." The frown on Victoria's face humored John. "That woman actually lived. Andrew's treatments seemed to have worked, but now he's ill from it. I think it's horrible he had to sacrifice his own health for hers."

"He'll be fine, Victoria," John said. "Don't get yourself upset over that woman. She's not worth it. Keep smiling. You're beautiful when you do."

"Yes, you are, dear," Shannon said. "Isn't our daughter beautiful this evening, Patrick?"

"She's *always* beautiful," the man grumbled. "Hand me another one of those biscuits!"

Shannon passed the biscuits and preserves to her husband. *It's no wonder he's so overweight.* "Are you enjoying the food, John?"

"Very much. You were right about Izzy. This is the finest food I've had since I arrived—with the exception of your

Irish stew." He winked at Shannon. A little lie never hurt. Especially when it might advance his chance of bedding her daughter.

* * *

"Oh, you flatter me!" Victoria's mama gushed more than necessary.

Victoria had grown tired of the attention John paid her. He needed to notice *her*.

She moved her hand under the table and placed it on his leg. "John, tell us more about some of the people you know in Bridgeport." As she spoke, she gently squeezed.

He turned toward her with an expression that made her warm from the inside out. *Good*. Their thoughts seemed to be headed in the same direction.

"One of the finest evenings I ever had was at a dinner party at Waldemere." John raised his chin in the air. "That's one of P.T. Barnum's estates. I'm sure you've heard of him. He's one of the more prominent residents of Bridgeport. Phineas Taylor Barnum, to be exact."

"You know P.T. Barnum?" The man impressed her even more. "Daddy, did you hear? He knows P.T. Barnum." She slid her hand further up his thigh and squeezed it firmly.

"I heard. He's a circus man, isn't he?"

"Yes, but more of a business man. He's done very well for himself. Bridgeport's growing. It's easy for a man to do well if he applies himself."

They finished the meal and Izzy brought out the cake. She sliced it and handed it around the table. Though it looked delicious, Victoria wanted something much more exhilarating.

"Just a small piece for me, Izzy," Victoria said. "I have to watch my figure."

"What about you, Mr. Fletcher?" Izzy asked. "You watchin' your figure, too?"

"Not *mine*," he replied and grinned at Victoria.

Izzy started muttering again and quickly went back to the kitchen.

"She seems irritable this evening," Victoria said. "What do you suppose is the matter?"

"I assumed she *always* acted that way," John said. "I wondered why you keep her employed."

"We couldn't do without Izzy." Victoria's daddy defended her. "She's a good woman. Must not be feeling well this evening. Hopefully she doesn't have what the doctor has."

"I doubt it," John said. "Maybe she just needs a day off."

"John," Victoria cooed. "I'm a bit worried 'bout my poor Andrew. Since we've finished our supper, do you suppose you could take me to see him?" She moved her hand further up his thigh, tempted to place it between his legs.

"That's a fine idea, Victoria," her mama said. "Andrew may need a bit of doctoring himself. Can you take her to him, John?"

"Of course I can." John's brows raised and he shifted against her touch.

"I don't know," her daddy firmly said. "I don't want her catching whatever he has."

"Now, Patrick . . ." Fortunately her mama was on her side. "He's to be her husband. He took care of her when *she* was ill. It's appropriate for her to do the same."

"Well, be careful," her daddy warned. "If he's runnin' a fever, keep your distance."

"I will, Daddy. So John . . ." She boldly placed her hand between his legs and smiled. "Are you ready to go then?" She moved her hand, feeling him, and pursed her lips. *He's ready all right.*

"I've never been more ready for anything." Turning his back to her folks, he lifted her to her feet and escorted her to the door.

Her mama followed behind them. "I'll understand if you don't come home this evening, dear. You take care of Andrew now."

"I will, Mama. I'll take care of everythin'." She hugged her.

"Enjoy yourself," her mama whispered in her ear. "Just remember what I told you."

Victoria peered deeply into her mama's eyes. "I will," she whispered. "I love you."

Victoria linked her arm through John's and he escorted her to his buggy. After lifting her in, he took his place beside her.

She rested her hand on his leg, ready to pick up where she'd left off.

"Not here, Victoria," he scolded. "We'll have plenty of time. You don't want anyone to see you, do you?"

"No, John. Only you." She placed her hands in her lap. Soon, she'd have all of him.

* * *

Victoria's heart raced.

John rushed her to his room. As they hastened down the hallway, she looked from side-to-side, attempting to see if anyone had noticed them. She didn't think they had, but then again, even if they'd been seen, she'd enjoy having folks spread this kind of gossip. She'd make every woman in Mobile jealous.

The moment they stepped through the door, John shut it behind them and locked it. He lit a lantern and the room glowed with soft warmth.

It was a simple room; a small sofa, overstuffed chair, a little eating table with two chairs, and an *enormous* bed with a plain wooden stand beside it.

He moved the lantern onto the bed stand and her heart beat even faster. She'd never been with a man. Only a boy who *thought* he was a man. Though she wanted this, she couldn't help being scared. She'd always been good at playing the game, but had never quite finished it.

She hovered by the door, too timid to take a step closer to the bed. John grinned, then leaned her against the wall and put his arms around her.

"Not yet," she said, moving from his arms.

"What are you doing, Victoria? I'm tired of your games." He followed her and encircled her once again.

"I'm not ready to take you off the shelf yet." Her heavy breathing made it difficult to speak.

"I think you are." He pressed his lips to hers.

She backed away. Maybe she'd taken on more than she could handle.

"What are you doing?" His harsh tone indicated frustration. "I know you want this."

"I told you. I'm not ready. I need to know your intentions." She took a seat on the sofa. Thank goodness she had an excuse to slow him down.

He shook his head. "You know my intentions. They're yours as well. You proved that at supper."

"What about *after* tonight? What then? If I'm to give up Andrew and choose you, I need to know what you plan to do with me." She forced confidence. After pretending for so long to be experienced and eager, he terrified her. Still, she couldn't deny he'd made her curious.

"I'll show you. I plan to do many things to you." He sat beside her and pulled her into his muscular arms. His musky cologne filled her nostrils and when his hands moved down her back she shivered. "Stop teasing me, Victoria." His lips brushed her ear; his warm breath whispered each word. "You promised you'd play." She gasped when his tongue circled her ear.

Her heart beat even faster. "I'll play . . . after you promise to marry me." There. She'd said it. Her mama would be proud.

"Marry you?" He backed away. "Is that what this is all about? You want me to marry you?"

"Course I do. You can't have me unless you promise to make me your wife. If you tell me you will, you can have me now." She tilted her head and looked at him coyly, her lips pouting. *Please say you will.* She wanted to learn from him.

"What about Andrew?"

"What about him? He doesn't love me. He doesn't even *want* to marry me. I think he's in love with that woman from the hospital."

"Claire?" John crossed his arms, facing her.

"You know her?"

"Yes, I do. It's a long story. One I don't care to share at this moment. I have *other* things in mind."

"Hmm, so did I. Thinkin' of that woman spoils the mood." She folded her arms and pouted even harder. She'd seen the way Andrew had looked at Claire. He'd never looked at *her* that way.

"Then don't think of her." John scooted close again and caressed her cheek.

She shook her finger at him. "Uh-uh," she said as he tried to kiss her. He hadn't agreed to marriage yet. Somehow she needed to convince him. "John, would it help at all knowin' that when my parents die, all the money will be mine?"

"All of it?" His eyes widened with curiosity.

"All of it. Every last penny." She smiled broadly. Yes, money mattered. They were very much alike.

* * *

Marry her?

John had vowed never to marry again. Since he never had difficulty finding a woman to share his bed, he didn't need a wife. But then again . . .

"Money always makes a woman more interesting," he said, gazing at her glorious cleavage.

It couldn't be all bad.

She'd make a stunning entrance on my arm at all the social affairs. Every man in Bridgeport would be envious. And . . . she'd save me a fortune in prostitutes.

"All right, Victoria. I'll marry you." He bent toward her and sealed the deal with a kiss. His heart beat faster. He loved the feeling—the anticipation—knowing in a very short time he'd have something young and fresh.

She no longer pulled away and willingly kissed him back. Yes, this night would end as he wanted. *No more excuses.*

He lifted her to her feet. "And now, you *will* keep your end of the bargain."

She looked at him the way a timid deer might stare down its hunter. He intended to remove her fear and release the animal deep within her.

"How old *are* you, Victoria?" His lips moved to her neck and he tasted her delicate, sweet skin.

"Nineteen." Her heavy breathing increased his desire. "How old are *you*, John?"

"Forty-six. But what *is* age? Just a number."

"That's true. Once a man and woman have developed all their workin' parts, age doesn't matter any longer. Your parts are workin', aren't they, John?" Her attempt at sounding bold didn't fool him. Her entire body trembled beneath his roaming hands.

"Let me show you." He loosened the scarf at her neck.

"No. *Don't!*" She grabbed his hand.

"It's all right, Victoria. I know what happened."

"You do? You know and you still want me?"

"I've never wanted a woman more." He tossed the scarf to the side, then moved his lips to the scar and gently sucked.

She moaned. The response he'd hoped for. This would be a very good night.

"You like that, do you? I think you'll like this even more." He unbuttoned her dress and pushed it to the floor. His mouth moved further down her body and stopped at her breasts. The full mounds crested above her corset. It would take time to remove it, so for now, he'd content himself with what he could reach. His lips and tongue glided over her form, tasting and teasing. He smiled at the sensation of her rapidly beating heart, pulsing against his tongue. No doubt he'd find moist heat between her legs.

She held his head to her breasts, twisting her fingers through his hair. "Yes," she groaned.

A heavy-handed knock caused both of them to jump. Focused on her breasts, John tried to ignore it. But when a second, much *louder* knock came—he couldn't take any more. "Damn it!"

"John! Open the door!"

"Oh, God," Victoria whispered. "It's Andrew. Why did he call you John?"

"Get in bed and I'll make him leave." He covered her mouth with a fervent kiss. "Think about what I'm going to do to you and I'll be there soon."

As she turned from him, he swatted her firm behind and received a naughty giggle from the girl. It increased his already-flaming desire.

Andrew will pay for the interruption.

Andrew beat on the door. "John! I know you're in there!"

John opened the door a crack. "What do you want? Come back for another swing at me?"

"No. I want to talk to you."

"We've done all the talking we need to. Go home, Andrew."

Andrew sniffed the air. "You have a woman in your bed, don't you?"

"That's none of your concern."

"You disgust me." Andrew leered at him. "I only came back because I want you to go with me to see Claire tomorrow. You owe her the truth. I'd tell her myself, but I want you to do it. I want you to face up to your lies."

"I have no responsibility any longer to you *or* Claire."

"What about your grandson? Don't you at least want to see him?"

John thought for a moment, curious to see what sort of offspring the two of them had produced.

It might be amusing.

"Very well, then," John finally said. "I'll go, but I'd like to get back to my business . . . if you don't mind."

"Enjoy your whore, John. I'll be by to pick you up in the morning. Make certain she's gone." Andrew shook his head. "I can't begin to tell you how thankful I am that your blood doesn't run through my veins. But I pity Claire that it flows through hers."

John slammed the door in his face.

Damn him for judging me. If he only knew which whore was in my bed.

He chuckled to himself and returned to the task at hand. He stretched, then rolled his head from side-to-side. Time to create the appropriate mood.

Victoria made it easy. She'd done as she'd been told and lay in his bed. Her clothes had been scattered here and there. The difficult corset lay to his right. That alone had taken some time.

How'd she undress so quickly? She must be eager.

He grinned at the nervous young thing. She toyed with her hair and lay there before him with the blanket pulled up to her chin. She didn't fool him. She pretended to be ready, but he saw how she trembled.

I'll make her ready. He'd learned long ago how to properly bed a woman. He considered himself quite gifted at it.

Her eyes were on him as he removed his clothing, but when he moved toward her, he found her to be distracted.

Instead of admiring his physique, she gazed upward. Her mind seemed to be elsewhere.

She nervously licked her lips. "John, I don't understand. Andrew . . ."

He pressed a single finger to her mouth. "Don't worry that pretty head with anything you heard. I'll explain it all later." He jerked the blanket from her body and scrutinized what he'd soon consume.

She lay there naked, with the exception of the gold heart necklace he'd seen on her before. It graced her flesh, sparkling in the lamplight. Her long red hair was tossed about on the pillow. Her arms were bent and raised over her head; her fingers twirled strands of her hair.

He moved his eyes downward and admired every perfect curve of her form. Her luscious breasts captivated him and beckoned him with pert nipples. He moistened his lips. "Good God, Victoria. Andrew's a fool."

Wasting no time, he lay down upon her impeccable flesh. He'd go slowly at first, but would eventually take her for a ride she'd not soon forget.

His mouth covered hers and she pulled him tightly to her.

"What do you want to do now, John?" She inhaled deeply. Her hands wandered down his back. The timid girl lost her inhibitions and firmly grabbed his buttocks.

"Everything." He kissed her deeply and probed her mouth with his tongue.

She responded readily, encircling it with her own.

He finished the kiss with a flick of his tongue on her chin, then pulled back slightly and stared into her eyes. Their lips were mere inches apart. Both breathing heavily.

He grinned. "You have potential, but I never doubted that for a moment."

She raked her fingers through his hair. He lowered his head to her neck and drank in the arousing scent of her perfume.

"John." Her voice shook. "I've never done *everything*."

"I'll teach you." Wanting to begin her first lesson, he parted her legs with his knee and easily slid into her with a slow, steady thrust. Yes, she was ready.

She gasped, but then wrapped her legs around him and grabbed on tight. He had no need to go slow with this one.

Andrew's more than a fool. John had taken the cream of the crop. Hot and delicious. He intended to enjoy every morsel.

He ravaged her through the night, taking little time to rest. They both got exactly what they wanted. Money and pleasure. Love had never once been mentioned.

CHAPTER 37

It had been difficult for Claire to leave City Hospital without telling Andrew goodbye, but she knew it was for the best. He had to forget her and move on with Victoria.

Even with a heavy heart, she managed to enjoy the trip home. The bright blue clear sky didn't have a trace of even one white cloud. The air was warm, but not uncomfortable. She wore no bonnet and let her hair fly freely in the wind, drinking in every sensation. Every smell. Every sight she beheld. She'd been reborn.

George offered to sit in the back of the wagon with Beth, so Claire sat in the front with Martha. She found his offer a little odd since he usually drove. What became even more unusual was hearing him speak more than one word. He was attentive to Beth, and Beth seemed to be enjoying the attention.

Claire questioned Martha with her eyes, listening to the two in the back carry on a conversation.

"Got me," Martha whispered. "First woman he ain't run away from."

Looking over her shoulder, Claire caught Beth's eye. She lit up with a large smile. *This is good*. Beth needed to smile.

The dirt road was bumpy and hard. It hadn't rained for quite some time and dust kicked up as the horses hooves trod along the winding road.

"What now, Claire Belle?" Martha asked. She stared straight ahead watching the road before them.

"I don't know. I need to find my way."

"Whatever you do, give yourself time. Don't make no hasty decisions and always follow your heart." Martha turned her head and gave Claire a sad smile.

"It hurts, Martha." Claire lowered her head. "I'm thankful to be alive, but livin' isn't very easy."

"It'll get better. Just give it time." Martha patted her on the leg. "You sure you want me to take you to Beth's?"

"Yes." No other place seemed like home.

"You know you're more than welcome to stay with me. Little Michael, too. I'd love havin' you there."

"Maybe soon. But I need to go to Beth's. I wanna see Gerald's grave and go back to where it happened. I can't explain it, but it's important to me."

"You don't hafta explain. Just know you're always welcome."

"Thank you, Martha. I couldn't have made it through this without you—or Andrew." The mention of his name sent her head reeling. Luckily she'd spoken softly enough. Beth hadn't heard her call him by his first name. But she had to be more careful.

She'd never forget the expression on Andrew's face when she'd told him about their daddy and wished she'd never had to tell. *Too much pain.*

The hours drug slowly on. Claire wanted to see Michael more than anything. To hold him and know he was fine.

As they neared her little town, she directed Martha to the boarding house where she pulled the wagon to a stop. Without waiting for the others, Claire got out of the wagon. Even though her legs weren't quite up to full strength, she rushed as quickly as she could through the front door.

"Mrs. Sandborn? Michael?" she yelled, heart pounding.

"In here, Claire!" Mrs. Sandborn's voice came from the kitchen.

Claire flew into the room. Michael sat perched atop the table eating applesauce Mrs. Sandborn was spooning him. Claire's breath hitched.

"Michael!" She scooped him into her arms and clutched him against her body. "Oh, my baby!" Breathing in the essence of him, she proceeded to kiss him all over his face. "Mama missed you so much."

He grinned and stroked her cheeks with his little plump fingers. "Mama!"

"Yes, Mama's here." She'd come so close to losing him and felt tempted to never set him down again.

"He sure did miss ya," Mrs. Sandborn said. She got a napkin and wiped the applesauce from the corners of his mouth. "Didn't take to cow's milk right away. You had him spoiled."

"I think he's grown. Has he?"

"Reckon so. He likes oats an' applesauce. I've been tryin' to get him to eat some pureed carrots an' squash. He don't like them much." Mrs. Sandborn pulled out a chair and nodded for Claire to sit.

"No—thank you—I've been sittin' all day. It feels good to stand." She rocked Michael gently in her arms and continued planting small kisses on his tiny head.

Mrs. Sandborn reached out her hand. "I'm sorry 'bout Gerald. I don't know what else to say. But, I *do* know what it feels like losin' a husband. I know it don't seem like it now, but given time, it'll get easier." Her eyes filled with tears.

Claire took her hand and gave it a squeeze.

Beth walked in, followed by George and Martha. They gathered around the baby and gave him their own love pats and kisses. Except for George, who stood in the doorway of the kitchen holding his straw hat in front of himself.

"George . . ." Beth motioned to him. "You can come in. The baby don't bite."

"'At's a'right, Miss Beth," George said and lowered his head. "I . . . I'll stay here."

Mrs. Sandborn let out a laugh, which caused George to cower. Claire thought he might bolt.

"Truth be told, Beth," Mrs. Sandborn chuckled. "Michael *does* bite! Had a round with the cat few days back. I scooped him up before old Midnight could take a swipe at him. He's teethin' again an' decided to chew on Midnight's tail."

Everyone laughed. Even George.

Mrs. Sandborn's cheeks glowed red from laughter. "Don't worry 'bout Midnight no more. He keeps his distance from the baby."

Beth smirked. "I would, too, if someone bit *my* tail."

George's cheeks flushed.

Martha walked over to him and gripped his shoulder, looking him square in the eyes. "Don't you be gettin' no ideas now."

His eyes opened wide and his mouth dropped. *Poor George.* Martha didn't spare a soul.

Martha grinned at him. "I hate to be difficult, but we best be goin'. It's a long way back home."

"I understand," Mrs. Sandborn said. "Claire, you come back another day and we'll get caught up. I'm just glad you're all right. Michael needs ya." She kissed Claire's cheek and gave her a hug. "Oh! Let me give you Michael's things." She packed a box with Michael's clothes, diapers, and toys, and handed it to Beth.

Claire kept Michael in her arms as they returned to the wagon. George took the box from Beth, then helped her up with trembling hands. Something had definitely sparked between the two of them.

"You all right, George?" Beth asked.

"Yep." After Beth smiled at him, he lowered his eyes, then grinned at her.

Once they arrived at Beth's, Claire instantly became light-headed. Everything struck at once.

She looked over to the fresh mound of dirt beside her mama's grave. Her body shook and tears began to flow. George and Beth had already gotten out of the wagon, but she couldn't move from the seat. She held Michael while her pain trickled down her cheeks.

Martha put an arm around her. "Baby—Claire Belle—it's gonna be all right. Let's get outta the wagon. You can go inside an' lie down."

Claire still didn't move. "I can't." She stared blankly forward.

"Yes, you can. Aunt Martha's gonna help ya." Martha got out of the wagon and went around to the other side. She reached up to take Michael from her, but she held him even tighter. "Claire, let me take the baby so you can get out. Beth'll hold him for ya." Again Martha extended her arms.

Claire turned and faced her. "This isn't my home. Where's my home, Martha?"

"Your home's wherever that baby is. For now, it'll be with Beth. Home's where love lies. It ain't a house. So you go on now and make this your home. Least for a little while."

With great care, Claire placed Michael in Martha's arms, then stepped down from the wagon. Martha handed him to Beth, then put her arm around Claire and walked with her inside.

Claire breathed in the woodsy smell. Though Beth's house now, it still smelled much the same as when she'd lived there. Beth had added a few new pieces of furniture, but otherwise it hadn't changed.

"Claire," Martha said. "George and I need to get goin'. You all right now?"

"I reckon so." She wanted to smile and reassure her aunt, but she couldn't.

Martha kissed her on the forehead. "I love ya. More than you know. You come an' see me soon. Even if you don't need anythin'."

Claire hugged her, then went to the bedroom and lay down.

She curled up and let her tears flow.

CHAPTER 38

Victoria opened her eyes. A small ray of sunlight seeped through a gap in the curtain over the window of their hotel room. Her body writhed, remembering the pleasure she'd felt through the night.

She giggled. She'd never been happier. She'd marry a man who truly appreciated her. A man who obviously *wanted* her. *More than once.* The fact he happened to be incredibly rich and handsome certainly didn't hurt.

Her silly tryst with the *boy* had been nothing compared to what she had with John. He knew how to use his body to please her. *Just the kind of man Mama described.* He'd given her gratification before taking his own. Until last night, she hadn't fully understood what that meant. But now . . .

I'm truly a woman.

John had done more than make love to her. He'd completed her.

He lay on his side, facing away from her. She pressed her body against his and ran her hands down his chest. Unlike Andrew, John had hair there. She found it desirable. She continued to be amazed that he had such an incredible body at his age.

He's handsome with clothes on, but I prefer him naked.

She giggled again. *I'm in bed with a naked man.*

The thought stirred her desires—ready for more play.

She pinched his nipple.

He jerked, then flipped over and frowned. "What are you doing, Victoria?"

She wrinkled her nose, then swirled her tongue around her lips. "I want more."

"You can't be serious. I gave you more all night. We've slept *perhaps* two hours." He stretched, then pulled her into his arms.

"I don't care. I like it and I want *more*." She nuzzled his neck, then moved her hand down his body until it came to rest between his legs. She whimpered. He didn't respond to her touch.

"Sorry, Victoria. You'll need to give me some time. I'm not as young as you are." He kissed her on the tip of her nose.

"You were young enough last night. I didn't know it could be so good. Now I understand the difference between a man and a boy. I much prefer a man." She wouldn't give up and continued to entice him with her hand. Much to her delight, he began to respond. The night of lovemaking had given her confidence. Made her bold. John had taught her well.

He laughed, gave in, and took her one more time.

After they finished, they both rolled onto their backs, exhausted.

"Thank you," she said, closing her eyes.

"Don't sleep *now*. I need to talk to you." He traced her body with his finger, then roused her in the same manner she'd used to wake him.

"Ouch!" She playfully slapped his chest. "Fine. I'm awake. What do you want to talk 'bout?"

"What you heard last night when Andrew came to the door."

"Yes, do tell. Why'd he call you John?" Her curiosity had been fully piqued.

"Because he found out I'm not really his father. He was adopted." John spoke without feeling.

She sat upright and leaned against the headboard. "Adopted? He may have no real breedin' at all?"

"I doubt he does from what I was told at the orphanage. His parents were nothing to boast about." He went on to tell her the most fantastic tale about Andrew's adoption. She'd never heard anything quite so intriguing.

"As for Claire," he said, looking at her with wide eyes. "She *is* my child."

"You're just full of surprises, John. So Andrew believed he was in love with his sister? That's priceless!" Victoria laughed. The story just kept getting better.

He explained in depth about Claire. Victoria loved this kind of gossip.

"Andrew will be here soon," John said. "I agreed to go with him to tell Claire the truth."

"Why help him? After the way he talked to you last night? And I could have sworn he called me a whore!"

"Don't worry. I'm not quite done having fun with Andrew just yet. And yes, he referred to the woman in my bed as a whore, so that would be you." He moved his hand over her body and lingered at her breasts. "Best whore I've ever had." He pulled her down and kissed her.

She kissed him back, wanting more.

"No. We need to get ready to go." His eyes narrowed, scolding her.

She pouted, hoping to get her way, but then a loud knock shook the door.

"He *is* punctual," John said. "You stay in bed. I'll tell him to meet me out front. Once I leave, get yourself home and cleaned up, and I'll see you this evening. I'd best be asking your father for your hand."

Victoria cast her wicked smile. "You've had everything else." She yanked him to her one final time and gave him a kiss to think about. "Have fun today with Andrew. Try not to be *too* hard on him." She coyly bit her lip, then lay on her side to listen.

John barely opened the door. "I'll be out in ten minutes."

"She's still here?" Andrew asked, disgusted.

"She's tired. I rode her hard last night."

Victoria tittered at the remark, then quickly covered her mouth.

"I'll be waiting out front," Andrew grumbled.

John shut the door. He dressed quickly, then gave her a brief kiss. "By the way, Victoria, my name isn't Fletcher. It's Martin. John *Martin*." He left her pondering one more mysterious detail.

* * *

It had taken him slightly longer than ten minutes, but John finally made his way to the buggy. Dressed in a three-piece suit and top hat, he hopped in next to Andrew.

"You didn't need to dress up for this," Andrew said.

"I always dress up." *It would be a very long ride.*

They went for miles without saying a word. The overcast sky threatened rain. Even though they were in a covered buggy, John didn't want to risk getting mud on his clean suit.

He was tired after his eventful night, but had no regrets. Victoria would serve him well. At least for a while.

"So . . ." John decided to break the silence. "Tell me again why you find it so important to tell Claire the truth."

Andrew looked sideways at him. "You're serious?"

He nodded.

"I want her to know so she'll stop condemning herself for what we did. She thinks I'm her brother and that we committed an unforgivable sin."

"You bedded her when you weren't married to her." John mustered up a heavy dose of spite. "Isn't that also a sin?"

"I know it was wrong. But we planned to marry. We would've made it right."

John laughed. "A sin is a sin. You don't just make it go away. Only God can do that."

"I believe He will. God knows our hearts. He knows our love."

Time to make him even more uneasy. "And what of Victoria? Poor, innocent, Victoria. She's the one slighted here. Didn't you profess your love to *her*?" *This is almost as much fun as last night.*

"Yes. But I never really loved her." Andrew refused to look at him, and squirmed in his seat. The ride had become much more interesting.

"So, you *lied* to her?" John stared at Andrew, amused.

"Yes. I lied. But I had every intention to *learn* to love her."

"You *had* the intention. Are you saying you no longer plan to?"

"I don't know!" Andrew's voice rose in anger. "O'Malley is insisting on it!"

"Then you have no choice. Marry Victoria and see Claire on the side. A lot of men have mistresses." John curled his lips into a devious grin.

"I'm not you, John!"

They rode silently again.

They were nearly there and Andrew stirred in his seat. He cleared his throat. "It's important you don't let on to Claire that I know the child is mine. Or to Beth either. And as far as Beth's concerned, you're my *associate*. Nothing more. She knows nothing of my relationship with Claire. Can I trust you on this?"

"This will be even more entertaining than I'd imagined." John laughed. "I'll try to behave myself, but I can't guaranty anything."

"Don't do this, John!" Andrew scolded. "This is the last thing I'll ever ask you to do for me. If you ever cared anything for me, please don't make a mess of this."

"You've done that yourself. I'm simply along for the ride."

John was familiar with this road. When they neared the house, memories of Ruth came to mind. He'd enjoyed her at first, but eventually tired of her. It had always been that way for him with women. Sooner or later they bored him.

Andrew stopped the buggy and John climbed out, shaking his head. The house hadn't changed much. Remembering being eighteen and newly married made him shudder. Thank God he'd left when he did.

* * *

Andrew regretted asking John to accompany him. It seemed the man delighted in tormenting him. He feared it wasn't over.

As he lifted his hand to knock on the door, it occurred to him that Claire could be elsewhere. But where else would she have gone? *Certainly not to Henry's.*

He rapped softly. His heart pounded in anticipation of seeing Claire *and* his son.

Beth opened the door. Her eyes grew wide. "Dr. Fletcher?" she whispered. "What are you doin' here?"

"Hello, Beth. My associate and I have come to check in on Claire. She's here, isn't she?"

John nodded at Beth, tipped his hat, and smiled his *charming* smile.

"Yep. She's sleepin' right now. Been sleepin' a lot since we got home yesterday. Poor thing's still worn out." Beth continued to whisper and looked at John. "You a doctor, too?"

"Yes, I am. Dr. Fletcher's patient made quite the stir at the hospital. I was away during her stay and wanted to see the miracle for myself."

Beth flashed a broad grin. "I never knew there was so many good-lookin' doctors in Mobile."

John chuckled. "You flatter me." He took her hand and kissed it. "It's a pleasure meeting you."

Beth's cheeks glowed red.

Andrew flashed John a look of displeasure, but it did no good. No doubt the man enjoyed their ruse.

Beth glanced over her shoulder into the house. "I s'pose you can come in. We all shared Claire's room for quite some time. We're almost like family." She stepped aside so they could enter.

Andrew's mind flashed back to the night in the rain. He pictured Claire lying in the bed behind the closed door. His longing for her hadn't diminished.

His eyes shifted to the woven rug.

Michael . . .

Andrew's heart skipped a beat. Though his son faced away from him, his raven black hair and dark complexion confirmed everything. Still, he wanted to see the boy's eyes.

"That there's Michael," Beth whispered. "Ain't he beautiful?"

John folded his arms over his chest, seemingly disinterested in his grandson.

Andrew stepped closer to the child. "Yes he is, Beth." He knelt down behind him.

Michael turned his head, grinned, and raised his arms to Andrew.

"Dada." The child's simple word made Andrew's heart dance, but he looked quizzically at Beth.

She grinned. "I reckon he thinks all men are *Dada*. You can pick him up. Seems he wants you to."

Andrew's heart thumped. He lifted Michael into his arms and held him close. Then he closed his eyes and breathed in his scent. Unable to help himself, he kissed him on the cheek.

Michael studied his face and patted it with his tiny hand. "Dada!" A sweet grin lit up his small features, though his eyes were dark as coal. *Just like mine.*

Tears welled in Andrew's eyes. "Yes Michael, Daddy's here," he whispered in his ear so no one else could hear. He didn't want to let him go.

Beth took him from his arms. "He likes ya. Usually don't take to folks so quick. I know he misses his daddy. Reckon he likes havin' a man hold him."

"I'm sure that's it," Andrew said. "And you're right. He's a beautiful baby." He cupped his hand over Michael's head.

Michael stretched backward in Beth's arms, once again reaching for him.

"I ain't never seen nothin' like it!" Beth exclaimed. "He never done that with anyone 'cept Gerald."

John chuckled, but covered his mouth when Andrew glared at him. Still disinterested, the man kept his distance.

"What's goin' on here?" Claire yelled, entering the room.

Andrew turned to look at her. Her eyes blazed with hatred toward John.

"It's all right, Claire," Beth said. "Dr. Fletcher and his associate, Dr. ...?"

"Smith," John said with a grin. "Dr. Smith."

"Yeah," Beth said dreamily. He'd managed to enamor the woman. "An' Dr. Smith. They came by to check in on ya. I invited 'em in. I knew you wouldn't mind. Not after all we been through at the hospital." She rubbed Claire's arm. "You up for company?"

"I don't know . . ." Claire moved her attention from John and glared at Andrew. Yes, she had every right to be furious with him. If only she'd give him the chance to explain.

"Beth," Andrew said. "Would you give us a few minutes alone with Claire? I'd like to give her a thorough examination. As long as *she* doesn't mind."

"I don't," Claire said flatly. "Beth, why don't you take Michael out for a walk? Before it starts rainin'."

"All right." Beth hesitated. "You sure you don't care if I leave you alone?"

"I'll be fine." Claire gave Beth a reassuring smile, then Beth walked out the door with Michael. As soon as it shut, Claire stepped within inches of Andrew. "Why'd you bring *him* here?" She scowled at John.

The man smirked. "It's nice to see you, too, Claire."

Andrew took her arm in an attempt to ease her, but she jerked away.

John bellowed with laughter.

Andrew did his best to ignore the man. "Claire, please. I had to bring him. There's something you need to know."

"There's nothin' I want from that man!"

"Please sit down and we'll explain." Andrew remained calm, understanding her anger. They both despised John.

She moved to the table and sat. Andrew took the chair beside her. John didn't budge and remained standing.

"Well?" she asked. "What is it?"

John strolled around the room, scratching his chin. "I know what happened between the two of you."

Claire's eyes widened and her nostrils flared. "How could you tell him?"

Andrew looked at her with sympathy, trying to come up with the right words to say.

"He told me about you a long time ago, though I didn't know it was you," John continued. "He wrote about a woman he'd fallen in love with that had left him. He was heartsick and asked my advice. I told him to forget you and move on. So, he did."

Andrew shook his head. He didn't want her to believe he'd *ever* forgotten her. "Claire, that's not all true—"

"Excuse me, Andrew. I'm still talking," John scolded.

"Tell the truth!" Andrew snapped.

"I am. In my own words." John cocked his head. "When I came to Mobile for Andrew's wedding—to a *very* fine woman I must add—I ran into your Aunt Martha at the hotel. To make a long story short, eventually I found out that the woman Andrew had been in love with and was caring for at the hospital was you, Claire."

John focused on Claire who remained visibly angry. How could she not be? At least now she directed the fire in her eyes at John, giving Andrew *some* relief. Still, he hated seeing her upset with *anyone*.

"Oh, simmer yourself down, Claire." John rolled his eyes. "The story gets better."

Claire crossed her arms over her chest. Anger hissed from her nostrils.

"The night you told Andrew the truth about your *shared* blood, he came to see me, ready to take my head off. I told him something I'd promised his mother I'd never tell. He was adopted. He's not my blood. So Claire, my dear, you can redeem yourself. For *that* particular sin."

Claire's expression instantly changed. The anger disappeared and she burst out sobbing.

Andrew stood and placed his hands on her shoulders. "Claire, don't you see? I'm not your brother. Please don't cry. You've shed enough tears for me." He attempted to pull her to him, but she pushed him away.

"I want you to leave," she said through her tears. "Please take that man out of my house and leave!"

No. Not like this. "Claire. I still love you."

"No! You love Victoria! Go to her and forget me!" She sobbed even harder.

"I *have* to marry Victoria, but it's you I love." He reached out again, but she blocked his advance with a firm hand.

Her brows furrowed. "You *hafta* marry her?" Her chin quivered. Her face contorted in pain. "Then go! You shouldn't a come!"

"You don't understand. Please let me explain." Andrew wanted to tell her everything.

The door opened and Beth walked through. "What did you do?" she yelled. "Why's she cryin'?"

Andrew found himself speechless. He couldn't say much of anything in front of Beth.

John stood back saying nothing, smirking all the while. How could he find pleasure in so much pain?

Claire took Michael from Beth. "I'm fine, Beth. Just make 'em leave." She went to her bedroom and shut the door.

"I'm sorry, Beth," Andrew said. "I didn't mean to upset her."

"Don't know what you did, but she said *leave,* so you'd best go. I'm sorry, too. I always liked you, Dr. Fletcher."

Andrew walked out the door with John behind him. John made a point of kissing Beth's hand again before shutting the door. The man had the nerve of a viper.

Andrew felt sick to his stomach. He'd left so much unsaid.

"That went well," John said as they hopped into the buggy.

"Don't say another word," Andrew growled and snapped the reins.

They rode silently. Andrew fumed the entire way, wishing there'd been something more he could've done.

"So . . . Andrew. . ." John's voice startled him after hours without a word. They were nearly home. "What would you say if I told you that you don't have to marry Victoria?"

"You love toying with me. Don't you, John?" He couldn't wait to be rid of the man.

"Let me just say that Victoria is *insatiable*. Honestly, you don't deserve her." John's smug tone said volumes.

Andrew stopped the buggy and turned to face him. It all made sense. The smell of the perfume. The game John had been playing. "It was Victoria in your bed, wasn't it?"

"You are a smart boy, aren't you?" John sat upright boasting with his body.

"I'm no *boy*. I'm a man. I stopped being a boy a long time ago." Andrew popped the reins.

"No, if you were a man you'd have taken Victoria to your bed. You'd never have had a second thought of Claire. Then again, perhaps Victoria is more woman than you can handle."

"And you can handle her. Right, John? What do you plan to do, marry her yourself?"

"As a matter of fact . . . *yes*. She asked me last night before I had my way with her. Funny girl. She insisted I vow marriage before spreading her legs." John spoke of her with little feeling.

"Please spare me the details." John's lewd comments disgusted him.

"Did you know she has a heart-shaped mole right on her—?"

"Do you wish to disgrace her even more? If she's to be your wife, at least show some decency and keep your private affairs to yourself."

"I thought you might want to know what you're missing. But don't worry, I'll satisfy her. *I* know how to satisfy a woman."

"I'm sure you do. And for how long? How long until you tire of her and toss her aside?" Andrew genuinely cared for her well-being. No woman deserved the likes of John Martin.

"Long enough. I'm sure she has quite a few good years in her. I'll take all I can get."

"She deserves better!" Andrew gripped the reins so tightly they burned into his hands.

"Like you? Sorry Andrew, she chose me. She wanted a man, not a boy. I proved to her just how much of a man I am."

"Bedding a woman doesn't make a man. *Loving* a woman does." With the hotel in sight, Andrew was nearly rid of the man who'd tormented him for years.

"Love? Love has nothing to do with it. I wanted a good time in bed and I got it. And I'll get plenty more of it. Don't you worry though—I'll take care of her. Just like a *daddy* would." He chuckled under his breath.

"God help her." Andrew stopped the buggy and John jumped out. "You could've had the decency to tell me all this before we saw Claire. She still believes I'm marrying Victoria."

"Makes it much more interesting, doesn't it?" John smirked. "I've enjoyed our time together, Andrew. I'll miss our insightful conversations. You know, it's quite intriguing. I came here for my son's wedding and will leave here with his bride. I can see clearly which one of us is more of a man." He tipped his hat and strutted into the hotel.

Andrew needed *decent* conversation, so he steered the buggy down the road to see Alicia. He hoped the coffee was already brewing.

CHAPTER 39

John stared at himself in the mirror hanging in his hotel room.

You are a handsome devil, aren't you? Women love you, and you love women.

He'd discovered early in life the joy of self-gratification. But he found it even more enjoyable when he used others to attain it. So, he prepared for a confrontation with Patrick O'Malley. Being two years older than Patrick, the man wouldn't take kindly to the idea of having him marry his only child.

But he never backed down from a challenge. He'd enjoy the evening and hope for a piece of Victoria for dessert. One taste of her and he wanted more. It'd take a long time for him to tire of her flesh. Young and perfectly formed. Ready to be molded into exactly what he wanted her to be.

He knocked on the O'Malley's door and removed his hat.

Izzy opened it. "You again?" She scowled.

"Yes, me again. And if I were you, I'd grow accustomed to *me*."

He strutted through the door and shoved his hat into her hands.

"What do I need this for?" Izzy leered at him.

"Put it somewhere!"

"I knows where I'd *like* to put it," she muttered, walking away. If it were up to him, he'd have her dismissed immediately.

The evening took an upturn when Victoria flew down the stairs and eagerly wrapped her arms around him.

"Slow down, Victoria." He chuckled at her enthusiasm. "I haven't asked permission to marry you yet."

"Mama already knows. I told her everythin'." The girl's eyes sparkled. *So beautiful . . .*

He traced her mouth with his finger. Then, after casting a look from side to side, he cupped her breast with his hand. "Everything?"

"Well, not *everythin'*. But she knows we spent the night together." Victoria bit her lip, batted her eyes then covered his hand with her own, pressing it to her body.

"That might as well be everything. She wasn't angry?"

"No. She wanted it to happen. She likes you, John. She thinks you're better suited for me than Andrew. Now we just have to convince Daddy."

"Do you think it'll be difficult?" He removed his hand from her breast and studied her face. *She's still very much a child.*

"Maybe. But Mama will help. Oh, John! Soon I'll be your wife!" She hugged him again.

He nearly walked out.

"Where are your parents?" he asked with a sigh.

"They'll be home soon. Let's go to the sittin' room and wait for them." She took him by the hand and led him to a bright warm room.

She sat on a settee and fanned her skirt, then gazed up at him with her gorgeous green eyes. However, he found her abundant cleavage much more interesting. He noticed she wore the same heart necklace that always seemed to be around her neck. "Where did you get that?" he asked, fingering the thing, then sat beside her.

"Andrew gave it to me." She giggled. "He said he was givin' me his heart. Funny, isn't it?"

"Why do you still wear it?"

"To remember that men lie." He'd never heard her so serious. "I'll never take it off."

"I see . . ." He looked away from her.

"You won't ever lie to me, will you John?" She ran her hand along his leg. Her art of seduction had improved.

"I'll always tell you the truth. Just as I told you everything about Andrew and Claire. I won't lie to you, Victoria." He meant it. He wouldn't lie. He just might not tell her everything.

"So tell me. Do you love me?" She accented her sweet voice with a kiss on his lips.

"I love every part of you." His desire flamed. He worked his hand under the fabric of her dress, then ran it up her leg until he found bare flesh.

"I'm not talkin' 'bout my body." She closed her eyes, becoming breathless. His caress had worked its magic. "I'm talkin' 'bout *me*."

"You *are* your body." The heat coming from her skin made his heart pound. "Why don't we get out of here? Go back to my room." He craved gratification. After gliding his lips along her neck, he moved lower and nestled his face into her bosom.

Her hands entwined through his hair. *Maybe I can take her here.*

"We can't leave yet," she rasped. "You have to talk to my . . ." She gasped. "*Daddy?*"

John jerked away from her and stood facing Patrick O'Malley.

The man blew steam out his nostrils. "What the *hell* are you doin' to me child?"

Victoria rose and wrapped her arms around John. "I'm not a child!" She stomped her foot.

"You're *my* child!" Patrick fumed.

Shannon ran down the hall. "What's goin' on here?"

"That *man* had his hand up her dress and his face in her bosom!" Patrick pointed a stiff finger at John. "I should *kill* you for touching me child!"

"Calm down, Patrick," Shannon urged. "Let him explain."

"Explain? Explain that he enjoys fondling young girls? Let me throw him out!" Patrick lunged, and John jerked back.

"No, Daddy!" Victoria stepped between them. "I *want* him! I *love* him!"

"You *love* him? What are you sayin'? You're to marry Andrew in just over a week. You want his *father* now? You've gone mad, child!"

"Stop callin' me a child! I'm a grown woman. He wants to marry me. Don't you, John?"

Her large soft eyes slowly blinked. And even though this hadn't turned out as he'd planned, he decided to go along with it. "Yes, I *do* want to marry her."

"You can't!" Patrick bellowed. His face had become redder than Victoria's hair. "I forbid it. It's ungodly. You're older than I am!"

Victoria inched closer to the man. "You can't forbid it, Daddy. He already bedded me. Last night. *All* night long." The look she gave him displayed masterful spite—hands on hips and breasts heaving.

That's my girl.

"You did *what*?" Patrick spewed. "You defiled me daughter? How dare you!" He pushed past Victoria and grabbed John by the collar.

John grabbed his hands and shoved him away, then brushed off his clothing. *You're no match for me.* "I defiled no one. She wanted it and so did I. We came together of our own free will. No one forced her. Truthfully, she rather enjoyed it." He pulled on his collar and lifted his chin.

"You bastard! You took advantage of an innocent lass!" Patrick breathed rapidly, clenching his fists.

"She's not that innocent," John said with a smirk.

A coy tilt of Victoria's head said everything that needed to be said. She linked her arm into his and placed her hand on his chest, then batted her eyes at her father.

"Now then," Shannon said. The woman seemed to be the coolest in the room. Without a doubt, she sided with them. "Let's all calm down and talk about this."

"There's nothing to talk about!" Patrick stomped his foot. "I want him to leave and never see our daughter again!"

"Mama?" Victoria's eyes pleaded with her mother.

Shannon took Patrick by the arm and led him down the hallway. The room fell to a welcomed hush.

"Don't worry, John," Victoria said. "Mama will make Daddy understand."

With her parents out of the room, they returned to their seated position. Victoria's lips enticed him to forget the difficulty with Patrick.

"Victoria!" Andrew's loud voice startled both of them.

This should be interesting.

They walked toward him arm-in-arm and at the same time Shannon and Patrick emerged from the study. They met together in the hallway at the base of the stairs.

"Andrew?" Victoria huffed. "Why are *you* here?"

He looked as though he'd run the entire way. His hair was tousled and sweat beaded on his brow. He cast a quick spiteful glance at John. "You don't have to marry him, Victoria. He's not what he seems."

"I can't imagine what you mean. I know you don't want me and he does." Victoria rubbed her hand over John's chest. "In case you didn't know, I was with him all night."

He'd never seen Andrew so bedraggled. *Desperate and unkempt.* "He won't be good to you. I know I wasn't what you thought, but there's *someone* out there who will truly love you. Don't throw your life away on John Martin."

"Martin?" Patrick asked. "I thought it was Fletcher?"

"No, Daddy. His real name is John *Martin*. I'll explain it all later." Victoria's firmness impressed John more than ever. She had no intention of letting Andrew spoil this.

Andrew turned to Patrick. "Mr. O'Malley, please don't approve of this. He'll only end up hurting her."

Why not just get on your knees and beg?

"You had your chance, Dr. Fletcher," Patrick snapped. "You're behaving like a poor loser."

"No. No—that's not it. I know him well. He lies about everything." Andrew glared at John. Finally a lasting look he could build on.

"You want to talk about lies, Andrew?" John laughed. "Shall we start with your *son*?"

John chuckled at the simultaneous gasps.

Victoria's mouth dropped. "Son? What son?"

"The son his *sister* bore him." John spat out the words. Knowing this moment would eventually come, he purposefully hadn't told her before.

This is so much more enjoyable.

Shannon clutched her chest. "Your sister? Good Lord!" She crossed herself.

"I take it you didn't tell them. Did you, Andrew?" John loved being in full control. "Who's the real liar, hmm?"

"I think you need to leave now, Doctor," Patrick said, pointing to the door. "You're not welcome here any longer."

With even more desperation, Andrew stared at Victoria. "You're making a big mistake. Please believe me."

"I don't believe anythin' you say. All that time with me and you never told me 'bout Claire. You made yourself out to be righteous and pure. Wantin' to wait until marriage to have me, like you were some sort of saint. You're no saint, Andrew. You're the worst kind of man. A man who tries to hide who he really is. I know you now and I thank God I found out who you really are. John's everythin' I've ever wanted. He'd never lie to me." She turned her back on Andrew, then took John by the hand and led him down the hallway.

John looked over his shoulder at Andrew with a satisfied grin. His *son* grimaced and headed for the door. When it slammed shut, John pulled Victoria into his arms and gave her a kiss that promised more to come.

"Izzy! Bring champagne!" Patrick's voice boomed through the house. Shannon had obviously changed the man's mind. It would be interesting to find out how she'd done it.

Victoria giggled. "Daddy wants to celebrate." She nuzzled into John's neck. "I've never had champagne. Is it good?"

"Never had champagne? You're in for a treat."

"Daddy always said I was too young. But now he realizes I'm a grown woman." Victoria beamed. *A child with the body of a woman.* He'd help her grow up quickly.

They returned to the living room to wait for the champagne to be poured.

John let out a satisfied sigh.

A game well played.

And won.

CHAPTER 40

When Andrew rode away with John, Claire wanted to race after him. The shock of their revelation had her head spinning.

All she could do was cry. She cried over the wasted tears and anguish. She cried over leaving him that day in Mobile. If they'd known the truth then, perhaps Gerald never would've died. He never would've married her and he'd still be working with his uncle at the blacksmith shop. He'd be alive and she'd belong to Andrew. And now, because of all of the deceptions, Andrew would marry Victoria.

By the time she came out of her room, it was nearly dark. Beth paused from eating and looked up at her, saying nothing. Claire pulled up a chair beside her at the supper table. The food smelled good, but she doubted she could eat.

Upon seeing her, Michael toddled over and raised his arms. She gladly lifted him onto her lap and held him tight. "I'm sorry, Michael. Mama isn't much good to you right now." She kissed him on the cheek.

"He loves you, Claire," Beth said. "He's happy long as he has you. Can I pour you a bowl a soup?"

"Thank you, Beth. I'll try to eat."

Beth ladled a bowl full of vegetable soup and placed it in front of Claire.

She leaned over it and inhaled the wonderful aroma. "Mmm—Beth—it smells like you outdid yourself." She took a bite. *Maybe it'll help.* "Yes, you're a much better cook than I am."

"I wouldn't say that. We just cook different." Beth grinned, but then frowned. "Claire, what happened with the doctor? If you don't mind my askin'."

"It's hard to explain. Can we just leave it at that?"

"I'm your best friend. *And* your sister. You can tell me anythin'." Beth reached across the table and squeezed Claire's hand.

"I know that an' I appreciate you more than you'll ever know. But I can't talk 'bout it right now. When I'm ready, I'll tell you, all right?" Claire forced a weak smile.

"That's fair." Beth continued to eat, but then paused and raised her head. Her grin returned. "Can I tell *you* sumthin'?"

"Course you can." She could use some good news.

"George asked if he could call on me. Can you believe it? I ain't never had a man call on me before. What am I gonna do?" Beth shook with excitement and nearly spilled her soup.

"Answer the door when he does." Claire let out a soft laugh. It felt incredibly good.

"I'm serious, Claire! You know, I figgered out why he don't talk much. He has a stutter. He's self-conscious of it, but I think it's sweet."

"That explains a lot." Claire bounced Michael on her knee. "I'm happy for you. He's a hard-workin' man for sure."

Claire took another bite, forcing herself to get some nourishment.

"Have you tried to get that thing off lately?" Beth asked, pointing to Sarah's ring.

"No. My knuckle's been too sore." Claire twisted it around her finger. *Such a tiny thing to hold so many bad memories.*

"What 'bout usin' lard? Might work." Beth went to the cupboard, removed a jar, and placed it in front of Claire.

"That's a good idea." After setting Michael down, she stuck her finger into the lard, then pulled it out, covered in the greasy mess. A simple tug on the ring and it slipped right off her finger. She grinned from ear-to-ear. Thank goodness she was rid of the thing. If only it could be that easy to remove the horrible memories.

She sighed. "Now, what should I do with it?"

"Can I have it?" Beth twisted her mouth. "Since she was my aunt, maybe I can wear it one day."

"You thinkin' 'bout George?"

"Maybe . . . Heck, Claire! He ain't comin' to propose, just to call on me." Beth tried the ring on her finger, but it was much too small. "Oh, well. May have to get a bigger one."

Claire returned her attention to the soup. Eating was almost impossible. Even after nearly starving to death, food didn't appeal to her. Even Beth's fine cooking. A broken heart made it unbearable.

She swished her spoon back and forth in the broth. "Beth, tomorrow I wanna go to the shore—to where it happened. Will you watch Michael for me when I do?" She stared at the vegetables floating in the bowl, then pushed them under with her spoon.

"Course I will, but don't you want me to come with you?"

"No. This is sumthin' I hafta do alone. I hope you understand."

"I do. I just worry 'bout you. I know your heart's broke. Sometimes, don't you just feel like he's gonna walk through that door any minute? He'd come over to me and give me a kiss on the forehead, then he'd give you a big ol' kiss on the lips. I can still see him. Just like it was yesterday when we was all here." Beth lit up with an enormous smile. "Remember him flexin' his muscles on the beach? I thought I'd just die . . ."

"I remember. I'm glad I remember everythin'. I'm grateful I had the chance to love him. Even if it was just for a short while." Claire meant every word. She'd truly loved him. Maybe that's why it hurt so much.

"He'll always be in your heart, Claire. And you have Michael as a reminder of his love. Michael, the miracle baby. Mr. Porter's mule didn't get the best of Gerald."

"No, he didn't," Claire whispered. "*I* did." She stood from the table, cradling Michael in her arms. Where would her heart lead her next?

* * *

The warm air embraced Claire's body, even though the wind blew hard across the sandy beach. This kind of day promised a storm.

She still moved slowly. Her legs hadn't become quite as strong as they once were, but she was making great progress. She stumbled a bit heading down the tiny path to the beach, until she reached level sand.

Walking by the spot where they'd put their blanket that day, she had a vision of Gerald once again, flexing his muscles. He'd entertained them with his wonderful charm. Then her chest tightened, remembering the panic she'd felt when Michael vanished and the horror when she noticed his tiny body in the water.

Her heart thumped as she walked to the water's edge. It lapped against the shore in strong waves. The winds whipped up the crests and the swells as they came to land. She slipped off her shoes to feel the cool water on her feet. The salt air filled her nose with the familiar smell she loved so much.

Something sparkled on the sand not far from her, so she walked over to it, bent down and picked it up. Her eyes instantly clouded with tears. *Gerald's glasses.* The frames were bent, one lens had fallen out, and the other had cracked.

"Oh, Gerald!" She dropped to her knees. "I'm sorry! You didn't deserve to die! It shoulda been me!" Flattening herself on the sand, she sobbed. "You were so good. You did everythin' right. It shoulda been me!"

She lay there and cried in nonexistent time. The burden of deceit weighed her down and tore her up inside. Though she'd loved him in the end, she'd used him in the beginning. She'd been wrong—*selfish.* She could never tell Beth, but she had to tell someone.

Finally, she knew what she had to do.

Sitting upright, she used the sleeve of her dress to wipe the tears from her eyes. Her hands were covered in sand. As she stood, her legs trembled and almost buckled beneath her, but she managed to make her way back to the little house. The house she'd always loved, but the one she could no longer call *home*.

She went inside—saying nothing to Beth—and found a small box to place the glasses in. Then she went back outside to the graves.

She knelt at her mama's. "Mama, you know where I'm goin'. Please understand. I hafta find my home. Look after Gerald for me. He's a good man. I'm doin' what Aunt Martha told me to do. I'm followin' my heart. I love you, Mama." She kissed her fingers and touched them to the headstone.

Then she moved to the loose soil of Gerald's freshly dug grave. Reverend Brown had carved a simple cross for his marker, which was perfect for Gerald. He never wanted to be fussed over. She dug a hole in the dirt with her hands and placed the box into it. Then she covered it up and patted it down.

She sniffled, closed her eyes, and took a large breath. "Here are your glasses. I know you don't need 'em where you are, but they belong to you. So I thought I'd give 'em back. Don't ever doubt I loved you. If you're watchin' over me, please understand. I'm doin' this for me *and* for Michael. He needs a daddy. I'm goin' back home. Where I belong." Tears ran down her cheeks. She kissed her fingers once again and touched them to the cross marking the grave.

She went to the barn and hitched Cocoa to the wagon. Cocoa; the beautiful, gentle mare Henry had given them as a wedding gift. She'd know the way home.

"We're goin' home, Cocoa," she said, patting the horse's neck.

Still, without one word to Beth, she went back to the house and packed her things. Nothing would stop her. Not now. Not even Beth.

"What are you doin', Claire?" Beth asked.

Claire looked over her shoulder at her dear friend. The confusion on her face wrenched her heart. "I'm takin' Michael an' we're goin' home." She continued to pack.

"Home? You don't mean to Uncle Henry's, do you?" Beth's voice rose, but it didn't stop Claire.

"It's my home, Beth. It's where we belong. All our things are there. We'll be taken care of."

"No!" Beth tried grabbing her arms to stop her. "Gerald wouldn't want you to. Not with Henry!"

"Beth, I'm goin'." Claire jerked away from her. "Don't say another word 'bout it. I've made up my mind. I can't stay here." She'd packed what she needed, so she scooped Michael into her arms. With him on one hip and her bag on the other, she walked out the door.

"Claire! Don't do this!" Beth frantically waved her arms, crying. But Claire hardened her heart.

"I love you, Beth. You'll always be my best friend. But I hafta do this." Claire climbed into the wagon, held Michael close beside her, and didn't look back.

CHAPTER 41

Andrew stared at his ceiling. He'd memorized every inch of it. He wanted more than anything to see Claire again, but as Alicia had said, Claire needed time to grieve. For now, he had to leave her be.

Still, he wanted to be with her. He'd waited so long. And now—knowing the truth—there should be nothing to stop their love, except the memory of Gerald.

It was good he didn't have to go to work, because he certainly didn't feel like working. Instead, he started unpacking the crates that he'd packed to move.

Had he not been so miserable over the last episode with Claire and his *father*, he would've been elated. Knowing Victoria was heading down a path darker than she could begin to imagine, added to his misery. But on the bright side, he could stay in his house. He loved it here. Aside from being more peaceful than the city, it was home.

After working steadily for several hours, he allowed himself a break and went out to the barn. Grabbing a brush, he groomed Charger's long mane. He hadn't been ridden for a while, so he jumped on him bareback and took him for a short ride. Right down the road to Alicia's.

He'd seen her twice the previous day. The first time upon his arrival home from seeing Claire, and the second time after he'd tried to warn Victoria about John. Both times Alicia had sat with him and talked, leaving him feeling better afterward.

When he rapped on her door, Samuel opened it.

"Samuel!" Alicia hollered. "I din't tell you to get outta that corner!"

Samuel's shoulders drooped. He walked back to a tiny stool in the corner of the room.

Andrew shook his head and stepped inside. "Samuel's in trouble *again*?"

"The boy keeps runnin' off. Don't know what I'm gonna do with him." Alicia stood with her hands on her hips, looking as though the sun might never shine again.

Samuel snickered.

"You want supper tonight?" Alicia scolded, pointing a finger.

"Yes, Mama."

"Then mind yourself an' hush. I'm still mad at ya!"

Samuel sat on the stool and put his head in his hands. He didn't make another sound.

"Am I intruding, Alicia?" Andrew asked.

"No, but if you keep showin' up at my door, folks is gonna start talkin'." She grinned.

"You're one of my only friends. I'm sorry I keep laying my troubles at your feet." He took a seat at her table and she poured both of them a cup of coffee. Just what he'd hoped for.

"That's what friends is for . . . to look after each other. You know you're welcome here anytime. So what's on your mind now? Victoria? Your da—I mean, *John*? Or Claire? Or is it all a them?" She sat down across from him after casting a wary eye toward Samuel.

"Mostly Claire. I doubt I can do anything about Victoria. She's made up her mind. Besides, I believe she hates me now. As for John . . . I never want to see him again. I hate to think of the kind of life he'll make for Victoria. But *Claire*. I *want* Claire. I don't have to tell *you* that."

"No, I've know that for what? Nearly two years now? How time flies . . ." She shook her head.

"Right now, not fast enough. How much time do you think she needs? To grieve?"

"Only she'll know. It's different for everyone. Your situation's different. But if you push her, you'll only push her away. You'll know when the time's right."

They talked all afternoon and Andrew stayed for supper. He played with the children and told them stories as they got ready for bed. Though he loved being there, it was well after dark and time to go home. Charger would be anxious to get settled in the barn.

Alicia hugged him as he prepared to leave. "Listen to your heart, Doc. It'll know."

As Charger approached the house, Andrew noticed a wagon pulled up in front of it with no one in it. Memories of Tobias made his heart pound, so he approached with caution.

"Steady there, Charger." Dismounting, he soothed his horse.

Cautiously, he peered into the wagon.

Oh, God!

His heart leapt. Before his eyes—like an answer to prayer—were Claire and his son. They lay curled up together, sound asleep in the back of the wagon.

As quickly as he could, he settled Charger in the barn, then returned to Claire and Michael.

Reaching over the side of the wagon, he lifted his little boy into his arms.

Claire stirred. "Andrew?" She rubbed her eyes.

"Yes. How long have you been here?"

She stood and jumped down from the wagon. "Awhile. I waited for you. I'm glad it didn't rain."

"Let's go inside," he said and opened the door. "I'll put Michael on my bed. I'll be right back." He carried him into his room and gently laid him down on the bed. Then he bent over and kissed him. "I love you, Michael," he whispered, then crept out of the room.

How could this be happening? He had his son in his house—on his bed—and the woman he loved with all his heart stood in the other room waiting for him. *Too good to be true.*

Her eyes were on him and it made him shiver.

"You know, don't you?" she asked, not shifting her gaze.

"That Michael's my son? Yes, I know." She lowered her eyes, then turned away from him.

"I should've told you, but it was all so mixed up. I've ruined everythin'."

He wanted to tell her it would be all right. And he wanted to hold her, but he knew she didn't want him to. So he stood there without touching her. "Why do you say that?"

"Andrew . . . I came here to tell you everythin'. I can't bear it alone anymore. I owe it to you *and* to Gerald." She walked across the room and sat down at the table. "Could I have a glass of water?"

"Of course. Or if you'd prefer, I have sweet tea punch. Someone I met once got me started on it." He smiled, attempting to make her feel better.

"That would be nice. Thank you."

He poured some for himself as well and sat down next to her. Her sweet honey scent filled the air, increasing his desire to touch her.

"I know it's wrong for me to be here." She stared at her drink. "I only came to say what I need to say, then I'll leave you, and you'll never hafta see me again. I'm sure Victoria wouldn't approve." She took a sip of tea.

"About Victoria—"

Claire put up her hand, stopping him. "No. Let me say what I came here to say first. Please?"

He nodded. "I'm listening." He sipped his tea and gazed into her eyes.

Their eyes locked for a brief moment. He had no doubt their shared feelings ran deep.

Looking as though she might cry, she took a large breath. "The day I left, I thought I'd die. I never knew I could love as deeply as I loved you. Somehow I made it to Martha's through my tears. I planned to stay there for a short while, then go home as if nothin' ever happened. But then I found I was carryin' your child. I made Martha believe I was heartsick over Gerald. When I told her 'bout the baby, she insisted I return home an' marry him. So I made a plan. I did a horrible thing."

She stopped speaking and stared at her hands. Then after taking another drink of tea, inhaled deeply again. She wouldn't look at him. "Gerald had never even kissed me at that time. I went to him, professed my love, and seduced him. I made him have me so he'd think your child was his." She burst into tears and laid her head on the table.

So that's how she'd deceived him . . .

Knowing she'd been intimate with another man had always caused him pain, but the ache he felt for her now, outweighed all other. He needed to reassure her, but he had to remain quiet until she finished.

She sniffled. "Andrew, I deceived him to save my own shame. I convinced myself I did it for the child. But I did it for me! I was ashamed of what we'd done and I used Gerald to hide behind. How can God ever forgive me for that? Why couldn't things have been different? If I'd just stayed with you and never left, Gerald might still be alive. He was a good man. He loved me an' died *because* of me."

"Claire—look at me," Andrew whispered. He *had* to speak.

She raised her head from the table.

"You can't blame yourself for his death." He penetrated her eyes with his own. "You did what you thought was right at the time and I know you loved Gerald. I saw it with my own eyes."

"You did?"

"Yes. The day I came to have my horse shod. I wanted to know he was good to you. What I witnessed was a man completely in love with his wife and his unborn child. As I left, I saw the two of you together. You were laughing . . . and then you kissed. I saw real love, Claire. How can you blame yourself for loving him?"

"I *used him* in the beginnin'!" she cried and folded into herself.

"But you loved him in the end. Isn't that what matters? That you *did* love him? You gave him more love in the time you were together than I imagine he had in his entire lifetime." She needed to listen to him and stop tormenting herself. He couldn't bear to see her in pain. "I know what just a few days were like in your arms," he whispered, closing his eyes to the memory. "I've lived off that memory for a very long time. He had you for nearly two years. He was in heaven then, and I'm sure he's in Heaven now. He may never have known love at all, if things hadn't happened the way they did. Maybe God gave you to him for a brief time so he could experience love."

"Andrew . . . How can you be so understandin'?"

"Claire, I—"

Once again she put up her hand. "There's more I hafta to say."

He'd let her continue, but every part of him wanted to hold and comfort her. He didn't care that she'd spent the last two years with Gerald, if only *he* could have her for the rest of his life.

She looked downward. "I'm ashamed because I deceived Gerald throughout our marriage. There were many times you were in my thoughts when I was in his arms. I couldn't let you go! I've *never* let you go. But now—I *hafta* let you go. To *her*." Her hands trembled and her tears streamed.

He'd heard all he needed to hear.

Taking her hands in his, he knelt beside her. "Claire. Look into my eyes."

She covered her mouth with one hand, but did as he requested.

"I'm not marrying Victoria. You're the only woman I've ever loved or wanted." He brushed his hand across her damp cheek. "I'll give you as much time as you need, but I'll wait for you no matter how long it takes."

"But . . . what about the child?"

"What child?"

"You said you *had* to marry her. I assumed—"

"No. Oh no, Claire. There's no child. I never *had* Victoria."

Claire gasped and her hand shook as she once again covered her mouth. "Never? But you were with her a long time."

"I won't lie to you. I was tempted."

"Why didn't you?"

"She wasn't you." Their faces were only inches apart. Her breath mingled with his. He wouldn't rush her, but could he at least hold her?

He moved even closer and she didn't back away. Their lips met. They lingered—barely touching—afraid to go further. Their breathing became even heavier and he placed his hand on the side of her face. "I *will* wait. You can tell me when you're ready." He backed away.

She stretched out a quivering hand. "God forgive me, but I've waited long enough. Andrew, please hold me."

Thank God.

Without a moment's hesitation, he wrapped his arms around her as tightly as he could.

"It's always been you, Andrew," she said, weeping. "Will God punish me for loving you?"

"How can God condemn love?" He held her even closer, not wanting to release her ever again. Their bodies shook with utter joy as they gazed at one another in disbelief. He thought he'd lost her forever, but she'd come into his arms once again.

He lifted her to her feet, then raised her into the air and slowly brought her back down again.

Though she continued to cry, the sparkle in her eyes told him what he needed to know. They'd become tears of joy.

"Wait right here," he said and placed her in a chair.

He went to the roll top desk and pulled out her ring, then returned to her and knelt at her feet. "Claire Montgomery Alexander, will you do me the honor of being my wife?"

"You still want me? Even after all this? Even after you know I gave myself willingly to another man?"

"I want you more than ever. Gerald was your husband. I expected you to love him. His memory will *always* be with you. I just hope that when we lie together, it'll only be me in your arms."

"Gerald was buried. I'll keep his memory, but only that. I wanna be yours again. I wanna be your wife. It's all I ever wanted." She stared into his eyes.

He slid the ring on her finger. "This time, promise me you'll leave it on."

"I'll never take it off. I swear." She stood from the chair and he rose from his knee. Tentatively, she touched his chest, trembling all the while. "I can't believe this is real. It feels too much like a dream."

Yes, he felt it, too. A dream come true. Her delicate hand shook against him and his knees were ready to buckle. "Would it be wrong of me to suggest we lie down? I'd like to hold you. I *need* to hold you."

"What 'bout Michael?"

His name covered Andrew like a warm blanket. "Yes, I'm a father now, aren't I? It'll take some getting used to, but I can't think of anything I'd rather do." He brought out one of the large crates he'd unpacked and folded a blanket inside it. "This should do for now."

"Poor Michael. He's been put in so many different types of beds recently."

"We'll have to get him his own—may have to add on to the house."

Andrew went to the bedroom and lifted Michael from the bed, studying his features. *So much like mine.* If he could, he'd stop time and make this joy last forever. Their love had brought this little life into the world. Now they'd all be together to create the loving home he'd been praying for.

Please don't be a dream.

He kissed Michael's cheek and laid him in the crate. His son barely stirred and continued to sleep.

"I forgot about poor Cocoa," Claire whispered.

"Cocoa?"

"My mare. Since it looks like I'm stayin', can you put her in the barn?"

She's truly staying.

"Of course." He pointed a finger at Claire. "Don't move." He hurried out the door and took care of the mare, then rushed back inside.

"Come with me," he said and reached out to Claire.

* * *

Claire willingly took Andrew's hand and followed him to the bedroom. Her heart beat hard in her chest. Was it trying to tell her to slow down, or did it know she'd finally come home again?

Whatever her heart tried to say, she had no doubt she wanted to feel the comfort of Andrew's arms and never leave him.

He lit the lantern beside the bed and stood there simply gazing at her. A smile warmed his face. He slowly pulled the pins from her hair. She shook her head and let it fall over her shoulders.

He cupped her cheek with his hand. "I'll just hold you, Claire. Nothing more."

Tentatively, she looked up at him. "Andrew?" Ashamed of what she was about to say, she lowered her head.

"What's wrong?" He put his arms around her trembling body.

"Gerald hasn't been gone long, but I've been mournin' you far longer. I reckon it's wrong, but I don't wanna wait. I wanna be with you. I know others wouldn't understand and would think poorly of me. But all that matters is what *you* think a me. If you want me now, I'm yours. Because I love you."

He held her close and his warmth comforted her. She remembered this. All of it. His smell. His touch. The beat of his heart against her cheek.

Though her hand shook, she started unfastening the buttons on his shirt. He held his breath, shuddering beneath her touch, but made no attempt to stop her.

Opening his shirt, she ran her hands across his bare chest. His smooth skin drew her in and she brushed her lips over his torso. Lightly at first, then her passion stirred and she kissed him harder—tasting the body she'd only been allowed to dream of. She pushed the shirt over his shoulders, down his strong arms, and let it fall to the floor.

He placed two fingers under her chin and lifted her face. "Are you certain?"

She nodded. "You're all I've ever wanted."

He bent down and their lips finally melted together in a warm and loving kiss. Tears fell from her eyes. Their love had never faded.

Taking his time—as though savoring every instant—he helped her remove her dress. She shivered as his fingertips glided along her bare back.

She closed her eyes and enjoyed the sensation of chills trickling along her spine. His lips brushed her neck, then moved to her upper body. *Oh, God . . . I remember this.* The way he made her feel. She'd always wanted to relive these sensations.

She slid her hands around his waist and his pants joined her dress at their feet.

He lifted her to the bed and laid her down on her back. Then he lay down next to her and propped himself up on one elbow.

He stared at her.

"What's wrong, Andrew?" *Why'd he stop?*

"I can't believe you're here. I can't stop looking at you. You're beautiful, Claire." With one finger, he traced the curve of her body, then smiled. "You've changed."

"What do you mean?" His gorgeous dark eyes held her captive.

His hands cascaded over her breasts. "They're larger than I remember. Not that I'm complaining."

"It's your fault," she said matter-of-factly, with a smile on her face.

He continued moving his hands down her body and stopped at her protruding ribs. "This isn't good. You'd better start eating more."

"Being unconscious for a week didn't help. Trust me. I'm healthy." She scolded him teasingly, then caressed his face. She remembered *this* Andrew. The playful one, who was also loving and irresistible.

His hands glided even lower. He removed her undergarment and tossed it on the floor. Then he reached underneath her and grabbed her bottom. "Hmm . . . it's bigger, too. Not that I mind that either."

"Andrew Fletcher!" she laughed. "You know my body changed when I had Michael."

"I wish I'd been there." He rested his hand against her belly.

"No, you don't. I wasn't very pleasant. And Sister O'Casey was—well—unusual."

He chuckled. "I know her. No need to explain."

When he fingered her stretch marks, she pushed his hand away. "They're ugly."

"No, they're beautiful. They're a reminder of the life you carried inside you. The life *we* created. Nothing's more beautiful." He bent down and kissed each mark. Then he raised himself back up to her and kissed her lips. Slowly. Fervently.

"What 'bout creatin' a little girl?" Claire's heart beat hard, anticipating what they were about to do.

"Now *that* would be very beautiful." He shifted and began to move onto her.

"Wait." She stopped him with a firm hand against his chest. "Don't I get to see if you've changed?"

He grinned. "I suppose it's only fair." He laid down flat.

She propped herself up and moved her hand over his body. First, she glided her fingers across his chest, then down his arms.

Her hand went lower. Across his abdomen, then down to his groin. When she touched between his legs, she found him already aroused. He needed no encouragement. "Hmm . . ."

His eyes were closed and his chest heaved. She'd been tormenting him and enjoying every minute of it.

"What's wrong?" he asked, breathing heavily.

"Strange. You seem larger, too."

"What?" His eyes popped wide.

"Your arms are *huge*. You've really built up your muscles." She giggled.

"Claire . . ." He laughed and rolled her over, moving atop her. "No one can make me smile the way you do." He pushed her hair back from her face, then kissed the tip of her nose. "You have no idea how much I've missed you."

"I'm just keepin' you on your toes. Someone's got to." Was it wrong to feel so happy? *Do I deserve his love?* Whatever the answers might be, she didn't care. She'd finally arrived at where she wanted to be. Nothing would ruin tonight. "I missed you, too."

"I love you." He kissed one eyelid and then the other. Then he tenderly kissed her lips.

She ran her hands down his back, making him shiver. Her body molded into his and she marveled at the chiseled perfection of his form. She opened to him, and he slowly entered her, while she closed her eyes and breathed in his essence.

They'd been given the ultimate gift. The ultimate expression of their love. The gift God made perfectly, to unite two bodies into one and make them one flesh.

He lay there upon her, not moving, so she opened her eyes. She found him staring at her, his coal black eyes penetrating her to the core.

"What's wrong?" she asked and raked her fingers into his hair.

"Nothing. I just realized something." His chest heaved.

"What?" She breathed in unison with him.

"I've been searching for where I belong. Claire, *you* are my home." He said exactly what *she'd* been feeling. They found their home in each other. She could stop searching.

He devoured her in a hungering kiss.

Their movement started and they became a symphony. It began slowly with soft rhythmic percussion. Then the strings added their melody. The bow slid across its instrument with ease and grace, back and forth as the tempo increased. The piano joined and the player's fingers rolled across the keys, tumbling into a new song. The tempo quickened even more. The drums beat louder. Then the horns blared and added their elation in the melody they'd created. Finally, their song rose into a loud forte. The percussion beat harder and faster and finally exploded with a crashing of symbols.

Then it began to fade away. They slowed until it became a simple note carried across the breath of a flute.

Their song ended.

Exhausted—but content beyond words—Claire glided her fingers through Andrew's dark thick hair. His head nestled against her breasts. Never had love been made with more passion or more genuine feeling. They were soul mates created for each other and they'd never be apart again.

Andrew moved his head onto the pillow. They stared at one another. Their hands hadn't stopped their tender caresses. He pulled her close and she rested her head on his chest.

"Claire?" He gently stroked her hair. "When you got here, you said you were only staying to tell me what you had to say, then you planned to leave. Where were you going to go?"

She wished he hadn't asked and laid there quietly for a short time. But she wouldn't lie to him. *No more secrets*. "I was goin' to Henry's."

"But why? After everything that happened."

"I didn't know where else to go. In my mind, it made sense. But I did as Aunt Martha told me and listened to my heart. It brought me here first. I never dreamed you'd want me to stay, though it was all I really wanted." She mindlessly traced patterns on his skin.

"I'm glad you listened to Martha *and* your heart. I would've had to steal you away from Henry." His fingers continued moving through her hair.

"You woulda done that?"

"In a heartbeat." He smiled and gave her a reassuring kiss. "I'll be right back."

He got out of bed, slipped on a pair of pajama bottoms, and left the room. When he came back, he held Michael in his arms.

Claire got up and pulled a gown from her bag. She put it on and crawled back into bed. Andrew had placed their son in the middle.

"What faults? I found *you* here. That made everything worth it." He took her hand. "Let's go inside and get us some coffee. Michael should be waking soon, shouldn't he?"

"Yep. I can teach you how to change him." She grinned.

"How about *I* teach him to use the outhouse?" He draped his arm over her shoulder. "The sooner, the better."

They closed the door to their little house and the sun rose high in the Alabama sky. They didn't live in a perfect world, but the love they shared could carry them through even the most difficult times. They'd face the world hand-in-hand, knowing that together they could weather *any* storm.

Acknowledgments

I'd like to start by thanking all of my readers! I received such wonderful feedback from many of you after you read *Deceptions*, Book 1 of this series. It thrilled me to know how much you were looking forward to the next book. You have no idea how incredible it feels to be able to share this saga with you all. It's been in my mind and heart for so long now that getting it out into the world is a blessed release.

A special thank you goes out to Mrs. Beach, the librarian in the local history and genealogy division, from the Mobile Public Library. Her help was invaluable. She sent me information about Mobile City Hospital along with photos and detailed documents regarding its history. I've fallen in love with this fantastic historic building. Though it's no longer used as a hospital, it's fun to step back in time and imagine what it had been like all those years ago.

Thank you to Cindy Brannam, my incredible editor. This book is my longest to date, and I know it consumed much of her time. I'm fortunate she's on this wonderful lengthy-saga journey with me.

Rae Monet managed to find the perfect Victoria for my cover. It was a tall order. Asking for the most beautiful woman on earth with red hair and a devious smile made it a little complex.

Jesse Gordon always comes through for me, too. My mind rests once I send my documents to him for formatting. I know that soon after I'll have a finished product to share with the world. Thank you, Jesse!

And to my Beta readers who have told me they're enjoying walking down the road with this cast of characters again, thank you for sticking with me!

Coming Soon!

Desires
Southern Secrets Saga, Book 3

The *Southern Secrets Saga* continues ...

Set in both Mobile, Alabama and Bridgeport, Connecticut, follow the five families you've grown to love and maybe even sometimes *despise*.

Emotions run rampant for the Alexanders and Fletchers. Undeniable love has caused excessive pain. Forgiveness is sought for wrong that was done, but hardened hearts may leave it unattainable.

New arrivals come to Mobile. Part of the Montgomery family that had nearly been forgotten. They'll ignite more than one kind of flame.

The O'Malleys and Martins have their own troubles. Long distance makes it difficult to know what's truly going on behind closed doors. Especially when the doors are locked.

Desires run deep. But that which is desired isn't necessarily what's best for those who try to attain it.

Coming Soon!

A Golden Life
By Jeanne Hardt

Writer's block.

Someone should come up with a four-letter word for it.

Traci Oliver may be a best-selling romance author, but for the first time in her writing career she can't type a word on the blank page. Book number fifty is supposed to be her best ever—her *golden* book—but inspiration joined her husband in the grave. How can she write about love with a shattered heart?

At the precise moment of the anniversary of his death, a knock on her door changes everything.

When characters from her books take on human form and tell her that they've come to help her, she doubts her sanity. Are they real, or has she lost her mind?

Her doctor says grieving is a process, but she never dreamed that part of the process would bring her heroes to life. She wonders if all people experience this kind of thing, or is it a weird phenomenon reserved solely for romance writers? Truthfully, the only hero she wants in her life is her husband, and she can never be with him again.

Or maybe she can ...

If you're enjoying the *Southern Secrets Saga*, you might also like these books by Jeanne Hardt!

The RIVER ROMANCE Series

Step back in time to 1850 and travel along the Mississippi River in the *River Romance* series!

Marked
River Romance, Book 1

Cora Craighead wants more than anything to leave Plum Point, Arkansas, aboard one of the fantastic steamboats that pass by her run-down home on the Mississippi River. She's certain there's more to life out there...*somewhere*. Besides, anything has to be better than living with her pa who spends his days and nights drinking and gambling.

Douglas Denton grew up on one of the wealthiest estates in Memphis, Tennessee. Life filled with parties, expensive clothing, and proper English never suited him. He longs for simplicity and a woman with a pure heart—not one who craves his money. Cora is that and more, but she belongs to someone else.

Cora finally gets her wish, only to be taken down a road of strife, uncertainty, and mysterious prophecies. When she's finally discovered again by Douglas, she's a widow, fearing for her life and that of her newborn child and blind companion.

Full of emotions, family secrets, and the search for true love, you'll find it's not just the cards that are marked.

Tainted
River Romance, Book 2

Despite her new position as manager of the *Bonny Lass,* Francine DuBois doubts her abilities. After all, the only skill she's ever been recognized for is entertaining men and giving them pleasure. But she'll never let her insecurities show in the presence of the new captain. He's too young to be a pilot and he'll never measure up to his predecessor. However, just below the surface, there's something about him she can't ignore.

Luke Waters may be young, but he's determined to prove he's more than capable. He'll show everyone he's the best pilot the Mississippi River has to offer. His only problem - the new crew manager. His religious upbringing taught him to frown on women of her profession, so how can he bring himself to overlook her way of life and give her the respect a workable relationship requires? Especially when he can't stop dreaming about her.

Which is worse? A tainted past, or a tainted opinion?

Forgotten
River Romance, Book 3

Rumor has it, the war is about to end. But that doesn't stop Billy Denton from running away to enlist. He's lived a privileged life on the Wellesley estate, where slavery is seen as a necessary means to operate their textile production. Believing no human should be enslaved by another, he's willing to fight—and even *die*—to change the future of the woman who holds his heart.

Living and working at the estate is all Angel knows. When Billy tells her he's joining the Union army, she begs him to stay, fearing she'll lose her best friend ... the only man she's ever loved. She'd rather remain a slave, than have him harmed in any way.

Angel attains freedom, but time passes and there's no sign of Billy. In her heart, she believes he'll come home to her. Their love may be forbidden, but can never be forgotten.

Holding on to hope ... Angel waits.

Also by Jeanne Hardt, another Southern Historical!

From the Ashes of Atlanta

After losing his Atlanta home and family to the war, Confederate soldier, Jeb Carter, somehow wakes up in a Boston hospital. Alone, desperate, and with a badly broken leg, he pretends to be mute to save himself from those he hates—Yankees.

Gwen Abbott, a student at Boston Women's Medical College, is elated when she's allowed to study under the guidance of a prominent doctor at Massachusetts General. While forced into a courtship with a man she can scarcely tolerate, her thoughts are consumed with their mysterious new patient. If only he could talk.

Two strangers from different worlds, joined by fate. Perhaps love can speak without words and win a war without a single shot being fired.

jeannehardt.com
facebook.com/JEANNEHARDTAUTHOR
amazon.com/author/jeannehardt

"I didn't want him to wake up and be frightened," he whispered, then reached over Michael and kissed her.

Seeing the two of them together affirmed they were where they belonged. Her heart burst with joy. She'd cherish her memories of Gerald, but she couldn't deny that her heart had always belonged to Andrew.

* * *

Claire woke before Andrew or Michael. She got out of bed and watched them peacefully sleeping. Andrew had Michael nestled in the crook of his arm. They shared identical features. Michael was a perfect copy of his daddy.

Feeling at ease and very much at home, she went to the woodstove and started a fire so she could make coffee.

While the water heated, she meandered through the house and took it all in. Then she opened the front door and peered outside.

The sun had started to rise over the breathtaking landscape. She loved it here and would never leave again.

Leaning her head against the doorframe, she breathed in the warm fresh air, then raised her hand and admired the ring sparkling on her finger. A sigh of contentment left her lips.

As she looked toward the heavens, her thoughts turned to Gerald.

I hope you understand.

Andrew encircled her with his arms. He kissed her neck, causing her skin to tingle.

"Good morning, Claire." He breathed her name into her ear. "Did you sleep well?"

"Better than ever. How 'bout you?"

"Me, too. Michael must like our bed. He's still asleep." He pulled her tighter against him.

"He's had a rough few weeks, poor baby. But it'll be better now." She turned in his arms. "I feel bad he won't remember Gerald at all."

"Gerald shaped who he is. He may not remember him, but he'll still be a part of him." He kissed her lightly on the lips.

"You're a wonderful man, Andrew Fletcher. How did I ever deserve you?" She gazed into his eyes.

"*I'm* the lucky one." With a contented-looking smile, he swayed with her in his embrace.

She nestled against him. They stood there for several moments before either said a word. Then she tilted her head upward and looked at him. "Andrew?"

"Yes?"

"What would you think 'bout gettin' a milk cow?"

"I suppose we could. Why?"

"Ever since I woke up in the hospital I've had unusual cravin's for milk."

"Honestly?" His head tipped sideways and his brows dipped low.

She laughed. "No. The cow's for Michael. But I like milk, too."

"We'll get a cow." He chuckled along with her. "Anything else?"

She thought for a moment. "You don't plan on leavin' Alabama, do you? I really love it here—at your home."

"No. I know I wasn't *blessed bein' born here*." He imitated her accent. "But I've grown to love Alabama."

"Even with all its faults?"

Made in the USA
Charleston, SC
20 November 2015